PLANET OF EDEN

PLANET OF EDEN

DAN WHICKER

TALIA
SEK

TALIA SEK

PLANET OF EDEN
Copyright © 2024 Dan Whicker

ISBN 979 8 9899359 0 1

Editing by Ann Marie Whicker.
Cover Photo by Dan Whicker.
Cover Design by Dan Whicker with art by Amy Zimmerman
(studentandwriter.com).
Modeling by Leslie Craven (instagram.com/g0ldenleslie).

Published by TALIA SEK
Kissimmee, Florida

Visit www.danwhicker.com

For Dad, from whom I inherited a love of science fiction.

CONTENTS

Prologue

Like enormous black arrowheads, two triangular spacecraft darted across the night sky. What was a chase had now escalated into an impressive aerial dogfight as each vessel sought to hit the other with beams of disabling violet light. Thousands of feet below, illuminated areas on the ground marked probable settlements—places that one ship wanted desperately to avoid but the other seemed eager to reach. With a well-placed volley, the pursuer sent a warning to the fleeing vessel not to venture there, hitting the triangle neatly on its rounded corner.

"Ey essa?" the captain of the pursuing craft asked in his own language. *A hit?*

"Ae!" confirmed a female crew member.

The captain waved his hand over a small screen before him, causing the display to magnify and show his opponent's vessel and its damaged section. Some hull was missing and blue sparks formed a shimmering trail from the gaping hole. He frowned and yelled out to his crew that they should prevent further damage. Somehow, their immobilizing beam was not functioning the same way in this planet's strange atmosphere. Instead of taking hold of the other ship, it was acting like a disintegration ray. How could he capture the renegade craft if he could not use his grappler? Perhaps a warning shot would be enough to convince them to stand down.

"Keah, yyiiii eh ahsooo ey heh?" *Keah, what if we force them to ground?* the first-mate asked.

The captain shook his head. "Ehe. Ne siiiii ah ouha Blue." *No. They must not step on Blue.*

Despite the crippling damage, the renegade ship continued its escape, defiantly sending its own volley of purple beams at its pursuer as a warning to stay away. The captain glowered as his prey zipped between clouds and descended in a flash toward the planet's surface.

Pursue! he commanded. *Prepare to step!*

In a split second, his vessel disappeared from its position and reappeared mere feet from the other.

The step was too close! warned his navigator. *Impact imminent!*

The captain dropped himself into his command seat and grimaced. *Crash positions!*

The crew barely had time to brace themselves before a dramatic collision rocked the entire vessel. As their ship melded into its twin, gaps appeared in the black walls of the bridge, and a cold alien atmosphere blasted through.

Hold! the captain yelled out above the noise of rushing wind. Despite the many hull breaches, he knew their craft was already repairing itself.

The first mate stood to acknowledge his order. *Holding!* Her white, knee-length hair whipped wildly in the blasts of chilly air as she directed two crew members. *Aai, keep us steady! Ua, expedite mending of the hull.* She turned to the captain with the hint of a knowing smile on her lips. *We can do this, Keah.*

Keah scanned the bridge and beamed with pride. He had an expert team, committed and focused. They were also his family—his wife and children. During their many adventures together, he had trained each to be the master of an individual specialty. But when it came time to work as a group, they still functioned as one. Even the walls cracking open could not distract them from the success of their mission.

Show me the renegade, Keah said. At once, a screen appeared in front of him, displaying the condition of the other ship. His prey was badly injured—too damaged to fly on its own. *It will crash if we let it go.*

If we do not, his wife cautioned, *we will reach the surface as well.*

Keah nodded. A crash was inevitable now. Since he could not prevent it, his new priority would be to preserve his own vessel by forcibly separating it from the other. That, at least, would ensure one of them would survive for the return home.

Tammah! he called out to his eldest son. *Let Ua handle the hull breaches. I need you to disengage us from that other ship.*

Ae! Tammah replied. He worked his controls while nervously glancing at the approaching landscape through the bridge's forward viewport.

All of them understood that a crash of both ships meant being stranded on an off-limits planet. It was bad enough they had to chase these rebels dangerously close to the single-mooned blue world. Now, both craft were in danger of reaching its surface.

We will not crash, Keah said, reading concern on the faces of his children.

One of his daughters cheered while slamming her fist down on a section of her control panel. *By the Ways of Ahey!*

Their vessel shuddered in response. Keah monitored the outside view of both ships' hulls. His daughter's impulsive act had worked; their craft was extracting itself from the other and repairing its own breaches. In a flash, it then pulled completely away, leaving the other to continue its plummet toward the ground.

Pursue, Keah commanded his relieved crew. *We must not allow them to reach the surface. Recalibrate the beams to minimize damage. We want to capture...not do further harm.*

Keah's opponent was clever. Her ship was damaged, but she still managed to fly it in a sporadic pattern that was difficult to track.

Why must you come here? Keah asked, wishing he could talk the other crew out of their disobedient and reckless act. *This is no place for any of us.*

While his ship struggled to catch up, Keah studied the dark landscape below. Trees with unusual shapes formed ominous forests that were separated by glowing areas of settlement. He then saw built places with what appeared to be lighted paths, possibly roads, connecting them. Small transports rolled along the illuminated routes, and boxy structures—buildings, no doubt—lined both sides. Keah marveled at the scene's eeriness. It was foreign, but also somehow familiar. *What people live here?* he wondered.

Winged craft detected! one of his sons called out.

Keah counted six small vessels that had indeed launched from the planet's surface. They were racing toward the same area where the damaged spacecraft was now attempting to land. *We must hurry!* He was interested in what sort of flying vehicles the inhabitants of Blue had developed, but he could not allow them to witness his activities. A covenant was at stake, and he would not violate it. If any of his people were discovered, there would be galactic consequences. He was already party to one rebellious act just by coming here; he would not make it worse by being seen.

CHAPTER 1

Crash

Alone in the universe. That was how Jay Harrison felt for as long as he could remember. Life was hard, people were unreliable, perfect families did not exist, and isolation was safe. A rough childhood taught him those things. Now, as a young adult, he actually valued his ability to accept loneliness. It was no longer something to fight against. He needed no one's help; he could handle most problems on his own. If he did not have friends, that was fine. If he made some, that was alright, too. But they had to give him space.

Even now, pushing through thick underbrush while night-hiking in his favorite nature preserve, all Jay wanted to do was get away from his group of campers and relax. He needed an escape. Deep in the forest, he could find peace and pretend to be somewhere else—distant and unreachable.

"Are we far enough yet?"

Jay grimaced at the sound of the shrill teenage voice behind him. He had almost forgotten that Cody was tagging along on his nighttime outing. "Why did I let him come?" He stopped his march through the dark woods and waited for Cody to catch up—again. "What are you complaining about now?"

"I said, are we—"

"Watch out!"

Cody heeded Jay's warning too late. Caught up in a nasty thicket, his pudgy form stumbled downward into the shadows, ending with a thump and a few choice words.

"Come on, Cody!" Jay chided. "I said you could go tonight if you agreed not to talk, make noise, or bother me. Ever since we left camp, you've been doing all three. And I also said *no flashlights.*"

"Well, I...can't...see!"

Jay helped Cody to his feet and brushed leaves and dirt from his red flannel shirt. "Well, you *could* see if you'd let your eyes adjust to the nighttime light."

"What light?"

"Moonlight. Starlight. Firefly light. Pick one!"

Cody wanted to say something sarcastic in reply. Instead, he thought the better of it and just snatched up his light and switched it off. "There. Happy?"

"Now wait for a minute to get used to the dark. This isn't your first camping trip, Cody. Can't you at least remember the basics?"

Cody sighed and rolled his eyes, reminding Jay they had this conversation far too many times.

Jay would not apologize for it; Cody needed to learn. "Let's just keep moving," he said, pointing in a direction easier for Cody to navigate.

They had reached a tree line that separated the woods from a natural clearing Jay wanted to explore. He briefly thought about hiding from Cody in the field's chest-high grass, not out of meanness but to teach Cody a lesson about paying attention. He decided against it, though, knowing it would only make him feel guilty. Friendships were messy.

Jay knew Cody was trying. He was not a bad kid. Of all the current boys at the youth ranch, Cody had made the best progress during the past two years. That was Jay's assessment, anyway. As a live-in counselor, the owners of the ranch valued his opinions, but he was no psychologist. He was, however, a pretty good judge of people.

Like Jay, Cody went there as a troubled orphan and at first had difficulty fitting in with the other teens. He took an instant liking to Jay, though, and Jay supposed they both had at least a few things in common. Cody was also the only one who ever expressed any sincere interest in Jay's favorite hobby, astronomy, which was the reason they were out in the woods that evening.

Some other kids at the ranch accused Jay of favoring Cody. Jay disagreed, but it was true he protected the portly youth. Overweight and quite clumsy, Cody was an easy target for the other boys. His gullible nature did not help him, either. With Jay as his twenty-two-year-old bodyguard, though, the playing field was level. Still, Cody was smart enough to know it would not stay that way. Soon, Jay would move on, heading off to the university or finding work somewhere else. So, for the past six months, Cody became Jay's shadow, hoping he could learn how to take care of himself from a survivor who seemed to need no one.

When Jay thought he was far enough into the center of the open field, he stopped his march and waited for Cody to catch up. It was a mild and breezy night that smelled of late spring. The only sounds were cricket song and the wind caressing the surrounding plant life.

"This must be the spot," Cody said as he appeared through a wall of grass.

Jay just stared into the starry sky. "Yeah...this is a *brilliant* spot."

"So? Now what?"

Moments passed before Jay shook himself from his distraction and scanned the field. "I guess I'll flatten a circle in the grass here and use it for a base."

Cody squinted incredulously. "Base for what? You gonna find some *girls* to bring out here?" He chuckled through a goofy grin.

"What have I said about that, Cody?"

"Oh, alright."

"What have I *said?*"

"'Show you respect yourself by respecting women,'" Cody recited.

"Right. Don't be like the other guys, Cody. A real man always shows respect—always. Girls aren't toys. Don't forget it."

"Okay. Sorry. So...what *are* you gonna do out here?"

"I'll bring my equipment tomorrow night. If you're good, you can come with me again. Then I'll show you some things that will blow your mind."

"Yeah? Like what?"

Jay grabbed the top of Cody's head, pulled it back, and made him look skyward. "Right up there is the constellation Cassiopeia, and over there is Ursa Major. Below that is Bootes. We'll need my telescope to see the planets, and you'll love seeing the moon close up."

Cody turned his head under Jay's light grip and squinted at the glowing moon. "Uh-huh."

"But what I really want to study is Mars, which is right...over...there."

Guiding Cody's head downward, Jay aimed his gaze toward the tiny pinkish light that was Mars.

"Okay. It'll be cool. I'll give you that," Cody said, slapping away Jay's hand. "Um...thanks. I mean...for letting me come."

"Sure." Jay kept staring into the sky. He wanted to lose himself in that darkness—to pretend he was somewhere else instead of being bound to the confines of his own hard world.

Cody appreciated the moment and let Jay enjoy it in silence. For a long time, they both stood there, gazing at the heavens. Then, when Cody could stand the quiet no longer, he shuffled around in the grass and decided on a good wise-crack that would lighten the mood.

"Can you imagine if—"

Jay raised a finger to his lips. "Shh!"

"I was just gonna say—"

"Quiet, Cody!"

Jay's sudden harshness startled Cody, but when he noted the concern on Jay's face, he complied with his command. "What's wrong?" he whispered. "What are you looking at?"

Jay froze in place, his eyes wide and darting about as if trying to follow the sporadic path of a flying insect. At first, the object he was tracking appeared as an indefinable shape. It was deep black and its blurred edges were difficult to distinguish. Jay only detected the thing while it moved in front of the stars.

"It's there!" he said. "No, *there!* Wait. Now it's *there!*"

Cody tried to follow Jay's gaze. "I don't see anything. If this is some kind of joke—"

"Get down!"

The object zipped straight toward them just as Jay tackled Cody to the ground, and a sudden blast of wind pinned them both down. When it abated, Jay rolled onto his back and gawked with disbelief. Hovering a mere twenty feet above them was a black triangular mass as large as the field where he and Cody lay. The air between was thick and energized with static, causing the hair on Jay's arms to stand up. An otherworldly hum filled his ears.

The monstrous thing hung above them for several seconds. It then spun in a circle four times, becoming wobblier with each spin, as if it was having difficulty hovering. Worried that he and Cody were about to be squashed, Jay scrambled onto hands and knees, grabbed Cody's arm, and yanked. "Cody, move!"

Cody struggled to get his stout body up and crawling. "Wait! I...can't get up!" His sluggishness was not the only reason; the giant triangle was slowly rising. Before either of them could stand, another blast of wind pushed their bodies to the ground again. "Look!" Cody pointed to a mangled corner of the craft just as it turned and floated past the treetops out of view. A cascade of blue sparks marked its path.

"It's damaged!" Jay noted, jumping to his feet. "Cody, are you alright?"

"I-I-I...uh..."

"Talk to me, pal. Are—" The sound of snapping tree limbs somewhere nearby interrupted him.

Cody's wide, frightened eyes followed Jay's stare toward the woods. "That...that *thing* almost landed on us! What was it?"

Jay studied the dark forest. "I don't know. But I think it just crashed."

"Then let's get out of here!" Cody demanded.

Jay shook his head. "Not until I know what is it. You stay here. I'll be back shortly." With that, he tromped away through the high grass.

"No! Jay, wait!" Cody stood up and waved, but Jay was already out of sight. "We should go back!"

Jay heard Cody's protest, but he did not respond. He had already re-entered the forest and was too busy navigating through the under-brush and trees—at an unusual speed. With each step, his body also felt lighter. "What's going on?" he wondered out loud. He was a quick runner, but not this quick. When he also noticed a spreading numbness in his arms and legs, he knew the strange triangle must have had some-thing to do with it. Now visible just ahead of him, it was indeed pulling him toward it, and all he could do was shift and twist to avoid colliding with the trees.

Leaning toward an opening between tree trunks, Jay risked a glance behind him and saw Cody being dragged along, too. Cody, however, was not as quick as Jay to assess his predicament and adjust to it. Rather than working with the pulling force, he was still trying to run away from it. As a result, he tumbled over uneven ground and bumped between trees like a pinball rolling through a maze of obstacles.

When Cody finally realized that struggling would not work against the pull, he went limp and allowed his body to be tugged along. In seconds, he ended up right on Jay's heels.

While dodging the passing trees, Jay tried to maneuver himself closer to Cody. "Lean toward me!" he yelled.

"I...can't!" Cody sideswiped another tree and screamed in frustra-tion. The sound came out muffled, as if he was underwater. "What in the..."

Jay reached for Cody's arm to pull him closer and avoid further col-lisions. Instead of grabbing it, though, his hand passed right through. This elicited another muted scream from Cody.

"Jay!"

Turning into a ghost horrified Jay, too, but as he opened his mouth to join Cody in screaming, the pulling force released them and they both fell to the ground. The object had risen above the tree line again and disappeared from view seconds before Jay and Cody were about to plow into it.

Jay got to his feet and patted himself down, relieved to feel sensation return to his body. Cody, meanwhile, had scrambled to a tree and wrapped his arms and legs around its trunk as if to prevent himself from floating away again.

"It's okay," Jay said as he brushed himself off. "It stopped now." He stumbled toward a spot where the object had flattened a copse of small trees. In the upturned soil, he noticed tiny blue electrical currents and sparks. "Part of it must have touched the ground here." The strange effect fascinated him, but his inquisitive and composed manner bothered Cody.

"H-how can you be so casual about...about *that?*"

"I'm not," Jay said. "I'm as freaked out as you are."

"Well, you'd never know it!"

"Shh! Listen!" Jay tilted his head toward the sound of more distant cracking and snapping of branches. "It came down again."

"*What* did?" Cody asked as he let go of the tree he was hugging. "What is it?" His face was still white with fright, and he was backing away, worried that Jay might put his hand through him again.

"It's *okay,*" Jay said. "See?" He patted himself again to prove to Cody that he was not immaterial.

Cody did the same, but remained unconvinced. "I don't care! I'm goin' back! This is crazy! *You're* crazy!"

"You're in shock, Cody, but we're fine! Stop being so scared. Aren't you the least bit curious about what we've just seen?"

"No! No, I'm *not!* Nothing natural could do that to us!"

"Exactly..." Jay turned toward the second crash and strained to hear what sounded like a faint mechanical hum. "I'm going after it."

"Are you out of your—" Cody did not finish because Jay was already running through the woods toward the next crash site. "Jay! Wait!" he yelled. "I can't...I can't find my way back!" Faced with sitting alone in the dark woods or following his crazy camp counselor, he threw his hands up in defeat and bolted after Jay. "Scared?" he asked himself. "Of course I'm scared!" But Cody wondered what frightened him more— Jay's rash actions, being lost, or what they might see next.

CHAPTER 2

Overtaken

"I hope Vince will be okay." April Theele stared out the passenger side window of the family's late model sport utility vehicle, overtaken by a sense of inevitability that something was going to go wrong with her plans for the weekend. Paul, her husband, shifted uncomfortably in the driver's seat.

"You said that already."

April turned toward him in time to notice a very visible sigh. "When?"

"Five minutes after we pulled out of your mom's driveway," Paul answered. He dropped his right hand from the steering wheel and placed it on April's knee. "Look. Both of them will be fine. As long as Dex has his video games, he'll be happy, and Vince enjoys helping Mom out in the barn. It's *her* we should worry about—"

"She'll handle them alright."

"Well, there you go then." Paul smiled in triumph and went back to the business of driving.

"I hate when you do that," April said.

"Do what?"

"Boil everything down to the most simplistic answer."

Paul considered that for a moment, but could not come up with a complicated reply. "I can't help it. You know how it is; men are wired that way. We think in terms of logic...it helps us worry less."

"So I should just be more logical?"

Paul smiled and shook his head as he changed lanes. "Babes, I love you exactly how you are. You balance me out perfectly."

"Good." April always loved it when Paul used her pet name. It reminded her of their early years together—before kids—when they were just two carefree lovers. That and his smile—more of an impish grin—were all it ever took to melt away any tension between them.

"I still do the same for you, don't I?" Paul asked.

"Of course." April leaned over and kissed his cheek. "Sorry for all the worrying. It's just...this is the first time I'm leaving my babies for so long."

"I know, but it's only four days. So let's try to relax and enjoy it."

"I will."

Paul became quiet after that. He was concentrating on driving or lost in thought, so April pushed her seat back and pondered over their upcoming retreat. The name *Marriage Invigoration Weekend* both intrigued and concerned her. The concern came from reading too many advertisements for it. She did not care for how the ads claimed good marriages like hers were still at risk of developing problems. Her relationship with Paul was strong, but she had to admit their *marriage* could use some fine tuning. The past seven years had been great, but both of them agreed on needing a boost, especially regarding romance.

Vince and Dex, ages four and six, demanded most of April's time and energy. Motherhood was not for wimps. The women who ostracized her for deciding to exchange a paycheck for being a stay-at-home mom could never imagine how much harder it was to deal with small children all day. Then again, when April considered the demanding and needy personalities she had to endure in past jobs, children did not seem as bad. During her first year of being at home, she had learned to enjoy her new role and was glad to trade office politics and stress for playground games and fatigue.

Paul supported April in every way, and he never took being a husband and father for granted. April could tell, though, that the past year had been especially hard on him. He had changed jobs and was also taking online courses toward his master's degree. That meant more fatigue and less time for the family. Both he and April felt burned out. When it began affecting them in the bedroom, they realized they had to slow life down.

Overall, they were fine. Most of their married friends even envied their relationship. April, however, wanted to make sure it stayed that way. Too many couples she was friends with in college had divorced already, never making it past their fifth year. April and Paul Theele would not let that happen to them. She began exploring ideas for a couple's getaway and came across an ad for a marriage retreat that was within driving distance. When she read more about it on the event's website, she knew they should go.

It was going to be fun. They were alone and on their way to a romantic mountain resort, sneaking away for some much-needed intimate time in the quiet of nature. It would be as close to paradise as they could get. Although the mother in her fretted over leaving her children behind, April was determined to immerse herself in this new experience and rekindle some fire in her marriage.

Paul, in his usual way, was easy to convince, especially when he heard that the retreat's theme included reviving romance. He agreed, though, that a marriage-building getaway would benefit their relationship. Once on board, Paul worked hard to ensure they could go, even taking two unpaid leave days from his new job. To reward his enthusiasm, April planned to add her own sensual surprises to their weekend escape.

Tired of thinking, April closed her eyes and hoped to doze while she listened to smooth jazz on the radio. It was so characteristic of Paul to choose something like that. He enjoyed variety. She opened one lazy eye and glimpsed him bobbing his head to the music as he drove. He reminded her of the younger Paul—high-spirited and carefree, looking sexy in his tight athletic t-shirt and with his handsome face shadowed by late-day stubble. The wife in her noted he needed a haircut. The lover in her adored how the passing streetlights made his eyes sparkle with a lust for life.

We need time away, she thought before sleep overtook her. *This is going to be a fun trip.*

* * *

"Now what?" Paul's voice and abrupt application of the brake pedal startled April from her brief nap.

"Are you okay?" she asked, rubbing the grogginess from her eyes.

"Yeah. Sorry, Babes. Looks like there's something going on up there."

April noticed that the vehicles ahead of them were slowing down, their red brake lights blinking on and off like fireflies in the evening darkness. "I hope it's not an accident. Where are we?"

"Route sixty-four west. Find Cottersville on the map. We passed that about thirty minutes ago."

April unfolded Paul's travel map and held it up, using the headlights of the car behind them for a reading light. For some reason, Paul still liked to employ what he called 'paper atlases' during their trips, rather than solely relying on electronic devices. April assumed it was nostalgic, perhaps reminding him of the many treks he had been on with his father while growing up.

"Okay. I see it," she said, planting her finger on the spot. "Looks like we still have about thirty to forty minutes before we get to our exit."

Paul frowned as he brought their vehicle to a stop behind a long line of traffic. "Are there any side roads so we can bypass this?"

"Um...well...kind of. Yeah. The next exit should be Greenwood Road. Get off and turn right on that. It goes north for a few miles, but then it curves and we'll be going west again, parallel to sixty-four."

Paul liked the idea of moving rather than sitting still. Noting the Greenwood Road exit sign ahead, he pulled out of his lane into the graveled shoulder and headed for the off-ramp.

"You could have let me drive some," April said. "Want me to take over now?"

"No. I'm fine. I just feel like we're never going to get there."

* * *

Greenwood Road was a two-lane, paved farm road that provided access to a nature preserve on the right and to small farms on the left. Moonlight substituted for better lighting, but on this evening it was bright enough to cast soft shadows behind roadside mailboxes and long wooden fences. Paul and April had only been on Greenwood for about ten minutes when again they encountered a traffic jam.

"So much for our shortcut," Paul said with a long sigh.

"This is weird." April strained to see around the cars ahead of them. "Flashing lights, like a roadblock or something."

"Another accident?"

"I don't think so...there's a big floodlight, too."

"Great." Paul lowered the window and stuck his head out to get a better view. A small pickup truck drove past them, heading in the opposite direction. "They're making people turn around."

April unfolded the map for another consultation. "Back to this, then."

"I'm driving all the way up. I want to know what's going on. Maybe I can ask a cop about a different road."

Within a few minutes, they had crept to a police blockade. Four state troopers stood in front of a wooden barricade, illuminated by as many patrol cars and by two construction site floodlights. A van and a few unmarked cars were on the other side.

Paul put their vehicle in park, opened his door, and wobbled on legs that were stiff from hours of sitting. Since there were no other vehicles behind them, April got out, too, and she was glad for the chance to stretch.

A trooper wearing a metallic name tag that read *Brenan* ambled toward them, his flashlight held up at shoulder height in police fashion and his other hand resting on his belt. The other three troopers disappeared around the barricade.

"Evenin', folks."

"Good evening," Paul said. "We're trying to get to the resort and thought this might be a good shortcut."

Trooper Brenan looked April up and down, smiled, and nodded. "Ma'am."

Paul was in no mood for the cop's obvious ogling. True, he often had to put up with unwanted attention toward his wife. She was young, fit, and naturally attractive. Even in her jeans, wrinkled t-shirt, and tousled hair, she would be a head-turner to most men. Paul agreed, but she was his. He stepped closer and wrapped his arm around her waist to make the point.

"Well?"

"I've been seein' a lot of couples tonight," Brenan said with a creepy chuckle. Leering and being caught did not seem to bother him. "Guess ya'll are goin' up there fer the romantic getaway thing, huh?"

"If we can ever get there, yes," Paul answered. "The interstate is jammed up. What's going on?"

"Ya'll aren't from the *media,* are you?"

"Hardly."

"Well, what they told me was that a plane went down in the park."

"The park?"

Brenan pointed at the woods alongside the road. "The preserve."

"Is it bad?"

"Must be. They called in the military to help."

Paul then noticed that the forest was lit up in places by floodlights. Out of the darkness behind the barricade, a man in a suit appeared, followed by a soldier in what looked like full combat gear.

"Officer Brenan!" the suit called.

Brenan spoke to Paul and April more officially this time. "You folks go back to the interstate and head west. Then look for one-twenty-seven north. It'll take you out of your way, but at least you'll get to where you need to go. Have a good night."

With that, Brenan turned his attention to the suited man. Paul tried to eavesdrop on their conversation while he and April sauntered back to their vehicle.

"This is my replacement, then?" Brenan asked, gesturing toward the soldier.

"Yes."

"As soon as that last vehicle is off the road," the soldier said, "we'll bring in the trucks."

"Fine," Brenan replied. "The main blockade is up now. No one else can get through."

Paul guided April to the passenger side door, opened it for her, and then glanced at the barricade. "Military trucks? What was it, a military plane?"

"Well, it looks like they have plenty of help," April said. "Let's get out of here before it gets any weirder."

Paul watched a helicopter circling overhead. Under its sweeping searchlight, he could see more military vehicles and a massive tent further up the road. "Quite an operation."

"I'm getting in," April said. She started to climb into her seat, but hesitated when she heard a voice calling out from behind them.

"Wait! Hey, there! Wait!"

A young man, followed by a teenager, came crashing out from the tree line at the edge of the road. They both stumbled toward Paul and April and then leaned against the fender of their vehicle while catching their breath.

"Did you...did you...did you see them?" the twenty-something asked. "Are they—"

"Take it easy," Paul said. "You're about to run right into a big mess up ahead."

"Mess?" He peered around Paul and studied the barricade. "Good...good."

"I told you, Jay!" the teen said to his companion. His face was red with exertion and his eyes wide with fear. "I told you something like this was going on!"

Jay ignored the comment while he scanned the surrounding area. "Did you see any people just come through here?" he asked Paul.

"Yeah. There are lots of them around here. Police, soldiers—"

"No! I mean any *strange* ones."

"How about telling us what you two are doing out here?" Paul suggested.

"Are the police looking for you?" April asked.

"They came out of the triangle ship. It crashed. Twice."

Paul pointed toward the woods. "Are you talking about the plane crash?"

"It wasn't a plane…"

April considered the barricade, leaned in close to Paul, and whispered. "Maybe they witnessed something."

"Jay—that is your name, right?" Paul asked.

Jay nodded. "People…came out of it," he said between breaths.

"We'll get to that," Paul said. "What are *you two* doing out here?"

"Camping."

"With a group?" April asked.

"Yes."

Paul pointed at the younger boy. "What about him?"

"His name is Cody," Jay answered. "He's with me."

"Good. Listen, Jay. We're going to take you and Cody over there and get some help."

Jay pointed at the pasture across the road, and renewed excitement flashed in his eyes. "There! There they are!" He grabbed Paul's arm and swung him around to look.

"What?" It was dark, but Paul could see some figures in the meadow, and they were too small to be livestock. "Those are probably—"

"What's going on here? You people have to leave!" It was trooper Brenan, and he was marching with purpose toward Paul's vehicle.

Jay took one look at Brenan and bolted into the pasture.

"Jay! No! Wait!" Paul hollered. He looked at April and shrugged his shoulders. "Wait here. I'll go get him."

Before April could protest, Paul was already running to catch up to Jay.

"No!" April called after him. "Paul! Come back!"

Trooper Brenan stormed up to April and Cody and aimed his flashlight into the pasture. Its long beam followed Paul as he hopped over a wooden fence beyond the edge of the road. "You!" Brenan yelled. "Stop there!"

In a flash, April impulsively dashed after Paul and Jay, leaving Cody sitting on the ground and babbling about going home.

"Paul! Paul! Wait!" April demanded. "I can't believe this." She cleared the fence in one easy leap, marveling at how her body remembered her days in college track and field. Within seconds, she was already about twenty yards behind Paul and both of them were gaining on Jay. A quick glance over her shoulder revealed that Brenan and at least six others were chasing them all, flashlights swinging back and forth and commanding shouts interrupting the quiet peace of the pasture. Ahead of Jay, she could just make out three other figures that were running away as well. She wondered if Brenan or the soldiers would shoot them all for refusing to stop. That thought gave her more speed, and she found herself right on Paul's heels. Then everything changed.

A great shadow spread across the meadow and blocked out the moonlight. April looked up and saw a triangular patch of black where the stars should have been. A warm wind buffeted her just before a wide beam of purple light shot down from the sky, enveloping her, Paul, and Jay. She yelled out to Paul, but her words sounded muffled, as if her ears had filled with water.

No longer able to feel the ground under her feet, April glanced down and discovered she was being lifted into the air. Ahead of her, Paul and Jay were also floating upward—blurry specters within the grasp of an eerie purple light. After a brief tingle, all physical sensation left her. Then her vision blurred.

Am I dying? she wondered. *They must have shot me for refusing to stop. Oh, God, I'm dead.*

CHAPTER 3

Mistaken

April was mistaken about being dead. She realized that when she regained her senses and felt pain. Every muscle ached, and her skin tingled everywhere.

If I did die, she reasoned, *I must have just come back to life. My brain is still working, so that's a good sign.*

Thinking was a start, but she could not speak or even open her eyes. Long minutes passed. When sensation returned to her body, she could tell she was lying on something soft. Warm air blew over her face, and dim light was on the other side of her eyelids. She raised a hand and rubbed her eyes until she got them to open.

Soft floor. Dimly lit room, she noted. All the surfaces were smooth and black, and there were no visible windows or doors. *Need to move. Wait...what's wrong with my legs?* A glance downward revealed that her lower body had become embedded in the floor. *Don't...panic. Just...don't panic.* She poked at the flooring and discovered the surrounding parts were pliable—like thick putty or memory foam. When she dug holes, they remained open until she could pull her legs free. As she scrambled away, she watched the stuff fill in the empty spaces and make the surface flat and solid.

Two large lumps bulged underneath the same pliant material a few feet from where April was sitting. She crawled to the first one, slid her hands over it, and felt the distinct features of another body.

"Paul?" she called.

The surrounding room absorbed the sound of her voice. Scared and frantic, she clawed at the flooring. It took some effort, but she cleared enough away to find Paul's head. To her great relief, he was breathing and regaining consciousness.

"Paul!"

"What...happened?" he asked.

"Help me get you out of there!"

April uncovered his arms, and he immediately began helping her to free himself the rest of the way. With that accomplished, he rolled over and dug his fingers into the other lump that must have been Jay. Once Jay was clear and April knew he was alright, she collapsed in tears.

"Where...where are we?" Jay asked them.

Paul pulled April close and scanned the room while trying to calm her. He had no answer for Jay. "What's the last thing you remember?"

"Chasing after those other people," Jay answered, checking himself for injuries. "When I was about to catch up to them, I felt myself rising, then my body was gone."

April raised her head and used the back of her hand to wipe away tears. "What do you mean?"

"How else can I describe it? I saw you guys behind me. We were all running through the field; the thing flew over us, shot a purple beam, and here we are."

April frowned. "What thing?"

"The black triangle," Jay answered, as if it was obvious. "The aircraft we're sitting in right now. I followed one until it crashed. I guess there were two."

"Another one crashed?" Paul asked.

Jay poked at the black floor, watching the indentations refill as he replied. "Yeah. In the woods. Close to where I ran into you. First, it touched down a few times, like it was having trouble staying in the air. After it finally came down, some figures stumbled out."

"What figures?" April asked.

Jay hesitated to answer. "I...don't know. People."

"Who?" Paul asked. He tested the floor before slowly rising to his feet. "How did they dress? Were they military pilots?"

"No."

"Well, what did they look like, then?" Paul prodded.

"It was dark and hard to tell. Give me a minute here...my head still aches."

Paul sighed and began a careful walk around the room, examining the walls as if looking for a secret opening.

"Be careful of the floor," April warned. "Paul, try your phone."

"Should have already thought of that." He reached into his pocket but found it empty. "No good. It's back in the truck. Do *you* have one, Jay?"

"No. I lost mine running in the woods."

Paul returned to the center of the room, and the three formed a huddle. "I can't find a way out of here," he said. "Until someone comes, we might as well piece this story together. Jay, tell us everything."

Jay recounted his experience with the first triangular object, beginning with his search for a good stargazing site and ending with what he called the *abduction.* When he finished speaking, Paul and April just gawked at him. Neither knew how to explain what Jay saw, but they both believed him.

"Tell me more about the people you were chasing," Paul said. "How many were there?"

"Only three...I think. It was really dark in the woods, even in the moonlight. Didn't you guys see them in the field?"

"I only saw some vague figures running ahead of you," Paul answered.

"Me, too," April said. "But I was too busy trying to catch up."

"What about *before* that, though?" Paul asked Jay. "You must have gotten close enough to see what they looked like."

"Uh..."

"Yes?" Paul pressed.

"This is going to sound weird."

"Go on."

"They were naked."

"Naked?"

"Well...they were only covering their privates, anyway. Some kind of little loincloths, I guess."

"Like Tarzan?" April proposed.

"Okay," Jay allowed, "like Tarzan."

"All males then," reasoned Paul.

Jay shook his head. "One of them was different."

"How so?" April asked.

"I could tell it was female." Jay's cheeks flushed.

"How?" April pressed.

"Because she was topless."

"Oh, um..."

"Okay," Paul cut in, "so Tarzan, his brother, and Jane, then. I'm not sure what to say about that."

Jay managed a brief smile. "Me neither. But they definitely weren't pilots, and they looked foreign. When a searchlight hit them, I saw that their skin was bronzed. Not like a deep suntan, but dark bronze. Unnatural."

"It just keeps getting better," Paul said. "Sorry, Jay. I'm not doubting your story. It's making me feel very uneasy, though. Both of you help me look for a way out of here."

April nodded to Jay, and the three stood up in unison. Each took an area of the closest wall, pressing in and trying to find a weak spot in the spongy material that might suggest an exit. After several quiet minutes with no success, April posed the question that no one else would.

"Paul?"

"Yeah, Babes?"

"Do you think...have we been...abducted?"

"Like...by who?" Paul asked. "By the military? That's *my* first guess. I'm thinking we all stumbled onto something that we weren't supposed to see. Now we're being held until they decide what to do with us."

April nodded her agreement. It sounded sensible.

Jay, however, believed something very different. "This is no *military* craft."

"Let's not allow our imaginations to run wild," Paul warned. "Purple lights and a strange room aren't enough to make me accept that—"

At that moment, a small slit formed in the middle of the wall across from them. The three backed away, watching as a vertical line of light sliced downward through the black surface until it met the floor. Then, two sets of white hands reached through, gripping at the edges of both sides and pulling them open like a stage curtain. What walked through the opening confirmed Jay's theory.

CHAPTER 4

Captor

Paul and Jay took defensive positions in front of April, and Paul motioned for her to stay behind him. When the four hands finished opening the aperture, a silhouetted figure rushed into the room...and stopped short at the sight of them.

It was a man, or at least it resembled one. His anatomy and physical features were quite human, but his skin was a radiant iridescent white. Shoulder-length hair, of the same coloration, covered his head and framed a handsome, chiseled face. His wide eyes were bright green, and below a narrow nose were milky pink lips, parted as if about to speak. Paul guessed he stood about six feet tall, and on his perfectly proportioned muscular frame was not a stitch of clothing. His nakedness, though somewhat alarming, seemed natural for his otherworldly appearance. He was like a well-sculpted Greek statue or a store mannequin waiting to be dressed. Despite the apparent humanity, *alien* was the first word that came to Paul's mind.

Paralyzed by fear, the three abductees could only gawk at their captor. He returned their surprised stares, just as taken aback by their presence. After a few long moments, he raised one hand over his head and glanced back at the opening in the wall. It was a signal that brought another figure into the room, this time a female. She slipped through the aperture, paused when she saw the strangers, and then maneuvered herself to hide behind the male.

Like him, she looked human, at least anatomically. Iridescent alabaster skin was the only thing that covered her curvaceous body. On her head was a mane of wavy white hair, cascading to her knees and covering her most feminine parts like a shawl. Her eyes were beautiful green orbs, filled with wonderment as she examined the visitors. After recovering from the surprise of seeing them, she stepped out from behind her companion and conversed with him in whispers.

Paul strained to hear their words but could not recognize the language. To his ears, it was just a bizarre mix of vowel sounds.

"What is this, Paul?" April asked. "Who...*what* are they?"

Paul reached back and pulled her close, all the while watching the strange pair with open distrust. "I don't know."

"They're like the other ones I saw," Jay noted. "Their bodies are similar, but with a different skin color."

At the sound of Jay's voice, the female ended her conversation with the male and addressed them all. "Ooo-oh-yee. Ooo-oh-yee ah-a-eee-yee," she said in a friendly tone. "Ooo-oh-yee. Ooo-oh-yee."

Her companion raised his hands as if imploring them to stay calm. "Ah-ya," he added. "Ah-ya. Ooo-oh-yee."

Their voices were pleasing to the ear—soft, elegant, and sensuous. Paul looked to April and Jay for encouragement as he summoned the nerve to reply. They both nodded.

"What is ooo-oh-yee?" he asked the female. "Who are you?"

She smiled at the sound of her own word being returned to her. "Ooo-ahh-you?" she asked, trying to mimic Paul's words.

"Yes. Who are you? Why are we here?"

She turned back to the male and seemed to suggest something to him. He shook his head in clear disagreement, and the two began a private discussion.

Paul looked at April and Jay and shrugged. "I tried. Now what?"

The strange couple continued to talk until a third figure appeared through the opening in the wall. It was another female, somewhat younger-looking than the first, but with iridescent ebony skin and a black knee-length mane that sparkled with blue glitter. Paul guessed she must have been around Jay's age; her firm and flawless body suggested the prime of youth. She had the same green eyes and physical features as the other two, like a twin, or at least a close relative.

Noticing the three strangers, the black-skinned female abruptly stopped her approach and gasped. More surprised than afraid, she studied the Earth captives with both wariness and curiosity while she spoke to the white male. By his expressions, it was clear that what the girl was saying troubled him. After she finished her message, she then rushed out of the room.

"What do you think that was about?" April asked Paul.

"Probably us. I'm getting the impression we're not supposed to be here."

"You've got that right," Jay said.

After looking Paul up and down, the male dared to take a few cautious steps toward him.

"That's far enough," Paul warned. "Are you going to tell us what's going on here, or what?"

"Ooo-oh-yee," the glowing man replied in a genial tone. He then began talking to Paul in his strange language, pointing at himself while he stressed certain words.

"I think he's trying to explain who he is," April whispered. With curiosity overriding her fear, she stepped from behind Paul and strained to interpret what the male was saying. Her courage seemed to please him, so he began speaking to her instead.

"April," Paul warned, "I don't—" He stopped short when he realized she might be understanding something.

At the male's suggestion, his companion pushed back her long hair to expose more of her body. Amazed by her unabashed action, Paul and Jay diverted their eyes. Although she was alien enough to scare them, she was also human enough to be stunningly beautiful. Such a complete unveiling made both of the Earthmen even more aware of her nakedness, and the shamelessness of it unnerved them.

"Paul," April said in a whisper, "I think—"

"Are you getting any of that?" Paul interrupted, stealing a few glances at the female.

"Aw? Paw?" the woman asked, struggling to repeat what April said.

April nodded at her before answering Paul. "I think they've been trying to say that they're *like* us."

"Not quite," Paul said.

Noting the discomfort of her captives, the woman pulled her hair in front of her body to act as a partial covering. "Paw?" she asked April.

April took hold of Paul's arm as she responded. "Paul." Then she pointed to herself and said, "April," and at Jay and said, "Jay."

"Aw...ay-ih...ay." Though the pronunciations were hard for her, she understood they were names. Pointing at each of them, she tried again. "Paw...Ah-eel...Ay."

Her companion guffawed at her attempt to pronounce the words. "Ahee, seee-ah-yoo ih-uh-ho!" he said between laughs. She covered her mouth with both hands and giggled at herself.

The abductees could not help smiling at the laughing pair. Their awkwardness made them seem more like amiable strangers than suspicious captors. Trust had yet to be earned, but at least they were communicating.

At the sound of laughter, the younger black-skinned female returned. Standing close to the other two, she scrutinized the visitors with keen eyes and intense curiosity. Jay was her first interest. She gave him a good looking over with a penetrating gaze that expressed utter amazement. Jay fidgeted and tried not to stare back at her uncovered form. Satisfied with her assessment, she then turned her attention to Paul and April, examining them with the same look of wonder.

"Kei-hee-ah-may," the girl said after completing her once-over. Then, grinning, she turned to the alien man, whispered in his ear, and hurried out of the room.

April tried asking a question again. "Can either of you understand me?"

Their eyes darted to her, and they both smiled. April could not determine if it was because they understood her or if they were just pleased that she felt comfortable enough to address them.

"Why are we here?" Paul added.

The man took a few more steps toward Paul.

"Ooo-ah-ayfe," he said, struggling with the sounds. "Ens. Ens."

Paul could tell by the way he held out his hands that *ens* must have meant *friends*.

"Friends?" he asked.

"F-ens," the man repeated. "Ooo-ah-ayfe. Ooo-oh-yee."

"I think he's saying, 'You are safe,'" Jay said to Paul.

"Okay. That's a start."

"Friends?" April asked, holding out her hands to the woman.

She smiled at April's understanding. "Ooo-oh-yee."

"Okay...Ooo-oh-yee to you, too."

April still could not translate that word, but she assumed the couple meant it as a greeting or as something to put others at ease.

The alien man nodded at them all, looking as though he had just decided on an important course of action. "Paw, Ay, Ah-eel," he said. "Oooooo-eee-ey-oi-i-heh." He then motioned that they should follow him and the female to the room's exit.

The three looked to each other for agreement, but each had already determined trust was better than captivity, so they complied with the male's apparent request. Beyond the opening in the wall, they entered a long, bright corridor with the same soft, black surfaces as the room they had just exited. The alien couple escorted them through it until they reached an open portal at its end.

At the prompting of the female, they all stepped through the entryway and found themselves in a busy command center, like a ship's bridge. The space was expansive and triangular, with an elevated floor along the back wall where they had entered. Two steps led down to the main floor. In the middle, there was a circular column surrounded by what appeared to be six workstations and seats. The three corners of the room were transparent and resembled massive viewing windows—

viewports—that reached from the floor to the curved ceiling. All across the walls, panels of flashing buttons and glowing displays splashed color into the otherwise ebon space.

"Looks like we're on the bridge," Paul whispered to April and Jay. Besides the two white-skinned ones, he counted seven other aliens there. Three sat behind the center workstations, and Paul recognized one of those as the younger female he had seen earlier. The four others stood in front of the viewports, looking out and pointing as if they were searching for something.

Like the host couple, the alien crew seemed to have no use for uniforms or coverings of any kind. The females—four in all—were clothed only in ebony skin and knee-length hair that was jet black and speckled with colors individual to each. The three males had a similar appearance, but their hair was much shorter and devoid of the colorful flecks. All of them—male and female—were of the same height and had fit muscular bodies. Statuesque and flawless, their unclad forms resembled living marble statues, carved by a master artist.

It took a few moments for the busy group to realize strangers were in their midst. When they did, each of them stopped working and just gawked at the visitors with surprise and wariness. Noting a sudden unease in the room, the white-skinned man addressed his people in their language. His commanding presence suggested he was their leader. With a firm but calming tone, he announced the foreigners and then gave a very brief speech. After he finished, they returned to their duties, trying to limit their curiosity about the new arrivals to occasional glances and discreet gazing.

Still stunned and now feeling like uninvited guests, Paul, April, and Jay remained in the back of the room until the white-skinned woman approached them and motioned that they should go to a viewport. Two females moved away to give them access, all the while gawking in silence.

"Okay, so now what?" Paul whispered to his companions.

"She's motioning for us to look out the window," Jay noted. "Want to go first?"

Paul shrugged and stepped closer to the transparent wall. Beyond it was only darkness, but when he peeked downward, he saw a glowing city—his city—from a height of at least five thousand feet. *So, we're in a craft after all,* he thought with growing amazement, *and we're flying!*

"What is it, Paul?" April asked.

When he did not immediately answer, she and Jay stepped next to him and followed his stare.

"Oh...man," Jay said.

April gripped Paul's arm. "I think we'd better reconsider our theory."

Paul nodded. "Yeah. Remember how you were looking forward to some excitement this weekend?"

"Not like this, though," April replied, suddenly shaking with renewed fear.

Paul pulled her close as they stared at the city below. "Try to keep it together, Babes. We'll get through this...somehow."

Jay shifted uncomfortably under the gaze of the two black females standing nearby. "Well," he said to Paul, "I hate to say I told you so, but..."

"I know, Jay. If it helps any, I no longer think this is a hoax or a military operation."

"Are you ready to say *alien abduction* now?" Jay asked.

"No. But if the shock wears off...I just might be."

CHAPTER 5

Intentions

The genial manner of the human-like beings and their cordial treatment of the abductees were not quite enough to keep April from feeling like a prisoner. Their gentleness made her want to trust them, but she would doubt their intentions until they could answer her many questions. Why were they being kept there? Who were these people? Were they even human? Would they eventually let her go? There were still too many unknowns.

At least we've been allowed to stay on their bridge, she thought. *They haven't tossed us into a cell.* She hoped it was out of kindness and not because they wanted to keep a close eye on the captives from Earth.

April guessed she had been on the bridge for about a half-hour before the white-skinned female approached her and tried to communicate again. This time, April recognized a few mispronounced English words, as if the woman knew something *about* her language but could not vocalize it.

Soon, both women grew frustrated. Their languages were just too different. It was not enough to imitate each other's pronunciations; the words needed to be understood. Fear created a barrier as well. April was apprehensive about letting the strange woman get too close to her, and that resistance seemed to cause resentment. The alien female, though cautious, clearly wanted to enter April's personal space. Was that important somehow?

A little later, during another awkward communication attempt, the woman abruptly walked away from April to speak to a black-skinned female who was working nearby. As they chatted, the white woman kept glancing back as if to suggest that April should watch the conversation. This April did, and after studying how the aliens interacted, she understood something new about how they communicated with each other.

They're very physical. Touch has meaning.

Sometimes it was obvious—touching or gesturing. At other times, they read each other's facial expressions and interpreted body language that was barely perceptible to April. She concluded that intimate awareness and physical contact were just as important as speaking words in their language—a type of nonvocal communication.

This revelation gave her more confidence. Staving off her fear as best she could, she raised her hand as if signaling her teacher to come over. "Let's try it your way," she whispered to herself as the woman approached.

Rather than keeping several feet between them, this time April allowed her to come as close as she dared. Without hesitation, the woman stepped so close that April could smell a fragrance emanating from her glowing body—like exotic tropical flowers. Fascinated and undaunted, she reached up and stroked April's hair.

April resisted showing any kind of aversion and willed herself to put aside her personal boundaries. As a reward, she could actually feel the other woman's emotions through her touch. Innocent intentions, honesty, and longing for understanding rushed into April's consciousness like a flood.

"How...?" April began to ask.

Green eyes stared back, and words that were not her own formed in April's mind. *Ooo-oh-yee. Be at peace. Learn.* The woman was communicating without even speaking. It was pleasantly intimate, but also unnerving. April was not sure how to react.

The woman, sensing April's confusion and discomfort, nodded and backed away. She then glanced at Paul and Jay, who were nearby and watching the strange scene. Without a word, she made a slight gesture with her hand and waited for one of the three to interpret it.

"I think she...wants us all to leave with her," April told them, taking a cue from the persuasion in her eyes.

"Okay," Paul said to the woman. "Lead on."

She escorted them off the bridge and back down the main corridor to another room. By its arrangement, they could see it was a place for resting. Odd-shaped lounges, seats, and tables demarcated a recessed seating area, and dim lighting created an atmosphere of spa-like relaxation. Unusual works of art added color to the otherwise black space.

The woman raised and lowered her hands as if to suggest sitting. With gestures and foreign words, she also tried to tell them something about one of the room's walls. It was apparent her guests did not understand what she was saying, but she explained anyway. When she finished, she gave them an apologetic smile and shrugged.

"Thank you. I'm sure we'll be fine," April said.

April's perception seemed to please her. "Ooo-oh-yee, Ah-eel," she replied, bowing and turning to leave. Somehow, the entryway had closed after their arrival. Instead of opening it with her hands, though, the woman pressed her body against its membranous surface and allowed it to pull her into its blackness.

"Interesting exit," Paul said as he tested a lounge.

Jay watched as the portal's undulations subsided and it returned to its formerly smooth appearance. "Looks like you can either stretch it open or just push against it to go through."

"I'd hate to pick the wrong wall and end up outside."

"Me, too."

For a second, April thought about using that as an escape, but the reality that they were flying thousands of feet above the ground quickly dispelled the idea. "I'm afraid to touch *anything*," she told Paul.

"The seats are safe enough," he said, patting the soft material. "Come and sit down."

He stood, and as April sat in his place, she shot him a look of surprise.

"Yeah," he agreed. "They conform to your shape. It's actually quite comfy."

April squirmed and the lounge changed to suit her feminine curves. It was indeed comfortable. She leaned back and let out a long breath.

"So...what was that all about...between you and the white female?" Paul asked.

"Language lessons," April replied. "It was strange. I do understand something, though."

"Really?"

"There's a lot of subtle communication going on. I mean, other than words."

"What then? Telepathy?"

"No. Not like that. But there *is* something about communicating through touch to share thoughts. Then again, I might be imagining it all. Am I acting like I'm in shock, Paul?"

"No. But just rest there a minute." He scanned their surroundings. "Jay and I will explore the room."

"Try the wall she pointed to," April said.

Paul walked over and tested different spots by pressing his hands against them. "It all feels firm."

"To the left," April suggested.

"How can you tell?"

"From here, the shade looks different."

Paul moved a few steps to his left and pressed against the surface. It offered less resistance, even allowing his hand to go all the way through.

April gasped. "Be careful!"

Paul took a deep breath, stuck in his other hand, and then stretched it apart like a curtain, enough to accommodate his head and shoulders. After another deep breath, he leaned his head inside the opening and looked around for a few seconds. Then he pulled away, and the hole closed.

"What is it?" asked Jay.

"It's another small room—only big enough for one or two people. There are a few holes in the walls and a few weird-looking seats."

"That's strange," April said.

"If I had to guess, I'd say it looks like a bathroom."

"How can you tell?"

"It's sort of configured that way—like a shower, sink, toilet. Just a guess."

"There's another spot to try...way over to the right," April said, pointing.

Jay stepped over to it and slid his hands across the surface. "Besides the difference in shade, this part is a little more spongy." Like Paul, he pressed through, made a hole, and stuck his head inside.

"Well?" April said when he finished his inspection.

"It might be storage, possibly for food. I saw boxes and plants with fruit on them."

"Well, at least we're not being treated like prisoners in a cell," April said. "That makes me feel better."

Paul returned to her and sat on the edge of a nearby lounge.

"What do you think we are, then?" he asked.

April considered that for a moment before answering. "Surprise visitors, I guess," she replied. "Like we dropped in unexpectedly."

"Did you get anything at all from your chat with the female?"

"Not much. I thought I heard some familiar words, but... I don't know."

"She seems to like you."

April recalled their unspoken exchange and the woman's gentle touch. "She seems sweet, like a young girl, but she also has such wisdom in her eyes. I don't see or sense anything negative or dangerous about her or *any* of them."

"Yeah. It's hard not to trust them," Paul agreed. "They all have this *thing* about them that makes you think they're as harmless as baby deer."

"But you doubt that?"

Paul leaned forward, resting his elbows on his knees, and let out a frustrated sigh. He sensed she was looking for some reassurance. "We'll just have to take it one step at a time."

Jay joined them in the seating area, choosing a seat next to Paul. "Want to know what I think?"

Paul and April shook off their fatigue and turned toward Jay, eager for a fresh perspective.

"Yes, we would, Jay." April said. "What *do* you think?"

"I think these people, or aliens, or whatever you want to call them, were trying to help their friends—the other ones who crashed their ship in the woods. It might have been a rescue, but we got in the way and they pulled us up instead."

"I hadn't considered that possibility," Paul said.

April agreed. "Me neither. I forgot about the others. I wonder what happened to them."

"Who knows," Paul said. "But if these aliens were trying to help the other ones, why were the others running away?"

"They might have been running from *our* people—the searchers—or from *us*," Jay guessed. "What if they were supposed to wait in that field to get picked up, but we scared them off?"

All three sat in silence for a few minutes while they considered Jay's theory.

"Maybe they'll let us go once they get their friends," April said.

The silence returned—an uneasy silence caused by doubt.

"Why wouldn't they?" Paul asked.

Jay scanned the room like someone who was being watched. "They might want to study us."

"Too much sci-fi, Jay," Paul said.

"I guess we'll find out soon enough," Jay countered. "But at least we know *one* thing for sure."

"What?" April asked.

"There is definitely other intelligent life in the universe."

CHAPTER 6

Witnesses

There was no shortage of witnesses to the evening's UFO activity. Hundreds of people had been frightened enough to contact the police departments in their communities after seeing one or two black triangular objects in the night sky. It would have been easy to dismiss the sightings as misinterpretations of natural phenomena, nighttime aircraft, or even a well-planned hoax. But then the military inquiries and strange calls from important-sounding government offices began. Clearly, something had happened in the forest that was much bigger than the usual UFO frenzy.

Because the military had already been tracking the unknown objects, it did not take long for their aircraft and ground vehicles to converge on the western boundary of the nature preserve. After arriving, soldiers discovered three areas with broken trees and shriveled vegetation. At the most heavily damaged site, there was also an unexplainable absence of soil about three feet deep.

Preliminary evidence pointed to either a plane crash or multiple meteor strikes, but there was no wreckage and no debris. Military personnel searched the woods until first light, and that is when they discovered something even more unusual—fresh sets of bare footprints near the site with the missing dirt. The prints were easy to follow since the ground in that part of the forest was wet. They led to Greenwood Road, close to the spot where soldiers had erected a portable command center. The trail continued on the other side of the road into a pasture where a traveling couple and a young man had purportedly disappeared.

While surveying the crash sites, investigators received a continuous flow of messages about a strange flying object, and the sightings were not limited to areas near the nature preserve in the mountains. People all along the interstate highway, which led to the state capital over eighty miles away, also claimed to have seen a UFO that night. Truck drivers and nighttime travelers saw it gliding silently overhead. Third shift factory workers, police officers on late-night patrols, college students coming home from the clubs, and even airline pilots all had similar reports. Whatever it was, stealth was not a concern; its purposeful movements and exploratory behavior suggested it was searching for something.

* * *

When the sun peeked over the horizon, it seemed like a typical early morning in the small city that was also the state capital. Commuters were already on the highways. Newspapers were being packed into their stands and vending boxes. Restaurants and coffee shops were opening their doors for business.

The first people to realize it would not be a normal day were motorists with an unrestricted view of the city while traveling to work. Their familiar cityscape now included a huge triangular object hovering above the financial district. From a distance, it could have been mistaken for a giant balloon or a new advertising gimmick. Up close, however, it looked otherworldly. The surface of the thing was the darkest shade of black, absorbing light into itself like a great hole in the sky. With rounded corners and edges, there were no seams or protrusions to show it was a machine. It had to be artificial, yet its hull moved and pulsated as if it was skin over a living creature.

The Triangle—a fitting name used by the news media—had been circling the city during the early morning hours before it came to rest over a high-rise bank building. Reporters were diligent in finding eyewitnesses. They also discovered the connection between the Triangle's appearance above the capital and sightings near the state nature preserve the night before. When they learned three people mysteriously disappeared in that area, journalists and newscasters made their habitual hasty speculations. Sensational stories soon spread around the world of a bona fide UFO, alien abductions, and the uncertain fate of an entire city.

Government officials urged citizens to remain calm but refused to offer their opinions about the object. For reasons of safety, they directed police to reroute traffic away from the financial district and evacuate everyone in the area. That response suggested concern about a potential terrorist attack. Most people, though, had already decided a *human* threat was improbable—they knew the Triangle had to be alien.

* * *

By late morning, camera crews were broadcasting live from nearby buildings, and the scenes were astonishing. What was happening in that unremarkable city resembled a movie, not actual news reports. While police cleared the streets, military planes circled in formation overhead, observing the UFO from above. Since no radiation or other harmful emanations were present, helicopters flew in for a closer inspection.

The object did not react to the circling presence of the other aircraft, even when a pilot guided his helicopter close to one of its rounded corners. There, he described the surface as being transparent, similar to a large window, but he could see nothing through it. Just as he was about to reposition his craft further away, though, two heads appeared behind the smoky, glass-like aperture.

The faces looked human, but their penetrating bright green eyes and unnatural black skin and hair made them look otherwise. Surprised at the sight of the hovering machine outside, the two beings pointed at it and turned away, as if alerting someone behind them. While they were doing this, powerful gusts of wind pummeled the helicopter. The sudden jolts shook its pilot and crew from their amazement, and they hurried to keep the aircraft stationary. By the time they regained control, the Triangle had moved. In an instant, it was on the other side of the downtown area near the state capital building.

All six helicopters followed the path of the UFO and surrounded it again, keeping a safer distance. From the ground, soldiers dispatched drones for closer photo and video surveillance. Just as they were approaching, however, the object sent rapid and directed beams of purple light toward the streets below.

Unsure whether this action was a simple warning or a prelude to an attack, the drone pilots recalled their craft and the helicopters executed defensive flight patterns. Then, in a flash of violet light, the black triangle darted straight up into the sky and disappeared.

* * *

After debriefing the pilots, a special investigative committee made up of thirty men and women held its initial meeting. They sat in silence, watching video recordings of the Triangle and enlarged photos of alien faces being projected onto a large screen.

When the viewing was over, the Defense Secretary was first to speak. "Any comments?" he asked as he scanned the faces of each person in the room. His eyes rested upon Doctor Doug Haines, a renowned scientist and the director of the national Space Agency. "Dr. Haines?"

"It's fascinating," Haines said, stroking his trim white beard.

"Could it be a hoax?" someone asked from across the long meeting table.

Haines shrugged his shoulders. "Without seeing the other data, I can't comment on that."

"Come on, Doctor," said another committee member. "There isn't a lot to compare this to. With all due respect, how much more information do you need? We have scans, pictures, video, and credible eyewitness accounts. Thousands of people saw the thing this morning."

Haines frowned. "Yes. You are correct. No one can deny that a large, black, triangular object of unknown origin appeared over the city. I have seen nothing like it, and there is no craft—at least that I am aware of—in the Space Agency, the Defense Department, or developed by foreign powers that can maneuver in such a fashion. But I have yet to see the data on the object's composition."

"You'll have that soon," the Defense Secretary promised. "What do you think about the faces?"

The projectionist returned the photos of the alien faces to the display screen, bringing another uncomfortable silence to the room.

"Like I said...fascinating," Haines replied.

"Does anyone here want to go out on a limb?" asked the Secretary. More silence. "Director Turgis?"

Laura Turgis was the director of a small government bureau known only as The Agency. Its purpose was to investigate unexplained phenomena that could affect national security. Because she and her staff worked in secret, they received little attention...until now.

"It's too elaborate to be a hoax," she replied, "which makes me consider subterfuge, spying, and intimidation."

She really wanted to say this UFO could represent alien life. After overseeing hundreds of investigations, only a few cases had shown any promise, and those were inconclusive. Until now, she was ready to give up her childhood dream of being the first person to prove the existence of intelligent beings from another world. The lack of indisputable evidence had almost turned her into a resolute skeptic. But then the Triangle happened. Right in front of them was all the evidence they needed. With no support in the room, however, she would not gamble with her reputation. Not today.

"Please explain," the Secretary said.

Rather than supporting her assertion of a foreign threat, Laura decided to discredit it by describing her investigation. Perhaps the recounting would raise doubts in the minds of the committee members. Then they would be open to considering the only remaining explanation for the UFO.

"My agency's investigation began last night after the first few phone calls about UFO sightings at the nature preserve," she said. "So far, we've interviewed twenty-eight witnesses from that area, and their descriptions are almost identical. Working with General Shepherd, we assisted the soldiers in searching the crash sites for debris, but as the early reports show, we found none."

"What about the disappearances of the three people outside the nature preserve?" someone asked.

Laura smirked. Everyone in the room knew that part of her job was to investigate abduction claims. Secretly, she enjoyed it. Such investigations appealed to her fascination with psychological studies. On the downside, they also hurt her agency's credibility.

"Paul and April Theele," she answered, "were on their way to a mountain resort when they stopped at a police roadblock near the nature preserve. From what we've been able to piece together, Jay Harrison, a twenty-two-year-old youth camp counselor, and a teen named Cody Milner, were camping in the preserve but wandered away from their group. Milner said they witnessed a UFO crash and followed three people—he guessed it was three—who came out of it. Their pursuit led them to the barricade on Greenwood Road. According to local patrolman Officer Brennan, Jay Harrison fled into a nearby pasture. The Theeles went after him. Brennan, a second officer, and four soldiers gave chase and saw the Theeles and Harrison being drawn up into what they described as a big black triangle. The UFO disappeared seconds after taking them."

Laura's summary brought silence to the room again.

"Do their families know?" the Secretary asked as he rubbed the wrinkles on his forehead.

"No, sir. We're leaving that up to higher levels to handle."

"Well...they'll have to be told before they see it on the news. We won't be able to keep their identities a secret for much longer. This story has already gone around the world, and people are asking a lot of questions. We've got to be very careful in how we proceed. We must not appear to be hiding facts, but we don't even know what we're dealing with yet. All communication regarding these events is top secret. Do you all understand this?"

Everyone nodded in acknowledgment.

The Secretary was just about to adjourn the meeting when a staff assistant entered the room and handed him a note. The committee members stared at him with expectation, but he read the contents to himself. When he finished reading, he placed the paper on the table and looked hard at Laura.

"It seems Miss Turgis has her work cut out for her on this one," he stated with the utmost seriousness. "Before the UFO disappeared, it abducted three more people from the city."

CHAPTER 7

Voices

April woke with a jolt, startled by the sound of hushed voices. Her lounge seemed to know she wanted to sit up; it released her from its soft embrace and even helped her into a seated position. Scanning the room, she saw that two black-skinned aliens—a male and female—had entered during her brief doze. Aside from their skin color and apparently younger age, they both had features similar enough to the white pair to imply a familial relationship.

"Ooo-oh-yee," the female said. She grinned apologetically when she noted April's surprised expression.

Her companion repeated the greeting with a wary smile. "Ooo-oh-yee."

Their nakedness caused April to divert her gaze. But as her eyes darted around to avoid glancing at certain parts of their anatomy, she could tell her discomfort perplexed them. *Don't ruin what you started with the white couple,* she warned herself. *It's okay to look.* Their exposed bodies disquieted her; she was not accustomed to such lack of modesty. Not that she was a prude. She simply did not like being bombarded with erotic thoughts, especially in her current circumstance. *Why do I always have to think of a naked body as something sexual, though?* she wondered. *And these are aliens, anyway.* She tried associating them with the people indigenous to Earth's untamed jungles, to whom nudity was nothing unusual. It helped...a little.

"Um...Ooo-oh-yee," she replied.

Checking on Paul and Jay, she saw that both were snoozing in nearby lounges.

How could we fall asleep during a time like this? she wondered. *Were we drugged?* She considered the two faces in front of her. *They've been so friendly and hospitable. I can't imagine them doing that to us.*

The female took a few steps toward April and pushed her long, black mane behind her body. As she did, specks of blue in her hair glittered under the soft light of the room. This time, April did not look away, and it seemed to please the young alien woman.

To push the hair back means something, April reasoned. *Gestures are almost as important as words.*

She recalled studying the bridge crew. When the females engaged in conversation, they often began by pushing their hair behind their bodies, exposing them from the front. April guessed it was a symbol of openness. To test her theory, she tucked her own shoulder-length locks behind her ears. It worked. The female's eyes brightened with approval, and April congratulated herself for trusting her intuition.

"You...ah...Ah-eel?" the female asked.

"Yes. I am April."

The girl pulled her hair in front of her like a shawl. "Ah." She motioned for the male to join her, and both stepped into the seating area and sat in lounges across from April.

"You're the one I saw earlier...with the white couple," April said.

"Ah...em...Eee-uh," the girl replied while tapping her chest. "Eee-uh."

April marveled that with only a bit of difficulty, the alien girl was speaking English. She glanced at Paul again and saw that both he and Jay were now awake and observing the exchange.

"Eee-uh? You are Eee-uh?" April asked.

Eah slid off her seat and knelt close, almost pressing against April's knees. Then she took hold of April's hand and placed it on her bare chest. "Eah."

April flinched and tried not to gasp. The girl's intimate gesture was unnerving, but in her eyes there was only innocent intention. "Eah," April repeated, spreading her fingers open and feeling Eah's skin. It was soft and warm, uniquely feminine despite its unusual color. April noted a subtle iridescence, like a rainbow mixed with black oil. Underneath, a fast heartbeat thumped with excitement.

"Yessss. Eah," the girl said with a penetrating stare. "And you ah Ah-eel."

"Eah…" the male warned as he shifted uncomfortably.

Eah frowned at his interruption and released April's hand, but April did not withdraw it.

"It's okay," April said to them both. "I want to be friends." With her insecurities in check, she took Eah's hand and placed it on her own chest.

Eah smiled with affection at the repeated gesture. "Yessss. Fff-ens," she told April. "Frens! Hooo-mah. Eah es hooo-mah, too…like Ah-eel."

"You mean…*human?*" April asked.

"Yessss."

April released Eah's hand. "Eah, are you able to understand me?"

Eah nodded, but April could tell she was struggling to form a response. "I know some woo-eds," she said.

"You know some words?"

"Yes! Sss-ay moh woo-eds."

"Ask her why we're here," Paul suggested to April as he and Jay both rose and moved to stand behind her.

Preoccupied with reading April's lips, Eah paid them no attention. "Wooo-eye…ah…weeee—"

"Eah, why…are…we here?" April asked.

Eah pushed herself back and shook her head with uncertainty, as if she was wondering how to respond. After a moment, she leaned in again and stared into April's eyes. She needed April to do…something.

No, to say *something,* April thought.

Eah nodded. "Woo-eds," she said. "Moh woo-eds."

"Words?"

"Werrrr-dsss. Yes, Eah...needs...wer-ds."

"She's not just mimicking you," Jay said. "I think she's trying to learn."

Eah broke off her stare to look at Jay. As she did, the seriousness in her face softened into something else—intense interest, accompanied by a charming smile. It brought a warm feeling to Jay's cheeks.

April continued. "Eah, are we here by mistake, or did your people want us here? Where are you from?"

Eah snapped from her quick examination of Jay and resumed concentrating on April. "Fer-ren-ds," she said as she brushed her hair back behind her ears. "Wer-ds. Say mo-re words, Ape-reel."

"Right...say more words."

"You seem to understand her," Paul said.

"A little. It's like trying to figure out someone with a heavy accent who's speaking in broken English."

"So, she knows the words, but not how to *pronounce* them?" Jay asked.

"Possibly."

"Yes," Eah agreed. "Eah knows some words."

"Eah, do your people—the other people—know our words?" April asked.

She took a moment to process April's question, then lit up when she understood. "Yes, Eah's p-peopoh know some words, but Eah knows words bettah."

Eah's pronunciation was improving with each passing minute. She was quite intelligent and only needed to hear April's pronunciations a few times before she could repeat them.

"Eah knows our words better than the others?"

"B-bet-ah. Yes. Bet-ter. Eah knows words better."

Jay leaned in closer to Paul and whispered. "Maybe she's a language specialist among her people."

"A linguist? Could be, I guess."

Eah noted the side conversation and sat back on her legs to observe Jay as he talked to Paul.

"On their bridge, it looked like they each had a specialty besides helping to fly the ship," Jay noted.

"So each one has a specific job," Paul guessed. "A work team."

"Assembled for a mission."

"Interesting."

"Well, she knows our language better than the white ones."

Eah was now scrutinizing Jay's appearance. There was something about him that seemed to fascinate her, and it made him nervous. "Why is she looking at me like that?" he whispered to Paul.

"Got me. Maybe she finds you attractive."

"Not funny," Jay shot back with a smirk.

April ignored the jest. "I don't know what to say now, Paul," she said. "They communicate differently."

"Like how?"

"The slightest gesture or expression has meaning. That's probably why they use few words or sounds. I'm just guessing here."

"Let's be careful, then."

"Exactly. So what should I do?"

"She's interested in Jay now," Paul answered. "Let *him* talk to her."

Jay stiffened. "I don't, uh..."

"I'll try again," April said. "Eah, why...are...we...here?"

Rather than replying, Eah abruptly stood. The male rose, too, and it was then April noticed the white pair coming up behind them, having entered the room unnoticed. They motioned for Eah and the male to join them. After a brief conversation amongst themselves, the couple and the younger male left while Eah returned to the seating area to address the Earth visitors.

"Yaw hep es needed," Eah said. "Now, you come wit me an hep...help...wit dah ooo-tahs."

"The *others?*" April questioned.

"Yes...uh-thers. You help with dah others."

April shot Paul a questioning glance.

"I'm not sure what it means, but it beats sitting in here," he quipped.

Jay nodded in agreement, so April grinned at Eah and rose from her seat. "Sure. Yes...we will help you if we can."

Eah wrapped herself in her hair and rushed the Earth humans out of the room and into the corridor. She then led them to a closed portal where the white-skinned couple and two younger males with black skin were already waiting. The two males created an aperture, and the couple motioned for the Earth guests to enter.

"I guess we go in first," Paul said.

All three sensed uneasiness from their hosts.

The room looked like the same one they had found themselves in when first brought aboard, and they understood the reason for the aliens' apprehension as soon as they stepped inside. There before them were three more people from Earth—two men and a young woman. The men were struggling to free the woman from being embedded in the floor. Nearby were lumps still under the black surface—presumably more bodies yet to be uncovered.

CHAPTER 8

New Guests

The men halted their rescue and froze in place when they noticed Paul, April, and Jay stepping into the room. Close behind were the two white-skinned aliens. They strode in, but stopped short at seeing the young woman embedded in the floor.

Alarmed, the alien male took a few tentative steps toward the new guests to help. "Ooo-oh-yee," he said, raising his hands in a gesture of peace.

Startled at the sight of the bizarre naked couple, the men grabbed the woman's arms and yanked her up in a panic. While they pulled, she writhed back and forth to loosen the floor's grip. It helped. But as her body began sliding out, the gummy floor clung to her clothes and threatened to denude her lower half.

"No!" the woman shrieked.

Her rescuers, misunderstanding the cry of distress, tugged even harder. This time, the rubbery material gave in to their frenzied struggle and released its hold. Unharmed and with her dignity still intact, the woman kicked her legs while the men dragged her to a spot where she could get a footing. Then, all three of them retreated to a far wall.

"Try to keep calm," Paul said, attempting to draw their attention away from the aliens.

One man stepped forward, his expressive blue eyes filled with both curiosity and incredulity. "Just what the devil is going on here?" he demanded with an angry British accent. "Who are you people?"

Paul guessed he was in his late fifties. Other than being well-dressed, there was nothing identifying about him. His pointed chin and defiant posture made him look like a highbrow who had just realized he was a prisoner.

"My name is Paul Theele. This is my wife, April, and this is Jay—"

"Harrison," Jay added, remembering he had not given the Theeles his full name. "Jay Harrison."

"Where are we? What are we doing here?"

Paul stepped closer and tried to block their view of the alien couple who had surreptitiously moved across the room to uncover the three lumps under the floor.

"I can't give you a lot of answers. We got here just like you...some hours ago. You're safe. Try not to be afraid."

"I demand to know what is going on!" the accent declared.

"Get in line," Paul said under his breath. He glanced at the white-skinned pair. They had already uncovered two torpid figures, a male and female, and were working on the third. Unlike the other new arrivals, though, these were not from Earth. Despite their apparent human-like anatomy, they still had a distinct, alien appearance. Dark bronze skin, manes of deep black hair, and simple loincloths were the only things covering their flawless bodies. "Jay?" Paul asked. "Are those..."

"Yeah," Jay affirmed. "They look like the ones I chased through the forest."

"Who are these...people?" the young woman asked in a shaky voice. Her lab coat and teal green scrubs identified her as someone in the medical field. Shoulder-length black hair framed her pretty face, and almond-shaped eyes suggested a Japanese heritage. Paul guessed she was in her late twenties.

"Well," Paul replied, "the white ones are our...hosts."

"What do you mean by *hosts?*" the second man asked. Oddly, he sounded quite levelheaded, despite the bizarre scene around him.

Middle-aged and fit, his neat appearance in a tailored business suit and confident demeanor suggested he could have been someone of importance.

"We don't know *who* they are yet," Paul answered. "All I can tell you is that they're friendly, and—as hard as it is to hear—not from our planet."

The woman in the lab coat pressed herself against the back wall. "You can't mean—"

"What do you take us for? Idiots?" the British man demanded. "If this is some kind of *joke*—"

"It's no joke," April said. "Trust us."

*　*　*

In efficient haste, the white-skinned couple completed their task of uncovering the third body. They then backed away from the groggy bronze aliens and watched as they bestirred themselves. The female was the first to notice they were not alone. She sat up, squinted at her captors, and recoiled at the sight of them. Her two companions did likewise, staring with expressions of recognition and revulsion, then all three jumped to their feet.

"Ahhhh-oiy-eeeeeii-uah-sah-uh, Ah-tee-Kee-uh!" the woman yelled at the white male. "Soooo-oh-yeee-ah-esa Blue!"

He frowned, took a step closer to her, and with a flick of his wrists, communicated an unspoken command. None of the bronzes reacted, so he repeated the action and added words to it. "Ria sah-eeye-oh-aaaho-ni. Ahey soh-ni-oooooie-wah Blue."

"Ehe!" the woman said, in apparent refusal.

He made more gestures, this time with the imposing stance of someone who commanded respect. No longer playing the role of genial host, he was reminding everyone in the room of his position aboard the alien craft. He was in charge, and they were to obey his orders.

With some hesitance, one of the bronze males at last relented and backed away from his companions. After adjusting his flimsy loincloth, he turned to study the Earth humans.

The female followed his stare. "Suisa ah Blue!" she exclaimed. Their presence in the room surprised her, but she also seemed to be awed by them. With wide green eyes, she examined each one. "Kah-e-oh-ya..."

The white male and his counterpart shared suspicious glances. By their expressions, it was clear the bronze woman's fascination with the other newcomers troubled them. Both stepped between the two groups to divert her attention.

"Yeh-he-oh-saaaah-eeeeeee-yoi-essa!" the female insisted. She said more through expressions and subtle gestures, but the result was the same; her captors would not comply with her demands.

The white female smiled, but offered no compromise. "Ria yoi-eh-eeee-sih-ah."

It was an obvious stand-off. The white pair stood their ground while the bronze woman and her two male companions argued with them non-verbally. At the moment of highest tension, Eah, who had remained in the passageway, strode into the room and positioned her black body between her pearly counterparts. Her presence ended the strange quarrel. All three bronzes gawked at her with recognition and wariness.

"Eah?" the bronze woman asked.

Eah said nothing. She returned their gaze and seemed to hold them in a brief, mystified trance. Her face expressed regal expectancy, like a monarch conveying explicit directives through a simple stare. While she did this, her body added a striking visual display to support her message by changing its color. In seconds, her skin transformed to an iridescent white, crowned by the same mane of blue-speckled, black hair.

After Eah's physical change, the bronzes surrendered themselves to her strange enchantment. More captivated than beaten, they tempered their aggression and allowed Eah to communicate with them through a nonverbal exchange of emotions.

"How did she *do* that?" the medical woman asked. "Her skin just turned from black to white! Did you *see* that?"

April maneuvered herself closer to the woman and whispered. "Don't speak or draw attention to us."

"Why?"

"Their communication is...tricky. One word—or even a gesture— could send the wrong message. I've seen a lot of threats passed back and forth here."

"And how do you know *that?*" the British man asked.

"We've been here longer than you," Paul said. "Just observe and stay quiet, like my wife suggests."

Paul's firm tone did not sit well with the new arrivals, but they believed he and April were saying these things for their benefit. So they refrained from asking more questions and observed in silence.

The white male directed another command at the bronzes. This time, they complied, allowing Eah to lead them out of the room. He then motioned for the Earth humans to follow him and his companion as they exited.

"I'm not going *anywhere* until I get some answers!" the British man roared.

"Then stay here and sink back into the floor," Paul said. He hoped the quip would shake the man from his obvious shock.

The medical woman poked her foot at the area of floor that had imprisoned her lower body. The hole had already filled, and she found the surface to be solid. Still, she leaped over it to join Paul and April at the open portal. "I'm not staying in here," she said to April, searching her eyes for assurance.

"You'll be fine," April said.

"Gentlemen?" Paul encouraged.

With some reluctance, the two men stepped gingerly toward Paul and April and followed them out of the room. Jay brought up the rear, nodding at the two black-skinned males who were still standing guard in the hall. With cordial grins, they both nodded back, closed the portal, and then disappeared down the opposite end of the long corridor.

The white-skinned couple led them all back to the lounge and then took their leave. Once inside, Paul urged the newcomers to sit while he, April, and Jay recounted what they each experienced the night before.

At his conclusion, everyone sat in silence for a few moments while they considered the stories.

"It's incomprehensible," the British man said. "I have no alternate explanation, but I can't bring myself to believe we are all victims of an alien abduction."

April offered a short, sympathetic smile. "That's how we felt at first, too."

"Accept it," Jay suggested. "So far, they've treated us very well. The ones with white and black skin have been friendly. The bronze ones, though...there's something about *them* I don't like."

"Me, too," Paul agreed. "They're different from the others. More aggressive."

"I still can't believe this," said the medical woman.

"I'm sorry," Paul interrupted. "We've been talking, and we don't even know your names."

"I'm Yori...Yori Shimizu," said the young woman. "I'm a medical student at the college downtown."

"My name is Ellis Minister," the man with the British accent said. "Please call me Ellis. I teach physics, probably at the same university."

"Capital U?" Yori asked him.

"Quite."

"Perry Carlson," offered the other man. "I, uh, work for the government."

Perry's eyes shifted with elusiveness. Even after a long pause that gave him ample time to elaborate, he did not disclose more about himself.

"So, what's the situation in the city?" Paul asked the newcomers. "What was happening before you got here?"

Yori answered first. "It was crazy. I didn't listen to any news during my drive in, and it was still dark when I arrived, so I couldn't see the thing right away. I watched a news report a little later on a friend's phone."

"The *thing?*" April questioned.

"The talking heads are calling it *the Triangle,*" Ellis explained. "There were sightings in many places throughout the night. In the early morning, it was hovering over the financial district." He nodded to Yori, allowing her to continue her story.

"We were told to evacuate our building," she said. "After all the recent terrorist threats, we took it seriously. Staff and students flooded the streets—it was chaos. I found a way through the crowds and got about a block away when…" She hesitated, unsure how to explain what happened next.

"You floated into the air?" April offered.

"Yes…something like that, I guess. I blacked out. The next thing I knew, these two gentlemen were yanking me up…and then I saw you."

"How about you, Ellis?" Paul asked.

"Much the same, for sure. I have a flat just a few blocks away from the university. Of course, I couldn't see the object—the Triangle—past the surrounding buildings. It wasn't until I popped into the cafeteria for breakfast that I found out what was happening. A crowd was around the telly, watching the morning news. When I saw the captured footage…well…it was both fascinating and terrifying at the same time. The room filled with people as word spread, but no one knew what to do. At first, we were told to stay where we were."

"Why didn't they evacuate your building, too?" Paul asked.

"To keep things orderly, I suppose. It didn't take long before the police came in and supervised an evacuation. They led us into the streets where I encountered the scene Ms. Shimizu described."

"Yori is fine," Yori said. "How were you…taken?"

"Amazingly enough, I believe I ended up near *you*. A crowd surrounded me and it was suffocating. I escaped into an alleyway where I followed a group in lab coats. I remember seeing a shadow from above that darkened the alley. Then there was a quick flash of violet light…and another. I saw windows passing by as I…well, I suppose I rose from the ground…and…"

"Then you were here," Paul concluded.

"Quite so."

"Mister Carlson, I'm thinking your story is about the same?" Paul asked.

Perry stood and began pacing. "Yes. Pretty much."

Paul waited for more details, but Perry offered none. His standoffishness was unsettling.

"So...what happened?" Paul prodded.

"Same thing. I was in a coffee shop when everyone ran out to see it. The cashier left, so I tossed some money on the counter and walked out."

"How did you end up here?"

"That's what *I'd* like to know. People were running around all over the place in a panic. I was near a small side street, so I ducked in. The next thing I knew...I was here." He returned to his seat, and the room became silent.

Ellis took over the job of pacing. When he could stand the quiet no longer, he worked on a theory. "What do you do for a living, Mister Theele?"

"Huh?" Paul had been deep in thought, and the question startled him. "Oh, please, call me Paul. Well, I teach computer science at a tech school while I'm finishing my master's degree."

"And Missus Theele? April, is it?"

"Yes. I homeschool our two sons."

"And you, Jay Harrison," Ellis said as he turned to Jay. "From your recounting, we know you like camping and astronomy. Do you attend university?"

"No," Jay replied. "I work as a live-in counselor at a youth ranch."

"I see. Are your parents of special prominence?"

"I don't have parents. I grew up at the same ranch."

"Oh. I'm sorry. Do you know anything about your family history?"

"Not really, no."

"What are you getting at?" Paul asked.

Ellis sighed. "I'm not entirely sure. I suppose I am looking for a link in our apparent abductions, but so far, they seem to be random."

"*Kidnapping* might be a better word than *abduction*," Perry said with heavy sarcasm. "I don't accept that these people are aliens from another world."

"Do you disbelieve your own eyes?" Yori asked.

Perry stood and positioned himself in the center of their little group. "Look," he said in a hushed tone, "I'll confide in you *this* much: I am a congressman on the Defense Committee, and I have a background in anti-terrorism." He glanced over his shoulder, leery of eavesdroppers. "Because of this, I'm the sort of person who our nation's enemies would love to lay their hands on. So please keep my identity to yourselves. The only reason I'm telling you is so you'll listen to me. I'd like to get out of this alive."

"So...wait a minute," April said with an incredulous chuckle. "You think some really strange terrorists have taken us hostage?"

Perry looked around the room. He wanted to defend his theory, but had to agree that it was just as hard to believe. Still, he was not about to accept quick and crazy conclusions. "I admit our situation appears to be a stereotypical alien abduction story," he said, returning to his seat. "But it's a trick. A colorless room, nudity used to shock us, a fake language— they're using mind games. So I think we should go forward carefully." He turned toward April and glared at her. "If this *is* an intricate plot, we shouldn't get too friendly with our captors, either."

"What's *that* supposed to mean?" April asked in defense.

"Mister Carlson," Paul said, intervening, "my wife can understand these people a little, and they're grasping *our* language—"

"Listen..." Perry cut in.

"No. Look *around* you. I was every bit as skeptical as you are now, but the facts are right here." Paul poked his finger into his spongy seat. "This is not *our* technology. And those people are *aliens*. Have you ever seen a human being change colors like a chameleon?"

"I—"

"People from another world have abducted you, Mister Carlson. As far as we know, they're friendly. We've gotten into the middle of something here, and I'm hoping they'll tell us more when they can. In the meantime, let's not be paranoid or defensive. One wrong gesture could get us into trouble with them. So why not watch and let this thing play its course?"

"Well said." Ellis nodded in agreement. "I understand your concern, Mister Carlson, but we must all be patient."

Perry scoffed at the idea. "Patience! Well, we seem to have little choice, do we? I've warned you, though, and I'm still not changing my mind. I don't buy the *alien* thing one bit."

"What else would it take to convince you?" April asked.

"Something bigger than a black room and weird body paint."

At that moment, three white bodies pushed their way through the entry portal. It was Eah and the host couple.

"See?" Perry said. "They've probably been listening to us."

Eah crossed the floor and plunged her hands into a far wall. Like a baker stretching dough, she manipulated the black material until she created a large hole. She then caressed the edges, which coaxed the opening to hold its shape. Satisfied that it would not close, she stepped back to admire her newly formed viewport. Then, turning to the Earth humans, she beckoned them all to inspect it. "Please...look here...and be at peace." Through an exotic-sounding accent, she was now speaking in clear English. "There is much to explain."

April eyed her with surprise and suspicion. Eah had either been pretending not to know their language, or she was much faster at learning than April had assumed.

Paul was the first to accept Eah's invitation. Trying to ignore a growing trepidation, he allowed his curiosity and impatience for answers to propel him toward the viewport. "Alright...let's see what we've got now."

Eah offered him a reassuring smile and stepped out of his way.

After taking a centering breath, Paul leaned toward the viewport and stared into the blackness on the other side. What he saw was both beautiful and frightening. It was his planet—Earth—but he was seeing it from a distance of many thousands of miles.

"Well, what is it?" Perry asked.

Paul scanned the black void for any evidence that would expose this as a hoax—wires, the edges of a projection screen, some overlooked detail. He needed something that would save him from having to accept he was no longer floating above a city, but flying through space.

"Paul?" April entreated.

He turned to his alien hosts. "Yes," he said to the male. "There *is* much explaining to do."

CHAPTER 9

Reasons

The alien hosts waited in the sunken seating area while the six abductees from Earth took turns peering through the viewport.

"Is this really happening?" Yori asked Jay. "Why are they taking us away?"

"They must have their reasons."

Eah stood nearby, smiling while she studied her guests' reactions. At the moment, she seemed to be especially interested in Yori.

"What's wrong with the girl?" Yori asked in a whisper.

Jay stole a shy glance at Eah. "Besides the obvious, you mean?"

"I don't like the way she's looking at me."

"She tends to do that," Jay said. "I think she's just trying to learn from us."

Yori half-smiled at Eah while struggling not to stare at her uncovered form.

"Try to stay calm," Jay said, noticing Yori's discomfort.

"Calm? I'm not on my planet anymore, and some naked alien chick is staring and making eyes at me."

Jay chuckled and glanced at Eah again, which drew her attention to him.

"See?" he whispered to Yori. "It's not just you."

Behind them, the others from Earth had finished viewing their distant planet and were engaged in hushed conversations.

"I'm telling you...it's a trick," Perry said, loud enough for everyone to hear, "and you're all falling for it. Don't—"

"Come," the white male interrupted. "Come...sit."

With some hesitation, they all returned to their seats.

"You ah hee by ack-see-den," the man explained. "Es-cuse my use of woo-eds—words. We undah-stand the rrrr-oots of your...lan-guage, and we ah abe-el to see and sense mee-nings. Now dat we hear your words, we also can put sound to dem and speak dem wit you."

"Who *are* you people?" Perry demanded.

"I em Ah-see-hee-uh."

"Aht...tsee...kee-uh?" April repeated. It sounded like a short string of vowel sounds, but she could pick out places where a consonant would make sense in English.

"You may call me *Kee-ah*." He pronounced the name with a soft K, almost slurred.

"Alright...Keah," April said.

He turned to introduce the females. "This es *Ah-hee*. She es the dyad of me, or en your words *wife*. An this es Eah, who es a daw-tuh—"

"Daughter," Eah corrected.

"Duagh-terrr. Dah others en this ves-sel ah also of us."

"You mean, you're a family?" April asked.

"Yes. We ah seek-ahs...trav-eh-lahs...travelers. Our home es—" He paused, struggling to find the correct words. "Our home planet would be tans-lated pur-pel—purple—en your words."

"A purple planet?" Jay asked. "Then that's outside our solar system."

"Yes. It is," Ahee said.

"In distance, it is very far off," Keah added.

April marveled at how Keah's use of English was improving with every sentence he spoke. "So...you said we're here by accident? How?"

Keah frowned and hesitated.

"Well?" Perry prompted.

"We did not mean to take you," Keah answered. "We only came here...to...app-hend...to app—"

"App-re-hend," Eah interjected.

"Yes. We only came here to apprehend the others—the Dah-Ahey. They used...took...one of our vessels and fled to your planet." He nodded to Eah, prompting her to continue the story.

"While we were trying to capture the Dah-Ahey," she said, "we also captured *you*. The *ayawaya*—the tool we use to transport people—was not working well. It was difficult for us to...eye-suh-lite them."

"Isolate?" Yori suggested.

"Yes. Isolate. You must have been very close to the Dah-Ahey when we used the ayawaya."

"We were right behind them in the field," April recalled. "So you got us...instead of them."

"But that was in the mountains," Ellis noted. "*We* were in the city. How did they get all the way there?"

"Maybe they hitchhiked," Perry quipped, "or caught a bus."

Ellis ignored his cynicism. "Regardless, the three of us—Carlson, Yori, and myself—must have been nearby when Keah's people were trying to nab them downtown."

"Yes," Eah agreed. "We *nabbed* them...but only after nabbing you first."

Jay chuckled at Eah's use of the word.

"I am using your words rightly?" she asked Jay.

"Sorry. Yes, you're doing a great job—"

"So, you *beamed us up* by accident," Perry interrupted, glaring at Eah. "How fascinating."

"Beam?" She squinted at him while struggling to understand his comment.

"Hear her out, Mister Carlson," April said. "Eah, who are the others? Who are the ones you were trying to apprehend?"

"They are the *Dah-Ahey*. Those who run."

"Run from what?" Paul asked.

"Run...from...*Ahey*."

Paul shrugged his shoulders. "And what is—"

"Ridiculous!" Perry blurted. "Every word. Why don't you people just level with us and lay down your demands? Enough of this *alien* gag already!"

"Gag?" Yori asked. "Mister Carlson, do you have any idea what this all means? Why can't you accept what is going on here?"

"Sorry. I'm not as gullible as you seem to be." He turned to Paul. "Mister Theele, they have held you here since last evening. Don't you think this game has gone on too long?"

Paul shifted uncomfortably under Perry's harsh stare. He agreed there must have been more to Eah's tale than just an accidental abduction. But he also knew that pressuring these alien people would not get answers. The situation required patience—and tact.

"The story isn't finished," he said to Perry. "Give Eah time to explain."

"And let's not insult our hosts," April added. She could tell by their confused expressions that they did not care for Perry's rough manner.

Paul returned to questioning Eah. "Eah, why are we so far from our planet?"

"Our *wa-ah-ahea*—our vessel—is unstable. It became...damaged...when we stepped to your world."

"Stepped?" Ellis asked.

"It is what we call the...movement...of the vessel. Sometimes big steps, sometimes small steps to travel between places."

Ellis leaned forward and studied Eah. With his initial shock and anger mostly subsided, he was now acting like a classic inquisitive scientist. "Exactly how was it damaged?"

"By your at-moose-fear—atmosphere. Entering and exiting the fire. We build wa-ah-ahea for waters...not so much for fire."

"Fire? You mean friction?"

"Fire and heat," Eah answered. "Most worlds we visit do not have this sort of covering. We did not expect it on Blue."

"This still doesn't explain why we are now *supposedly* thousands of miles away from our planet," Perry reminded.

"The wah-ah-ahea... We cannot return you to your world," Eah said in an apologetic tone.

"What do you mean by *cannot return?*" Ellis asked.

Keah answered for her. "The wa-ah-ahea would not hold together again in your atmosphere."

"Well, perhaps our people could help with that," Ellis suggested. "We have vehicles that can pass through the atmosphere. If you at least get into a safe orbit—"

"There is too much damage," Keah said. "To return from this distance would mean remaining on your planet...and that cannot be."

"Where does that put us, then?" Perry asked.

"The wa-ah-ahea can only go in one direction," Eah replied.

Ahee brushed some long strands of white hair behind her ivory shoulders and regarded them all with a reassuring gaze. "You must come with us to our world," she informed. "There, we can...repair. Then...we will return you to Blue—to Earth."

April felt a familiar tightness in her chest as fear crept back into her heart. "How...how long will we be away?" she asked Keah, bracing for the answer.

"Long?"

"Ahua," Eah explained to him. "Time es eeh-yiii-oh-ahhhhh-ahua."

Keah nodded. "I understand. Measuring the passage of events, yes? That is different in *ahea*—space. Out here, lengths are...ih-reh-liv-int."

"Irrelevant," Eah corrected.

"Irrelevant. So, it is difficult for me to answer."

"We measure time according to the rotation of our planet," Ellis said. "One rotation is a day. We divide one day into twenty-four periods that we call hours."

"I understand, but I do not know your planet." He placed his hand on his chest. "We...*feel* the passage of moments...inside. Is it possible for you to do this?"

"Yes," Ellis answered. "We have a way of measuring time internally...in our bodies."

"Then...in the same time that Paul and April and Jay have been with us, we should reach Hourou—our world."

Paul calculated how long he had been aboard the alien craft. It was late evening when their abduction happened—between eight and nine o'clock. The other three abductees arrived just after eight in the morning, and about one hour had passed since then. So Paul reasoned he had been there for about thirteen hours.

"Around thirteen hours then," he told the Earth party.

"We *will* return you to your world," Keah assured. "Now...you are guests—friends—and we wish you to be at peace with us. You must...trust us, as we have trusted you. The Ways of Ahey have allowed this...cir-cum-stance. So there will be good at its completion. In this you must also trust."

Keah's confidence and soothing tone had a comforting effect on the Earth party. As he mastered their language, he could somehow use it to convey and compel emotions. At that moment, he was projecting the idea of sublime peace. The feeling was further enhanced through his expressive green eyes, which bored into each of them with an enchanting force.

"So...what do we do now?" Jay asked, shaking off the momentary daze.

Perry seemed to be the only one not affected by Keah's strange ability. "We stop playing along with this game and walk out of here," he said as he stormed toward the portal where the alien humans had entered.

Before he reached it, however, his left foot sank into the floor. Perry swore and struggled to get free, but it would not budge. "I'm stuck!"

Keah and Ahee jumped up and ran over to help him. The way they clawed in desperate seriousness at the soft black material around Perry's ankle was frightening.

"What is this, a booby trap?" Perry yanked against the strong suction and raged. "How dare you keep me here against my will!" The floor reciprocated by pulling his leg in—half the distance to his knee.

"Cease struggling," Keah warned. "You will go further in."

"Yes, I see that. Wait! It's getting hot under there!"

"Be calm. We are freeing you."

Besides the floor, the room's air temperature had also risen. Paul wiped beads of sweat from his forehead as he stood to offer assistance. "Can we help?"

Eah stuck out her arm, signaling Paul to remain in the seating area. "You are safest not to move." She whipped her long hair behind her body, then nimbly leaped over a seat and ran to assist Keah and Ahee.

Despite being warned, Perry continued to struggle and his leg sank further down past his knee.

"Oh-esa-eeeeeeee-ah-ho," Keah said to Eah.

"Ae." She took over digging around Perry's leg while Keah and Ahee stood and began yanking him up by his arms.

"What are you doing?" Perry demanded, trying to resist their grasp. His reaction made it clear he did not like being touched by them.

"Cease struggling," Keah repeated.

Perry relented, and with one big tug his leg slid out of the hole. "It worked. Now let me go."

Eah backed away as Keah and Ahee released him and he fell backward onto a more solid part of the floor.

"What...what is this?" Dumbfounded, Perry gawked at his naked leg. "It tore off my shoe...my sock...my pant leg!"

Ahee examined him for signs of injury. "You have not been harmed." After a non-verbal exchange with Keah, she and Eah dashed out of the room.

Keah helped Perry to his feet and guided him to the seating area. "Sit here."

"Why should I think the chair is safe?" Perry asked.

"It is safe."

Looking at the others, Keah noticed the beads of sweat on their foreheads. He wiped his own and regarded the dampness on his hand. "The wa-ah-ahea es becoming more unstable," he said to them all. "The heat will increase. I must go now and direct the repairs."

Ellis rose and stepped gingerly toward Keah. "I was wondering if I might...that is...it would interest me to—"

"I see you are very curious, Ellis Meen-eh-ster," Keah said, anticipating his request. "Yes, you may come with me, but walk very close and only in my steps." He then turned to address the rest of the group. "Please remain only in this seating area. It is safe. We will return to you after we have made repairs."

With that, Keah and Ellis left the room. April, Paul, Jay, and Yori sat nervous and motionless on their lounges while their searching eyes scanned the floor around them for any signs of deterioration.

Perry removed his jacket and loosened his tie. "What are you all looking for?"

"Weak spots," Jay answered. "The area where you sank looked a shade lighter than the rest of the floor."

"Right. And let's also start thinking about our options."

"Options?" April asked. "What options do we have but to go along with this and do what we're told?"

"We look for opportunities," Perry replied, "and when the time is right...we act."

April shot Paul a skeptical glance. He dismissed Perry's paranoia with a shrug and went back to scanning the floor around their lounges. Yori and Jay just smirked and did likewise.

"Fine...we'll play it your way." Perry shook his head and frowned, disappointed by their lack of support. "For now," he added under his breath. To offer some good will and prevent the need for another rescue, he helped them look for discolored areas.

The mishap had angered Perry, but the accompanying adrenaline rush also cleared his thinking. He now accepted the truth of his situation: they were aboard a damaged spacecraft that was headed to an alien planet. Since that was the case, he reasoned, he might as well position himself in a leadership role. That was his job and his area of expertise. The others in his party would need someone in charge. They did not realize it yet, but they were all about to become Earth's ambassadors. Perry Carlson was not about to leave that responsibility to amateurs. He would lead them. And when they all returned safely to Earth, he would be a hero.

CHAPTER 10

Adjustments

April was usually accurate when counting the passing minutes on her internal clock. She had honed the skill while competing in high school and college sports. Back then, timing was everything—the difference between a win or a loss. As Keah had said, though, time was indeed different in space; it moved much slower. Now, she found it hard to estimate how long Ellis had been gone. It must have been at least a half-hour, but her body kept trying to make adjustments to her guesses.

He's been away longer than that, but it also seems like he just left. Her thinking was not sluggish; thoughts still came fast, and she was glad for that. But deep inside, she noticed a weird deceleration—as if every atom in her was slowing down. *I'm going to ask Ellis about this when he gets back.*

During Ellis's absence, Eah had returned to inform her guests that the structure of their room was now stable. Keah was still working on the problem with the air temperature, but it was alright to move around. Other parts of the vessel, she said, had yet to be repaired, so they were not to leave. She also explained how to use the adjoining lavatory and encouraged them to eat what they found in the food repository.

April was relieved to hear their area was safe again, and Eah's hospitality helped to soothe her misgivings. Despite the rising temperature, she even managed to doze for a little while. When she awoke, not much had changed. Eah had dropped in again and invited Jay to accompany her while she inspected the vessel. Perry and Yori were in the middle of a heated argument about something. Paul had stationed himself at the viewport, staring out into space and interjecting an occasional opinion into the debate. Ellis was still gone.

April pushed herself to a seated position on her lounge, frowning at how her sweat-soaked t-shirt clung to her skin. "I'm a mess."

Paul's head snapped around at the sound of his wife's voice. "Are you okay?" he asked, wobbling toward the seating area.

April gasped when she saw how Paul was fighting the heat: his blue jeans were now cut-off shorts, his shirt was missing its sleeves, and he was barefoot. "What have you done?"

"We all got a little more casual...to cool down."

Yori and Perry had also transformed their clothing. Yori somehow had made a crop top out of part of her lab coat and turned her pants into shorts. Perry, likewise, had removed his suit jacket, cut the sleeves of his dress shirt to make them shorter, and trimmed the remaining leg of his trousers to match the damaged side.

"You look like castaways," April said with a chuckle. "Gilligan's spaceship."

Yori toyed with the frayed edges of her new top. "It beats being soggy with sweat. Eah told us her planet is always warm, so this should help there, too."

"How did you cut the fabric?"

"Jay found some kind of sharp tool in the other room," Yori answered. "We took turns." She was unusually calm for someone who now resembled a shipwrecked waif.

"Well, I can't take this heat anymore either," April said. "So I guess I'll join the beach party."

Paul helped her to stand. "Come to the restroom. I'll create some new fashions for you in there." He led her to the portal of the lavatory and stopped. "We can't knock, so we make a small hole and ask if it's vacant." He did so. There was no response from inside, so he enlarged the opening and motioned for her to enter. "It's okay. Just step in."

April complied. The walls of the narrow room were black, like everywhere else in the spaceship, but she could still make out its features in the dim light. There was a type of commode, a wash basin, what could have been a shower, and storage. It was a functional space, yet the lighting, cooler air, and scent of exotic flowers made it pleasant. "So...how do we use this?" she asked.

"You forgot?"

"I'm tired, Paul." She also felt disoriented and grumpy. In that condition, it would have been easy to let her guard down and collapse into Paul's arms like a sobbing mess. But she knew having a healthy emotional release would have to wait. Instead, she took a deep breath and forced herself to slip back into her *Adaptable April* mode—the one where she could handle pretty much anything. "Sorry. I'm just really exhausted."

Paul ensured the portal was closed behind them. "I know. See the sink in the corner? You'll feel better after you wash up."

"Wash up? You've already used it, then?"

"While you were sleeping, yes."

"How do you know it's safe for us?"

"The water? It's fine. Otherwise, why would Eah suggest that we use it?"

"Maybe she doesn't really know."

"It's plain, clean water. See the colored buttons above it?"

"Yeah."

"Just wave your hand over them. One's on, and the other means off. The temperature is pre-adjusted. You wash up, and I'll work on your new attire."

"I don't know. This is strange."

"Would you rather stay hot and sweaty?"

"No, but I'm about to strip inside in a *spaceship*. How much weirder can things get?"

"Come on," Paul said. "Give me your clothes. Our hosts obviously don't care about naked bodies."

As long as Paul was with her, April supposed she would be safe, so she gave in and undressed. "Cut away then. But remember...you bought these jeans for me for seventy-five bucks."

Paul grinned. "That's my girl." He then went about the business of converting the pants into a pair of shorts.

"Those cut awfully easy," April noted.

"You're right." Paul tossed them back to her. "The tool is sharp, but still... It's as if the fabric has gotten weaker."

"Great. In a few more hours, we'll be looking like our hosts."

April slipped on her new shorts, rolled cuffs into them, and stepped to the sink-like basin that jutted out from the wall. Waving her hand over a blue button produced a stream of water from a hole below it. She cupped her hands under the flow. It was tepid, soft, and smelled wonderful, like tropical flowers. "So far, so good," she whispered. Leaning over the tub, she splashed her face, neck, and chest and sighed as the water relieved her hot skin. In an instant, the heady fragrance also calmed her racing mind. No longer anxious, she became highly aware and peacefully carefree at the same time.

"Okay," Paul said as he tossed her shirt back to her. "You're all set. Feeling alright?"

"Yeah..."

Paul raised an eyebrow at the sensuous tone of her voice. "Enjoying the water, huh?"

"Either that or I'm hallucinating."

"Use it sparingly. We want to stay alert."

Despite Paul's warning, April continued to splash and rub the water all over her body.

"I'm stepping out now," Paul said. "I'll be right outside."

"Okay." April scanned the room and a slight smile creased her lips. The setting brought back a memory. For a birthday gift, Paul had sent her to a ritzy spa for women near the beach. She and her best friend

Jen spent a wonderful weekend being pampered with every kind of treatment the place offered.

How long ago was that? she wondered. *Maybe six years? Too long.*

After she finished washing, she waved the water off and searched for a way to dry herself. On the opposite wall, there was a human-sized air vent grille and control button. Since there were no towels, she assumed it was some sort of blower. With a wave, she activated the button and a pulsating current of fragrant air buffeted her.

Pretty efficient, she thought. *No laundry to worry about.*

She slid off her shorts and then held her clothes in front of the vent to dry them. The air quickly removed the dampness, and to April's amazement, it even cleansed them. When her skin was also dry, she dressed in haste and looked around for somewhere to stash her underclothes and shoes. A few cubbyholes, already stuffed with discarded items from the other Earth guests, provided storage. Bundling her effects, she placed them in one of the empty spaces before approaching the room's exit and considering how to get out.

Rejuvenated and a bit more courageous, April decided not to use her hands to create an opening. Instead, she wanted to try the other way of passing between rooms. "If they can do it, I can do it." She held her breath and leaned against the portal. With rippling and sucking sounds, it drew her body in and surrounded her.

It's like moving through a thick gel, she thought. As soon as she entered, the portal instantly pushed her through to the other side. The sole discomfort was from how it tugged at her clothing. Evidently, the portals preferred only bodies to pass through them. When Perry lost his shoe, sock, and pant leg to the gripping floor, it was because the damaged spacecraft had placed a random portal there and intensified its filter. *No wonder it concerned Keah and Ahee so much. Stepping into one of those could have sent a body into space.*

Ellis was standing nearby when she exited, waiting for his turn in the lavatory. "Ah! I see you're adapting to your environment."

"Just feeling a bit more daring." April glanced back at the portal, assuming he was referring to her use of it. But he was gesturing toward her scant outfit. "Oh...this," she said shyly. "Yeah, it helps."

"Good. I suppose I'd better do the same. The heat is becoming quite unbearable."

"How was your tour?"

Ellis smiled as he stretched open the portal. "Perhaps the best word would be *humbling*. These beings are so far ahead in knowledge of the universe... It's rather difficult to take in fully."

April nodded. "Yes. You can see it in their eyes."

"An interesting observation. They certainly do share many physical similarities with us."

"So, you think they're not human?"

Ellis ducked halfway into the lavatory before answering. "I don't see how they *could* be." With that, he disappeared behind the closing portal.

Paul approached and slipped his arm under April's. "Babes?"

"Hmm? Oh. I was just chatting with Ellis."

"Yeah. He hasn't stopped talking. I think he has information overload."

"I hope he did alright with them."

"You mean communicating? I think he mainly observed them. He's going to tell us about it when he comes out." He guided her toward the room's single viewport. "Come over here. You've *got* to see this."

April's bare feet sank into the floor with each step. The effort was almost like walking through dry sand and took a bit of getting used to without shoes. When they reached the viewport, Paul gestured for her to look out. She hesitated, unsure if she wanted any more surprises.

"Go ahead," Paul said. "Few people will ever get to see what we're seeing."

Her apprehension gave way to curiosity, and she peered out. Paul was right. There before her, filling half of the view, was the planet Saturn.

"It's...it's—"

"Saturn," Paul confirmed. "Can you believe it?"

"I...um..."

She and Paul had once watched a documentary about the solar system. The pictures of the planets were amazing, but nothing like this. The giant globe was so close, she could see movement in its gassy atmosphere: swirling clouds of milky brown in a sky streaked with silky pastels. Saturn's famous rings, resembling one massive flat disk, circled the planet's equator, and several of its moons were visible.

"Paul, is this...for *real?*"

"I know. It's hard to fathom," Paul answered. "I've given up over-analyzing and doubting it, though. The sooner we can accept what's happened, the sooner we'll get something good out of it."

That did not sound like Paul's usual way; he should have been nervous, like her. Instead, he was passive and accepting. What was changing him? She snapped her head around to look at him and smelled flowers as strands of her damp hair fell across her face. Was there something in the water? After washing with it, she was more at peace, too. What was happening to them?

"Paul..." She was about to question him, but a sudden concern distracted her.

"I know that look," he said. "What's wrong?"

"I'm thinking about the kids."

Paul frowned and nodded. "At least they weren't with us when all this happened. They're safe, Babes."

"But if our abduction is all over the news... What about our families? And what if we don't make it back?"

"Easy. Take it easy," Paul said. He stared at the viewport while pulling her into a hug. Saturn was beautiful, but seeing it was also a reminder that they were very far from their home. "It'll be okay."

"Will it?"

"Yes. We're supposed to be in the mountains at our retreat, right? No one expects us to call, and we're not due back until Monday night. Hopefully, we'll be home well before then."

"Do you think anyone knows what's happened to us?"

"Besides the cops who chased us through the field? Who knows? We have to stay focused on the here and now...and on getting back. We *will* get back, Babes."

"Alright." April needed to hear Paul's confidence. It strengthened her—at least enough to accept the present situation. She took centering breaths to further calm herself and joined him in gazing at Saturn.

Moments later, the room's main entry portal made a rippling sound, which signaled that someone was coming through. Everyone turned and watched as Keah's white body pushed through the cloudy membrane.

"Ooo-oh-yee." He crossed the floor to join Paul and April at the viewport.

"So...are we there yet?" Perry asked with a snort. He shot a knowing glance toward the others. The question was not a joke, but a test; he was still probing for a slip-up that would expose Keah and his people as frauds.

Keah just stared at him, his head tilted to the side in contemplation.

"That was supposed to be funny," Perry said. "You know. Humor?"

"Hume-or?"

"Words or ideas that make one laugh," Yori explained.

"I understand. To laugh, yes. But our word for humor is—"

"Never mind," Perry interrupted. "I guess you really *are* an alien."

"On this vessel, *you* are the alien, Perry Carlson," Keah said with a sly grin.

April snickered at what she understood to be a jest from Keah. "I believe Mister Carlson is wondering how much longer it will take to reach your planet," she explained.

Keah stepped closer to the viewport and considered the view of Saturn. "We are passing your *ha-ah-heee-ah*—greatest—ringed world now," he said. "Just past this is where we *step*."

"Step?" Yori questioned.

Ellis appeared behind her, having just returned from the lav. "It's their word for how the spacecraft moves."

"So...what happens when we *step?*" Paul asked.

Keah pointed his index fingers toward each other. "Our *eekaoa*—our galaxies—touch." He pressed his fingertips together.

"And we step into yours," Paul surmised.

"Yes. You understand. Perhaps Ellis Meen-eh-ster can explain it with better words. I must make...preparations. The wa-ah-ahea will require more care as we step."

With that, Keah left the room. Everyone else turned to Ellis, hoping he could tell them what to expect next.

"How does one explain the purposeful moving together of entire galaxies?" Ellis wondered, scratching his head. "My new friends, I believe this journey is going to be replete with surprises."

CHAPTER 11

The Tour

"Why are so many rooms empty, Eah?"

"Empty? If you examine closer, Jay, you see that *none* of the rooms are empty."

Rather than argue the point or appear dense, Jay just nodded and allowed her to continue their tour of the spaceship. Evidently, every room was important, even the ones that looked unused.

Circular corridors and cramped stairways gave easy access to each level of the vessel. Jay counted five floors before he lost his sense of direction. There must have been more; the ship was enormous. He wondered how such a small crew could manage it. Eah said the size and shape had something to do with the way the craft traveled through space. Also, it often carried cargo, so having the extra rooms was useful.

"What does your spaceship use for fuel?" Jay asked, being careful not to step on Eah's flowing hair while they descended a tight stairwell.

"Foo-el?"

"Uh...power. What powers it?"

"Ah...*hoono-heeoh.* That which *propels* the wa-ah-ahea?"

"That's it. Yes."

"Come. I will show you." She chose a side exit from the stairway and led him into a long, descending corridor. Halfway down, she stopped beside a wide access tube with a ladder in its center. "We go all the way," she said, pointing downward.

Jay entered first, grasping the rungs with care. They had a gummy texture, which he assumed was for a safer grip. From their position in the round shaft, the floor was not so distant as to cause concern; they must have already been close to the lowest level. Jay wondered how high it went, but since Eah was directly over him, he respectfully refrained from glancing upward.

At the bottom of the tube, Eah opened a portal and took him even deeper into the belly of the vessel to show him the ship's principal source of power. When they arrived, he expected to see some sort of high-tech machine. Instead, he found an alien tree growing in the center of a cavernous room. It stood at least twenty feet tall and almost touched the domed ceiling. Alive and ambulatory, its bulbous trunk pulsated with an eerie green light while hundreds of thick vines reached out and penetrated the surrounding walls. Every so often, the snake-like branches withdrew from certain spots and reinserted themselves into others, causing harmless colorful sparks to cascade onto the floor and fill the air with the smell of ozone.

Eah said the plant was transferring power to other areas of the vessel and that the entire ship was a living organism. Jay nodded, but he wondered if she was using his language correctly. The spaceship was alive? How could anything live in space? Again, rather than question her, he smiled and tried to show appreciation.

Eah's use of English improved with every new description and commentary. She still struggled with many words, but it was clear she was determined to work out the pronunciations with minimal help. So Jay resisted correcting her too much. He enjoyed listening to her, anyway. Her attempts were cute, and the sound of her exotic voice pleased him. To let her do most of the talking was easy.

The harder thing for Jay to deal with was Eah's penetrating gaze. Though she had beautiful and expressive eyes, he found it difficult to stare into them for very long. Doing so caused a strange dizziness, and his thinking became clouded by a jumble of emotions. Somehow, Eah had the ability to impress her thoughts and feelings on others through a simple look. She could also draw them out of people, which accounted for Jay's mental fog. After discovering this, he decided to avoid making extended eye contact until he could better understand this unusual power of hers.

Unfortunately, Eah's other stunning features were just as hard to evade. Her skin had remained pearly white, like her parents, so her body stood out against the black surfaces of the spaceship. No matter where Jay looked, the glowing girl was always within easy view, and it was hard not to gawk at her beautiful, naked form. To keep himself in check, he spent much of his time scrutinizing blank walls and meaningless spaces.

After a while, Eah picked up on Jay's distraction and suggested they visit the bridge to observe ship operations. He agreed, so she led him up a narrow, spiraling companionway in the vessel's core that allowed for quicker access to the upper levels. The stairs ended in the middle of the passageway that bisected the triangular spacecraft from the bridge in its forward-facing vertex to its rounded aft.

"Now that I've gotten a closer look," Jay said as he walked behind Eah, "I really appreciate your shape... Your *ship!*"

Eah stopped and stared hard at him.

"Uh... I mean, it's pretty...pretty impressive...this ship."

Eah continued her gaze, impassive save for the hint of a smile at one corner of her mouth.

"I might not be using the best words here," Jay admitted with a nervous chuckle. Flushed with embarrassment, he wondered how he would survive such a gaffe.

Eah uttered a soft, amused giggle and flipped her hair back. "Come." Her blue-speckled mane trailed behind her like a long cape as she resumed their walk along the corridor.

Jay followed, inwardly chastising himself for being so gauche. When they reached the bridge's entry portal, he waited and watched while Eah pushed herself through. "I have to get a grip on all of this," he whispered. "No more embarrassments." He leaned against the portal and allowed it to draw him into its jelly-like embrace.

On the other side, Eah took hold of his arm to steady him as he passed through.

"That takes some getting used to," Jay said, glancing around the busy command center, "but it's actually—" He froze and gaped when he saw the forward viewport. "Is that what I think it is? Is that really *Saturn?*"

Eah waved him on as an invitation to cross the bridge.

"This is...amazing." As he rushed past the crew, they all looked up from their tasks, distracted by the sudden intrusion.

"Ooo-oh-yee," Eah said, nodding to her curious siblings. With a few gestures, she signaled it was alright for Jay to be there.

One of them—a female—chuckled from the back of the room. A smirk from Eah silenced her, and they all returned to their work while Eah joined Jay at the viewport. "Sah-*toon?*" she asked, trying to imitate his pronunciation. "Sa-*tun.* Sa-*turn.*"

"That's good!" Jay praised. "Sa-turn." He turned and risked a lingering look into her mysterious eyes.

Below her black feminine eyebrows and long lashes, wide green orbs stared back at him, sparkling with light and reflecting his own excitement. The flawless white skin on her delicate face dazzled him with its subtle streaks of iridescence. Full, pink-tinted lips formed a gleeful grin after the tip of her wandering tongue briefly moistened them. All of it fascinated Jay, and Eah seemed to enjoy the attention. In fact, through her gaze, she was imploring him not to turn away.

Jay submitted to her unspoken urging and became lost in a strange enchantment. It was as if a magical power radiated from her eyes, seeking an intimate connection that he was unsure how to accept. He felt as naked as her, fully exposed under her scrutiny, with his every emotion laid bare.

"Eah—" He tried to speak, but words would not come. Her eyes held him there, filling him with something—visions—but there were too many to receive all at once. Just as the bizarre exchange was threatening to make him swoon, a sudden surge of raw emotions erupted from deep inside of him. In an instant, he became the stronger of the two, and a desire to take control overcame him. Without realizing what he was doing, he opened his eyelids wide and forced his own chaotic feelings into Eah. A brash and selfish part of him wanted to flood her mind the same way she had sought to fill his. Before he knew it, he was also reaching out and stroking her soft cheek.

In a flash, their psychic connection ended. Eah pulled away from his touch, wrapped herself in her hair, and turned aside toward the viewport. Jay dropped his hand and did the same. A long silence passed as they both watched Saturn and tried to sort out what had just taken place between them.

Disgusted with himself for what he decided was a momentary loss of control and some poor judgment, Jay summoned the courage to speak. "I'm sorry, Eah. I didn't mean to offend you."

"Offend?" Eah asked from within her cocoon of hair.

Jay scanned the room and was relieved to find that no one was paying attention to them. "I've made you uncomfortable. I apologize."

"Why did you push into me?" she asked.

"Push in? I don't understand. What just happened between us?"

"Communication. It is a way that our people communicate without words."

"I see that now, but I'm not used to it."

"Yes. You were forceful. You...pushed in. Only the Dah-Ahey do that."

"The Dah-Ahey? I didn't even know what I was doing. I wanted to try it, but I guess I couldn't control myself. Man, I feel horrible now. Are you alright?"

Eah brushed her hair behind her back as she turned to face him. Jay did not yet recognize the alien gesture, but her smile was enough to tell him that their new friendship was undamaged. He tried hard not to stare at her exposed body. Likewise, he did not want to make eye contact again. So, he continued to watch Saturn, which now filled half of the viewport.

Eah studied his facial features as she spoke. "You are not like the Dah-Ahey," she said. "I can see this. You have the Ways of Ahey inside. In that we are much...the same."

"I don't know what that means, but I'm glad you're not offended." Jay risked a glance at her luminous face. "And I'm honored that you think we're alike somehow."

"Alike, yes," she said, "but different. Yet...we tried to bond."

"Bond?"

"To...be...and communicate...on the inside." She touched her fingertips to her chest. "It is how *our people* unite."

"You say 'our people' as if you're including me," Jay noted.

She nodded. Her smile conveyed kindness, but Jay also detected wariness in the expression. That was understandable; to her, he was strange and foreign—even barbaric compared to her gentleness and elegance. In Jay's eyes, though, she was just as much a mystery. He wanted to trust her—to like her—but she was so...different.

"All people are related," she said.

Jay's lips formed a doubting smirk. "I believe that on *my* planet, but until now we didn't know life existed anywhere else."

"*Ehe*...no!" Eah reached out and placed a firm hand on Jay's chest. "I am not just 'life,' and we are not 'aliens,' as Perry Carlson says. I am human...like you, Jay. Your people and my people are the *same.*"

Jay struggled not to pull away from her intimate, yet innocent, touch. "Not *exactly* the same, though."

"No...not exactly the same." She said it with a hint of disappointment, but there was something else behind her words. Curiosity? Suspicion? Either way, her coy pout suggested interest.

"Well, since we're stuck with each other for a while," he said, "maybe we'll be able to sort it out."

Eah shot him a mysterious smile. "Yes...I believe many things will be *sorted out.*"

CHAPTER 12

Step

*W*hat happens when we step? Paul Theele's question echoed in Ellis's mind while he paced the floor and pondered how to explain an alien technology he did not understand. *What happens, indeed? I have a PhD in physics and over twenty years of teaching it, but I still don't know where to begin.*

The aliens' ability to travel through space defied the laws of science —at least the ones Ellis knew and taught. What they were doing should have been impossible, yet here he was in an incredible spacecraft flying through the solar system. *All this time, we've been wrong,* he concluded. *Even Einstein was only scratching the surface.* He walked to the viewport and considered the planet Saturn. *Impossible. This is simply impossible.*

"Are you okay, Ellis?" Paul asked. Like the other abductees, he had been waiting patiently for a scholarly explanation.

"Hmm? Oh...yes." Ellis turned back to face them all. "I apologize for my hesitation. It's just that...well...according to everything we know about the behavior of matter on our planet, what is happening to us right now should not be possible."

"That's what *I've* been trying to say," Perry said, "but maybe they'll believe *you.*"

Yori placed a finger to her lips, signaling Perry to keep quiet. "Go on, Ellis. At least tell us what you can."

Ellis returned to the sitting area and chose a seat near Yori, while Paul and April joined them from the viewport. "Well, as our...host...explained, this vessel will reach a predetermined point in space and *step* into a different galaxy."

"Is it like some sort of science fiction thing—going into *hyperspace* or something?" Paul asked.

"What you're referring to is faster-than-light travel, but this is different. Our own galaxy is over one hundred thousand light years from one end to the other. So even at the speed of light, it would take thousands of years just to travel from Earth to the edge of the Milky Way."

"Let alone going into another galaxy," Yori added.

"Precisely."

"So, how do they do it?" Perry asked.

"Are any of you familiar with the theories of dark matter?" He received a few uncertain nods and a few blank stares.

"Dark *what?*" April asked.

"Dark *matter.* It's the stuff that many scientists think makes up *most* of our universe." Ellis stood and pointed around the room. "For example, consider this area. We know that matter comprises protons, electrons, atoms, particles, elements, and all the rest. Everything in this room is matter, being held together by invisible bonds. But what is *between* the tiniest of particles? What exists between a proton and an electron?"

"Nothing," April suggested.

"Many have accepted that idea through the years. But there are indications of an unobservable matter—a dark matter that fills the emptiness of known matter."

"If it's unobservable, how do they know it's really there?" April asked.

"Because we can observe its *effects* on known matter. We've seen something *affecting* visible matter, but until now we could only make guesses about the cause."

"Until now?"

"If my observations aboard this spacecraft are correct, these aliens have proved that dark matter exists."

"Right. So what does this dark matter have to do with how they travel between galaxies?" Perry asked.

"Everything!" Ellis exclaimed. "They base their technology on it. From what I've seen, they *manipulate* dark matter. Doing so allows them to travel through space, covering impossible distances in short amounts of time. They also use it to build things like this spaceship and to transport people and things, like they did to bring us aboard."

"Did they tell you how they manipulate it?" Perry asked.

Ellis sat down hard in his seat. "How could they? Even without the language barrier, it would be like explaining the laws of physics to a child. They've probably been studying and experimenting with dark matter for hundreds of years, whereas our scientists have only recently *hypothesized* about it."

"Keah said that our two galaxies would *touch*," April recalled.

Ellis smiled as he considered the idea. "Quite right. Besides moving smaller objects and people, they can do the same with enormous objects, even to the size of a galaxy."

Paul was still incredulous. "I can accept transporting smaller things, but *galaxies?* Are you sure you understood them correctly? They do have a unique way of communicating."

At that, Ellis frowned. "Your wife is not the only person in this room who can understand them, Paul."

"I'm just asking a question."

"I'll admit that I had a troublesome time with Keah's accent and use of our language. Communication was problematic, but not impossible."

"If I could add something here," April said, "watching their movements is as important as listening to their words. They communicate with subtle gestures more than half the time."

Ellis considered that and nodded. "Yes. That would account for much. Thank you, April. I hope I didn't offend you."

"Not at all. I'm here to help."

Perry stood and began pacing behind the seating area. "So, they can move galaxies? What are they...gods?"

"I haven't decided *what* they are," Ellis answered. "I accept what is observable, and what I have observed is that they are super-intelligent beings from another world...as difficult as that is for me to say...and for you to hear."

Perry stopped and faced Yori. "Miss Shimizu, you are a medical student. Do *you* think they are human?"

"By outward appearances, their bodies *look* human. They're flawless, like perfected masterpieces. It's hard to believe."

"Elaborate, please. *What* is hard to believe?" Perry asked.

"Well, human biology is my specialty. I've studied hundreds of bodies—every type, from every background, and in every stage of development and decline. Just looking at these alien people makes me think of *perfected* humans. It's as if there isn't a defective gene in their bodies. That's why I say it's hard to believe."

Perry shrugged. "Any *other* observations?"

"Too many to go into. I'm still sorting this whole thing out in my head. At the risk of sounding too unscientific, I suppose we should consider that they may have taken on the outward form of a human being, especially since they can manipulate matter."

"I think you're wrong there," April said. "Eah *told* me they are human. She was emphatic about it. From the moment we first met them, they wanted to impress that on us."

"Maybe Jay will find out more while he's with Eah," Paul suggested. "Can we get back to the dark matter thing? I'd like to hear more."

"Yes, let me explain it differently," Ellis said. "Perhaps a demonstration will help." He pulled a handkerchief out of his pocket and with his free hand formed a fist, as if he was grasping an invisible mug handle. He then draped the square cloth over it. "As I push my fingertip lightly into the center of this handkerchief, tell me what happens."

"It forms an indentation," Paul noted.

"And if I keep pushing?" Ellis pushed the cloth into his hand like a magician performing a disappearing hanky trick.

"It folds in."

"What of the edges? The corners?"

"They move. They get closer together."

"Good. Now imagine there is a small marble attached to opposite corners. What would happen to them?" He pushed the cloth through his fist and then pulled it from underneath.

"The marbles would move closer to each other," April said.

"Exactly!" Ellis praised. "Think of the handkerchief as an area of space between two celestial bodies—two planets, or even two galaxies. Those are the marbles." He stretched the cloth back over his hand. "In the nothingness of that space is dark matter, represented here by this handkerchief. Create a force that will act on that matter. Aim it between two distant objects..." Ellis repeated the pushing action with his finger. "The space between, or dark matter stretches, and the objects move closer to one another. Remove the force and space springs back, and the objects return to their original positions. Actually, a thin sheet of rubber would make for a better representation of such spacial elasticity, but you get the idea."

Paul rubbed his damp forehead. He was still hot, still sweating, and still fatigued. Now he was getting a headache. "Ellis, I have limited knowledge of physics, but wouldn't *gravity* cause a problem with this? And the size of a galaxy? I mean...I would think that forcing planets or galaxies out of their normal locations would—"

"Quite right," Ellis agreed, "but gravitational forces and the sizes of objects do not affect dark matter in the same ways as normal matter. Thus, size becomes irrelevant. In fact, we can toss out everything we thought we knew about matter—both seen and unseen. That dark matter exists and can be manipulated changes our very laws of physics—of nature."

"So, if I understand you," Perry concluded, "they shorten the distance between two points by temporarily displacing the dark matter *between* the two points?"

"That's it, Mister Carlson. They even do it to travel through space, which they call *stepping*. Somehow, they displace dark matter between their point of origin and their chosen destination. For much shorter trips, they use the vessel's inertia—it's forward motion—which is created by a *step*. It's sort of step-coast-step-coast movement, I suppose."

"How did they bring us into their ship?" April asked.

"I posed the same question to our friend Keah. He didn't call that a *step*, but something else. They latched on to us by grabbing hold of the dark matter in and around us—"

"So, they *beamed us in* then," Perry interrupted.

"No. Not dematerialization in the fictional sense. More likely, I'd say they...turned us inside out."

"*Excuse* me?" April asked in disbelief.

"The dark matter between the atoms making up our bodies enveloped the...the...*hard* matter, if you will. For a short time, I suppose we became almost immaterial—at least regarding the matter we know of."

April shook her head and looked at Paul. "This is giving me a headache."

"I've had one for a while now," Paul said.

"Mind you, this is all quite hypothetical and based solely on my limited observations and understanding. I believe, however, that it is what Keah showed me."

"Their knowledge is so far beyond ours," Yori said. "Imagine what else they must be able to do. Think of what their planet is like. I'm not sure I'm ready for it."

"Well, they're taking us there regardless," Perry noted. "Look. I can't help being a skeptic, and I intend to remain cautious, but I do appreciate the incredible nature of it all."

"So, you're accepting all this as real?" Paul asked.

"I'm being open-minded. If it is for real—and that's a big *if*—I'm thinking of all the things we could learn from such aliens. It would be an opportunity to begin a relationship that could change life on our planet forever." He walked over to the viewport and stared out as the vessel passed the last of Saturn's outer rings. "And we'll all be famous when we get back."

The room became quiet as the five Earth humans considered Perry's last words. Paul's head was throbbing, and he was having difficulty grasping it all. He wanted to believe Keah and his family. They were so genuine and peaceful. But how could he trust beings with the power to do the incredible things Ellis had just described? Were they trustworthy? Were they indeed human? How could that even be? His belief system taught him to discount the existence of life outside of Earth. So where did these people come from?

Is everything I believe turning out to be wrong? Paul wondered as he massaged his throbbing temples. *There must be more to this. There has to be an explanation.* He looked at each of the others. Like him, they were all lost in their own thoughts, and their expressions conveyed confusion and doubt.

I've got to find Keah and Ahee, Paul decided. With all that was happening, he needed at least one certainty; he had to know he could trust them. The more he fretted about it, the stronger the sense of urgency grew to seek them. When he could bear it no longer, he stood and headed for the exit portal.

"Where are you going?" April asked, alarmed by his sudden departure.

Paul turned to regard his wife. Other than during the births of their children, he had never seen her so exhausted. The sight of her sitting there, rubbing her aching forehead and pulling at her sweat-soaked clothing, strengthened his resolve to find answers. They had been aboard the alien vessel for too long without knowing. He had to be sure about who these beings were.

"I'm going to look for Keah and Ahee," he replied in a shaky voice. The heat was draining him, and he was having difficulty maintaining his balance. "I have to get at least *one* answer—to put something to rest— for all of us."

"What is it?"

"I'll explain when I come back," he said, stumbling toward the room's portal. He stuck both hands into it, but then yanked them out when he encountered resistance. Someone was coming through from the other side.

A white hand appeared first, followed by a foot, then a leg, then a female chest and abdomen, and at last a head. It was Eah. Once she was through, Jay pushed his way in behind her.

"You were leaving this place?" Eah asked Paul. "Is there something you require?"

"I...uh..." Paul studied her for a moment while forming his reply. Her physical perfection was hard not to notice, but it was her eyes that captivated him. They expressed a deep sincerity and a longing to be understood. As she held his gaze, Paul felt dizzy. "Well...I was...just..." He stumbled forward and almost fell into Eah.

"Paul!" Jay grabbed his arm. "Are you okay?"

Paul shook himself from his momentary daze. When his vision cleared, he realized he was now sitting on the floor. "What happened?"

April and Yori rushed over and eased him back onto his feet.

"It looked like you fainted," Yori answered. "It's the heat and stress. Let's get you to a seat." She and April guided Paul to a lounge while Jay followed close behind.

Eah disappeared into the adjoining repository and returned with a handful of what looked like small plums. "You should eat this," she said, offering one to Paul. "It will strengthen you."

Paul hesitated, wondering if it would be safe to eat the alien fruit.

"The *water* was fine for us," April reminded. "Try one."

He took one and bit into it. The texture was like a pear and it tasted nutty and sweet. After a few more bites, his head cleared and strength surged through his muscles. "Thank you," he said to Eah. "I'm getting better."

"I will bring more. This helps when you feel weak. I will also bring another—one that comforts from the heat." She went back into the repository just as Keah and Ahee appeared through the main entry portal.

Ahee noticed the group huddled around Paul right away. Concerned, she rushed over to them. "Is Paul...*okay?*" she asked April.

"It's the heat," April replied, wiping her damp forehead. "The high temperature is affecting us."

Ahee frowned and glanced at Keah. They communicated silently for a few moments until Eah returned with two large bowls of fruit. She served the Earth humans while Keah and Ahee sat down next to Paul.

"Keah," Paul said. "I'm sorry, but I was coming to speak to you when I..."

"The food will strengthen you. Eat."

Paul complied, taking fruit from each bowl and tasting it.

"I can see you have many questions," Keah said, studying Paul's expressions.

"Yes...I do."

"It is the same for us. Perhaps answers will come while we travel together."

"Well, it's comforting to know you're just as perplexed by it all as we are, I guess."

"Yes," Ahee agreed. "Purr-plexed. But there is a reason for all of this. In that, you must find comfort. Ahey has—"

"I take it we're about to experience what you call a *step?*" Perry interrupted.

"Yes," Ahee answered. "We were coming to tell you that...and to be with you."

"What's going to happen?" Yori asked.

"Much the same as when you came into the *wa-ah-ahea*," Keah replied. "It is a...fast thing." He motioned toward the room's viewport, which Eah had enlarged during their conversation. The viewing area was now six feet high and about eight feet across, offering a magnificent view of Saturn's outermost rings. "You can watch the step from here."

"We are still learning your language," Ahee said. "Are we saying the words...*okay?*"

"Oh, yes!" April answered. "We've been very impressed by how fast you've picked up on it."

"Picked up?"

"I mean, with how fast you're understanding our language."

Ahee smiled with great appreciation. "Eah understands even better. Her gift is in words, and she studies comm-ooon—"

"Communication," Eah suggested.

"Yes. Communication. She has been...teaching...all of us. Now, Eah will talk and es-plain what you see."

Eah smiled at Ahee and pointed to her own lips. "Ex-plain."

"Yes," Ahee agreed. "*Explain.*"

"Jay has told me he studies *ahea*—space," Eah said as she stood next to the viewport.

Jay shrugged. "It's just a hobby."

"Come." Eah held out her hand and motioned for him to join her by the viewport. "You can help with words and names."

"Alright. I'll try."

Everyone else in the room positioned themselves in the seating area to face the viewport. They had finished all the fruit, which had somehow satisfied both hunger and thirst and even cooled their bodies. Paul and April no longer had headaches, and both were more at ease as they gave Eah and Jay their full attention.

"Since you're into astronomy, Jay," Paul said, "seeing Saturn up close must impress you."

"Yeah. I've seen it a few times through my telescope, but nothing compares to *this* view."

Eah exposed a control panel on the wall. She touched it, and the transparent material of the viewport changed into a colorful swirling pattern, like oil moving across the surface of water.

"I will...mag-nee-fy, so you can see our *eekaoa*—our galaxy."

A second touch of the control panel brought an image of a spiral galaxy into view. It was a typical galaxy, with a bright center and rings of cloudy dust embedded with trillions of stars. This galaxy, however, had what looked like a long tail coming out of it, as if one of the spiraling rings had broken and stretched out into a long line of clouds and clusters of stars.

"That looks like the Tadpole Galaxy," Jay said.

"The *what?*" Perry asked.

"The Tadpole Galaxy," Jay repeated. "It has a numerical reference, but people call it the Tadpole Galaxy because it looks sort of like a tadpole. It's in the constellation Draco and is one of the closer galaxies to ours."

Keah and Ahee nodded as they listened and were both enjoying Jay's descriptions.

"Tad-poh?" Keah asked.

"Tad-*pole*," Jay corrected. "A tadpole is a baby frog—an animal on our planet. This galaxy has a shape that looks like a tadpole."

Jay hoped the alien humans would understand. It was awkward having to describe such a simple thing.

"Yes. Yes. We are understanding," Keah said. "To us, this is Eekaoa *Ehuah. Galaxy Ehuah* is the name. In your words, *Ehuah* is...clouds. Cloudy. The cloudy galaxy."

"Hourou—our world—is here," Eah said, pointing to the mid-section of the galaxy's tail.

The viewport changed its magnification, and the area to which Eah pointed filled it. Beautiful blue star clusters appeared as sparkling diamonds amid massive pastel clouds of purple, green, and blue.

"The step will take us to this area." Eah pointed to one star cluster, and the magnification brought it into view. "Here are Tahah and Tameen. They are twin stars. Around them is our...planet system. Hourou is the third planet."

"Like our Earth," Jay noted.

"Two suns?" April asked.

Jay nodded. "Binary stars. Two stars close together, with one often drawing energy from the other."

"How interesting," Yori said.

"It's not as unusual as you might think," Jay added. "I've read that two out of every three stars might actually be binary stars, or even a system of three stars close together."

Eah was about to say something but stopped short when one of her people entered the room. It was a male with black skin. He waited at the portal until he saw Keah and Ahee sitting amongst the Earth humans. A slight gesture from Keah told him it was alright to approach the group.

"This is Tammah," Eah said. "He is here to tell us we will now step."

Eah touched the control panel, and the viewport returned to normal, showing only the blackness of space dotted with stars. She then walked over to Jay and stood beside him.

"Here we can see our progress," Keah said, nodding toward the viewport. "To step is not such a strange thing. Rather, it is *natural*."

After Keah spoke, the Earth humans noticed a slight vibration in the material that made up their seats and the floor. As it grew stronger, April grabbed Paul's hand. The other Earth humans looked at each other with trepidation, and Jay took a few nervous steps closer to Eah.

"The step begins," Keah said in a soothing tone. He gestured toward the viewport, and everyone in the room turned their attention to it. The star field changed in a bright display of colored streaks. Then, after a few seconds, it showed only blackness.

"Your galaxy is behind us," Eah said. "We are now in void."

"Space between galaxies?" Jay asked in amazement.

"Yes."

A tiny speck of light appeared in the center of the viewport. It grew rapidly until it formed into the swirl of another galaxy. A long tail identified it as the Tadpole Galaxy. In seconds, it filled the entire viewport and then morphed into streaks of colored light.

"We have entered our galaxy now," Eah said, "and will turn toward our home...toward Hourou."

The Earth guests were all captivated by the view. What they saw was awe-inspiring and terrifying at the same time. April glanced at Paul, who sat wide-eyed and dumbfounded as if he wanted to say something but could not form the words. She tried to give his hand a reassuring squeeze, but found she could no longer feel it. Looking down at their intertwined hands, she gasped as she gripped right through Paul's fingers. The effect that brought her aboard the alien vessel had returned.

Jay also noticed their sudden change of state. As he watched the brilliant display in the viewport, he reached up to touch his face and found that he could no longer feel with his fingers. The shock of that caused his legs to buckle, and he stumbled toward Eah. Instead of knocking into her, however, he fell right through her body, landing with a soft thud on his hands and knees.

Yori, having witnessed Jay's fall, screamed and pointed at him, but the sound of her voice was so muffled that it failed to attract anyone's attention. Though Ellis and Perry were seated next to her, they were too enamored by the display in the viewport to notice much else.

Eah came down on one knee beside Jay and was saying something he could not understand. Her expression showed concern, so he gave a quick grin to show that he was alright. He then pushed himself up into a kneeling position.

Somehow, the floor and the other structures in the room had remained solid. Jay looked down at the floor and wondered why he was not being absorbed into it. The idea worried him, so he turned to Eah and reached for her hand. This time, he could feel and take hold of it. Eah nodded, accepted his grip, and helped him to his feet.

Sound returned to normal. The first noticeable noise came from Yori, who was still yelling at the top of her voice. The other Earth humans were slow to come out of their stupefied states, but April picked up on Yori's terrified rant and followed her stare over to Jay

"It's okay. I'm alright," Jay said as he patted himself down. "I'm still in one piece."

"What happened?" April asked Yori.

"He...he fell right *through* Eah!" Yori exclaimed.

"Yeah. That was bizarre," Jay admitted. "But it was just like how we came into the ship. I remember my body going numb, and then it was like I turned into a ghost or something."

"Incredible!" Ellis said. "A temporary asomatous state for us, yet our surroundings remained solid."

"The wa-ah-ahea is made up of both matters, Ellis Minister," Keah informed.

"It also has living qualities," Jay added. "At least, that's what I saw when Eah was showing me around."

"Yes," Keah agreed. "The wa-ah-ahea is also a living thing."

"I would like to see more of it," Yori declared, having calmed herself from her previous fright.

"We will show you *many* wondrous things while you are with us," Ahee declared as she stood and pointed toward the viewport. "Welcome, new friends, to a new galaxy."

CHAPTER 13

Alien

True to Ellis's explanation, the alien vessel's steps caused it to travel at incredible speeds. The Tadpole Galaxy was only a pinprick of light mere minutes ago. Now, it filled the bridge's forward viewport. The Earth party hardly had enough time to appreciate the view before the ship engaged in another step and almost instantly moved into the center of the galaxy's tail. An impressive purple and green nebula lay directly ahead. Inside, hundreds of stars lit its cloudy shroud to reveal the enormous depth. Somewhere in that nebula was a planetary system that was home to the planet Hourou.

"What a beautiful nebula," Jay said, wobbling a bit while he gaped in amazement.

Yori caught sight of his instability and became concerned. "Are you sure you're alright, Jay? Any dizziness?"

"What? No, I'm fine. It's just the soft floor."

Yori beckoned him to sit next to her and he obliged. "Can you feel this?" she asked, poking various areas of his body with her fingertips.

"Yeah. No problems."

"Do you have residual tingling anywhere?"

"No. Really...I'm okay."

"Good. Tell me and Eah if any strange symptoms return, though."

"Like falling through someone else?"

"Funny. You know what I mean."

"During a step, we have seen many unusual things," Eah said to them both. "But there have never been injuries."

Jay poked Yori with his elbow. "Good to know. Right, Doc?"

"I'm not a doctor. I'm a..."

Yori became distracted when another alien female appeared through the main portal. Besides her black skin and the orange speckles in her hair, she looked much like Eah. After pushing her hair behind her body, she approached the seating area to speak with Keah.

"This is Uio," Eah told the Earth guests.

Although Uio spoke in the alien tongue, April heard insistent concern in her voice. "Something is wrong with their vessel again," she whispered to Paul.

"Great." Paul prepared himself to receive the bad news.

When Uio finished her report, Ahee rose and signaled for Eah to do the same, implying the problem would require immediate attention. Ahee then gave instructions to Uio, hurried her out of the room, and said something to Eah that seemed to include the Earth visitors. Keah stood and nodded his agreement. While Ahee rushed toward the exit portal, Eah scanned the floor as if searching for a path.

"What's wrong now?" Perry asked.

"The wa-ah-ahea has again become unstable," Keah replied. "I will take you to the...*bridge*. It is safest there."

The Earth humans exchanged concerned glances as they rose to follow Keah. In haste, he ushered them out of the lounge and into the ship's main corridor. On their way to the bridge, both Keah and Eah pointed out unsafe areas that appeared as indistinct blurs on the otherwise black surfaces of the floor and walls. The spots were more pronounced toward the forward sections of the vessel. They were also more dangerous. Several times, the group had to leap over sections of the floor that were dissolving.

"Is this thing going to make it?" Perry asked as he peered into a deep hole near his feet.

"You will be safe on the bridge," Keah replied. "By now, it has been stabe-uh-lized."

"I hope that means we won't all get sucked into a floor."

Keah stopped in front of the open bridge portal. "We will concentrate our remaining energy here to prevent—"

"*Remaining* energy?" Perry asked. "What? Are we running out of gas, too? I mean—"

"Carlson!" Ellis interrupted. "I think I can speak for everyone here in stating that your ill-placed remarks have become quite more than annoying. In fact, they are *intolerable!* There is obviously an emergency here! Now, will you *please* get into that room and cease with your negativity and taunting?"

An awkward silence followed Ellis's rebuke. With bright red cheeks and hands clenched into tight fists, he had clearly reached his limit in patience with Perry. Paul, April, Jay, and Yori communicated their own annoyance through stern glares. They were all fed up with his jeering, and he would have no defenders among them.

"Fine." Perry said with a smirk. He quickly ducked through the portal and the others accompanied him.

Nervous energy filled the bridge like a thick fog. The crew monitored their assigned workstations with an intense determination, hardly giving notice to the Earth humans when they entered the room. Keah hurried to his command chair while Eah steered their guests to a rear corner that contained little more than a large viewport.

"You can watch our return to Hourou from here," Eah said. "We shall pass quickly by our system's outer planets. Perhaps, when on Hourou, I can tell you more about what you will see."

Ahee called out to Eah from across the room, prompting her to leave her guests and take her place at a small control station. Before she sat down, she wrapped herself in her hair as if it was a shawl.

"Does the hair wrapping mean something?" Paul asked April. "Or is it for comfort?"

"Probably comfort," April replied. "Have you noticed the temperature drop since the *step?*"

"Now that you mentioned it, yes. It's much cooler in here. Either they fixed the problem or—"

"Let's not think about the *or*."

Ellis moved up next to Paul, needing some conversation to settle his nerves. "What are you two on about?"

"Hair and temperature," Paul answered.

"Ah, yes. The females have an advantage over the males in the colder air."

"You feel the difference, too," April said.

"Yes. The spaceship has been gradually losing heat."

"My guess is that the hair wrapping also comforts them psychologically," April added. "They're still a little awkward around us. We're the ones out of place, after all."

"Quite right," Ellis agreed. "Do you think this is all of them, then?"

"If it is," Paul answered, "there are nine, including Keah and Ahee."

Ellis considered the alien crew and noted that something was amiss. "I wonder what happened to the three bronze-skinned ones."

"After the tension they caused when they were brought aboard, they're probably locked up somewhere," Paul said.

Ellis frowned. "Hopefully in a *safe* part of the ship."

"I don't think now would be a good time to ask about all that," Paul warned.

April glanced at each of Keah's people. "I wonder if these really *are* their children. They all look to be around the same age."

"How could they pull *that* off?" Paul wondered aloud.

Ellis made an exaggerated shrug. "They *are* aliens."

"They're *humans*," April corrected.

"I note your conviction, April. However, based on observation, I am only willing to concede that they have...similarities. Perhaps in educating us, they will allow Yori to examine them. She could tell us much more."

"*That* would be interesting," Paul said with a bit of sarcasm. "The *abducte*es examining the *aliens?*"

"Paul—"

"I know, Babes. I'm just trying to lighten the mood."

"April," Ellis said, "if I may ask without compelling a defense..."

"Go ahead."

"You seem to have become attached to these beings, and you also understand them better than any of us. How did this all come about?"

April could tell Ellis was being sincere in his questioning. She also guessed that Paul was wondering the same thing. "I wouldn't say I'm *attached*," she answered. "I understand them a little, but I'm sure I've only scratched the surface." She watched Eah as she operated her control panels. "As for *how*...I don't know. I can't explain it other than to say it's like how a mother relates to her child, or how people who've been married for a long time can understand each other without even talking."

Ellis ruffled his hair and considered her answer. "Relational. Interesting."

"That's how it feels," April said, "and why it's hard for me to see them as just being *alien*." With that, she stepped away to talk with Jay and Yori, who had both moved to the viewport in the other rear corner of the bridge.

Ellis rubbed his tense neck and surveyed the room. Despite what April said, the scene before him looked bizarre and otherworldly. These alien beings were fellow humans? That seemed unlikely. Their bodies, though beautiful and captivating in their very naked state, were too perfect. Ellis could detect not a single defect. Nor could he point out any physical features he would find more attractive. Other than their glowing white or deep black skin, they represented all the best human traits. Surely, natural selection could do nothing more to improve these creatures.

As he observed them, though, he noted something familiar about how they worked together. He imagined being aboard a ship at sea. The captain was Keah. Proud and commanding, he called out orders while monitoring the status of their crippled vessel. Ahee was his first mate. It was her job to oversee the crew and ensure they stayed focused while they worked in unison. Each person had an individual task to perform, but operating this unusual vessel also required a synergy that only intimate connection could provide. They were much more than just a team. If they were indeed a family, Ellis thought, they had powerful bonds.

"A family of experts," he said to himself.

Paul had turned his attention to the nebula in the viewport, but overheard the comment. "Pardon?"

"Hmm? Oh. I said *experts*. They're each an expert with a specific task. It's as if they have spent many years training for this one event."

"Efficient and focused," Paul noted. "The technology that runs this ship must be incredible."

"Without a doubt."

"It must make our best computers look like simple toys, Ellis. I mean...even how they interface with it is different. They wave their hands over the controls and caress them like they're alive."

"It's indeed amazing," Ellis said. "What also impresses me, though, is how *mature* they are. They act with a maturity that only age can bring, yet they appear to be young adults."

"How old do you think Keah and Ahee look?" Paul asked.

Ellis regarded Keah, and then looked to Ahee, who was assisting two young males at a nearby workstation.

"I would guess they are scarcely older than you and April."

"We're in our early thirties."

"Interesting. I would be inclined to believe that these are *not* all children of Keah and Ahee, were it not for the family resemblance. Aside from skin color, you can see the genetic similarities plainly."

"I suppose—" Paul wanted to bring up something more important that had been bothering him when Perry walked up from behind and cut in to the conversation.

"I feel like I'm in a room with a bunch of walking, talking store mannequins. That's the only similarity *I* see."

Paul looked at Ellis and grinned, relieved that Ellis was also smiling.

"Indeed," Ellis said with a chuckle. "Carlson, that is a wonderful observation. I must admit that I have had a troublesome time finding an appropriate comparison."

Perry frowned with obvious disappointment. "I'm the sarcastic one. Remember?"

"I'm being serious, Carlson," Ellis said. "Often, my immersion in science prevents me from recognizing the simplicity and clarity of everyday life. I appreciate input from those who are in the thick of it."

Perry's disposition changed when he saw Ellis was being genuine. "Thank you," he said. "You might think I'm being difficult, but I'm just as concerned for all of us as you are."

"I believe you, Carlson."

"I also appreciate having a scientific mind along. Your observations will be invaluable...especially after we get back."

Bonding complete, Paul thought. *Hopefully, they'll start getting along better.* "You know," he said to them both, "I'm still confused about something. Despite all the weirdness, April and I are compelled to trust these people. I can't explain why. For me, maybe it's because I have little choice."

"But you do still have some reservations," Perry remarked. "I can tell."

Paul let out a sigh and nodded. "I suppose I do, yes."

"We must all remain open-minded," Ellis warned, "as well as cautious."

"That's what I've been saying," Perry quipped.

"But there is no need for paranoia, either."

Perry shrugged off the comment with a chuckle.

"There's something more to all of this than we know," Paul said in a hushed tone. He watched April speaking to Jay and Yori on the other side of the bridge. She looked content, as did Jay and Yori, but Paul could tell they were all hiding a deep anxiety. "I don't know. I just have a sense of foreboding."

"Why?" Perry asked. "Things have been going so well. What could you possibly be nervous about?"

Paul ignored his sarcasm. "My gut tells me we're in for a bumpy ride."

CHAPTER 14

Evidence

Laura Turgis knew what she had seen and investigated so far proved the existence of intelligent extraterrestrial life. But she still needed conclusive evidence. Eyewitness accounts, photographs, and video recordings were just not enough—even if they came from hundreds, or thousands, of sources. Those things could only prove that a good many people saw an aircraft of unknown origin. Likewise, the images of the unusual faces in the craft's windows only showed that someone piloted it. What Laura really wanted was something tangible—hard proof that would provide an undeniable link to another world.

The disappearances of the six unrelated people bothered her as well. Try as they did to keep that quiet, her investigators could not prevent the story from overshadowing all other news about the UFO sightings. There were just too many witnesses to the abductions in the city. A few bystanders even shared photos from their camera phones that were clear enough to identify two of the abductees—the college professor and the medical student.

Laura tasked a team from her agency to investigate the disappearances while she led a separate one in search of the evidence she needed. It had been less than twenty-four hours since the incident, but she was already becoming impatient. Without an irrefutable link to extraterrestrial intelligence, her government could explain it all away through creative downplay, blatant cover-up, or worse—complete silence. Laura would allow none of that to happen. The *Triangle* was not simply an experimental military aircraft, nor was it an elaborate hoax. She knew it, and so did the other twenty-nine people who swore to secrecy after viewing the video recordings. This was the real thing—a bona fide visit by beings from another planet along with human contact. She could accept no other explanation, and neither would millions of people who were watching the story unfold in the news. They deserved to know the truth, and Laura believed it would eventually fall upon her to give it to them.

* * *

Laura exited Route 64 via the Greenwood Road off-ramp—the same route the Theeles had taken before they disappeared. It was easy enough to uncover that the couple had been on their way to a marriage retreat in the mountains. How they came to be involved with the missing Jay Harrison was still unknown, though. Laura assumed they may have found him and his friend wandering around lost and were trying to return them to the nature preserve. What happened next was hard to believe: a police officer and several soldiers chased Harrison and the Theeles into a nearby pasture and witnessed their abduction by the Triangle. Their accounts were all identical, but they sounded more like science fiction than fact—beams of light, people floating and demateri-alizing, a strange spacecraft. Laura had heard it all before. At least this time, though, the witnesses were credible.

She pondered these things as she pulled her car up to the first barricade. A young Marine slung his M-16 and approached her, while a second began writing on a tablet. Laura rolled down her window and held out her agency identification.

"Director Laura Turgis," she said. "General Shepherd is expect-ing me."

The Marine scrutinized her ID, scanned the interior of her car, and nodded approval to his comrade.

"Yes, Ma'am," the second said. "Sign at number eleven, please."

Laura accepted his tablet and stylus and signed her name on the eleventh line, noting the other names above hers. She recognized two. One was Doctor Haines from the Space Agency. The other was a colleague of hers from the Department of National Security. Evidently, terrorism and foreign spying were still not being ruled out. It made sense. Perry Carlson, an abductee, was a member of Congress and the Defense Committee.

She exchanged the tablet for her ID and waited for them to open the gate.

"Continue on to the next checkpoint," the soldier instructed her. "Someone will escort you to the site from there."

"Thank you."

"Good evening, Ma'am."

A good evening? Laura thought as she drove away. *Only if this turns out to be what I'm hoping it is.*

The second checkpoint was an ominous military-style roadblock, erected in front of the same spot where the Theeles had parked their SUV. Laura stopped her car at the gate and saw that the vehicle was still there—no longer on the road, but moved onto the grassy shoulder. She wondered if the couple would ever return to drive it again.

"Ma'am?" The voice startled Laura from her pensiveness. Three Marines had approached and were now staring in at her. The one who had spoken wore a captain's insignia on his uniform. "I'm Captain Lawrence," he said. "I'll be escorting you to the site from here. Just leave your keys in the ignition and we'll move your vehicle."

"I'm supposed to be meeting General Shepherd," Laura said as she exited the car.

"Yes, Ma'am. The General sends his apologies. He was called to a briefing. You'll be meeting with Colonel Richter."

Laura shrugged off the change of plans. Most important was the discovery at the crash site. The rank of her tour guide was inconsequential.

Captain Lawrence led her around the barricade to a white car with government license plates. "The site isn't far from here, but I'll drive you over."

Lawrence opened the passenger door for her. After she seated herself, he shut it and spoke into his headset while going to the driver's side. "Yes, sir," he was saying as he entered the car and turned on the ignition. "I am transporting Director Turgis to the site now, sir."

Military personnel had cleared away scrub and debris from the thick forest to form a road. It was rough, twisting in directions that made little sense. The car bounced and jostled as Lawrence swerved it between the trees.

"No offense," Laura said, gripping the dashboard, "but couldn't they have done better with clearing a path?"

"Ma'am? Oh, the road. We had to compromise with the nature preserve people. This section of the forest is the oldest, and they didn't want us to damage the environment. Sorry about the rough ride, Ma'am."

"No problem. I have yet to see a map of the site, but I understand that it's in a natural clearing?"

"Correct, Ma'am. The pilots probably chose it as a safe place to attempt a landing."

Laura wondered how much Captain Lawrence knew. "What is your clearance, Captain?"

"Top Secret, Ma'am," he replied as the car entered the field, "but it would be better if you directed further questions to Colonel Richter. We're here already."

The vehicle rolled to a stop in front of another barricade. Two Marines approached with rifles slung. After recognizing the Captain, they saluted, gave a nod to Laura, and returned to their posts. The gates opened and Lawrence drove through.

"The site measures about fifty square yards," Lawrence said. "It's fenced and patrolled. After we park, I'll escort you to the command center to meet Colonel Richter." He pulled something from a side pocket and handed it to Laura. "This is your security badge." It was on a lanyard, which Laura hung around her neck. "You must wear it at all times. I'll retrieve it when I return you to your vehicle later."

Lawrence parked the car, and they both exited.

"Thanks for the ride," Laura said.

"My pleasure, Ma'am. This way, please."

She followed close as Lawrence led her to a massive army tent. Behind it stood a twenty-foot wall of scaffolding that resembled the framework around a building under renovation. Laura could see soldiers atop the wall, pacing back and forth as if guarding something beyond it. Inside the tent, field operation electronics and workstations filled most of the space. Doctor Haines was in a far corner, talking to an officer whom Laura guessed to be Colonel Richter.

Haines saw Laura enter and rose from his chair as she approached. "Hello, Director."

"Doctor Haines," Laura replied.

The officer stood and offered his hand to Laura. "I'm Colonel Richter."

"Laura Turgis."

"General Shepherd apologizes for his absence. He wanted to show you the site himself, but was called away to a briefing."

"No need to apologize, Colonel. I *am* eager to begin my investigation, though."

"Good. I'll be interested in what you think of the *find*."

Laura's heart skipped a beat. She tried to hide the anticipation that suddenly filled her. "The *find?*"

"There's no official name for it yet. Doctor Haines and I were just trying to decide what to call it in the documentation."

"I already know about the site, but what is...*it?*"

"Colonel," Haines interjected. "Why not *show* Miss Turgis what we have instead of describing it? I'd like to see her initial reaction."

"Please do," Laura said with an excited grin.

Colonel Richter nodded in agreement. "Follow me, then." He led them out of the command tent and then to a spiral staircase that was attached to the scaffolding. Richter went up first, followed by Haines and Laura.

"Does the wall surround the entire area, then?" Laura asked.

"Yes, it does," Richter answered. "From up here, you'll get a good view of the operation, and it's easier to access what we found."

At the top of the stairs, they stepped onto a small platform that hung above the enclosed site.

"As you know," Richter said, "this third crash site is like the first two...with one exception. Here, exactly three feet of dirt is missing."

Laura surveyed the ground below her and gaped at the enormous triangular pit. To her, it seemed as if someone had meticulously dug out the soil to ensure that every square inch was the same depth. Just as strange, something had withered all the vegetation around the hole.

Laura's eyes followed a string of yellow caution tape along all the three sides, marking a perimeter. Ten feet beyond was a similar boundary.

Doctor Haines pointed at the tree line. "Over there is where they discovered the footprints. They go all the way to the road that brought you here."

"Where does that catwalk lead?" she asked, motioning toward a suspended walkway.

"That's where the *find* is," Richter replied. "Let's go."

The catwalk crossed over half of the site before declining to form a steep ramp. At ground level, it continued downward into a large cavity that resembled the mouth of a cave. The Colonel stopped at the opening, anticipating Laura's next question.

"The cavern beyond was not here before the crash. It's safe, though. Something compacted the surrounding dirt so tightly that it's now hard as rock."

"Since we're going in, I assume there's no danger from radiation," Laura noted.

"Correct. There has been no radiation of any kind."

Richter led them through the opening and into a dark tunnel. Work lights turned on as they entered, illuminating a long metal walkway suspended from above and lined with railings and wiring harnesses.

"I'm impressed you were able to secure the site and complete these structures in such a short amount of time," Laura said.

The Colonel nodded before ducking under a low-hanging wiring harness. "We spent the time we had while tracking the object to prepare for every plausible scenario. So assembling materials and placing assets was simple enough. And most of it was already close by. Just outside the capital, there's a company that specializes in rescue equipment for mining accidents."

As they continued on, the tunnel's decline became more pronounced and constrictive. Laura began using the railings for support while she stooped to avoid hitting her head on the ceiling.

"We're passing the last set of work lights," Richter said, "but as you'll soon see, we won't need them."

He was right. When they walked a little further, the tunnel was still illuminated, even after the lamps behind them had turned off. They should have been standing in complete darkness, yet a dim light remained.

"Where is the light coming from?" Laura asked.

"We don't know," Doctor Haines answered. "We could not locate the source. It's simply...there. Reflecting off the surfaces, perhaps."

"But they're black," Laura pointed out. Unlike the first section of tunnel, this was not of rock and dirt. The surfaces were different—coated in a deep black substance with the porousness and overall appearance of acoustic foam.

"Black indeed," Haines agreed, "and yet there is still a reflective quality."

"What's up ahead?" Laura asked. She could not see past Haines and the Colonel on the narrow walkway.

Richter moved aside and gestured toward an odd doorway a few feet ahead. "We're already inside the remnant," he said. "Just inside there, though, is something much more interesting than this strange hallway. Be careful not to touch the sides as you pass."

Laura followed the two men through the doorway and marveled at its design. Where there should have been some kind of door frame, the walls on each side of the opening were rolled back like curtains. Just above her head, shreds of a black membranous material stirred in the currents of her passing.

On the other side, Laura found she was now in a spacious chamber. It was triangular, and in front of her was a transparent corner—like a window from floor to ceiling. It seemed to be unbroken, and beyond it she could see compacted dirt. In the center of the room was a circular bank of colorful panels. Behind each one was a large black blob that resembled a beanbag chair. Laura stood in silent awe and struggled to make sense of what she was seeing.

Richter and Haines gave her a moment to process her thoughts before Haines broke the silence. "It's an intact room—a part of the craft," Haines said. "But we haven't any idea of its function."

The walkway that Richter's team erected inside the tunnel continued to the far side of the room, so Laura walked to the center. "The air in here is different," she said. "It's clean, like pure oxygen."

Haines nodded. "It's close to that, yes. Tests have shown a perfect air quality. No contaminants. Nothing harmful to us. Notice also that the temperature is more comfortable than in the tunnel and warmer than outside. It has remained constant, even adjusting to bodies entering and exiting."

Laura leaned over a rail to inspect the area around a flashing panel. "Almost every surface looks like it's covered in the same black material, and—"

The sound of creaking metal interrupted her. By the time she realized it was coming from the shifting rail, she was already falling and landing on the room's floor.

Richter and Haines scrambled to the spot where she had been standing.

"Laura!" Haines shouted as he reached for her.

"Are you alright, Miss Turgis?" Richter asked. "Doctor Haines, be careful!" He took hold of Haines's arm to prevent him from falling in after her.

The catwalk was only about three feet from the floor, but Laura had rolled far enough away that they could not reach her. "I'm fine," she said, pushing herself up to a seated position.

"Don't move!" Richter warned. "Let us try to reach you."

"No, wait!" Laura ran her hands over the surface of the floor. "It's spongy, like...like one of those memory foam mattresses that conforms to your shape and springs back."

"Don't touch anything!" the Colonel demanded. "We don't know about possible contamination yet. We've only just sent samples for testing."

Laura ignored his warning and crawled toward the flashing panel she had been trying to examine.

Richter frowned and turned to Haines. "Doctor Haines?"

Haines just watched Laura for a moment.

"Really Doctor, I—"

"We have to know, Colonel, and it might as well be now," Haines said. "She'll be alright. I'll monitor her. In the meantime, maybe you should get some help to fish her out."

"Radio communications don't work in here," Richter informed. "I'd have to leave, which I will not do. We'll break off the railing and pull her up with that."

While the two men examined the broken metal, Laura tested what she now realized was a seat. "This is actually a chair," she said. "It faces what must be a workstation. There are colored areas and large buttons."

"Definitely don't touch those!" Haines warned. "Just have a quick look and get back over here."

As Laura observed the workstation's position, the purpose of the room became apparent. It was the command center of a spaceship.

Another ship, Laura thought. *We assumed there was only one.*

"What do you make of it, Laura?" Doctor Haines asked while he assisted the Colonel in disassembling another piece of railing. "Any ideas?"

Laura stood and let her feet sink into the floor before attempting to walk on the strange surface. After steadying herself, she stepped toward the workstations that were closer to the large window. "I think this room is the control center of *another* alien spacecraft."

"So the early eyewitness accounts about *two* UFOs were accurate," Haines said.

"Yes." Laura caressed the edge of a control board in front of her. "Everything in here is made from the same material. It's like nothing I've ever seen—"

"Miss Turgis, we're going to pull you back up using this piece of rail," Richter said as he maneuvered it toward her.

"Yes, Laura," Haines agreed. "Enough exploring. Best come back now."

Laura turned to face them. "So there were *two* flying craft. We're in the remaining section of one that crashed. What do you think happened to the rest of it?"

Haines gestured for the Colonel to wait. Richter put the rail down and let out a loud sigh to show he was losing his patience with the two of them.

"Doctor Haines has a theory," Richter said to Laura. "I agree with it, and so does General Shepherd. In fact, the General is briefing the special committee about it right now."

"Well?" Laura pressed.

"We think the extraterrestrials destroyed the rest of the craft on purpose," Haines said. "That explains the triangular blast."

"What about the missing dirt?"

"It's possible they destroyed that, too."

"And *this* section?"

Haines rubbed his neck while he thought about it. "Well, I'd say either they didn't see it buried under the ground or they rushed off and didn't finish the job."

Laura turned her attention back to the main workstation. "As alien as it may be, there is logic to this."

"What do you mean?" Haines asked. "Do you recognize anything?"

"No. It's hard to explain. The layout feels...well, it looks as though it could have been made for humans."

"Alien and human at the same time?" Colonel Richter asked.

"Well, consider the design here." Laura motioned toward the rest of the room. "You have a doorway, seats, a command chair, workstations, a window—"

"You're assuming an awful lot," Richter said. "We have nothing to compare this with. You say it's the bridge section of a spaceship, but for all we know, you could have just been sitting on a toilet."

His comment drew a laugh from all three. Although the current situation was frightening, none of them could stop from being excited and awestruck. The discovery—the *find*—was the greatest in history, and they were among the first to explore it.

Laura became quiet as she wrestled with the implications. She now had the evidence she needed to prove intelligent life from another planet had visited Earth. This would change mankind's knowledge of the universe forever. Nothing would ever be the same.

Richter extended the rail toward her again. "Alright, Miss Turgis, it's time to get you out of there."

"Do come, Laura," Haines agreed. "We should get topside now."

Richter gave him a sideways glance. "That will have to wait."

"Why?" Laura asked, standing and making her way to the end of the rail. "What's wrong, Colonel?"

"Contamination. We don't know anything about this material yet. You're the only one who's touched it. There must be quarantine until the test results are back."

"What about the technicians? What about the people who constructed these walkways?"

"Nobody came into contact with it during the process. The teams and the techs all wore protective suits."

Laura felt herself becoming anxious. "You don't mean that I have to stay in *here,* do you?"

"I'd be afraid you would try to take off in it," Haines said in jest, anticipating an answer from the Colonel that Laura would not like.

Laura took hold of the rail and used it as a support while she stepped gingerly up to the catwalk and pulled herself onto it. When she was standing with them again, Richter and Haines backed away to avoid contact. Their reactions perturbed her.

"Come on! It's pretty clear that I'm fine. There's no radiation, remember?"

Richter shook his head. "I'm sorry. You know about protocol. We should have the test results in a few more hours—three at most. I'll go up and arrange for a quarantined waiting area. Doctor Haines can stay here to keep you company for now. But *no contact.*"

"Can you send down two laptops?" Haines asked. "We can at least use the time to get this all into a report. And please wire us up a link down here as well...for access to our research."

Richter nodded and exited the room. Haines waited for a few moments and then spoke in a hushed voice. "Anything you want to say without a military presence?"

The question surprised Laura. Up to that point, she had assumed they would all continue working together. Haines, however, just exposed a coming power play. One of their three organizations would have to take control—the military, the Space Agency, or Laura's agency. She wanted it to be hers, but Haines had already been positioning himself and the Space Agency. The military more than likely would defer to either of them, being bogged down with other responsibilities.

Laura knew that an agency showdown would come, but now was not the time. At this stage, they had to be unified—at least until she was free from quarantine. "No," she answered with a chuckle, as if to brush off a silly question. "You?"

Haines turned away from her, struggling with an answer. "No...I suppose not. They're...doing a superb job."

"I can tell you have some reservations."

Haines glanced at her and smiled. "They have no idea what this truly means."

"I do."

He raised an eyebrow. "What, my dear?"

Laura sat on the edge of the catwalk and slid back down onto the floor of the alien room. "Evidence."

CHAPTER 15

The Planet

The planet Hourou was still too far away to identify within its surrounding purple and green nebula. But its binary suns, Tahah and Tameen, shone like orange pinpricks from the cloudy center. As Eah had described, these marked the planetary system her family called home.

"Like the view?" Yori asked Ellis. He had been staring out the forward viewport for some time.

"Hmm? Oh...quite so."

"You look puzzled about something."

"I'm still wrestling with how all this is possible."

"Traveling through space? I thought you had it basically figured out. You explained it pretty well to the rest of us."

"Not even close, my dear." Ellis chuckled and glanced at her. Like himself, she was looking at other things while they were talking. He followed her gaze and saw she was studying one of the male aliens who was working nearby.

"I'm listening," Yori said, sensing Ellis's eyes upon her.

"Unlike your friend there, *our* people are still striving to return to the moon, and we're only using robotic vehicles to explore Mars. But to these beings, such endeavors are child's play. A mere solar system does not confine them; they've truly reached for the stars and conquered interstellar travel."

"That's not all they've conquered," Yori noted. "With such perfect bodies, they must have eradicated disease. I wonder what they could teach us."

"Much," Ellis guessed.

The two fell silent as they went back to admiring their choice of subjects. Ellis was about to walk across the bridge and ask Eah a question about the ship's speed when one of her brothers shouted at her from his workstation.

"Ehe!" Eah replied. She waved her hands over her control board and studied it. "Eh-eee-na. Ehe." Agitated, she spared an apprehensive glance at Keah.

Keah turned in his seat and communicated an offer to help, but Eah shook her head and tried her controls again. Unsatisfied with the results, she stood and began searching the bridge for something.

"This looks strange," Yori whispered to Ellis.

Eah stepped gingerly toward the group of Earth humans. "Are you now able to identify unsafe areas of the wa-ah-ahea?" she asked. Each of them nodded. "Good. We are concerned that the room may become unstable. You can help us by telling Ahee if you see such signs."

From across the bridge, Ahee offered a reassuring smile. "Ooo-oh-yee."

Perry was about to comment, but he stopped short when the bridge became illuminated by a soft, lavender light coming from the main viewport. The vessel already entered the nebula, and Hourou was directly ahead, growing larger by the second.

Ellis gaped at the view. "Incredible! So fast..."

"Yes, we will be there soon," Eah said, checking the floor for weak spots. "The wa-ah-ahea is...straining. Keah desires to reach Hourou before—"

"We understand," Ellis said. There was no need for Eah to elaborate on what was obviously a critical situation. The vessel's structural integrity was weakening—dissolving around them—and Keah was rushing to get them to the planet's surface. "Is there anything else we can do?"

Eah shook her head, wrapped herself in a cocoon of hair, and stepped away to examine a far corner. As she left, Ellis heard her speaking to herself in a hushed tone. Though her words were foreign, he recognized one of them: *Ahey*. She repeated it with reverence—like a prayer, Ellis thought.

Long minutes passed on the alien vessel while everyone busied themselves with their assigned tasks. Besides occasional melodious beeps from the ship's controls and whispers between the crew members, the bridge was quiet. Then, responding to a command from Keah, Eah and two of her brothers rushed out of the room. When they returned a short time later, they had the three bronze-skinned people with them. Eah led the newcomers to a far corner and conversed with them there. Unfazed by the presence of the bronzes, the rest of her family continued their work, while the Earth humans shared curious glances.

"I forgot about them," Paul whispered to April.

"Things have been so weird that I did, too."

"Can you make out what Eah is saying to them?"

April gave a heavy sigh. "I wish I had more focus. I've been bouncing between disbelief and being scared to death since we got here."

"Me, too," Paul admitted. "Don't think about anything else but the here and now, though. What do you see?"

April studied Eah as she talked to the bronze ones. They stood in the corner sulking, like children who were being warned not to misbehave. "I'm guessing here," she said, "but it looks like Eah is explaining the situation with the ship."

"Ship?"

"Well, that's what we're in, right—a spaceship?"

"No. It's a wa-ah-ahea."

"Funny."

"Hey. I'm learning, too. What else is she saying? The other ones don't look happy."

April watched Eah's lips. "I can't figure it out. I hardly know any of her words."

"What about the others? Are *they* giving you anything?"

"A little. They use a lot of the same gestures, but the way they do them is different."

"How so?"

"They make motions that are...harsh. There's no beauty in their movements."

"Beauty?"

"Compared to Eah's people, they're crass."

Paul observed the conversation and noted subtle differences in the way the alien humans communicated through body language. As April said, the bronzes were much less graceful. Their use of gestures and facial expressions was more explicit, even audacious. Paul found it familiar, though; it reminded him of how people acted back on Earth.

"It seems to me like they're being held by Eah's family under a sort of house arrest," April said.

"Well, that explains the hostility."

"They *did* steal a ship."

"True. But how are you *getting* all this?"

"I don't know. Maybe it's intuition. Their expressions suggest things to me. Every movement—even a twitch—has meaning."

"We've probably either insulted them or humored them hundreds of times since coming aboard," Paul quipped.

"I hope not. Anyway, we should make sure the others understand this so they don't unknowingly—"

"I get it. I'll help with that. Can you infer anything else about the bronze ones?"

"Eah warned them about how they should behave and about the condition of the ship. Then she invited them to help, but they each refused."

"I guess they're holding a grudge."

"Well, they're the ones who stole a ship and broke the rules."

"Yeah. I'd like to know more about that."

"Me, too. But I'm going to stop eavesdropping now. Let's get back to helping the people who can take us home."

"Right."

Both of them returned to searching the bridge's surfaces for signs of deterioration. When anyone noticed a spot, they called out to Ahee. As she waved her hands over her control panels in response, the dissolving areas became solid again. Tension grew on the bridge each time a new fissure appeared. On two such occasions, several of Keah's children had to abandon their workstations when the floor crumbled beneath them. The way they dashed from their seats was warning enough that it would be very dangerous to fall into one of the holes.

Soon, Hourou filled the forward viewport. Jay interrupted his scanning of the room's interior to observe the alien world. It was a magnificent planet. The outer atmosphere reflected the surrounding nebula's dominant shades of green and purple. Underneath, dazzling hues of violet marked seas and lakes across a single massive equatorial continent. The only other large landmasses capped the globe at each pole, separated from the ringed one by expansive lavender oceans that were dotted with tiny islands.

The vessel's approach placed it in line with the equator on the day side of the planet, offering a stunning and colorful perspective. From its present distance, Hourou resembled a giant pearl, swirling in purples and greens while suspended within pastel mists. Its single moon was also visible, likewise reflecting the nebula's color palette.

Ellis joined Jay in appreciating the view. "Fantastic, is it not?"

"It looks like a purplish version of Earth," Jay replied, "if our continents were all at the equator."

"Yes. Similar to our ancient Pangaea...as proposed by...Wegener, I believe."

"Alfred Wegener. 1912. In 'The Origin of Continents.'"

"Very good, Mister Harrison!"

"There's no sign of broken continents or drift, though," Jay noted.

"No. Not from this view."

"So this planet has a single large ringed continent along its equator and a small one at each pole."

Ellis nodded. "Assuming it continues on the other side of the planet, which we cannot see, it suggests a ringed continent, yes. Good observations, Jay."

"I wish I had a camera."

"As do I. Your memory will have to suffice, though. Hold on to this image. Indeed, study everything we see and commit it all to memory. We'll have much to describe and explain when we get back home." Ellis allowed himself one more long moment to enjoy the planet.

Jay smirked, wondering if anyone on Earth would believe any of it. He was still having a hard time believing it all himself. When Ellis stepped away to join the others, Jay also returned to the task at hand, checking his immediate area for discolorations on the surfaces. Everything around him was the normal shade of black. Satisfied, he scanned a path on the floor that would take him to where Eah was working at the rear of the bridge. His way looked solid, so he went to her, wary of any surface changes with every step.

Eah was repairing a control panel that was embedded in a rear wall. As Jay approached, he noticed her shiver a little before wrapping herself in her hair.

"It feels chilly back here," he said, looking over her shoulder at the strange controls.

"Chilly? Oh...the cold, yes. Some parts of the wa-ah-ahea are...shedding...heat into ahea—space...as it loses some structure." She glanced at Jay, and her eyes lingered on his clothing. "Are you alright, Jay?"

"Me? Oh, fine. I'm more concerned about the ship."

"Ship? You mean the wa-ah-ahea?"

"Sorry. Yes."

"The *ship* will be...fine, too. Some controls are *hasha-ah-ao*. You would say *frozen*. But..."

Eah looked back at the control panel, drawing Jay's attention to it as well. Her delicate, white fingers caressed its colored buttons in a deliberate, repetitive order. She seemed pleased with her repair. "Ah! It is...fixed.

"Nice job."

"The...ship...will have enough structure to pass safely through Hourou's waters now."

"Waters?"

"Waters. We say...*wiihee.*"

"*Wy-hee,*" Jay repeated.

"They are the waters that cover Hourou."

"You mean oceans? Your people live under the water?"

"No," Eah said with a chuckle. "The waters of the wiihee *surround* Hourou. You say *at-mos-phere.*"

Jay nodded and assumed Eah's language had different meanings for the same words. He turned back toward the forward viewport and considered the view of Hourou. "Your planet looks amazing, Eah."

Eah understood his comment as a compliment. She stepped away from the control panel and its surrounding cold pocket of air to appreciate her home world with Jay. Paul and April joined them, as well as Perry, Ellis, and Yori.

Across the room, Ahee announced something in the alien tongue that brought visible relief to the crew. She then approached the group of Earth humans and offered the translation. "The wa-ah-ahea is stable," she stated. "We can now pass safely through the atmosphere of Hourou."

Keah stood and joined them. "It will be our pleasure to have you as our guests on Hourou. Our people will welcome you as brothers and sisters."

"Thank you, Keah," Yori said. "We appreciate what you've done to keep us comfortable...and safe. I, for one, am excited about seeing your home."

Keah gave a quick bow and returned to his seat.

"Please sit there," Ahee said, pointing to the edge of the raised floor at the rear of the bridge. "It will be best for you to sit, as some movements may cause you to...lose balance."

The Earth party complied with Ahee's suggestion, seating themselves and watching the viewport with much interest. Eah joined them and sat next to Jay. "All is well," she whispered to him, having noticed the uneasiness in his body language. "Soon, we will be home."

While the wa-ah-ahea approached the outer edge of Hourou's watery atmosphere, it hesitated and dramatically slowed its speed. Mistrusting of its structural integrity, the living vessel vacillated when it should have begun reentry. This sent violent tremors throughout its frame that shook and startled the unprepared occupants.

"Here we go!" Paul exclaimed.

The convulsions knocked several of the standing crew into their seats, while those already seated had to struggle to remain so.

Jay lost his grip and bounced into Eah, causing them both to fall backward against the rear wall. "Sorry, Eah!" he said, scrambling to untangle himself from her long hair.

Paul wrapped one arm around April to keep her from falling while he dug the fingers of his free hand into the edge of the raised platform. The others in their party did likewise, helping each other to stay seated while being jostled together.

The events that followed happened in a chaotic blur. Keah called out a series of commands just before the alien vessel slammed into what appeared to be a wall of clear water. Despite their efforts to brace themselves, the collision threw all the Earth humans and the bronze-skinned people to the front of the bridge. Paul yelled something, Perry cursed, and April let out a scream as they all landed in a heap.

Inside the watery layer that made up Hourou's outer atmosphere, the vessel bounced back and forth like a submersible caught between conflicting currents. Water, forced in by pressure outside, entered the bridge through small cracks in the curved walls. More came in through tiny holes, creating crisscrossing jets that shot in and soaked the room. Cold pools quickly formed, slippery as wet ice.

The vessel did not stay submerged for very long. Its speed had decreased, but it was still moving fast enough to shoot out the other side with a breaking force that sent all of its occupants tumbling to the rear wall of the bridge. Having broken free of the shallow ocean suspended above the planet, the ship was now plummeting through the air toward the edge of a green landmass below.

"What is happening?" Jay asked Eah.

She did not answer him. With arms spread wide, she just closed her eyes and muttered. "Ahey, yoi esa wah-hah-matua." Her wet hair whipped wildly as blasts of air entered through more cracks in the walls.

Alien terrain rushing at him was the last thing Jay saw through the forward viewport before he lost his footing and stumbled across the room, smashing into other bodies. A side wall then completely dissolved, flooding the room with bright, lavender-tinted light. Several voices called out to each other as large pieces of black, foam-like material joined the tumbling mass of people.

Jay heard Eah call out his name, her voice sounding strangely calm amidst the chaos. His frantic eyes tried to locate her, but all he could see was a glimpse of her white hand gripping his forearm. Then he felt himself become weightless, like he was floating.

No, not floating, he thought. He was plummeting through the air. Chunks of black material fell alongside him, which he assumed were pieces of the spacecraft. With some effort, he aimed his body toward a large piece of debris. Eah was still holding onto his arm in a death grip, and her added weight allowed him to overtake his target and grab hold of it. Somehow, he climbed atop the thing and pulled Eah next to him.

There was a sudden flash of purple light, the green of vegetation whipping past, and more water. Jay blacked out before he hit the ground.

CHAPTER 16

Returning

Laura gripped the steering wheel and fixed her drowsy stare on the empty lanes ahead while her car sped down the Interstate toward the city. She had spent the night in quarantine, working with Doctor Haines, reviewing documents, taking notes, and writing her own official report while trying to connect the crash site in the forest with the UFO sightings elsewhere. All the while, and especially now during her long drive, one question kept nagging her: would the aliens be returning?

Test results from the material that was taken from the alien craft showed no radiation and no evidence of potential biological contamination. Although it was of an unknown origin, scientists said at the molecular level it was close enough to compounds found on Earth to be deemed similar. The larger mystery, as Haines explained it, was that *the matter was turned inside out.* Because of such inversion, it was impossible for them to examine it further.

For Laura, it was sufficient that she was not in danger. The speed of her release from quarantine, however, meant she now owed several higher-ups some big favors. She hated being indebted, but this time it was worth it. She was out of confinement and free to conduct her investigations away from Haines and other prying eyes.

An incoming phone call interrupted Laura's contemplation. The screen on her dashboard identified it as being from her deputy director, Alex Vaughn.

"Answer," she said to accept the call. "What's up, Alex? Do you have something?"

"Good morning to you, too."

"Alex, I—"

"You're wound awfully tight this morning."

Laura paused before replying. She had worked through the night with no sleep and coffee was her only dinner. She was tired, hungry, and stressed, but she was not about to let herself become nasty. "I'm sorry," she said with a sigh. "It's been a long night and I've lost some time. Where are you?"

"Waiting for you."

"Where?"

"At a little coffee shop on Seventh and Main. I'll order you breakfast if you call when you get off the highway."

"Sounds good. What have you found out?"

"Haines has been on the up-and-up with you, but he's holding back something vital."

"How convenient," Laura quipped.

"He probably told you all he *could*."

"Yeah...it's never personal."

Alex understood Laura's sarcasm. It was not the first time another agency kept important information from her. Sometimes, it was unintentional. She rarely worked in the open, and that meant it was easy to forget about her. She had hoped such secrecy would insulate her from the usual cross-departmental politics. Instead, it made playing that old game even more difficult.

"Well, the race is on." Alex continued. "Haines wants notoriety and the spotlight for the Space Agency."

"So, what did he leave out?"

"Hold on to your steering wheel; we have a truck driver who picked up what he called 'three half-naked druggies' on Thursday night after the major sightings. He drove them from the Greenwood Road exit all the way to the city. He claims they had strange colored skin, and that they didn't seem to understand him."

"Could be the ones who left us the footprints," Laura guessed.

"Probably."

"That's a long drive," Laura said. "I'm making the same one right now. They must have talked."

"Must have."

"This is good, Alex," Laura praised. "Where's the trucker?"

"*We* have him."

Laura's spirit lifted. "How did you manage that?"

"We got there first."

She could tell that Alex was beaming with pride at the other end of the call, and so was she. "Alex, I love you!"

"Really? We'll have to talk more about that later."

They had talked about it many times. In fact, they would have married a few years back if Laura had not been so in love with her career.

"I think we should."

Now it was Alex's turn to pause. "How...close are you?"

"I'll be to you in another forty-five minutes."

"Okay. First, we eat and compare notes. Then we'll talk to the truck driver."

"Alex, do you know anything yet...about what he's already said?"

"Only enough to make me believe the whole incident is far from over."

Laura felt her stomach drop and her eyes widened. "You mean—"

"Laura, just get over here. I'm sorry, but Jacobs is calling me, and she's the one watching the guy. Drive safe, you hear?"

"I will." Laura ended the call and resumed staring at the highway ahead.

First a piece of UFO and now someone who probably talked with extraterrestrials, she thought. *Someone's looking out for me today.*

* * *

After an uneventful and peaceful early Saturday morning drive on the Interstate, Laura was soon enjoying the company of her co-worker and secret boyfriend, Alex, at the popular downtown cafe named Joe's Java. Alex refused to discuss work until they had finished their breakfast, so between mouthfuls, they talked about fun things, eventually touching on their relationship.

It did not take long to reach the usual impasse. Alex was ready for marriage, even at the expense of moving further up in his career. Laura was not. She wanted one more chance to make a major contribution in her field before settling down. Alex argued that getting married did not mean living in obscurity, but Laura had to overcome deep-rooted values taught to her by an emotionally wounded feminist mother who always put work first. During Laura's college days, friends reinforced that message—friends that lived the high life and pursued lucrative jobs while shunning committed relationships.

Laura felt caught between two conflicting desires. To avoid choosing one, she distracted herself by running in the same race to the top as those around her. It did not work well. She realized there was something more to life, and that included Alex. She tried to keep him happy while she pushed forward in her career, but he was not the type of guy who would settle for only a physical relationship. Alex was deep, and that is why she loved him so much. She had a good man—not like the losers she wasted her time with in college and in her earlier jobs. Alex was a lover, but he was also a friend who knew her inside and out. He was a keeper. Laura did not want to lose him, but she felt trapped into having to make a quick decision.

Most of the time, when the relationship conversation became too intense, Laura could appease Alex with her well-refined feminine charm and a long night of intimate play. But she sensed those days were coming to an end. Alex wanted—no, he needed—more. He wanted all of her, and she appreciated his honest insistence. She would rather walk away from her job as the director of her agency than to leave him. With the current events as they were, though, she wanted one last chance to make a big impression on the world. After that, she could handle a life change. She hoped Alex understood and would wait...one more time.

Alex said he understood, but losing the argument again disheartened him. Laura rubbed his knee under the table and gave her best alluring look until he perked up. They then made plans for a secret rendezvous that evening and pushed aside their breakfast plates, communicating a mutual desire to move on to other topics.

"So," Laura said, "who's trailing Haines?"

"Donich."

"Good. Donich won't be noticed."

Alex glanced at a table where four noisy patrons had sat down.

"Friends of yours?" Laura sneered.

"Media people. They're all over the downtown district."

Laura shifted in her seat for a look at them. The newcomers were oblivious to anyone or anything outside of their own loud conversation.

"We have agents shadowing most of them," Alex noted. "That's how we found out about the truck driver."

"Alex, you should see the alien craft. It's amazing."

"You can get me in, can't you?"

"Probably. If you're a good boy."

"So, it's not fake this time, huh?"

"It can't be."

"How can you be so sure?"

Laura thought for a moment, remembering every detail of the strange room into which she had fallen. "It's hard to explain. It felt like it was made for humans. There's a design to it that looks familiar, but it's also *very* foreign. And the materials used to build it are unlike anything I've ever seen."

"Interesting."

"Plus, the way the military and other departments are handling it shows that *no one* can figure out what it is."

Alex squeezed her hand and checked his watch. "Time to go," he announced as he dug some rolled up bills out of his pants pocket and tossed them on the table for a tip. "I already paid. We're meeting the truck driver around the corner."

"We're *holding* him?" Laura asked with concern.

"No...*entertaining* him. We put him up in a room at the Astra last night and told him we needed his help with a secret government investigation that had to do with a terrorist plot. He talked himself into thinking that he stumbled into something huge—a conspiracy theory type—and asked us to protect him."

"Alex, that's terrible!" Laura scolded.

"I didn't lie! I just let him go on with his crazy theories. Poor guy watches too much news."

"Whatever. Let's see what we can get out of him. After that, you'd better think of something to set him straight, or at least keep him quiet about us."

* * *

The truck driver was waiting for them in the hotel's chic restaurant, having just finished breakfast as well. He rose as Laura and Alex approached his table.

"Jerry, this is Laura from the Agency," Alex said.

Laura offered a handshake. Jerry was tall, thin, in his late fifties, and had a weathered face that came from hard living. Dressed as he was in faded blue jeans, an old t-shirt, and an over-sized flannel shirt, the image of him clashed against the backdrop of the posh hotel restaurant. He looked Laura over, shook her hand, and motioned toward a chair.

"Have a seat. You want some coffee or somethin'?"

"No, thank you," Laura replied. "We're fine."

"Jerry," Alex said, "we have little time. So, if you don't mind, Laura and I would like to get right to our questions."

"Okay. Go ahead."

"Start from the beginning," Laura prompted. "Tell us about how you picked up the hitchhikers."

Jerry took a sip of his coffee and pushed aside his folded newspaper. "Okay. Well...I was on my usual route when I saw these three people standin' next to the highway."

Laura did not bother to take notes or ask about times and places. Alex had already seen to that the night before and he was most likely recording the conversation, anyway. Right now, she was listening for details that would only come out in story form. "Go on," she said. "Give us as much description as you can remember."

"Well, I wasn't gonna stop at first. I just slowed down to have a look. The girl was wavin' her arms and arguin' with the two guys. Then I saw all three of 'em were hardly wearin' anything. I guess I wanted to make sure there wasn't any bad stuff goin' on. You know...like the guys attackin' the girl or something. So I stopped."

"You weren't concerned for your own safety?" Laura asked.

"No. I had my forty-five close by. Got to nowadays."

"Right," Laura said. "Then what happened?"

"I hung out the window and asked the girl if she needed any help. Can't figure out if I scared 'em or if it was my rig, but they were all shakin' like leaves."

"What did she say?" Alex asked.

"I dunno. She was a foreigner. She started talkin' in some foreign language and pointin' in the direction that I was goin'. So I got the idea she was askin' fer a ride."

"Did you recognize the language at all?" Laura asked.

"Nah. I'm not real good at that. It was different, though. Never heard anythin' like it."

"What were the other two doing?"

"Standin' there...lookin' scared. It was like they all just got robbed or something, which is what I figured."

"Why did you think that?"

"They didn't have nothin' on but their underwear for one," Jerry said with a grin. "Weren't carryin' anything either. Strange, don't ya think?"

"So, you offered them a ride?"

"Couldn't just leave 'em like that."

"Did they understand you?"

"Not really. Seemed like they didn't know English."

Laura paused with her questioning to allow Jerry to gather his thoughts. He assumed she was waiting for him to add more.

"So, anyway," he continued, "I waved 'em into the cab and they got the idea easy enough. Had a hard time gettin' in—like they never rode in somethin' like my rig—but they sat down and behaved themselves. For what it was worth, I warned 'em not to try anything stupid."

"Did they understand that?" Alex asked.

"Who knows? The girl, though, kept babblin' on about who knows what. She looked like she was half frozen, so I grabbed my coat and tossed it on her. I'll never forget the sight of 'em...good lookin' and buck nekkid."

Alex wanted to comment, but sat back in his chair after a warning look from Laura.

"Jerry," Laura prompted with all seriousness, "what I am most interested in right now is what they *said*. Your ride with them took at least forty-five minutes. In all that time, is there anything *significant* about their speech—their language—that you can remember? Could you make out *any* words? Even if it sounded *a little* like English?"

Jerry pushed back in his chair and stared down at the table as he considered Laura's questions.

"This is the most important part, Jerry," Alex said. "It could help us figure out where they came from."

Laura got the idea that Alex had been over this with Jerry already, and that Jerry had been holding back something.

"Jerry?" Laura urged.

"I didn't think they were bad people," he mumbled.

"What?"

"They were like three kids—scared. Foreigner kids that got taken advantage of—a rotten joke, robbed, I don't know. But...they were okay."

"We understand," Laura said, "but we can't put the pieces together without these clues. You have them, Jerry. Don't you?"

Jerry looked up at her like someone who was about to betray a friend. Laura showed him her best comforting smile and held her breath as he answered her.

"Yeah. I kept talkin' to 'em and askin' questions, hopin' they might figure it out. Well, they did alright. At least the girl did. By the time I dropped 'em off, she had some words figured out. She said somethin' that sounded like 'Stop here.'"

"What else?" Alex asked, unable to hide his excitement.

"The two guys jumped out of the cab. She stayed for a minute and rubbed her hand on my face, lookin' at me all sexy like. She said..."

Laura tilted her head and raised an eyebrow. "Yes?"

"She said somethin' like, 'You and us. You *like* us.' So I said, 'What are you talkin' about?' I mean, I could sort of figure her out. She had these big green eyes. When she looked at me...I dunno...I started feelin' weird."

"Weird? Like how?" Laura asked.

"Like...dizzy. Hard to explain. She was pretty enough alright...too pretty. The more I looked at her...at her eyes, I mean...it was hard to stop. I got embarrassed." He looked at Alex. "You know...young enough to be my kid and all that. Shouldn't stare."

"Go on," Alex said. "What else did she say?"

"Yeah. So then she says, 'They will come back. They will come back for it.' At least that's what it sounded like. She babbled a bunch of other stuff I couldn't figure out, too. In between, though, she kept grabbin' my arm and saying, 'They will come back for it.' Then she jumped out and all three of 'em took off running. That was it."

Jerry lowered his head, signaling that he had nothing more to say. Neither Laura nor Alex could conceal their shock, so they were glad he was not looking at them. After a long, awkward silence, Alex stood up and cleared his throat, motioning for Laura to follow him.

"Well...thanks, Jerry," he said. "That helps a lot. It's, uh, quite possible that you're helping us to break up a major terrorist cell."

Laura turned away to conceal the range of emotions that were being displayed on her face. Jerry looked up at them both with a deep cynicism in his eyes. He glared at them as he also stood to leave.

"I'm not as dumb as you think, Alex," he said. "I know what's goin' on here."

Laura spun around, alarmed, but refrained from saying anything.

"These people weren't from *here* at all," Jerry asserted. "That's what this is all about. I know it...and *you* know it. And now you know that more are probably comin' back—back for that thing in the woods that them three were runnin' from. Or back for *them*. Either way, it ain't over yet, is it?"

Laura turned and headed for the restaurant exit, unable to focus her thinking on anything but one idea: *They're coming back.*

CHAPTER 17

Hourou

LATE MORNING: DAY 1 ON HOUROU

"Jay? Jay? Ah-hoo-eee-es-oi, Jay! O-eh-ay-ooo-ee-is-Ah-hey-se-Hourou!"

At the sound of Eah's excited voice, Jay's eyes shot open. Bright light made him blink while he stared up at the silhouette of her body kneeling over him.

"Jay? Eh-yah-ah-eee-heh-oh-hah."

As his senses returned, Jay realized he was lying on something soft, warm, and damp. Eah hovered over him, shaking his shoulders and speaking in her native tongue.

What is she saying? Jay wondered, fighting off his stupor. *It's noisy. She's trying to talk above the noise. Waves? Wind? People laughing?*

All at once, Jay remembered the alien vessel and the moments leading up to its crash. "Eah!" he shouted as he sat upright. "What happened?"

"Ooo-oh-yee, Jay. Ow es aye...afe...s-afe."

"I don't understand. You're using your own language." Jay scanned the immediate area and saw that he was sitting on a beach. "Where are we?"

Eah sat cross-legged and faced him. Her entire body was wet and the sunlight reflecting from her white iridescent skin made her look radiant. As she gathered her matted hair and tossed it behind her, the light of Hourou's suns highlighted her feminine curves and defined muscles. Jay allowed his eyes to linger on her for only a moment before checking himself for injuries.

"Mah wo-eds...words...reh-turn to Hourou," Eah said as she watched him. "I em sorry. Be-ing home. Yes, being home...brrrrrr-ings...my own words back. You ah...uninjured?"

"I think so." There was no pain and his limbs were working. Like Eah, he was wet, and purple-tinted sand covered his skin and clothing.

"Where are we?" he repeated. It was a needless question. He was on Hourou, on a beach, at the edge of its surf line—and alive.

"Hourou weh-comes you, Jay," Eah replied with her usual charming smile. "You ah safe."

As Jay took in his environment, unfamiliar sights, sounds, smells, and feelings overwhelmed his bewildered senses. All around him were things that were foreign, yet also familiar. The beach was like those of Earth; a vast sea reached to the horizon, its small waves rolling onto a sandy shore that stretched for miles. The colors were quite different, though. The water was lavender, just like the cloudless sky, and the sand was a mix of tan, purple, blue, and white granules.

Jay heard the sounds of sea birds but did not see them. Behind him were tall dunes dotted with unfamiliar plant life. A short distance beyond, towering trees topped by impossibly gigantic leaves formed the border of a thick jungle.

Besides Jay and Eah, the only other people on the beach were two from her family, a male and female. They had changed their skin from black to iridescent white to match Eah and were frolicking in the ocean waves like carefree children. Jay squinted at them as his eyes adjusted to Hourou's unusual sunlight. Were they playing a game? The girl was whipping her wet, knee-length hair in wild circles and trying to ensnare the male with it while he expertly dodged her attempts.

"Where are all the others?" Jay asked.

Eah rested a reassuring hand on Jay's shoulder. "All ah safe. They ah a-part from us now—sep-a-rated in the...fall?"

"I would say crash."

"Craaa-sh."

"Where's the ship?"

Jay looked up and down the beach, but all that remained of the alien craft, at least nearby, were a few large chunks of black material dissolving into the sand.

Eah followed his gaze, and a small frown formed on her wet lips. "It is no more and has returned to Hourou. We will make a new wah-ah-ahea."

"How are we going to find the others? How do you know they're safe?"

Eah stood and motioned for him to do likewise. "Wah-ay-u-iiee. I know it inside...from Ahey."

"So you can feel them? Sense them? Then we have to find them!" Jay jumped up and stumbled to get a footing; his legs moved faster than usual. He guessed that the alien planet had a different gravitational strength. He seemed to weigh less, and his body movements were quicker and awkward.

Eah steadied him and giggled. "Ooo-oh-yee, Jay. Everyone will be together again. Come! We bathe in the *oa-hah* and Ahey will strengthen us. Come!" She grabbed Jay's hand and led him to the water's edge, but he paused while she entered the surf.

"Sorry. I need a minute."

Eah tilted her head to one side, as if trying to make sense of his words.

"What I mean is...I'm feeling kind of strange. I'll just wait here."

She studied his body language for a moment. Then, with a nod, she turned away to join the others in their splashing romp.

Jay watched them in a detached manner, caught up in his thoughts and anxieties. Everything seemed so surreal. Being in the spaceship was one thing; at least there he was confined and with other Earth people. Out here, though, he was exposed and alone. To make it worse, despite Eah's cheeriness and hospitality, he immediately felt as if he was somewhere he should not be—like a trespasser. While he surveyed his new surroundings, he could not think of himself as a visitor or simple observer. Rather, he was an intruder, seeing things that were not meant for his alien eyes to see.

He stared at a chunk of the spaceship's hull melting into the sand and wondered where Paul and April had ended up. He hoped they were alright, and the thought puzzled him. Even in the short time they had been together, he was regarding them as friends. Sharing such a harrowing experience, he supposed, could bring people closer. *Eah says they're all safe,* he thought, *but how does she know? What if I'm really the only one who survived the crash?*

He observed Eah and the two others as they jumped and splashed. *How can they be like that after everything that just happened? Aren't they worried about the rest of their people? Don't they care about mine? About me?*

At that thought, Jay walked away from them and headed further down the beach. It had been a long time since he felt so lost. Memories resurfaced of a young boy orphaned by the cruelty of death, living with several temporary families. As he grew up, there was a job, a mission, and what some called a tribe—the other kids like him who lived and worked at the youth ranch. Jay kicked at the odd sand, chuckling at the idea that fate might have played its ultimate joke on him, being marooned on an alien planet with more people who would never understand him.

Except maybe Eah. He turned back to look at her and the others. It surprised him that he had walked so far already. The three of them were now small figures in the distance, still playing in the water and unconcerned about him or anything else.

Careful to keep them in view, Jay stopped and sat on the wet sand with his toes touching the foamy edge of the surf. The ocean was warm, like the surrounding air. It was a perfect, tropical climate—not too hot, not too cold, not too humid, not too dry, not too windy, not too still, not too noisy, not too quiet. Jay had seen little of his own world aside from photographs in books and online, but he imagined the islands of the Caribbean or the South Pacific might make close comparisons. He reached out and scooped up some water.

Plain old water. Nothing weird yet. When he brought his hand to his face, the similarity lessened. *There's no sea smell. It's pure.* He touched his tongue with his fingertip. *And no salt. A fresh water ocean!*

Although he was thirsty, Jay stopped short of drinking it, deciding he would first ask Eah if it was safe for consumption. It was fine for bathing, which she was already showing. Coated as he was in sand from head to toe, he wanted to do likewise, so he rose and surveyed his surroundings. Satisfied with the apparent privacy, he entered the water and waded out until it was up to his chest. Then, he stripped off his clothes and did his best to wash the sand out of them and off of his skin. With the job done, he lingered in the small rolling waves and marveled at their soothing effects. Somehow, he was experiencing both calmness and invigoration.

Before Jay could fully relax into the sensation, something touched his leg. With a yelp, he jumped aside, and his anxious eyes searched the sandy bottom. Nothing. Though the water was as clear as glass, he could see no intruder or floating debris. He waited and then noticed movement near his feet.

Now what? While backing away, he dressed in haste and checked his position. *Great. It's between me and the shore.*

Before he could circumvent the spot, the sand underneath him rose. His reaction was immediate; he dove toward the area where Eah was bathing and swam hard, parallel to the shoreline. Between frenzied strokes, he risked a glance back and saw a giant mass of what appeared to be blue rock emerging from the waves right where he had been standing. When he faced forward again, two hands gripped his shoulders while his head bumped softly into a white female torso. He pushed backward, found his footing in the chest-high water, and wiped his face. "Eah?"

"I am here, Jay." Despite the terror that was rising from the waves near them, she was giggling.

"Eah, we have to get out!" Jay lurched toward the shore, but Eah did not budge. Instead, she turned him around to face the monster that had now fully surfaced and displayed itself before them.

Jay froze at the sight. It dwarfed any animal back on Earth. The closest comparison he could make was to a giant crab. The creature had a flat triangular shell for a body and stood on four pointed legs. Other spiny protrusions jutted out of it at hard angles that almost made it machine-like. Where claws would have been on a normal crab, it had two long antennae similar to those on a lobster. With these, it felt its surroundings, skimming the water and whipping the air. Jay could distinguish no eyes or mouth, though there were areas in the beast's frontal region that could suggest logical locations. Its entire body was a shade of blue he had never seen before.

"Shouldn't...shouldn't we be running?" Jay cringed as the creature stood to its full height and lashed at the water with its antennae.

Eah said something in her native language.

"What?"

"It is aaaaaah-ah-pah-sah. Stand firm, Jay. It es wanting to give—to show—its beauty."

Jay gaped at the beast, but not in appreciation. To him, it was not beautiful; it was terrifying. Then, to make the situation even more bewildering, Eah's two companions ran from the safety of the beach toward the colossal sea monster, laughing and kicking up water as if to taunt it.

Eah chuckled at the bizarre scene, unconcerned.

"Eah?" Jay knew he was missing something important.

She pulled him toward the beach just as one of the creature's long antennae reached the spot where they were standing. "We will keep you from him. You are new to Hourou. If he touches you, he will be...cur-eye-us? Yes, curious. He will then follow us all over Hourou."

Jay stumbled onto the dry sand, never taking his eyes off of the monster. "No...I don't think I would like that."

Eah stayed at his side, wringing water from her hair and laughing at the antics of the two antagonists. At first, it seemed to Jay that they were teasing the beast, tempting it to reach out to them with its antennae and then dodging its touch. As he watched, though, it became apparent that the creature was toying with *them*. It could have easily lashed them with its feelers, crushed their tiny bodies under its legs, or impaled them with one of its other parts. Instead, it was playing with them.

After a while, Eah yelled to her siblings in the alien tongue and gestured that they should return to the beach. In response, they stopped dodging the antennae and stood still, allowing the crab creature to touch them at last.

"Aren't they afraid of being smashed...or eaten?" Jay asked.

Eah placed a warm wet hand on his shoulder, and it sent a small chill through his body. "Now I am not understanding *you*, Jay," she replied. "Have you no an-eee-mals—animals—on Blue?"

"On Earth?"

"Earth, yes."

"We have a lot of animals. Nothing that big, though. And the wild ones fear people. Some we can tame, but you always have to be careful around them."

Eah considered his words and pulled back her hand. Jay could tell she wanted to ask more, but what he said somehow discouraged her. A brief sadness appeared in her eyes just before she turned away from him.

"What's wrong?" he asked.

Before answering, she drew her hair in front of her body like a long shawl. Jay wondered if the action represented being uncomfortable with the conversation. "What is rooo-ong? Heee-eh-ii, Jay. Your words have so many meanings."

Jay could not determine if she was being evasive or if she did not understand his simple question. "Oh. I mean...is there something bothering you? Did I confuse you?"

"Oh...I understand."

Jay waited for an answer, but Eah just stood there watching her companions, who now were caressing the crab creature's giant antennae. Satisfied that their game was over, it moved toward the beach, passing over the two with great care to avoid injuring them.

"Well?" Jay prodded.

Eah smiled at his persistence.

There was so much about Eah and her people Jay did not understand. Still, he found himself unable to resist thinking of her like a girl from back home. Unlike most of them, though, Eah seemed to have taken an immediate liking to him. He wondered if her attention should concern him. Deep inside, though, it pleased him. "It's okay," he said. "Sometimes I forget that I'm so alien to you."

Eah tossed her hair behind her body and spun around to face him. "Neither of us is *alien*, Jay."

Dumbfounded and unsure what to say, Jay averted his eyes and hoped for a quick end to the awkward moment.

Eah tried hard to get him to make eye contact. When he showed her no response, she let out a little sigh and walked past him toward the others.

Great. I blew something here, Jay thought. *What have I gotten myself into? Is she mad at me now?*

Eah glanced back at him and smiled. "Come, Jay," she called. "We leave now to find the others."

She's right, he thought as he followed her. *Eah's not really all that alien. She's just a complete mystery...like all girls.*

* * *

Jay had no way of keeping track of the passing time, but he guessed it must have been many hours since their encounter with the crab creature. To keep his restless mind occupied during their long march beside the sea, he questioned Eah about everything he saw. Fortunately, she never tired of answering him. She often asked for clarification or giggled at his choice of words, but she always made sure they were understanding each other. He could tell she was curious, too, especially about his planet, yet she held back her own inquiries. To make it less one-sided, Jay interjected simple facts whenever he noted her interest. This seemed to please Eah, as did Jay's willingness to stop redirecting his gaze whenever he looked at her.

In studying Eah and the two others, Jay discovered they put considerable emphasis on viewing each other's bodies. He remembered April saying they communicated with visual cues as much as with words. Body language, then, was important, and it called for each communicant to be diligent in observing the other. Diverting one's eyes—like Jay often did—would be an insult to them; it communicated indifference. That was not his intention, though, and he hoped Eah understood he was just trying to be respectful. He did not want her to feel uncomfortable under his curious glances, nor did he want his mind to wander with indecent thoughts.

As they walked together, Jay struggled to change his thinking about the beautiful naked girl beside him and her two attractive siblings. The exotic environment around him aided in distracting his attention. It also helped to provide a context for their natural state. In such a place, their nakedness seemed to make sense. It was practical, for one thing; the climate was warm, and Jay had yet to see anything on the beach or in the dunes that would require them to wear protective coverings. Wherever they walked, the sand was never hot, and there were no sharp rocks or seashells to avoid. The sunlight, too, felt harmless. Though there were two suns, the watery upper atmosphere filtered their rays, creating a soft light just warm enough to be pleasant on the skin without burning it. No wonder they felt so comfortable having nothing on their bodies.

Jay found it was much easier to look at Eah and the others when he kept it all in that proper perspective. He still had to strive to maintain innocent thoughts. But when he did, his rewards were more calmness, less loneliness, and a better acceptance of his situation.

After some time, Eah halted their march and motioned for Jay to rest on the sand. She sat with him, presumably to keep him company, while the other pair waded into the water to resume their strange game. Eah had made some sort of formal introduction between them and Jay after they left the giant crab, but Jay was so shaken by the experience that he had forgotten their names.

"So...tell me their names again," he said, nodding toward them.

"Tammah and Uio."

"Tammah is your brother, then."

"Born of Keah and Ahee, yes, like me. So in your words...brother."

"And Uio is your sister."

"Yes, but that is different."

"I don't understand."

"Uio is of another dyad—another pair. She came to live with us. I can call her *sister*, as you use the word, because all people are related."

"So...is she part of your family, then?"

Eah thought for a moment before replying. "Family is all, and all is family."

"You're all related somehow?"

"All have come from the same, yet each comes from the two."

A riddle? Jay wondered. Was she testing his intelligence? He wished April or Ellis were there to interpret her unusual sayings. He must have sounded dimwitted to Eah, especially when he said things like his next statement. "Uh...I don't get it."

Eah looked at him and giggled. "Get?"

"Sorry. I'm not understanding."

She smiled, toyed with her hair, and pushed it behind her. "It is...okay, Jay. There is much I am not understanding. So...together we will...as you say...figure it out?"

Jay smiled back, amused that she was picking up on the many uses of his native words. "Yes. We'll figure it out together."

Though his hair was short, he had enough of it on the sides to tuck behind his ears, so he tested a theory. While making eye contact, he made a combing motion and pulled some strands behind one ear. The result was immediate; Eah's face expressed surprise and elation. She said nothing, but turned back to watch Tammah and Uio at play.

Jay grinned in triumph, proud that he had done something to so please her. Since she was looking the other way, he allowed himself a few glances at her exposed body. Black hair cascading down her white back made for a stark contrast in the bright sunlight, and her skin sparkled under the rays of the Hourou's suns. Something unusual on her shoulder caught his eye, though. It was a small tan-colored patch of skin, nearly the same color as his own. *Where did that suddenly come from?* he wondered. Then, as quickly as it had appeared, it faded back into iridescent white.

By now, Jay knew Eah could change her skin color. When he first saw her on the alien vessel, it was a deep black. Later, she changed to the same iridescent white as her parents' bodies and kept that color ever since. The other members of her family had the same ability. Tammah and Uio had black skin aboard their spaceship, but now both of them had changed. Tammah's skin looked just like Eah's and Uio's was similar, but with a blue tint.

Eah did not acknowledge the change in her shoulder. Though Jay was curious, he decided against bringing it to her attention. It was more important that he was learning how to communicate with her better. Now, he wanted to concentrate on their similarities as much as he could and not on their differences. Their verbal exchange pleased Eah, so that was enough.

Jay observed Tammah and Uio's antics in the water and wondered what Eah found so amusing about them. To him, they were acting like silly school kids, but Eah was obviously seeing something else. Like before, Uio was pursuing Tammah in the thigh-high surf and trying to get close enough to entangle him in her long hair. As she whipped her head around and stalked Tammah like a cat hunting its prey, Eah giggled and muttered commentary to herself. More than once, Eah jumped to her feet when it appeared Uio was about to ensnare Tammah. He was too quick, though, and Eah had to settle for yelling out what sounded like either praises or taunts.

It looked to Jay as if Eah wanted to join them and that she was having a hard time holding herself back. He assumed she was only staying on the beach because of him. Then again, he might have been misreading the situation. For all he knew, it was a game that was meant for two. It vexed him not being able to interpret what should have been common sense cues.

Tammah was doing well at avoiding Uio's stealthy advances, but more than a few times, he lost his footing and only narrowly escaped her whirling tresses. Eah cheered Uio on, but when it was apparent that Tammah had escaped yet again, she sighed and plunked herself down on the sand next to Jay.

"You don't have to stay here for me," he blurted.

Eah drew her knees to her chest and rested her chin there. As she did, her hair cascaded down each side of her body, encasing her like a cocoon. Jay saw just enough of her face to note she was smiling.

"I mean, you could go out there...if you want to."

"Tammah ii-o-mah-eeee-u. Tammah would not prefer it."

"Why? Two against one?"

Eah shifted her weight in the sand. "Tammah would lose the game, yes. But Tammah also still seeks dyad with Uio."

"What is *dyad?*" Jay considered the meaning. "A pair? A couple?"

Again, Eah fidgeted, which Jay took as a signal of uneasiness. When she did not respond, he got the idea that he was supposed to figure it out himself.

"So, they're together then," he reasoned. "But I thought you consider Uio to be a part of your family. Is that sort of thing normal here?"

"Uio is not from Keah and Ahee," Eah reminded. "She is from another Two in a different place on Hourou. She came to live with us to learn."

"Learn what?"

"Travel. Exploration."

"I understand. On Earth, some students live with other families while they're learning, too."

"Yes."

"So...Tammah and Uio are trying to be a couple, and joining them would be awkward."

Eah nodded and let out a quiet sigh. "It is a game for twos."

"Oh."

A flock of unusual sea birds flew overhead, diverting Jay's attention. They looked reptilian, like a bird's body covered with long, colorful scales instead of feathers. The flock landed near the dunes and plucked at some scruffy vegetation with their long beaks, ignoring their human neighbors.

When Jay looked back at Eah, he saw she had reclined on the sand and was staring up at the sky. He did likewise. She was quiet for a long time, so he just listened to the sounds of the waves, the laughter of Tammah and Uio at play, and the strange clucking of the bird creatures. Eah's world was quite alien, but Jay found enough similarity to Earth to ease his anxieties about being there, at least for the moment.

"Dyad is not play, though," Eah said, startling Jay from his own deep thoughts.

He turned to face her. "Sorry. What?"

"Dyad is not play. Do you understand?"

Oh, we're back to that, Jay thought. "Not really, no. I thought their game was a flirting thing, and that's why you're staying out of it."

"I do not know that word, but dyad is not a game."

"Tell me about it, then."

Eah sat up and regarded the two at play, and Jay did the same. "Like the game," she said, "Uio pursues Tammah. Sometimes, Tammah pursues Uio. They are matched—much alike. Uio is...bold, and Tammah is also bold. They compete much. They make a good dyad, but I wonder if it would be balanced...and dyad must be balanced."

"Too much the same. I see. To me, Uio seems like a tomboy and Tammah is super competitive. That would make a relationship difficult."

"I do not know those words, but, yes, Tammah and Uio are much the same."

"So this is just a game, but we can still tell something about their dyad."

"Yes. It is only for play. Are there no such games on Blue?"

"Earth."

"On Earth?"

"Yes," Jay said with a chuckle, "but this kind of thing is usually for kids...children...little ones, not adults."

Jay considered the game and admired the simplicity and purity of it. Watching the young man and woman frolicking in the waves together made him miss something that seemed almost ancient within him.

Pure fun for fun's sake, he concluded. *Good clean fun, like little kids back home that have no hang-ups and no agendas.* He frowned as his admiration turned to an inner chastisement. *And, earlier, the first thing that came to my mind was less than innocent. What's wrong with me?*

"Do you understand now?" Eah asked.

"I'm starting to. They're just playing, not flirting. A dyad has nothing to do with it. Tell me more about the dyad."

Eah smiled. His curiosity obviously pleased her. "Dyad is...seed...already planted," she explained. "We must discover and nurture it. Dyad must also be balanced."

"Do Tammah and Uio think they're balanced?"

"Maybe. These things are difficult to see when you pursue someone."

"I can definitely understand that. It sounds like starting an intimate relationship here has the same challenges as it does on my planet."

"Bonding in dyad is a challenge, yes. But the challenge can be...enjoyable."

Jay did not know how to take that statement. The wistful tone in her voice and the dreaminess in her eyes as she gazed at the sky confused him. After an awkward silence, he continued with his questioning.

"So...what will they do if they find that they're not really compatible —that their dyad won't be balanced?"

Eah considered the two at play again. "Tammah will look for dyad in another. He will seek other Twos."

"Twos? What do you mean?"

"Each comes from the Two. There are many Twos on Hourou."

Jay thought hard, and the interpretation became clear. "Families? Twos are families?"

"All is family—"

"And family is all," Jay finished. "I remember. Clans, then. Units? Your parents form a unit that we call a *family* on Earth."

"The Two, yes."

So Tammah will look for a girl from another clan or tribe, Jay thought. "I understand. See? I take a while, but I eventually get it."

"Get...is to understand."

"In this case, yes. I am getting the dyad."

Satisfied with his answer, Eah jumped up and scampered into the water to coach Uio on her hair whipping tactics. Tammah laughed as the girls spun their heads around while trying to appear menacing. When Uio finally snagged Tammah's arm, he stopped laughing, though, and reevaluated his defenses.

Jay could tell that Eah did not mind him being a spectator. In fact, it did not take long for him to figure out she was actually performing for him. The way she snuck glances to see if he was still watching was telling. More than once, too, he caught her gazing his way when she assumed he was not paying attention.

I might not really be getting the dyad after all, he thought. *Or am I?*

CHAPTER 18

The Jungle

LATE MORNING: DAY 1 ON HOUROU

"Let's not get too far away!" Paul called out the warning to April, unsure if she was even listening to him. Despite Keah and Ahee's insistence that it was safe, he did not like the idea of his wife exploring their new environment by going deeper into the jungle alone. April's thinking was not clear; she was probably experiencing shock from their traumatic introduction to Hourou. Both of them had blacked out during the crash of the spaceship. The only memory Paul had after the walls of the bridge dissolved was a foggy recollection of falling, floating, and of seeing April tumbling through the open air beside him. After that, he woke up next to her on a bed of soft multicolored moss at the base of a giant tree.

Keah and Ahee were nearby, reclining on the expansive carpet of moss and engaged in a quiet chat. Paul assumed they had rescued him and April from the wreckage of the spaceship and then moved them to safety. After checking himself for injuries, he roused April and did the same for her, relieved to find that both had only suffered bumps and scratches.

The alien pair ended their private conversation and turned to watch, but said nothing. Then again, Paul guessed, perhaps they were communicating with him through facial expressions and indistinct gestures. If so, he must not have been interpreting them correctly, for the two of them looked just as calm and composed as always. They did not seem to be injured. Neither did their behavior suggest shock. They simply lolled under the tree, bare yet unoffensive, like a couple that had sneaked into the woods to find some quiet time alone.

Paul asked them if they were alright. Keah answered in his alien tongue mixed with English words, and he sounded oddly relaxed. The traumatic experience did not affect his ever-present smile, and that perplexed Paul. Did Keah and Ahee not recognize that something life-threatening had happened to them all? Feelings of distrust and insecurity soon returned. To distract himself from falling into despair, Paul buried his anxieties and focused on their surroundings.

There was very little left of the spacecraft. Some large chunks of black material littered the jungle-like area around him and were dissolving into the ground. Besides the ship, there was something else missing, too—the other members of their party. When Paul mentioned it, Keah told him they had become separated in the crash, but that he was certain everyone was safe. Paul doubted it. That he and April had survived such a crash was miraculous enough. Surely there must have been a few casualties. Keah, however, was adamant that everyone was fine.

"How can you know that, though?" Paul had asked.

Keah's answer was ambiguous. To Paul, it sounded as if the people of Hourou could send each other messages through the natural environment somehow. Of course, that was hard for Paul to believe, but so was everything else he had recently experienced. Rather than ask Keah more questions, though, he accepted what he could and hoped they would all be reunited soon.

It was April who suggested having a look around while Keah and Ahee discussed what to do now that they were back on their planet. Paul wanted to listen in on the planning, but he followed April to ensure her safety.

"Let's not get too far away," Paul repeated.

"They're probably nearby somewhere," April mumbled, scanning the surrounding jungle.

"*What* is nearby? What are you looking for?"

"I told you," April answered, "my shoes and other clothes."

"No, you didn't."

"Whatever! Just help me look."

"What makes you think we're going to find anything around here? The entire ship broke into pieces and what's left looks like it's melting. Our stuff could be scattered across miles of jungle for all we know."

April stopped walking, looked up at the massive, alien-looking trees above her, and considered Paul's logic. "Paul, help me look...please. They still might be around here."

Paul took hold of her arm and turned her toward him. "Babes, they're gone. What you have on will have to do."

April let out an exasperated sigh.

"Listen," Paul continued, "Keah and Ahee don't wear a thing, and they don't care about going barefoot."

"Paul, *we're* the aliens here. We don't know *anything* about this place!"

"You think I don't know that?"

Paul looked back toward Keah and Ahee. They seemed to be engaged in a small debate of their own, albeit with much less tension. He chuckled as he considered the scene. *Two couples stranded in the jungle and arguing. We're so different and yet so similar.*

"What's so funny?" April demanded.

"Nothing." He kissed her on the forehead. "Let's check around a little more, but try not to touch anything that you don't see those two touching."

April gave him a quizzical frown. "Okay. Why?"

"It's their planet. We'll have to follow their lead."

"Do you think the others are really alright?"

"I hope so."

"Do you still trust Keah and Ahee?"

Paul looked back at the couple again. "I'm trying to, Babes. I'm really trying."

"They got us here safe."

"As safe as crash landing on an alien planet can be. I'd say we're lucky to be alive."

April could not argue with that. Neither she nor Paul understood how they could be thrown from a flying craft into the open sky, plummet, crash through enormous trees, hit the ground, and still live. Yet here they were, and everyone else in the spacecraft supposedly survived as well. "Nothing has made much sense since we ran after Jay in that field," she admitted. "Is this even real?"

"Real enough to give you scratches on your legs. And we're both in our right minds. It's no dream, Babes."

"I know that. It's just so surreal. I mean...look at this place."

Paul looked up into the trees and at the purple sky beyond. "Well, we're here. So, we'll take one thing at a time like we did on their ship. You tell me the moment you see or sense something wrong with our two hosts."

"So you don't completely trust them, then."

"Like I said...I'm trying."

"Okay. I still trust them, though."

With that, April resumed her search of the area. Paul shrugged off his apprehension and humored her by helping, though he felt it was a futile effort. During the disintegrating vessel's long descent over the jungle, he knew April's shoes and clothes were probably miles away, dangling from the branches of a colossal tree. They might have even vanished like what remained of the spaceship.

Paul's first concerns were survival and getting back home, not footwear. He considered his own bare feet while stepping with care over a flowering shrub. Everywhere he walked was soft and devoid of anything pointy, hard, or otherwise uncomfortable to tread upon. Colorful mosses covered every inch of the jungle's floor, creating a plush carpet, even over fallen limbs and uneven ground.

Still uncertain about his footing, Paul steadied himself by placing his hand on a thick tree trunk, inadvertently scraping off a small piece of bark in the process. The fragment fell onto the moss at the base of the tree, and within seconds, the moss absorbed it. Amazed, Paul reached into a bush and broke off a stick about the thickness and size of a pencil. He then walked away from the tree into a partial clearing and dropped it onto the moss right in front of his toes. Again, the moss consumed the stick. Squatting down, he dared to poke his finger into the same spot. The moss allowed an indentation, but did not draw in his finger. Evidently, it only ingested fallen vegetation.

Paul stood and looked for April so he could show her the amazing trick.

"April!"

His voice sounded loud in the jungle's quietness. Until that moment, he had not noticed how peaceful it was in that place.

"Did you find something?" April asked, hurrying to his side.

"No, but you have to see this." Paul turned to the bush and removed another stick.

"I thought you didn't want us to touch anything."

"Just watch." He dropped the stick in front of her and the moss did its trick again; the stick disappeared.

"That explains why there isn't much debris lying around," April noted. "The jungle has a natural cleaning system."

"Yeah. It keeps you from stepping on anything that could hurt your feet."

April pushed her toes into the moss and tested the resistance. "It's really soft."

"That's probably why they don't bother with shoes."

"And clothes?"

Pail smirked and shrugged his shoulders. "With bodies like that, they—"

"Paul! April!" Keah called out. "We must travel now to join the others." He and Ahee joined them. "Has your strength returned?"

"We're fine," April replied. "My legs feel really strong. I could hike for miles."

Ahee nodded and studied April's body. "You are stronger on Hourou because your *eu-uaua* are of Blue."

"What is eu-uaua?" April asked.

For an answer, Ahee pushed her hair back and gestured to various places on her body. "Eu-uaua is this."

"Muscles?" April guessed, pointing to her bicep. "You mean muscles?"

Ahee rose and gripped April's arm. "Yes, Eu-uaua. Muss-els."

"And Blue is what again?" Paul asked.

"That's what they call Earth."

"Got it. Our muscles were made for Earth, so we're stronger here on Hourou."

Keah nodded and gestured toward the jungle. "You will need strength for the distance we must travel. Are you ready?"

"Ready," Paul said. He leaned in close to April as Keah and Ahee took the lead. "So that's the end of the clothes hunt. You going to be okay?"

"I guess so...as long as the trail stays soft, and it doesn't get cold here."

"I'm hoping they'll consider those things. But if they don't, we'll have to speak up, or take care of our own needs. Okay?"

"Okay."

Paul watched Keah and Ahee as they walked ahead, navigating through the thick jungle with ease. As out of place as their white naked bodies looked in that environment, they seemed to be built for such trekking. Their movements conveyed confidence, and that was what Paul was going to need to get out of this bizarre situation. He would have to trust the alien couple. He wanted to, but it was going to take more than attractive bodies, smiles, and comforting talk to convince him they were trustworthy.

"Paul," April said, interrupting his anxious thoughts. "They're a lot like us, you know."

"I hope so, Babes. I hope so."

CHAPTER 19

On the Edge

LATE MORNING: DAY 1 ON HOUROU

"Absolutely incredible!"

Ellis Minister was standing on the edge of an enormous boulder, yelling his observations down to Yori and Perry as they stood below him in a field of green chest-high grass.

"What is it you see?" Yori asked.

"A vast steppe—a prairie—stretching several miles in every direction."

Perry had hoped for something more. "And beyond that?"

"Nothing behind us," Ellis observed, "but ahead it meets the border of what appears to be a substantial forest."

"And there's nothing between us and the forest?"

"I can only see more boulders—like this one—scattered about. Otherwise...miles of grass."

"Any sign of the others?" Yori asked.

Ellis squinted in the bright light of Hourou's suns, searching for any movement in the great sea of green.

"Well?" Perry prompted.

"No signs of them in any direction. The grass hides everything. It has even reclaimed the area where we came down."

"Where are the kids?" Yori was referring to the four members of the alien family that ended up with them in the crash.

Ellis chuckled to himself. In his eyes, Yori was no older than those youths. "They're on the other side of the rock...waiting to help me back down."

"You needed little help getting up there," Perry quipped.

"True. Gravity must be less here. I feel lighter."

Yori asked, "Do you think they know where we are?"

Ellis thought about how the four Hourou natives seemed to be untroubled about the crash or about being lost. After accounting for everyone and ensuring the Earth humans were unharmed, they had hurried into the surrounding vegetation and returned with armfuls of small fruits and strange shells filled with water, which they shared with the group. Otherwise, they had acted like nothing unusual had happened. Even now, they were simply sitting around and talking amongst themselves as if only passing the time.

"I don't know," Ellis said. "They certainly don't look concerned."

"They don't look the *same* either," Perry noted. "Didn't they have black skin before?"

"Yes," Yori agreed. "While we were on the spaceship, they all had black skin. Only the parents were white. There was the one girl, though —Eah—who changed to white in front of us."

"So they are *all* able to alter their skin color," Ellis said.

"What?" Perry asked. A light breeze blowing through the grass made it hard to hear.

"I'll come down so we don't have to yell." With that, Ellis moved to the other side of the rock, where it was easiest to climb down.

"Did he say they can *all* change color?" Perry asked Yori.

"Yes. Probably all of them can do it."

"Black to white and white to black. *That's* different."

"It's fascinating. I wonder if—"

Perry interrupted her with a heavy sigh.

"What?"

"Why did I have to get stuck with the two science nerds?"

Yori bristled at his rudeness. "I'm not a *nerd,* Mister Carlson. I'm in my last year of graduate school, and my interest is in human anatomy and physiology. Forgive me if changing one's skin color happens to intrigue me."

"Okay. Whatever."

Perry seemed to back down, which pleased Yori. There was enough tension among them already. They did not need quarreling to distract them from what was most important—survival.

"New subject," Perry suggested. "What do you think happened to the others?"

"I guess there's no way to know. I'm hoping they survived by some miracle, like we did."

"Miracle?"

"Figure of speech. But how else do you explain it? We should be dead after such a crash."

Perry looked up into the purple sky. There were no clouds, but he saw flocks of birds in the distance.

"I *can't* explain it," he admitted. "Let's see if Minister can. It's a different planet. Different rules. My guess is that we got lucky...really lucky."

"Maybe."

Ellis pushed through the tall grass and joined them. "Maybe what?"

"We're trying to figure out why we are even alive," Perry said.

"Well, lacking proper data, I can only offer conjecture, but—"

"Data?" Perry interrupted. "Now *there's* a scientific word. Okay, let's hear a best guess, professor."

Yori shot Perry a sideways glance and stepped closer to Ellis, who was frowning at Perry's brusqueness. The congressman liked to manipulate people with his words; he had already shown that on the spaceship. Since crashing on the planet, though, his tone was becoming even more antagonistic. Both Yori and Ellis were no longer hiding their irritation at his pushiness and incivility.

"Now look here, Carlson," Ellis said, "your position back home might be one of authority, but here—"

"Yeah, I get it," Perry jeered. "Here, *none* of us is in charge. Or are you proposing that the *scientist* should lead the party?"

"Wrong, Carlson. This is not about political posturing, as difficult as that may be for you to believe. It's about survival. If the three of us are going to continue to survive in this alien world, we have to get on better."

"Okay. Okay. I get it," Perry said. "So what's the plan—*our* plan?"

Yori gestured toward the area where the alien youth waited on the other side of the boulder. "I don't think it's up to us. We're in the hands of the natives."

"I don't like the idea of following children," Perry warned, "even if they *are* from here. There's something wrong with them, anyway. They haven't shown concern for their missing family, and they've been treating the crash of their ship like a trivial matter."

Ellis chuckled. "It is quite disconcerting—their obliviousness to danger."

"And you trust them to lead us?" Perry asked Yori.

"They showed they care about us," she noted, "by bringing food and water."

"Which hopefully won't harm us."

"Are either of you experiencing any negative reactions?" Yori asked.

"Only to our situation," Perry quipped.

"Not me," Ellis said. "Actually, after eating the fruit, my strength came back to me."

"Anything else?" Yori asked him.

"It seemed to clear my head...like giving clarity of mind."

"Perhaps Mister Carlson here needs a few more bites, then."

Perry grinned at Yori's wisecrack. "Touchè."

"At least we know we can eat something here and drink the water and not become ill," she said to them both. "That's a start. Plus, the locals have shown an interest in our safety. As aloof as they sometimes seem to be, they're paying attention."

Ellis scratched his head and looked back toward where he had left the young alien humans. "I have to agree," he admitted. "Despite their apparent youth, they display spurts of wisdom and high intelligence. Like Carlson, I have my reservations about entrusting myself to their total care, but I also recognize that we haven't much of a choice. I wouldn't even know what direction to walk in...or why."

"For all we know," Perry said, "the slightest misstep here could end very badly."

Yori agreed. "True. That goes for dealing with the locals, too. We don't know how we're going to be received by the rest of the population."

"If there is one," Perry added.

Ellis raised his hands in simulated praise. "Then it's sorted. Let's go round up our guides and prompt them to take us somewhere. Perhaps we'll be able to communicate enough to direct them."

"Adult supervision," Perry said with a snicker. "Reminds me of being a chaperon during one of my daughter's high school volleyball trips."

"See there?" Yori said. "Your human is coming out. The fruit worked on you, after all."

Perry grinned at her comment. Ellis and Yori did likewise, signaling their desire to accept a truce. Both, however, nodded knowingly at each other when Perry pushed past them and took the lead toward the spot where the alien youths were waiting.

* * *

Time on Hourou conflicted with the visiting humans' internal clocks. None of them could guess how many minutes or hours had passed since their arrival. With two suns, it was also difficult to measure time by the movement of shadows. The two stars, Tahah and Tameen, were at different distances from the planet. Tameen led the larger sun, Tahah, across the sky, meaning that Tameen was the first to rise. As the more distant sun, it appeared smaller and would cast a softer light until Tahah rose above the horizon to join it in creating day. Neither were as bright as Earth's sun, but when both were in the sky together, their combined light resembled Earth daylight.

Yori wanted to mark the time of their arrival. She considered the two suns and noted that the larger one was still low. Did that mean it was late in the morning? A glance at her wristwatch reminded her that its digital screen had gone blank after the crash; it must have gotten damaged somehow. At least it was not her fault this time. She had ruined her last one during a lab experiment. This watch, however, was a birthday gift from her father. She hoped someone could repair it once she got back home—if she got back home. With a sigh, she removed the timepiece and shoved it deep into her pants pocket.

Perhaps the time of day did not matter on this planet, anyway. Her young hosts did not seem to care about it; they were more interested in playing. At least, that is what she assumed the four alien youths were doing. They had flattened the tall grass into a large circular area by stomping it down with their feet. When the circle's size was satisfactory for their needs, they each stepped to opposite sides of the perimeter. After laying down, with eyes closed, they began rolling their bodies across the circle. The object of the game was apparently to stay in motion, avoid collisions, and remain in the makeshift arena. Rather than being a competition, it was just lighthearted fun. The players rolled and tumbled, missing collisions by inches but often passing right over each other, all the while taunting one another and laughing.

Early in the game, Ellis and Perry had stepped away for a private conversation, leaving Yori as a lone spectator. After a while, Ellis appeared through a wall of grass and sat down beside her.

"Well, this has been going on for a while now and there is still no clear winner," he said, playing the part of a sports commentator. "The men's team, led by brothers—what are their names again?"

Yori grinned, appreciative of Ellis distracting her from restless thoughts.

"Ua and Aai," she replied. "Ua is the taller one and most likely the older of the two. His height gives him a little disadvantage, but it's made up for in his mature musculature."

"Well said, Miss Shimizu!" Ellis joked.

"It's Yori."

"Well said, Yori," Ellis corrected, pleased by her informality, "and please also call me Ellis."

"Thanks, Ellis."

"So...the two males are Ua and Aai. What about the females?"

"Mahah and Maiha," Yori answered. "Maiha is the quieter one. Mahah is a bit more physically mature, so she must be the older one."

"Well, it's hard to tell, but it seems we've been here for quite some time now. Other than their names, do you think you've been able to understand anything else that they've said?"

Yori considered her awkward communications with the four alien humans. Speaking to them like small children did not produce results. Likewise, slow and short sentences did not help. Yori only achieved some success after she remembered April Theele's observation that the aliens used body language as much as words. Of course, she did not know what gestures to use. After studying them and trusting in her own intuition, though, she made a few important breakthroughs.

Ellis and Perry had even less success in communicating with them. At first, she thought the two men simply lacked patience. Now, however, she understood it was because they needed more perceptivity. She could only communicate with the aliens if she was concentrating on a deep enough level to discern more than words and verbal cues. Somehow, this had come naturally to April. Yori was learning as well, but she wondered if the males in her party could do so.

"Their words are very difficult to pronounce," Yori said after pondering her attempts. "Many of them sound the same. Like April said, though, they also use gestures and other physical cues that are sometimes a little easier to interpret."

"Such as?"

"Most of them are subtle. A simple twitch of a facial muscle can convey an entire thought."

"I suppose we do that on our planet as well," Ellis noted. "Body language tells much."

"This is similar, but much more precise. Unlike our body language, with them you never have to wonder about vagueness or second meanings."

"They communicate with intention."

"Exactly. If I wink at you from across a room, there are several things you could infer. It might mean a shared understanding, a personal recognition, or an attraction."

"But the context and environment would also play a part, would they not?"

"To us, yes," Yori explained, "at least a little. If we didn't know each other and the environment was a nightclub or party, interpreting the wink might be less ambiguous. So for us, the situation is important, but it doesn't seem that way for these people. To them, such a gesture can only mean one thing. It's part of their language."

"I see," Ellis said with a nod. "So, have you been able to interpret many of these gestures?"

"No. I can understand a few very rudimentary ones. I need more time to observe and interact."

Ellis watched with interest as the four alien youths rolled about in the grass. "Well, since they don't seem to be in a hurry to go anywhere, observation is all we can do."

"This whole thing is scary, but it's also fascinating...isn't it, Ellis?"

"Yes, it is. What do you make of their unusual game?"

"I can't figure it out at all," Yori admitted. "I mean...they survived the crash of their spaceship and became separated from the rest of their family—who may not have even lived through it. Instead of caring, here they are rolling around naked in a field and laughing."

"I hope it isn't the fruit," Ellis said with a chuckle. "Do you feel any strange effects?"

"Well, I have no desire to join them."

"Oh, I don't know. It looks a bit fun, actually."

Yori smiled. As bizarre as it looked, the game was only innocent play. "Seriously, though," she said, "don't they look a little too old to be acting this way?"

"Not to me."

"Come on, Ellis. You're not that old."

"No, but I teach undergraduates who are about this age. Speaking of which, you can't be much older than those students, my dear, or these alien youths."

"Would you put these in their early twenties, then?"

"I would say that's about right if they were from our planet. And I can imagine that many of my students would find this game worth trying...after an adequate amount of alcohol consumption, that is."

"You're probably right," Yori said. "What appeals to me, though, is their innocence. We think they're acting improperly, and I have to admit that when they started I wasn't having innocent thoughts—"

"I'll meet your confession with one of my own," Ellis interrupted. "My observations were, at first, based on less than wholesome ideas."

"Yet there isn't anything wrong with it," Yori continued. "They're just having some good, clean fun, like kids playing together. We're the ones who are imposing our conclusions on *them*."

"Quite right. While not fully understanding."

"It makes me feel guilty in a way."

"Science is about observation without personal judgment—without bias. That's difficult to do when the environment is so foreign and potentially hostile."

"There's more to it than the scientific observation, but I agree with you. I guess I'm talking about moral judgments and the filters we see life through."

"Too much psychology for me, Yori," Ellis said. "Given our strange circumstances, I'm more comfortable staying with scientific inquiry."

"Okay, but why this game right now? Are they that irresponsible, or is it a social thing? Is it some sort of tradition? Is it religious? Maybe it's just stress relief?"

Ellis looked back to check on the whereabouts of Perry. "It's too bad we don't have an anthropologist with us instead of a politician."

"*Baka*," Yori said.

"Pardon?"

"It's Japanese. Means he's an idiot."

"Agreed. Let's hope he doesn't get us all into trouble."

Yori nodded and returned her attention to the game. The players were getting tired, as evidenced by their inability to continue avoiding collisions. Lighthearted wrestling matches replaced the rolling when two players became entangled. The females' long hair was both a handicap and an advantage, depending on who the match favored. The males fought harder against each other, but seemed to go easier on the females, which was not a smart strategy for them. In the end, it looked as though the girls claimed the victory. The game ended in a heap of good-natured laughing.

Yori laughed with them and nodded to Mahah and Maiha to signal that she understood and appreciated their win. Her show of solidarity pleased the two females so much that they rose and rushed over to sit close to her.

"What's this?" Ellis asked in jest. "Preferential treatment?"

"Girl power."

"Okay, lads," Ellis said to the males, "we had better stick together."

Ua and Aai acknowledged his comment with a laugh.

"Wait...do you understand me?" he asked.

"Ssssss-tik?" Ua questioned. "Sss-tik tooo-geth-ah."

"Brilliant!" Ellis exclaimed.

Aai stepped forward. "Bri-lant."

Then the girls got involved.

"Bri-lant," repeated Mahah.

"No, Bril-lee-ay-ont," Maiha said.

"Brilliant!" Ua pronounced correctly.

Ellis jumped to his feet. "That's it! Brilliant!"

The youths continued to say the word until each could pronounce it properly.

"Now we're making progress!" Ellis declared.

"Yes, it es brilliant," Ua said.

This elicited a round of laughter from all of them.

"I...feel...brilliant...a-boat it," Mahah said, giggling.

"Meen-eh-stah es brilliant," Ua added.

"Well, I—" Ellis began.

"We...ah...unner-stanning woo-eds—words—an... it es brilliant," Maiha said like a proud pupil.

Their ability to learn a new language so easily amazed Yori. "Ellis, they're getting it! It's like back on the spaceship."

"Eah taught us some...woo-eds—words," Ua explained. "We liss-en...we learn."

"Speak *our* woo-eds!" Maiha said.

"Okay," Ellis replied. "Give me one."

"Give?" Maiha asked.

"Oh, sorry. I mean, say a word in your language."

"Oooooo-eee-ey-oi-i-heh."

Ellis shot a tentative glance at Yori, but her bright smile encouraged him to make an attempt.

"Oooooh-eee-hay-oi-het," he repeated.

All four youths laughed, but not with mockery. How Ellis was grasping their language excited them.

"Brilliant!" Ua praised. "Meester Minister es learning."

Ua's use of English was improving by the minute. Ellis even thought he detected a hint of a British accent like his own.

"What is Oooooh-eee-hay-oi-het, then?" he asked Maiha.

Maiha rose and pushed her hair behind her body. "Oooooo-eee-ey-oi-i-heh," she said with all seriousness, "means joining." She motioned toward Ellis and Yori. "You joining us."

"Sticking togeth-uh," Ua added with a smile.

"I like the sound of that," Yori said, feeling more of her anxieties wash away. Successful communication brought her some much needed confidence. Just as she was enjoying the moment, however, a sudden realization threatened to ruin it. "Ellis," she said, "where's Perry?"

Ellis scanned the immediate area and only then realized Perry had not been with them for quite some time. The youths did likewise and seemed to understand Ellis and Yori's concern.

Yori recalled Ellis's comment about Perry getting them into trouble. "Why would he go off alone?" she asked him.

"We must stick together," Ua said.

Ellis nodded at Ua, admiring his newfound command of words. He also noted a hint of authority in Ua's voice. "Yes, Ua," he said. "We had better find him."

* * *

Perry Carlson was no fool. Although he had deserted the group to be alone and do some thinking, he stayed close enough so as not to get disoriented. He also marked his path by picking handfuls of grass, rolling it up, and placing the wads where he would see them upon his return. He knew he would not become lost, and the need to clear his head overrode the fear of his new surroundings, at least for the moment.

My next move, he thought to himself. *What's my next move?*

Perry prided himself on being able to stay one step ahead of damaging situations. This time, however, he was far too removed from his element to develop effective strategies.

"Strategizing," he said out loud, scoffing at the idea. "A lot of good it does here. I might as well just strip down and start rolling in the hay like the crazy natives."

As he left the higher elevation near the base of the giant boulder, the height of the surrounding grass changed from chest-high to just above his head. It reminded Perry of one of his political advertisements in which a cameraman followed him through a cornfield while he talked about supporting local farmers. He could not see where he was going, so he and the camera guy kept walking in what they believed to be a straight line. When they completed the filming, they found themselves lost in the boundless corn fields and Perry had to call the authorities to extricate them. It was an embarrassing yet humorous outing that made for some good cocktail party conversations.

Perry grinned at the memory as he reached into his pocket to feel for his mobile phone. Of course, it was not there. During his abduction, it must have fallen out, or the aliens confiscated it. Either way, it would not do him any good in a different galaxy.

As he stopped to uproot some grass and make another path marker, Perry looked up at the sky and wondered what people back on Earth thought about his sudden disappearance.

Plenty of people saw my abduction, he recalled. *The aliens didn't care if anyone saw it. Why me, though? Oh, their story is that it was accidental, but how do I know for sure? What if they targeted specific people and just made up the story about chasing the supposed runaways? Perhaps their plan was to bring us here for an examination. In that case, the whole crash of the ship was a ruse to test us somehow.*

Perry considered the missing members of his party. *They wanted to split us up to see how we would react. Maybe they want to study how skillfully we can survive. That would explain why they embedded some of their own into our party. The others from Earth are in the same fix and have their own observers.*

As he balled up the grass between his hands and recalled his abduction and the details he had learned while aboard the alien vessel, Perry's present theory made more sense. In his usual strategic way, he filled in the unknowns with best guesses and planned potential responses and actions until he convinced himself of the logic of his ideas.

Well, I won't be some lab rat for these aliens to study, he concluded. *They're going to deal with me on my terms.*

Perry dropped the wadded-up ball onto the ground and considered the wall of grass in front of him. Though there was nothing ahead but thick green crisscrossing blades, the back of his neck tingled with the unsettling feeling that he was being watched. As he reached out to make a hole, he uncovered a bronze female face staring at him from under a mane of long black hair.

Startled and frightened, Perry swore, stepped backward, lost his footing, and fell with a muffled thump onto the soft ground. The intruder pushed through the grass and stood before him, somewhat surprised by his reaction.

"Sa-eee-aha-i-sohore-wher-ri-ai?" she asked.

"You nearly gave me a heart attack!" Perry shot back. He rose and regained his composure. "What are you doing out here sneaking around? Why aren't you with the others?"

The young woman did not answer. Instead, she just gawked at him in astonishment.

"Which one are you anyway?" Perry demanded.

"Wiiiiii-sh wonnnn."

Perry ignored her gibberish and continued his verbal assault. "Why'd you change color? Trying to camouflage yourself to be a better spy? Well, you're wasting your time. I will not give you anything to—"

"Shee-hei-ai-oh-sa-nah!" she demanded.

"I don't understand you!"

"Unner-stan you! Unner-stan *Dah-Ahey!*"

"Dah-Ahey?" Looking her over, Perry realized she was not one of the youths in his party who had changed color. Her physical features were almost identical to theirs, but she was wearing a tiny loincloth. "You didn't change color," he noted. "You're the other kind—the Dah-Ahey."

"Yes! Ria es Dah-Ahey!"

"I thought the crash must have killed you and your friends. Obviously not. So what are you doing running around out here alone? Why not join us?"

"Ehe! You join *Dah-Ahey!*"

"Alright, calm down. The last thing I need right now is an agitated woman on my hands. What are you trying to tell me?"

"Sa lass tingg you need es an ageeee-tated wo-man, Par-eee Car-elson. Unner-stan Dah-Ahey."

Perry staggered backward in surprise at her use of his own words, and especially at hearing his name come out of her mouth. "So...you know more than you pretend. Why the act, then? It might have worked on the others, but not on me, honey."

The woman shot him a look of pleased amazement and pushed her hair behind her bronze body. "See me, Car-el-son."

"Whoa now!" Perry warned as he tried to avert his eyes. "Let's not have a misunderstanding. Why don't you just tell me why you're here for starters? Why aren't you with the others?"

Sudden concern brought a frown to her beige lips. "Others?"

"Yes," Perry replied with impatience. "The others. The white ones."

"Others white?"

"Yes."

"Carlson shhh-ood not go wit sa white ones."

"Huh? What are you talking about? They're *your* people, not mine."

"Carlson shoood come wit Dah-Ahey. Come wit me. Come wit Ria."

"Is that your name? Ria? Go with you where?"

"Carlson comes now!" She grabbed Perry's arm and tried to pull him along with her as she searched for a direction.

It was then that Perry heard distant voices calling his name. "Hold on!" he said to the woman. "It looks like they've found us, anyway. Let's just go back and sort this whole thing out, shall we?"

Ria tugged on his arm, but when the voices sounded closer, she let go and turned to leave in the opposite direction.

"Wait! What are you doing?"

Before stepping into the high grass, she turned back toward him and offered an enticing smile. "I am Ria, Carlson. Find me. Come to dah Dah-Ahey." Not waiting for a response, she disappeared into the wall of greenery, leaving Perry alone with his confusion.

Seconds later, Ellis and a young white-skinned male entered Perry's alcove. "Ah," Ellis said. "There you are. We worried you had gotten yourself lost."

"Huh? Oh. Well...why would I do something as stupid as that?"

"I meant no offense, Carlson," Ellis said. "We were just concerned, that's all."

"Alright. So, here I am anyway."

"Are you alright? You look like you've seen a ghost."

"I'm fine," Perry said with his best fake smile. "You startled me, that's all. I wanted to be alone and think. Seeing as how that's ruined now, though, let's just go back." He rushed Ellis and the white-skinned young man back onto his marked path.

Ellis studied him with a wary expression. "You didn't see anything strange out here, did you?"

The question startled Perry. He thought his ploy had worked, but Ellis was not that easy to fool. Neither was the male alien; his green eyes kept scanning the surrounding area as if searching for something.

"No...just me and the grass."

Ellis studied Perry's face for hints of evasiveness, but Perry Carlson was a master at masking his emotions. "Good," Ellis said, satisfied. "We need to get going. I think our friends are finally ready to take us somewhere."

"Fine by me," Perry said as he continued to push the two along his path. With a quick glance back, he glimpsed the strange woman's face behind the grass, watching him with great interest. *Dah-Ahey,* he thought. *So there is another culture here besides that of the white-skinned ones. How interesting.*

As if reading his thoughts, the woman smiled invitingly before disappearing into the vegetation.

Ria, I think we'll be meeting again.

CHAPTER 20

Convinced

"You're doing a superb job." Alex watched Laura fidget with her mobile. "The committee is convinced about everything else. Why not this?"

Laura jammed the device into a pocket of her blazer and frowned. "Because *this* is different. Now we're talking about the visitors *coming back*. They're not even thinking about that."

"If not...they will."

"Why? Because of a truck driver's story? That's *not* enough."

"The committee has accepted everything so far—concrete evidence and personal testimonies. Considering the various personalities, that shows a lot."

"Sure. They can't deny the crashes or abductions, but there's not enough proof to support the idea of a return visit. Unless we can find the aliens that Jerry talked to, we've got nothing to show."

"We have a piece of the craft they left behind," Alex reminded.

"Inconclusive. The committee already assumes the rest of it burned up or something."

"*That's* what is inconclusive, Laura," Doctor Haines said as he approached their cafeteria table with two trays of food.

For the past four hours, Laura and Haines had been answering questions in front of a special government committee that was studying the extraterrestrial visitation and tasked with suggesting an appropriate response. The committee's mandate was ominous. Its recommendations would affect science, politics, global relations, religion, and every other area of human life. Laura felt the full weight of that responsibility while presenting the findings of her own investigation.

It was a rainy Saturday in the nation's capital—the third day after the very first sightings of the Triangle. Since then, Laura had been working nonstop with very little sleep. She had hoped to return to the second crash site that day to re-examine the remains of the spacecraft. Then, her superiors called her in to attend the special meeting and present any recent information that might be useful to the committee.

The first half of the meeting had gone smoothly. Because the committee chairman demanded that the presenters focus only on facts, it was difficult to use opinions, politics, or grandstanding to sidetrack or hinder the proceedings. Laura answered many questions, but her allotted time to give a full presentation was to be after the lunch break. She appreciated the delay. It allowed her to clear her head and consider her approach to a subject no one had mentioned yet—a second visitation.

Her sixth sense told her the alien visitors would come back. It was hard to explain, but harder still was the deep *need* she felt for them to return. Of course, she had a personal agenda—everyone did. She wanted to score big; it was time for a woman like her to get some professional respect. Besides that, though, she needed an answer to a question she had since the start of her ten-year career chasing down strange phenomena and supernatural experiences. She needed to know if there was something bigger at work in the universe that pointed to a better existence. A quick drop-by from alien beings only created more mystery. If they visited this planet again—if she could see them, communicate with them—that would show her a greater meaning to it all.

Laura snatched a paper-wrapped burger from one of Haines' food trays and a cup of what she hoped was something caffeinated.

"What do you mean by 'inconclusive,' Doctor Haines?" she asked, unwrapping the burger. "I'm saying the remains of the alien craft are inconclusive evidence for their return. We need to explain why they would come back for it."

Haines sat down across from her and gestured for Alex to help himself to their fast-food meal.

"There are many reasons for that, Laura," he said. "They might not want a piece of their technology to remain in our hands. Perhaps what's left is dangerous. They might also have need of it."

"Maybe there's something *inside* it they need," Alex suggested.

Haines nodded. "That's possible, too. We haven't even examined it yet to see if there are other rooms still intact."

Laura was unsatisfied. "The committee will tear all that apart. For each possibility, there's also an alternative explanation. What if they don't realize they left a part of the thing behind? Or...they don't care. Maybe they never tried to retrieve it and the rest of it just burned up. Or they can't recover it because it's buried too far in the ground. I could go on and on and—"

"Hey!" Alex interrupted. "I thought you're convinced they *are* coming back."

"My gut tells me they are. But that won't convince anyone else."

"That's what I meant by *inconclusive*, Laura," Haines said. "The committee can't state conclusively that the alien visitors will *not* be returning either."

"Exactly," Alex agreed between mouthfuls. "They must at least accept the possibility."

Laura considered Alex's statement as she hurriedly devoured her burger. Until then, she had not realized how hungry she had become.

"What? No fries?" she asked Haines, feigning a sudden chagrin.

Haines laughed and rose from his seat. "Sorry, kids. I'll go back."

Laura and Alex watched Haines until he returned to the cafeteria line.

"What are you thinking?" Alex whispered.

"I'm thinking," Laura replied as she stuffed the last bite of the small burger into her mouth, "that Haines can't wait to get his hands on this project."

"What project?"

"The one that comes next!"

"I'm not following."

"He *wants* me to convince the committee of an imminent return so he and the Space Agency can run the show."

"They'd still need *us*."

"Yeah, and we'd be working for *him*."

Alex shrugged his shoulders.

"Alex!" Laura chastised. "You know how long I've been trying to get respect for our agency! This should be *us,* not the Space Agency, the military, or anyone else!"

"Look," Alex said in a soothing tone, "I get the notoriety part—"

"Not just notoriety, Alex. It's about *legitimacy*."

Alex pushed himself back in his chair and let out a heavy sigh.

"What?" Laura demanded.

"Nothing."

Laura eyed him with suspicion, but did not press further. She could tell what was bothering him. His eyes betrayed something she had seen many times when the two of them would discuss advancing their careers.

Alex understood she wanted to be in charge of this thing to the end, so he forced a smile to show support. "Hey, I'm with you. Okay?"

"I know."

"Listen. At least Haines is backing you up. We can use that. I mean...here's the full weight of the Space Agency behind us."

Laura had to agree. "True."

"So you *keep* it behind us. Haines is unwittingly propping you up."

Alex's revelation injected a sudden confidence into Laura's weakened resolve. He was right. Haines was giving her the platform. All she had to do was stay on it. Her smile showed Alex that she understood well how to do that.

"So...you've got this. Right?" he asked.

"Yes. Thanks, Alex. How did you get so wise, anyway?"

"Sometimes, it comes with patience," he replied with a wink. "When this thing is all over, I'm going to take you someplace far away and teach you everything I know."

"The escape sounds great," she teased, "but as for the teaching—"

"Is this the table that requested three orders of artery-clogging fries?" Haines asked as he reappeared. "Sorry for the delay. The rest of the committee just discovered that there's a cafeteria in this building. What'd I miss?"

"Only a little pep talk," Alex answered. "Laura's going back in there to hit one out of the park."

Haines nodded and sat down. "Of course she is. She's a pro, and this is her moment."

"I appreciate the encouragement," Laura said, picking through the fries she did not really want.

"What will you say, then?" Haines asked.

"I'll wing it. In the end, they'll just have to trust us."

"Well...I've got your back," Haines said. "If you get into a corner, kick the ball to me."

"And I'll be in the peanut gallery projecting positive energy," Alex quipped.

"A prayer would do better." She grinned and glanced upward.

Haines gathered the litter onto the trays while he finished the last bites of his burger. "Well, kids," he said as he rose, "I need to say hello to someone and make a pit stop before we go back in. I'll see you in a few."

"Thanks for the food," Alex said.

Laura took a last sip of her drink, stood, and pushed her chair under the table. "Yes, thanks, Doctor Haines. I'm going to stretch my legs and get some fresh air for a few minutes."

Alex collected his briefcase and jacket and followed Laura through the cafeteria toward a pair of glass doors that opened into a garden courtyard. He hesitated before accompanying her outside.

"What's wrong?" Laura asked. "The rain stopped."

"I'm just watching Haines," he said, looking over his shoulder. "I want to see if he really talks to someone...and who."

Laura grabbed his arm. "Come on. Walk now. Spy later."

As they exited the cafeteria, Alex glanced back in time to see Haines dash out of the room, nervous and fumbling with his mobile.

* * *

Laura and Alex returned to the meeting and pushed through a crowd to get to their seats. An enormous conference table dominated the center of the rectangular room. With the high-backed chairs that surrounded it and a single row of them along each wall, there was little area in which to walk. Laura assumed the smaller space was to ensure a short invitation list. Indeed, there was hardly enough seating for subordinate attendees like Alex, who negotiated for a chair right behind her.

Alex patted Laura on the shoulder before taking his seat. On either side of her sat Haines and General Shepherd. Both were engaged in conversations, so she unpacked a few things from her briefcase and settled in to prepare for the next round of presentations. Earlier in the day, she had no time to appreciate her surroundings. Now she studied the details of the meeting room to calm her nerves.

The chamber looked and felt very official. Polished wood columns divided the ivory-colored walls into several sections, with lighted paintings of famous historical scenes displayed between each column. The stains of the columns, the framed artwork, and the conference table matched perfectly, creating an ordered and professional appearance for the place. The lighting, too, was just right, as was the temperature. A slight breeze from the air conditioning system circulated the smells of wood polish, newly laid carpet, and fresh coffee.

Laura still needed a boost, so she reached for a carafe of the coffee and poured a cupful for herself and Doctor Haines. As she did, she glanced toward the front of the room. The committee chairman and three others occupied the head of the table. Behind them was a large optical projection screen displaying a photograph of the alien Triangle.

As the other attendees took their seats, Laura sipped on the coffee and closed her eyes to center herself. *You've got this, girl. This is your time and your platform. So, go for it.*

The banging of a gavel interrupted Laura's momentary peace.

"Please take your seats," the committee chairman said. "It's time for business."

The noise level in the room dropped to a hush. When the doors were closed, the chairman glanced at Laura.

So, I'm next on the agenda then. Good. Let's get this over with.

The meeting resumed with the usual protocol. The chairman re-stated the purpose, mission, and importance of the proceedings. He then reviewed procedure and reminded the committee of the enormity of what they were discussing. Laura hoped the ensuing weightiness in the room would help with her presentation.

"With that, I will turn it over to Director Turgis."

"Thank you, sir," Laura said. "I would like to begin by thanking the committee members and my colleagues and presenters for their questions and observations during the first session. As I mentioned in my previous reports, the work of my agency has been vigorously supported by all the others represented in this room, and I've been thankful for the eagerness of my fellow directors to share information and to create an environment of cooperation. Thanks to that spirit of collaboration and partnership, my agency, which has operated in relative isolation and obscurity, is now being seen as the vanguard in our shared quest to understand the unprecedented events that have brought us all together."

Laura paused and glanced around the room at the attendees.

"The recent interest in my agency's work has been both appreciated and energizing. As you know, we have been investigating unusual phenomena—including alleged UFO sightings, extraterrestrial visitations, and alien abductions—for quite some time. Until now, the best cases left us with only questions and doubts. Any evidence that we collected was inconclusive. Eye witness testimony, though sometimes highly credible, was still suspect.

"On Thursday of last week, that all changed. Our planet being visited by intelligent life from another world is now undeniable. My agency has a multitude of eyewitness accounts, corroborated and nearly identical. We possess hours of video footage from private citizens, businesses, local governments, military sources, and satellite operators. There is also credible testimony from someone who spoke to the extraterrestrial visitors. We even found a section of the crashed spacecraft, and it is intact enough to give us insights into what the visitors are like.

"These are truly remarkable days for my agency, but also for the field of science, for those organizations and individuals who search for life beyond our planet, and for every human being who has ever asked the familiar question: 'Are we alone in the universe?' I am proud of our work and to be a leading part of this committee on such a momentous occasion."

Laura paused for effect. *Leadership fully established.* She glanced at Haines and noticed a hint of surprise being hidden by a smile of support.

"Well said, Director Turgis," the chairman said. "You and your agency have had your work cut out for you. Some acknowledgment and respect *are* most appropriate, and your reports and observations are appreciated at the highest levels."

"Thank you, sir." She was proud of her introductory statement. *Credibility firmly established.*

"I don't mean to interrupt your presentation right at the start," the chairman noted, "but I would like to steer you toward the subject on page thirty-six of your recent report, specifically paragraph number—I guess it's the third paragraph?"

"I apologize for the format," Laura said. "Doctor Haines and I wrote parts of it while we were in quarantine at the crash site."

"No need to apologize, Director," the chairman replied. "I believe future generations will forgive our loosening of procedure, understand-ing the need for haste. Hopefully, these reports will remain classified for a long time, or at least until we are all too old to care about proper report outlining."

The committee members and other attendees allowed themselves a chuckle. Laura was unfazed, knowing that a strong composure at this moment was essential.

"Thank you, sir. Yes, in paragraph three, I mention the possibility of a repeat visit."

Mumbling replaced the quietness of the room.

"Quiet, please!" the chairman urged, tapping his gavel to signal a return to order. "Yes, to save time, Director Turgis, please elaborate on what the rest of the committee has already interpreted to be a controversial theory from your agency."

Here we go then. "Cutting right to the chase, my agency is proposing that this committee should consider a repeat visitation—"

More mumbling in the room interrupted Laura. This time, the chairman allowed it.

"You believe the aliens are coming back?" asked the committee's vice-chair.

"I prefer to use the term *visitors,*" Laura said. "I'm sure the committee will also find that the public will receive that word better than the word *aliens.*"

The chairman smiled, impressed with Laura's persuasive abilities. He could tell she was no stranger to politics. Not only had she cleverly positioned her agency as the leader of investigations, but now she was also defining the terms.

"Agreed," the vice-chair replied. "You believe the *visitors* will come back, then?"

"My agency's position is that there is satisfactory evidence to warrant a serious consideration of the possibility."

"Carefully stated," the vice-chair noted, "and judging by the various reports, no one is able—or willing—to make an unambiguous proposal."

"My agency's proposal is that the committee should earnestly consider the possibility."

"Then what?" asked another committee member.

Laura looked at her with as much command presence as she could muster. "Then...we make preparations."

The room erupted into loud talking between members. The chairman allowed it to continue for several seconds before once again using his gavel. "Please!" he bellowed. "This committee has maintained decorum and respect. Let's keep it that way. Director Turgis has the floor. Address your comments to her."

"With all due respect to Director Turgis," another member said to the chairman, "I would like to ask Doctor Haines if his agency supports that proposal."

The chairman looked to Laura for her consent.

Not so fast, Haines. Let me prime them for you. "Doctor Haines and the Space Agency have investigated all of this with my agency from the beginning," she said to the inquiring member. "Our two agencies have had access to all the evidence, and we reached the same conclusions about the knowable facts of the extraterrestrial visitation. In fact, it was Doctor Haines' work at the crash site that first led me to consider a return of the other craft."

Try to leave me hanging now, Haines. She turned to him and grinned. "Although Doctor Haines has his own presentation, I will yield a minute so that he can tell you this himself."

The chairman nodded at Haines to signal agreement.

"Thank you, Director Turgis," Haines said to Laura.

He fumbled with his notes before addressing the inquiring member. It was obvious to Laura that he was buying a few extra seconds by pretending he was nervous.

Now act like you're not in league with her already.

"Your question is regarding the Space Agency's agreement with Director Turgis' agency, uh, Representative—?"

"Nanchez."

"Of course. Representative Nanchez."

So smooth. Laura despised deceit, especially coming from someone who was usually a friendly colleague. *Keep your friends close, but your enemies closer, huh?*

"Yes, Doctor. Does the Space Agency support Director Turgis' proposal that the committee should consider a return visit by the ali—uh, the visitors?"

And your answer?

"After careful consideration of the evidence—especially the remnants of the spacecraft wreckage—my agency feels it would be advisable to consider all possibilities, including the potential return of the alien visitors, no matter how unlikely some might deem it to be."

Not bad so far, Laura thought. *Now you'll side with the doubters in the room, won't you?*

"I agree with what some of you are thinking—that it is more probable that the extraterrestrial visitation was a once in a lifetime event," Haines continued. "However, they have something that we want—the people that were taken aboard their craft, and we have something that they may want—a piece of their downed spacecraft."

"But what makes you so sure they would return for either reason?" asked the vice-chair. "And how do we know the people were abducted and not annihilated somehow?"

"My minute is up," Haines replied. "I will defer to Director Turgis on those questions."

Haines turned to Laura and smiled.

All you did was to side with doubt, Laura thought, smiling back. *I'm still leading this.*

"Thank you, Doctor Haines," she said. "Sir, no one in this room can do more than speculate about these things. Take the remaining portion of the spacecraft, for example. From investigating the site, it seems the vessel crashed. The section that remains was embedded in the soil and rock and somehow fused with it. The crash could have destroyed the rest of the craft. Another possibility is that the visitors used their second spacecraft to either destroy the wrecked one or to recover it. The reports submitted by General Shepherd, Colonel Richter, and our military engineers seem to show they were attempting to retrieve it."

"We already know that from reports, Director Turgis," the vice-chair noted. "I agree with that opinion. We could interpret the disappearance of exactly three feet of soil in a triangular pattern, matching the size and shape of one of the spacecraft, as the visitors scooping up the remains of the second one."

"Yes, sir, and they missed the part that was buried."

"With such technology, how could they miss it?" someone else asked.

"Again," Laura responded, "we can only speculate. They might have been rushing the retrieval. Perhaps they could not extract the other portion. Or...they left it on purpose."

"We've been over these subjects before," the chairman said. "Let's focus on why this would mean a return visit."

"Of course, sir. If the visitors made an attempt at retrieval and had to abandon their work, we can deduce they wanted it back. If they made that kind of first effort, there is a *possibility* that they'll make a second one. Likewise, if they *deliberately* left a section of the craft behind so we could find it, then it's *possible* they will return and reveal that purpose."

Several heads were nodding, which showed Laura that many of the committee members agreed with her.

"What I am proposing to the committee is that we should at least *consider* the possibility of a second visit and prepare ourselves accordingly."

Laura sat back in her chair and waited for the next round of questions, but the room remained quiet. She had made her point, and the members now needed time to contemplate what she said.

"Nicely done," General Shepherd whispered.

Laura smiled and hoped that her presentation would soon be ending.

"Are there any more questions for Director Turgis?" the chairman asked.

The members looked around at each other, shuffled papers, and shifted in their seats, which the chairman took as a collective negative reply.

"Well, then—"

"Excuse me, Mister Chairman," Representative Nanchez said. "I would like to ask the Director just one more question."

The chairman nodded his approval.

"Director Turgis, your report and your tone in this meeting display a certain amount of confidence in the idea of a return visit by the alien visitors."

She's about to put me on the spot. This is Haines' big gun. He must be worried. "Unbiased speculation better describes my position, Representative Nanchez."

Nanchez took the stealthy jab well, but now Laura had made herself a bigger target, and Nanchez was an expert in the arena of politics.

"Are you willing to back up your *speculation* with something more tangible than an educated hunch?"

"What is the Representative proposing?" Laura asked with open suspicion.

"Part of this committee's mandate is also to recommend further action. If the committee suggests making preparations for a potential return visit...is your agency willing to support such preparations with a portion of your own budget?"

The room erupted with verbal comments and criticisms. Again, the chairman allowed the disruption for a few moments before tapping his gavel. Laura still seemed to have the sympathy of a majority of the group, but a political bomb had exploded and now she needed to dig out of the debris.

During the commotion, Laura turned her chair a little, glanced over her shoulder at Alex, and saw him mouth the words *be careful.*

So, either I stay the course and risk bankrupting my agency if nothing happens, or I back down now and commit career suicide. Well done, Haines. You'd take over what's left of the agency either way.

"Director Turgis," the chairman said. "I recognize you have just been put on the spot, which was not my purpose in asking you to give a presentation or discuss the idea of a potential return of the alien visitors."

"Thank you, Mister Chairman," Laura replied. "It was inevitable that the subject of financing an uncertainty would surface."

"I do not require you to answer Representative Nanchez's question, and no one here is expecting you to commit the funds of your agency. In fact, the question is out of line. It goes beyond the scope and purpose of this committee. We are here to plan a public response first. If the committee offers limited recommendations regarding possible actions to be taken, it is a secondary priority."

"I was merely trying to ascertain the commitment level of Director Turgis and her agency," Nanchez said. "If this committee is to propose a return visit, and even make suggestions related to preparations, it would be prudent to have the *full* cooperation of the agency."

Nanchez's tactics amazed Laura. *Wow. First you drop the big bomb and then you snipe at the survivors. I'd like to show* you *full cooperation.*

"The subject is closed," the chairman declared. "Director Turgis, if there is no more to add, I will continue this meeting with some insight from General Shepherd."

"I would like to make one last comment, Mister Chairman," Laura replied. "Today marks a very historic occasion, and I would hate to think that many years from now students of history would study these events and assume political maneuvering was more important to this group of decision makers than dealing rightly with a situation that is unparalleled in our time or in any other." *Right back at you, Nanchez.*

"Agreed," the chairman said, trying to hide his admiration of Laura's political counterattack.

"I will simply restate the proposal of my agency: This committee should at least consider the possibility of a return visit and prepare ourselves accordingly. I am proud of my agency's investigation. We will support any efforts in planning for a second visitation. The Agency was created to explore possibilities, and this committee should do the same."

"Thank you, Director Turgis," the chairman said. "With that, we'll move on to other related topics. I asked General Shepherd to brief us on security and safety concerns..."

Laura stopped listening. She was too preoccupied with analyzing and predicting the political fallout from her sparring with Nanchez.

That was way too close, girl. If the chairman hadn't stepped in, I would have been forced into one of two really dangerous positions. It's a good thing this committee doesn't get the final say.

Laura spent the rest of the meeting listening to the remaining presentations while inwardly strategizing about where to take her agency's investigations next. The committee would report to higher decision makers, and Laura would be forced to accept whatever action or inaction they would mandate. Her agency would remain involved; that was a given. Whether it would lead or follow remained to be seen.

* * *

It was early evening by the time the committee adjourned. In the end, Laura had to trust that the chairman would convey her proposal to those in higher positions of authority. She should have felt satisfaction with getting this far, but annoyance with Haines denied her a sense of victory. How could he lower himself to engage in such dirty politics? Was supplanting her agency just to gain some personal fame so important? Most of the committee members had to know he was in collusion with Nanchez. He was so obvious. Still, even if his ploy failed, he might have planted seeds of doubt into the minds of key officials. Those doubts could affect the future of Laura's agency, her career, and the historic reaction to humanity's first contact with extraterrestrial, intelligent life.

"Come on, Laura," Alex said as he refilled their wineglasses. "You were brilliant and you know it."

Laura pushed her empty dinner plate away and surveyed the restaurant she and Alex had escaped to right after the meeting. It was a cozy little place within walking distance of the government building where they had spent the afternoon. The early crowd was leaving, making room for latecomers and pub-crawlers. She appreciated not recognizing anyone. For her, politicking was over for the day.

"I have to admit…I wasn't half bad," she said between sips of wine. "I wish you could have seen the look on Haines' face. He had no idea I was going to posture us like that."

"It was great," Alex agreed. "Of course he was prepared, but using the big guns doesn't always mean a guaranteed win. The attack was obvious to everyone, and even though his department wasn't seen as pulling the trigger—" Alex took a sip from his own glass. "His passive approach is going to keep him in second place."

"How so?"

"Laura, he will not lead this thing. It'll be us or Defense or some other quickly formed government entity. Haines' mistake is staying in the shadows."

"Or maybe he already knows something."

"Like what?"

"He's using Nanchez. How many others must he be playing with?"

"You're projecting too far ahead, Laura. Haines doesn't want to take over our agency. He just wants everyone working for *him*. He wants to be in the history books—himself and his people. That's all. He's not out to destroy us."

"Then why did Nanchez bring up our budget?"

Alex gulped down the rest of his wine and poured himself more.

"Like she said, she was testing your commitment."

"No, Alex. She was placing an idea in people's heads, getting them to think about money. After that, they start thinking about your position and power. 'What kind of clout does Laura's agency have? Is she ready to take the lead on something this big? What do we really know about her agency's work?' Those are what she wanted the committee to mull over. It wasn't even about our budget. She did it to cast doubt...plain and simple."

"Maybe so," Alex said. "It doesn't mean it worked, though. Anyway, you were on fire in there. You should consider a career in politics."

"This job has enough of that for me."

"True. So...what now?"

Laura finished her drink and stared at the empty glass. It was symbolic of how she felt—drained of energy and ideas.

"I guess all we can do is wait," she replied. "If the higher-ups accept that the visitors will return, we still have to see who they'll put in charge of the preparations. I'm not doing anything with that yet."

Alex poured the remaining wine into her glass.

"Well, I can't just sit behind my desk. I need to do more field work."

Laura looked at him appraisingly. She appreciated his energy and his loyalty. The wine was also helping her set aside her position as his superior and see him as her soul mate. Her heart warmed along with other parts of her body.

Why does everything have to be so complicated all the time? she wondered.

"I know that look," Alex teased. "Should I get excited...or worried?"

"Both."

"Oh, great. I'd better order us some coffee."

"One more work thing, then we'll be off the clock," Laura said. "I want to talk to the truck driver again."

"Jerry? Okay. Why?"

"His testimony is the strongest link we have to a return visit. I mean, the aliens—"

"Visitors. Remember?"

"The visitors—they actually *told* him they were coming back. It's possible he left something out of his story. Anyway, I want another chat."

"No problem. I'll set it up in the morning, and we'll meet with him somewhere."

"Thanks."

"Now, can we punch out and go home?"

Laura reached over and stroked his hand. "I thought you might take me dancing first."

"Your timing is something else." Alex understood she did not really mean dancing. "I'm gonna need some coffee if we're staying up late."

Laura looked at her watch and smiled. "Well, I am now off the clock. Order me a drink and yourself a coffee, lover. When I get back from the little girls' room, you can tell me what happens next."

Laura got up and headed across the restaurant. As she did, Alex searched for their server and his eyes stopped to rest on a booth occupied by two shifty men. They were watching Laura cross the room. When they noticed Alex staring at them, they hurried to turn their attention elsewhere. Alex understood what it all meant; he and Laura were under surveillance. He decided to keep the incident to himself so as not to ruin what he hoped would be a great evening. Being tailed was nothing new to either of them anyway, and Alex knew just how to handle it. In fact, he was looking forward to thwarting whoever set it up. The mastermind was underestimating their resources and capabilities. If it was to be a cat-and-mouse game, Alex was more than happy to play it.

Alex flagged down his server and ordered two light cocktails. Then, he sent a few discreet text messages to some colleagues that would start the contest on his end. Laura returned, and it pleased him to see the dinner and wine had loosened her up.

"Miss me?" she asked flirtatiously as she seated herself.

"Yes...and I've got quite an evening planned for you."

"Sounds exciting."

"Oh, it will be. It will be."

CHAPTER 21

Wilderness

MID-DAY: DAY 1 ON HOUROU

Eah led Jay, Tammah, and Uio along the shore of the purple ocean for a long time before finally turning toward the dunes and the vast wilderness beyond. Crossing the sandy hills was easy enough. Soft, colorful grasses and flowering shrubs were the only obstacles, and there were no sandburs to avoid. Besides the colors of the sand and the unique plant life, the dunes had familiar qualities that, like the beach, made them seem a little less foreign to Jay. That all changed, however, when the group reached the tree line and Jay stood before a wall of towering trees that warned of a very different ecosystem behind their massive trunks.

"The size of these is amazing," Jay said as he followed the others into the forest.

The trunks were at least as wide and tall as those of the great redwoods back home, and Jay guessed just one of their leaves could cover the roof of an average-sized house. He was glad there were no signs of the colossal foliage on the ground, taking it as a sign they did not shed. To walk under the expansive green canopy in constant fear of being crushed by a giant leaf would not help him to acclimate to this new world.

Eah smiled at Jay's wonderment, in her usual appreciative way. Tammah and Uio, who were understanding more of Jay's language, also expressed their pleasure with his fascination and commentary about what he was seeing.

"Is dar no such a-auh-hi-ooo-ah on Blue?" Uio asked Jay as she caressed the bark of a colossal trunk.

"Trees," Eah corrected. "On Earth."

"Ter-ee-zz," Uio said. "Errr-th." Eah and Tammah giggled at her elocution. Unflustered, Uio repeated the words, but this time with perfect pronunciation. "Trees on Earth."

"Good, Uio," Jay praised. "No, we don't have trees like this on my planet. There are some that grow almost as high and wide, though."

"Are there *many* trees?" she asked.

"Yes, but it depends on where you are. In some places, there are large forests. In others...none at all."

"Then—" A subtle glance from Eah stopped Uio from asking another question. Looking a little disheartened, she turned toward Tammah, who had taken the lead and was waiting for them all to catch up. He nodded at her as if reading an unspoken request.

Jay knew some sort of communication was going on between the three of them, and it frustrated him. He felt left out. Many of their gestures and expressions were obvious, but others were only a twitch or a shift of body position. He wondered if they were having long, non-verbal conversations while they were walking. With no way of knowing for sure, he kept talking and hoped that it would encourage them to engage with him by using words.

"So," he said, "if we're going into a jungle, won't we need some kind of protection?"

Eah tilted her head, perplexed. "Pro-teck-shin? What do you mean?"

"Sorry. I mean...it's a jungle—plants, trees, animals. Shouldn't you have clothes? Shoes? Something to protect yourself?"

Eah just stared at him, still not understanding.

Jay hid his frustration under a half-smile. "Look. The beach is one thing, but if we're going in *there,* you should cover yourselves, right?"

"Cover?" Eah asked with a puzzled expression.

"Cover," he said, patting his shirt and shorts.

Eah pushed her hair behind her body, looked down, and examined herself. Blushing, Jay directed his attention to his feet.

"And...and for feet," he said. "I don't have my shoes anymore. I can't go through a jungle with bare feet."

Tammah and Uio regarded their bodies and feet, just as confused as Eah.

"I am not unner-stan-ing," Tammah said as he considered his own uncovered state.

"I do not understand," Eah corrected.

"I do not understand," Tammah repeated. "You are not without what you need, Jay."

"Yes," Uio said. "What is missing from you?"

All three of them just stood there, staring at him.

Jay shook his head. *Are they really this naive? I can't just run through the jungle with nothing on!* "Listen," he said. "This is not *my* world. I'm not like you. At minimum, my feet are going to need some protection. What if I step on something sharp or twist my ankle?"

"Why 'not like you?'" Uio asked.

"Huh? Well...I'm not, am I?"

Uio frowned at him and put her hands on her hips. "Yes, you are."

"No, you're wrong. What I mean is...it's easy for you guys to run around like that, but I'm new here."

"You *are* like us, Jay," Uio stated. She seemed agitated now.

Jay noticed a quick nonverbal exchange between Uio and Eah. "What?" he asked Eah. "What's wrong?"

"It's okay, Jay," Eah answered. "You have all that you need. You must trust this."

"What's wrong with Uio?"

Uio glared at him while wrapping herself in her hair. If he was reading her right, she looked offended.

Eah pulled Uio aside, and the two discussed something in their language. Jay could tell Uio was questioning Eah about something he had said. He heard the word *wrong* mentioned several times.

Now what? he wondered.

As Eah talked with Uio, Tammah stepped closer to Jay and nodded his understanding.

"Tammah, what did I say to upset her?"

"Many of your words we do not understand."

"Which word?"

"The word is *wrong.*"

"Oh. That just means *not correct.*"

"Yes. Eah and I understand your meaning, but for other people on Hourou, like Uio, the...idea...means something else."

"So tell me what it means to her, then."

"It is difficult to explain. *Wrong* and *not correct* are ideas we do not think about. There is only *right*...and *correct.* Do you understand?"

"I'm catching on. That is...yes." Jay had already noticed from earlier conversations that they always seemed to focus on the positive nature of things. It was as if pointing out the opposite brought too much attention to it, and that made them uncomfortable.

"You said that Uio is *wrong,*" Tammah said. "Also, she is...confused...because you call yourself *not* when you *are.*"

"Because I said that I'm not like you?"

"Yes. But we can see you *are* like us, Jay."

"Uio must think I was insulting her."

Tammah chuckled and placed a hand on Jay's shoulder. "You cannot know what Uio thinks, can you?"

"No."

"Then why do you...guess...at what she thinks?"

Jay felt as if he was getting trapped in a giant semantic spider web. "I don't know," he admitted. "These are just things that people say. Well, on Earth anyway."

"Can you *know* the thoughts of others on Blue?" Tammah asked.

"Earth," Jay corrected. "No, we can't read each other's minds."

"Yet you guess?"

"Yes."

Jay began to understand something important about communication, not just with the alien humans, but among his own people as well.

"Why guess?" Tammah asked. "Why not see? Why not ask?"

Jay smiled as an epiphany formed in his mind. Conversation among these people was simple, be it through the use of words or gestures. There were no double meanings, no other interpretations, and no subterfuge. People on Hourou communicated just what they meant in plain forms. There was no guessing, and there was no possibility of projecting one's own perception into another's message. It was direct, genuine, refined communication. Jay had not transgressed by using incorrect words. His problem was that he was bringing contamination into the language of Hourou. He was forcing them to think in a way that was not only foreign to them but also somehow corrupt. He hoped understanding this would make it easier to converse with them.

Eah and Uio had finished their brief conversation and were watching Jay and Tammah.

"You're right, Tammah." Jay pushed his hair behind his ears and addressed all three of them. "From now on, I want you to teach me *your* words...and how to talk *without using* words. Don't try so hard to learn *my* language—my words. I want to use the words of Hourou."

Tammah and Uio smiled with appreciation, but Eah was beside herself with joy. Unable to restrain it, she launched herself at Jay and hugged him. "Aaaaaah-saa-eh-saa-iiiioo-hah-eeeeah-eh-seeee, Jay," she whispered into his ear. "You see? You *are* like us."

"Uh...yeah." Jay struggled to keep his balance, unsure what to do with his hands, while she continued her spirited embrace. His awkwardness caused Tammah and Uio to burst into hysterical laughter. They had good reason; Jay's embarrassment was obvious as he fumbled with how to return the hug of a euphoric, naked girl. He regained his footing and gave in, returning the hug and careful to appear neither overly eager nor too shy. To ease his discomfort, Eah pulled back and their eyes met, causing yet another delicate moment as he fought against the dizziness that a deep look into her eyes could cause. Eah seemed to remember it, too, so she released him and stepped backward.

After a warning glare from Eah, Tammah and Uio stopped laughing and Tammah motioned toward the jungle, signaling them all to resume their hike. He took the lead again while Uio held back to take up the rear. Jay was glad to be behind Eah so he could study her movements for signs of communication. She seemed like her usual self, but he noticed a slight spring in her step that had not been there before she hugged him.

I'm imagining things, he thought. *Or maybe not reading her right.* He decided her hug resulted from over-excitement—a friendly gesture. *So why am I still grinning about it like a silly teenager?* He chuckled at his question and looked behind him at Uio. She winked, as if she knew what he was thinking.

These three are amazing to be around. Funny…I had a tough time making friends back home. It's hard to trust people when they always let you down. Things are different here, though. Different with them.

Jay stumbled as he stepped over a protruding tree root, and Uio gave him a gentle nudge to keep him from falling.

"Thanks for the assist," he said.

"You are safe with us, Jay," Uio responded with another wink.

"Thanks." Jay wanted to believe her. He wanted to let himself trust these three and to be their friend.

Maybe I had to come all the way here to learn how to trust again.

* * *

As they traveled deeper into the jungle, wonderment over the enchanting nature of Hourou lessened Jay's concern about protection. Instead of threats and dangers, he discovered a pristine environment that invited exploration. The air was fragrant, and despite the towering trees and giant plants surrounding him, a light breeze caressed his skin. It was as if the jungle itself was exhaling pure, life-giving oxygen as he passed through its splendor.

Some of the vegetation resembled that of Earth, but some also looked quite alien to his eyes. The shorter leaf-bearing trees reminded him of palms, bamboo, and flowering bushes, as found in the tropics. Others, though, were like giant mushrooms or sea vegetation. Most were green, but many had colors he had never seen, as if from an other-worldly palette.

Jay paused to get a better look at one plant that was radiating light—a white, fuzzy, man-sized mushroom topped with an upside-down cap. Eah noticed he had stopped to inspect it, so she joined him while Tammah and Uio continued on ahead.

"This is amazing," Jay said. "It's lit up like a lamp."

"We call it ah-ho-rho-to-Ahey," Eah explained. "That means *light inside from Ahey*. At night, we walk by their light. They show—mark?—yes, mark paths."

"How do they create light?"

Eah reached out and stroked the fuzzy hair-like filaments that covered the plant. At her touch, they flickered in multiple colors.

"It changes colors, too?" Jay asked.

Eah gestured for him to touch it, so he traced a line across its surface with his finger. A row of colored light followed the trail through the filaments. "This is amazing! It's *making* its own light."

"Ahey fills it with light, so Hourou sees the light of Ahey always," Eah said.

Jay appreciated her supernatural description, but he wondered about the scientific one.

"It...collects and holds light," she explained. "Not reflects light, but keeps light."

"Then not phosphorescence—or glowing—but storage of energy that is converted into light by the plant. It's like a giant flashlight."

"Flash-light?" Eah asked.

"A flashlight is a small device for putting light in dark places. Power comes from batteries, and when you switch it on, electricity moves into a little bulb, and it emits light."

Eah mulled over Jay's description for a few moments while they both toyed with the plant's filaments. "I do not understand the flashlight-de-vice, but the meaning is similar, yes..." She seemed reluctant to ask a question.

"There's something you want to ask," Jay said, interpreting her subtle body language.

Eah nodded. Jay had been noticing that she and her people were very willing to tell him about themselves and their planet, but they hesitated in asking questions about Earth.

"Is it about plants?" he asked.

Eah nodded and smiled.

"Ask me," Jay prompted, relieved that the subject would not be something uncomfortable.

"Do you have ah-ho-rho-to-Ahey on Earth?"

"This plant? No. We have some strange phosphorescent plants, but nothing like this."

Eah tried to hide a brief frown, but Jay picked up on it. He was learning.

"That disappoints you?" he asked.

Eah avoided his stare while she toyed with the plant. "Dis-appoints?"

"Makes you sad. You were expecting something better."

"Yes," she agreed. "Expecting and being made sad. But not sad for Eah—me—or Hourou, but sad for Jay and Earth."

"I understand. But we have other amazing plants and things on Earth. Still, they don't compare to what I've seen here so far."

Jay could tell by the sudden change in Eah's expression that his comment pleased her. With wide eyes and an excited grin, she also seemed to be having a realization.

"You are enjoying Hourou!"

"Um...yes...so far," Jay answered. "This is all strange for me, Eah. The more I learn, though, the better I feel about it."

"I will teach you more. Come."

With that, Eah turned away and headed in the direction Tammah and Uio had taken. Jay followed her, puzzled yet curious. When they caught up to the others, he stopped short when he saw what they were doing. There, along a wide path of red and blue moss, Tammah was wrestling with what appeared to be a small dinosaur. Uio stood by laughing while she fed something to six more of the creatures crowding around her.

The animals were reptilian, standing on two muscular legs and having two shorter fore limbs with five-fingered hands. Their feet also had five digits and seemed to have retractable claws. On their small lizard-like heads was a ridge of bumps that extended down their backs to the base of a long tail. They stood about waist-high, no taller than the largest breed of dog back on Earth, and they played with Tammah and Uio like domesticated pets.

When Eah realized Jay was no longer right behind her, she turned and beckoned him to approach. "Come, Jay!" she called, trying to be heard over the odd squealing of the lizards and the laughter of Tammah and Uio. "They are *ohri*. They always want to play."

One creature ran over to Eah and nudged her hand with its head, as if it was asking her for a petting. She pushed her hair behind her and obliged by crouching down in front of it and cradling its face. While she spoke to it in soothing tones, she rubbed its smooth, leathery skin and giggled at its affectionate responses.

Jay remained frozen in place. He wanted to join Eah, but he was also afraid of how the animals might react to a stranger.

"It is okay, Jay," Eah said. "The ohri will accept you."

In a few moments, Jay's curiosity overcame his fear, so he stepped closer to Eah and the ohri. It was enjoying her attention and ignored his approach. She reached for Jay's hand and placed it on the ohri's head.

"Well, he seems to be alright with me touching him," Jay said, petting the animal.

"Eeee-saah—of course."

"He's just like a little dinosaur on Earth."

"You have ohri there?"

"Not anymore, no. There were, though, many years ago."

"Where did they go?"

Jay stroked the animal's tough skin, following Eah's example. Her delicate white hand was a stark contrast against its dark brown and green stripes.

"They became extinct," he answered, hoping it would not sadden her. "We don't know why they all died off. People have theories. Some say there was a great catastrophe that killed them. Others say we hunted them to extinction. No one knows, though."

Eah considered what he said and looked confused. "I do not know some of those words."

"Extinct means—"

"It's okay, Jay. That there once were ohri on Earth and now no more I understand. It is enough."

"Oh. Okay." Jay redirected the conversation to the subject of ohri on Hourou. "So, these ohri seem harmless enough. Tammah isn't worried about getting hurt."

Tammah had just finished his wrestling bout with one of the larger animals and allowed it to run over to Uio to be fed.

"Getting hurt?" Eah asked with a chuckle. "No, there is no hurt in play. Just play. Ohri know this."

"What is Uio feeding them?"

Eah stood from her crouched position and pushed the ohri toward Uio.

"Wooo-rooo-too," she answered. "You say fruit, or plants. The ohri climb the trees for it, but Uio has done it for them. Sometimes, *mahtee* drop them for the ohri as well."

"Mahtee?"

"You will see them as we go."

Eah glanced at Tammah and he turned his attention to her as if she had called his name aloud. They looked at each other for a moment. Then Tammah nodded and moved toward Uio, waving off the ohri. Jay assumed it was time to be moving on again.

* * *

Jay had no way of measuring time other than by his own internal clock and physical fatigue. If he was back home, it would certainly be nighttime by now. His legs told him he must have walked for many miles since leaving the beach. Although he felt strong here, his body was reminding him of its limitations.

Throughout their journey, Eah was quite attentive to his needs, offering to stop and rest, showing him how to find food and fresh water in the jungle, and teaching him the names of the plants and animals they encountered. After a while, Jay stopped asking questions because most of what he saw was so foreign. Instead, he listened and observed while enjoying the sound of Eah's exotic voice and language.

Soon, Jay had to deal with the uncomfortable business of needing to relieve himself, having been well-hydrated and fed throughout the day. He waited for as long as he could, but reached a point where he had to bring up the troublesome matter. When he communicated his need, he learned an important lesson about how the people of Hourou viewed the natural processes of the body.

His three new friends understood what Jay needed to do, despite his verbal stumbling and awkwardness. With impassive expressions, they led him away from the moss-covered path they had been following and into a sunny glade. Blue plants, standing about chest-high and resembling giant flower blossoms, filled the open space. Eah, Tammah, and Uio each chose a separate flower and pressed their bodies through the huge leaves—or petals—until the plant enclosed them. Jay continued to observe until, to his great embarrassment, he realized they were using the giant flowers as vessels for elimination.

He singled out his own giant flower and pushed through the petals to the open center. Inside, there were natural receptacles and basins at varying heights. The duty of the receptacles was clear enough, and he assumed the basins, which were filled with clear water, were for rinsing hands. Large bulbs also hung near Jay's feet from thick stems. He squeezed one, and it shot out a long squirt of fragrant water like a bidet.

I'm about to use a giant flower as a toilet, he thought. *Can this planet get any stranger?*

Adding to his embarrassment, he noted that the flowers Eah, Tammah, and Uio chose were uncomfortably close to his own. Even crouching down, he could see glimpses of their white skin between the giant petals. To Jay, bathrooms, no matter what the type, should afford privacy. He usually tried to avoid using public restrooms back home, yet here he was doing the deed out in the open and in mixed company.

Physical need defeated his self-consciousness. It helped that his three new friends paid no attention to him. For them, there was no shame, embarrassment, silliness, or requirement for much privacy. They treated the situation and environment as if it was all normal and acceptable. As difficult as it was for Jay, he did his best to do the same.

Later, as they continued their trek through the jungle, Jay got up enough nerve to question Eah about the natural lavatories. She told him the giant flowers grew all over Hourou and that their purpose was to remove debris from the environment. Through internal processes, they broke down excreta and decaying matter, converted it to useful minerals and nutrients, and deposited them back into the soil through a networked root system.

Jay thought about how it was a reverse process compared to what he knew about plants on Earth. Those extracted what they needed from the ground and used it to grow. On Hourou, this plant received waste from the environment and turned it into sustenance for other ones, sending it to them through its own roots. In addition, it produced a liquid antiseptic. Eah said it was one of only a few plants on Hourou that was not suitable to consume.

"Speaking of eating," Jay said as they traversed a bridge of fallen logs, "I notice our meals have been only fruits and plants. It's okay. I mean, I've met some vegetarians back home—but is that all you eat here?"

"There is something else besides plants?" Uio asked as she leaped from log to log.

"Well...what about meat?"

"What is mee-eet? Tammah asked.

Jay considered explaining it, but from what he had seen on Hourou so far, animals were like beloved pets. He was not sure that he wanted to talk about eating them on a planet of probable vegans.

"Never mind," he answered. "We just have...more variety. That's all."

Eah eyed him as if suspecting he was trying to use tact.

This girl's smart, Jay thought. *Not only can she read me like a book, but she's also learning my language really fast.*

His appreciative expression must have given his thoughts away, because Eah smiled like a girl that had just been flattered. He held her gaze. *Can you read my mind? I hope not, because a lot of what goes on in here might chase you off. Let's test it: I think you're the most beautiful thing I've ever seen.*

Eah stared into his eyes but did not respond.

No reaction, huh? So mind reading is out. That's good. I prefer the usual boy-girl mysteries.

Eah grinned, showing Jay that something in his facial expression had sent some sort of message. Rather than turning away, though, he kept studying her, hoping she was enjoying his attention.

Not sure what I'm doing, he thought, *but your communication is certainly...interesting.*

Uio interrupted the pleasant moment by coming alongside Jay and playfully bumping into him. "Almost all plants on Hourou have parts to eat."

"Huh? Oh...yeah," Jay said. "Eah explained that."

"All life on Hourou eats plants."

"You're getting better and better at using my language, Uio."

"Thank you, Jay." Now it was Uio's turn to be flattered.

Some sort of unspoken message went back and forth between Tammah and Eah. Uio must have picked up on it because she halted, turned toward them, pushed her hair behind her body, and stood glaring at them with her hands on her hips.

Uh-oh, Jay thought. *What's* this *all about?*

Eah and Tammah laughed, and soon Uio did as well.

They were teasing her about my compliment, Jay guessed. *I wonder if...* As a test, he focused his thoughts on communicating with Uio and allowed his mind to place the right expression, however slight, into his body language. *It's okay, Uio. Don't let them tease you.*

Uio snapped her head toward Jay in surprise, and Eah and Tammah did likewise.

It worked. They all understood me.

Uio sent him an appreciative signal. *Thank you.*

The exchange dumbfounded Tammah, but Eah beamed with delight. Jay tried to interpret her expression, but he could not determine if her excitement was about his growing skills...or something else.

* * *

By the time evening arrived, journeying through the alien jungle had exhausted Jay. Although the paths were easy to navigate, his new friends often led him through areas of the wood that required a good amount of athleticism. Whether swinging on thin vines over deep ravines, climbing through towering trees, or swimming across rivers and small lakes, Jay overcame every challenge. But now his body was tired; his feet and legs ached, and muscles he did not even know he had were begging him to rest.

The mental challenges had been just as strenuous. Throughout the day, Eah taught him words for what he was seeing and doing, but most of them were too hard for him to pronounce. Likewise, the subtle inflections and modulations of the language were complex and difficult for him to imitate.

Eah did her best to add consonant sounds to the words Jay could not repeat. This helped him to say them in ways the three Hourou natives could understand. Eah also tried to exaggerate her physical gestures and signals so Jay could better interpret those unspoken parts of her language. Sometimes, he astonished them with his quick learning. At other times, his awkward attempts provided them all with comical entertainment.

Their expedition created quite a bond between the four young adults. Tammah and Uio put aside competing with one another to help Eah in educating Jay. Their restraint further exposed the deep affection they had for each other. Though they tried to temper their true feelings, it was obvious they were in love. That seemed to please Eah very much. Jay, likewise, hoped that a mating—a dyad—between the two would happen. He guessed their extreme competition was just a false front, only a childish device to conceal what they truly felt. It was endearing to Jay. First, because he could relate to their subterfuge, and second because he was seeing something they could not—that they had much more in common than either realized.

Then there was the bond between Jay and Eah. Something was changing with them, too. He no longer felt like a project or a special pet. Eah's interest in educating him went deeper than a challenge or simple curiosity. Jay caught her studying him a lot, especially his reactions to Tammah and Uio's intimate affections. Why would that be important?

Though Eah was still a mystery to him, Jay enjoyed her company. By day's end, he did not even think of her physical appearance as alien any-more. Her flawless iridescent white skin, her large and bright green eyes, and her long blue-speckled black hair were quite befitting. He admired the strength and athleticism of her perfectly proportioned frame, with its lean pronounced muscles and hourglass shape. Jay had never seen a woman that was anything like her. She seemed to represent all woman-hood in one body—the ultimate female archetype.

Eah had a true natural beauty that would accept nothing less than admiration. Jay immediately felt ashamed if his thoughts tried to go in an unchaste direction. This was not because he was under some strange enchantment or spell. Rather, Eah possessed an inherent dignity that was even more glorious than her outward beauty. She was like royalty—to be admired, adored, and honored.

During that long day, Jay discovered much about Eah's personality and overall character. She was childlike in her innocence and curiosity, yet wise, like someone who had already lived a full life. She never acted anxious about anything, but exuded a calm confidence in everything she said and did. The only exception was in how she related to Jay. He detected less certainty there and a mysterious restraint, as if she was sometimes unsure how to act around him. He attributed this to the fact they were from different planets and cultures, but he also suspected there was something more to it.

Jay knew he was lousy at establishing interpersonal relations. He preferred to be a loner, having only a few friends. As for girls, he made it through the awkward teenage years unscathed by immature relationships. He dated a little and even kept a girlfriend through his senior year of schooling. Still, he was far from being an expert in understanding the complexity of the fairer sex. Love was a great curiosity, but he was ever cautious about diving in too deep.

To Jay, Eah's mysterious side was something to which he could better relate. He had always preferred the company of girls who were different. Eah was the ultimate in unusual females. To him, she was also the ultimate enigma—open, honest, and sincere, yet keeping a part of her inner self hidden and reserved. She was not unapproachable or withdrawn. Quite the opposite, she often embarrassed Jay with her openness and uninhibited nature. Back on Earth, she would have been an easy target for guys with no scruples, but Jay knew Eah was no conquest or prize to be won. She was a special treasure box that needed to be unpacked slowly by someone with the highest levels of appreciation and purity, and each rich jewel discovered should be cherished and cared for with honor.

As he followed Eah through the ethereal jungle, he became more curious about the hidden side of her.

She's still an alien, he thought. *No, she's* human. *That's been established...and then some. She's human alright, but she's an alien human. Still, shouldn't human be human even if you're a human on a different planet? I still can't believe I'm thinking about these things!*

Jay struggled with his thoughts throughout the evening as his expedition walked in silence. No longer squeamish about gazing for too long at Eah, Uio, or Tammah, he watched them walk ahead of him with admiration and camaraderie. Somehow, despite the strange circumstances, the alien environment, and his own awkwardness and distrust, Jay had made friends that day. He liked everything about them. They accepted him with no conditions, and he was feeling the same way toward them.

What about Eah? he asked himself, tracking her white body as it dodged in and out of the jungle's underbrush. *I'm not dense; she likes me. How in the world did* that *happen?*

Ahead of him, Eah turned around to make sure he was not falling too far behind. When she spotted him, she smiled, and he recognized in her expression an affection that both excited and confounded him.

So...do you like her, *Jay?* He wondered.

Eah pushed her hair behind her body, and Jay made the same motion as he approached her.

Like I said, he answered himself. *I'm not dense. She's gorgeous. Actually, she's absolutely perfect. Of course I like her. But...*

Eah reached out and took hold of Jay's hand. "We will stop here for the night."

Jay scanned the area and noticed no special reason to make it into a campsite. There was no shelter, no protection, no nearby water, and no strategic positioning. It was just a random spot along the mossy path they had been following through the woods.

"Okay," he said. "Well, I guess we can use branches to build some shelters and get a fire started."

"Tammah and Uio will gather what we need," Eah said as she sat at the moss-covered base of a giant tree. "Sit and rest, Jay." She patted a spot next to her on the ground and leaned back against the smooth trunk.

"I can help," Jay said, plopping himself down beside her. "I know a lot about wilderness survival. In fact, I was on a camping trip when your ship took me in—"

Jay stopped at the thought. It seemed like a week had passed since he had been running through dark fields with Cody, chasing after a mysterious flying aircraft. How long had he really been gone? It was only his first day on Hourou, yet his internal clock made it feel like he had been away from Earth for many days. He glanced at Eah. She had her eyes closed and sat as if meditating. Jay let out a huff and leaned back against the tree, looking past the high canopy above into the darkening sky. The first stars were already becoming visible as the light changed.

Those stars aren't even in my galaxy, he thought with a mix of wonder and trepidation. *Neither am I.*

He felt Eah's warm fingers as they located his hand and entwined with his own.

She sure likes to hold hands, he thought, studying how her white skin contrasted against his own. *Best not make too much out of it. I see Tammah and Uio doing it a lot, too. Maybe it's just a friend-thing here...or more of their physical communication.*

When Jay looked up, Eah was gazing at him. Warmth coursed through his body as their eyes met. He swallowed hard, admiring the flawless features of her face. Her stare made him nervous, but it also excited him in ways he was not ready to permit.

Eah's lips parted, and she spoke in a whisper. "Jay, I—"

Before she could continue, Uio pushed through some tall undergrowth nearby and dumped an armful of what looked like soft, raw cotton at their feet.

"Rey-heee-ah, Eah?" she asked Eah with a tone Jay interpreted as a tease.

Eah smiled at her and released Jay's hand. "Uio seh-lay-ooo, ei-os-fooo-es-ah-mah oy-aaaaaaa-oui."

"Ah." Uio considered Jay. Her expression showed she did not believe whatever Eah had just said. "Seh, Jay," she said to him with a sly grin.

Eah stuck her foot out and kicked some of the cotton into the air toward Uio. "Eeeeee-eh, Uio!"

Laughing, Uio turned and disappeared into the woods.

"What was that about?" Jay asked as he picked up some of the cotton and rolled it between his fingers. Their intimate moment passed, and he was not sure if he regretted it or if he was relieved.

Eah rose. As she watched Uio leave, she slowly wrapped herself in her hair.

The hair thing means frustration or some other discomfort, Jay thought. *I've seen that before.* "You okay?" he asked as he stood.

"Yes, yes," she said dismissively. "Uio es tee-neee-hah."

"Sorry?"

"Oh. Tee-neee-hah means to..."

"To tease? Like joking in fun?"

"Perhaps." She seemed flustered. "Come. I will show you camping on Hourou." Kneeling, she gathered up the cotton-like material. Jay helped her, smiling as he noted how much humanness he was now seeing in his new friends.

"So," he said, hoping to recapture a relaxing mood, "I take it this is to use as bedding."

"Yes. Uio will bring more, but when you put water on it, the *meeroh*...es-pans?"

"Expands."

"The meeroh expands, and it is very soft." She spread some in a circle at the base of a glowing lantern plant.

"Where will we get the water?" Jay asked.

"Here," Tammah answered, appearing from the woods. He was carrying an armload of large pink balls. After dumping them onto the ground, he chose one for himself and tossed another to Jay.

It was a coconut-like fruit. Jay even heard liquid splashing from within the hard, fibrous shell when he shook it. "How do I open it?"

Tammah showed him by locating a dark spot and pushing his thumb through it to create a hole. Jay did likewise, but found it difficult to penetrate the shell. Tammah's thumbs must have been much stronger than his own. With a little effort, though, Jay made an opening and waited for further instruction.

Tammah handed his fruit to Eah, and she sprinkled some of its liquid onto the meeroh. In seconds, the cottony fibers expanded, combining and forming a fluffy mat. Amazed, Jay walked over and poked at it with his toe.

Just like a thick, down comforter.

Uio returned with more meeroh and spread it around the mat's perimeter. Eah sprinkled more liquid, and the added meeroh combined with the mat, enlarging it to accommodate four bodies. Satisfied, Eah drank from the fruit and handed it to Jay.

Jay took a sip and smiled. "It tastes just like coconut water back home."

"Co-co-noot?" Uio asked.

"Co-co-nut," Jay corrected. "It's a fruit on Earth much like this one."

"Say Soso-naaah-ha," Uio said, instructing him.

"Sosonah-ha."

"Good! Soso-naaah-ha is good for many things on Hourou."

"I see."

"Yes?"

"I mean...I understand."

Uio chuckled, grabbed Jay's hand, and pulled him toward her. "Come! We will find food now."

"Umm..." Jay shot a questioning look at Eah, but she just smiled and nodded, evidently comfortable sharing him. "Well...okay."

Uio dragged him away from the path and through the surrounding underbrush. She was much less gentle than Eah, and her grip was strong and persistent. She let go of his hand when they reached another natural moss-covered trail that was perpendicular to the one they had left.

"We will follow this," she said, breaking into a trot. "It leads to open space."

"Have you been here before, then?"

"Ehe—No. These are my first steps in this place."

"What about Tammah and Eah?"

"Ehe."

"Then how do you know there's an open space nearby?"

Uio slowed her pace and pointed at the multi-colored moss under their feet. "The *eeeeemoo.*"

"E-moo?"

"Yes. The eeeeemoo is...many colored. It brings light to the...what you call...jun-gel?"

"Jungle."

"Yes, jungle. And the light comes from the open space."

"I don't understand. It's a different color? Or does light travel through the eeeeemoo?"

Uio waved him on as she trotted away. Jay assumed she was just in a hurry to get to the open space, since the jungle was darkening. She probably wanted to collect their food and return to Eah and Tammah before nightfall.

Their path, which had twisted into a glowing trail of moss, ended at a wide glade filled with green knee-high grass and dotted with clumps of trees. Jay stopped short before he left the tree line of the jungle. Even in the twilight, he could make out large shapes crossing between the groups of trees.

"Uio, wait!" he called out as loudly as he dared. "Something else is out there!"

Uio paused and scanned the area, waiting for Jay to catch up.

"I see things moving around," he said as he came alongside her.

"Yes, others come here to feed...like us," she whispered.

"You mean your people?"

"No." Uio crouched in the grass and tugged on Jay's arm, signaling for him to get down. "We are still far from them."

"Then who is here?"

Uio began searching the surrounding area for something.

"What are you looking for?"

She did not answer, but took hold of his hand and led him toward a spot several feet away. There, the grass was flattened, as if by something enormous. Uio mumbled in her language while watching the far end of the glade.

"Are these...footprints?" Jay asked. "If they are, I don't think I want to see what made them."

Uio stood and pointed to the closest copse of trees. "Come! We will go there, Jay!"

Jay needed no further prompting, nor did he have to strain to keep up with Uio. In a dash, they ran straight for the nearest thicket, plowing through the grass like a blast of wind. When they reached the first tree, Uio stopped and shoved Jay against its trunk.

"Wait," she said. In haste, she gathered her hair and twisted it into a long braid.

Jay averted his eyes, feigning a protective sweep of the surrounding area. For the first time, he noted similarities between Uio's body and that of Eah, and the idea of it unsettled him. *If they're not biological sisters,* he wondered, *why do they look so much alike? And...whoa...what am I staring at here?*

"What?" Uio asked, noticing his sudden discomfort. She was now wrapping the long braid around her neck like a scarf, apparently to keep it out of her way.

"Huh? Oh...nothing. So...what are we going to do?"

"You will lift me there," she said, pointing into the tree.

Jay looked up at the tree's lowest row of branches. They seemed strong enough, but Uio would have to be standing on his shoulders to reach them. The prospect of struggling to get her up there embarrassed him. "Sure...okay." He was no stranger to climbing, but this was the first time he was about to be doing it with a girl—a beautiful and very naked one. "I thought I was getting over this," he mumbled, examining the tree.

"What?"

"Nothing." Uio just stood there, waiting for him to do something, so he clumsily put his hands on her waist. "So, um, I'll just pick you up and—"

"Down!"

"What?"

Uio started laughing, then covered her mouth as if to hush herself. "You. Down."

"I, uh, don't understand."

She pointed to the base of the tree and then bent over as a demonstration.

Act as a step stool, Jay reasoned. *Of course.* He got down on his hands and knees. The moss under him was soft, but he was sore from the day's activities and hoped Uio was light.

She stepped onto his back, careful and balanced. "Up!"

Jay pushed himself to a kneeling position, while Uio, using the tree trunk to steady herself, walked up his back.

"Up!" she repeated, standing on his shoulders and grasping them with her toes.

Jay grabbed the tree and pulled himself upward until he was standing, marveling that he still had the strength. "Now what?" he asked, but Uio was already climbing onto a low branch. Jay backed up a bit and watched her scurry into the tree. "You look like a tall white monkey," he called up to her.

"What? What is mon-kee?" With her limbs spread wide, she grasped different branches in a simian-like pose that made Jay laugh. "I look like Uio, yes?"

Jay gazed up at her for a long moment and felt himself blush. *Change the subject, Jay,* he warned himself, *and mind your eyes.* "Yes, you look like Uio," he said. "I was just joking."

"Jook-ing?"

"Forget it! What do we do next?"

Uio shot him a playful smile before continuing her climb. As she disappeared into the darkness of its branches, he stopped watching her and began searching the glade for signs of movement. Other than a breeze blowing through the grass and trees, there was little sound out there. He looked toward the other small clumps of trees and saw definite shapes moving around them. After his eyes adjusted to the dimming light, Jay recognized they were very large animals lumbering in the other groves.

"Hey, Uio!" He maneuvered himself behind the tree. The trunk was not much thicker than his body, but at least it hid him. Uio did not answer. He could hear her, though, rustling in the leaves and grunting. "Are you okay up there? I could try to come up—"

A soft thump interrupted him. Alarmed, Jay spun around and saw that it was only a small, fruit-laden branch Uio had broken off and dropped to the ground. While she continued her work above, he went to examine its clusters of purple berries. Crushed ones underneath gave off a pleasing yet incomparable fragrance. He grabbed the branch by its broken end and walked backwards, dragging it closer to the safety of the tree's trunk. When his back bumped into something large and soft, he dropped the branch and stood frozen in place.

I got confused in the darkness. I'm not under the tree anymore. He turned to face what he hoped was a different tree, but found himself staring at a giant leg. "Uh...Uio!"

Behind him and from atop the tree, Uio was laughing. "Stay, Jay!" She rustled around in the leaves and said soothing words in her language.

Jay backed away from the massive limb with caution. As he did, he looked up and took in the entire form of its owner. "Another dinosaur," he said out loud to himself. "Like an Apatosaurus."

The animal stood on four thick legs and its body was as large as a full-grown elephant. A small lizard-like head and a long neck extended into the tree. At the other end was an equally long tail. To Jay, it indeed resembled the famous Earth dinosaur Apatosaurus. Unlike the creature depicted in textbooks and movies, however, this one's shape was proportionate and its skin was bright with a mix of vibrant colors.

"Jay, stay!" Uio repeated from somewhere in the treetop.

"I'd rather not get stepped on down here, Uio." He glanced up at the tree and caught glimpses of her white form as she moved across a large branch toward the creature. When she was as far out as she dared go, she reached out and coaxed the beast to draw closer. It responded by sticking its head and neck further into the tree. "Uio, are you...?"

Uio leapt from her branch to the animal's neck, laughing and rubbing the top of its head as if it was a pet. The big lizard responded with a deep rumbling groan and its tail flicked back and forth behind it.

Okay, so it's another friendly animal, Jay thought, relieved. Mustering his courage, he stepped closer. "Can I touch it?" he called up to Uio.

"Yes! Yes!"

He reached out and rubbed its leg. The skin was thick and leather-like, but also soft and dry. Submissive, the beast just waited there, accepting their caresses and appreciation with occasional moans. After a few moments, Uio said something, and it slowly lowered its head toward the ground so she could slide off its neck. Once back on the ground, she ran over to Jay and hugged him from behind while he continued to stroke the animal's leg.

"You are not afraid, Jay!" Sensing his discomfort from her embrace, she giggled and released him. "Or maybe only afraid of people."

Jay turned around to face her, startled by her comment. He smirked as if she was teasing him again, but her eyes told him that avoidance would not work. Behind him, the creature moved away, its giant feet thumping in the grass. "Wow," he said with a sigh. "You really nailed me."

"Nailed?"

"I mean...you're right about me. All day long, you, Eah, Tammah—you've all been able to understand things about me, even without us knowing each other's languages very well. I'm glad, but I—"

"You desire to do the same."

"Well...yeah. But it's not as easy for me."

"There is a thing said on parts of Hourou: A closed hand receives no more."

"What does that mean?"

"Like the hand, Jay, you must be open to receive."

"Do you think I'm a closed hand, then?"

Uio stared at the ground, her white toes toying with the grass as she considered his question. "You are a hand that is always opening and closing. Being that way...you receive little."

"I understand. I have to be more open. That's kind of tough for me, though."

Uio reached out and took his hand, caressing it with her strong fingers. When Jay returned the gesture, she turned his palm to face up. "Like this hand," she said, "stay open, Jay. There is so much happening all around you—so much to receive." She placed her free hand over Jay's heart. "But you will not if *this* hand closes."

Jay did not know how to respond, so he just nodded. Pleased with his reaction, Uio smiled, gave him a playful tap on the chest, and then hurried back to the tree.

"Come. We will return to Eah and Tammah."

Jay joined her in picking up the branches she had broken off.

"These smell good."

"Yes, you will make Eah happy with these," she said as a tease.

"What are you talking about?"

Uio giggled and handed him some branches to carry. "Eah likes this fruit. It is good for the body, but it also warms the insides—makes you happy."

"So...it's also an intoxicant?"

Uio smirked, reminding Jay of his foreign words.

"Sorry. It relaxes you, then?"

"Yes...but also happy." She crossed her arms over her chest in a self-hug and swayed her hips a little. Jay knew it could not have been a suggestive expression. He had never seen her people do anything provocative. "Get it, Jay?" She was trying to explain something about the fruit, but she was also teasing him again.

"You know...sometimes you sound and act very much like an Earth girl, Uio."

She laughed, picked up her pile of branches, and jogged toward the path of glowing moss that had led them to the glade. She was still laughing when she disappeared into the jungle. Jay ran to catch up, convinced that Uio had some ulterior motive in finding the mysterious fruit.

Wise like a mature woman and then she turns back into a young girl, he thought with amusement. *Be an open hand, Jay. Be an open hand.*

* * *

By the time Jay and Uio returned to the makeshift campsite, Eah and Tammah had prepared a meal of various berries, nuts, and fruits they had collected. They filled four wooden bowls—round pieces of tree bark—and arranged them on the mat along with some pink coconuts. Tammah was sitting close to the lantern plant, making designs in its glowing filaments and watching as its light made multi-colored dots on the surrounding trees. To Jay, the effect was like a disco ball in a nightclub.

Eah reclined nearby, staring into the jungle canopy and lost in thought. She jumped to her feet when she saw Jay and Uio lay their branches on the mat. "Soh hasah keerehpee!" she said to Uio, pleased with the addition to their meal.

"Ae," Uio replied. "Ooooo ai-i-ci-uh-iii-eeee-ah-oi Jay sheh-sah."

Tammah crawled over to the branches and chuckled as he plucked off berries and added some to each bowl.

"Okay. I heard my name in there," Jay said to Uio.

Eah sat back down and answered for Uio. "She wonders if you will like the *keerehpee*." Eah seemed a little embarrassed, so Jay assumed Uio's comment was also another tease.

"I'm sure I will," he said to Uio with a wink. "So...what's the secret? This keerehpee is a special fruit?"

Uio just giggled through a sly smile and sat down next to Tammah.

"We say it is like a *slow wind*," Eah explained. "Keerehpee calms the body and also the mind. It is...pleasant."

"Sounds good to me."

Eah smiled and motioned for Jay to sit with her on the mat while Tammah handed out the food and drink. She sat cross-legged, placing the large bowl in her lap, and Jay did likewise.

"Eat this one first," Uio said to Jay as she held up a keerehpee.

Jay watched as she peeled back its skin and bit into the flesh, then he followed her example. The skin was thick and zesty like that of a lemon. Inside, it was juicy with the consistency and flavor of a grape. After eating just one of the keerehpee, Jay understood what Eah meant by *pleasant*. The fruit had an intoxicating effect, but not in a way that dulled the senses. Instead, it cleared and calmed his thinking while stimulating his physical perception.

Though Tammah, Uio, and Eah talked together in their language while they ate, Jay did not feel left out. He enjoyed listening to their voices and challenged himself to recognize words in their conversation that he already knew. By the time he finished his meal, the surrounding jungle was dark with the night. The lantern plant in the center of their campsite gave off just enough light to illuminate the immediate area. Further into the trees, Jay could see other lantern plants and patches of glowing pastel mosses. Currents of exotic fragrances filled the air. Above him and beyond the high canopy, stars filled the cloudless sky. It was a true dreamworld, yet in it he remained lucid and aroused, sensing everything.

Jay liked how the soft light from the lantern plant made the white bodies of his friends seem to glow. He took a last gulp of his drink and decided to remove his tattered and dirty shirt.

"Jay yoi aaaaaah sah yee-muh-ssssah!" Uio said to Eah and Tammah after examining Jay's bare torso.

Tammah poked her in the ribs with his elbow, eliciting a loud yelp. "Hee-ah-ma iiee ooh, Uio." He scooted away as if daring her to retaliate.

Uio tossed aside her bowl and reached for his leg, preventing an escape. Then she crawled to him and they began wrestling on the moss mat.

"Eeeeee-eh!" Eah said. Their silly contest was too entertaining to interrupt, so she turned her warning into coaching. "Uio...Yah-yoi oh ooooooo-eh!" She looked at Jay and they both chuckled.

Jay became lightheaded and wondered if it was being caused by Eah's eyes, the keerehpee, or fatigue. He decided it was the berries, since he was also quite stimulated. As he became emboldened by the effect, he allowed his eyes to linger, admiring the way the colored light of the lantern plant played across Eah's body.

Eah did not seem to mind Jay's flattering attention. While he gazed at her, she even scooted closer and turned so he could see more of her. Both enjoyed the moment until the sound of Uio kicking over a bowl interrupted it.

Jay smiled and stretched out his legs, only then realizing that Eah's hips were touching his own. *How did I end up so close to her?* he wondered. Her hair, blown by a slight breeze, tickled his back. Nervousness threatened to steal his enjoyment. *There's nothing wrong with this. We're friends having fun.* He glanced at Eah. She was delighting in Uio and Tammah's roughhousing, giggling at their antics. *Man, she is absolutely gorgeous. Wait...what am I thinking here? This has got to be the keerehpee. That's it...I'm a keerehpee light-weight. Breathe. Just watch the game, Jay.*

Soon, Tammah and Uio called a truce to their friendly match and returned to sitting peacefully on the mat. They talked again with Eah in their language and did not concern themselves with her closeness to Jay. At first, he was worried about more teasing and prepared for it. When it did not happen, he doubted his interpretations of what kinds of joking were acceptable and what they considered being impolite.

Maybe the joke is old now, he thought. *More likely...I just didn't get it.*

He listened to them talking, but they did not mention his name. Neither did he recognize any more of their words. Soon, he became lost in his own thoughts, allowing his eyes to wander from person to person, taking in every detail and wondering what it would be like to be one of them. When they noticed his stares, they did not become uneasy, but smiled and continued their conversation.

There's not a shy or self-conscious bone in their bodies. They're confident, brave, and they have no secrets. I wish I was like that. I wish I could learn it while I'm here. Can I, though? Can I change and be like them? Or is this something only for people here on Hourou?

Jay considered the nighttime sky and the surrounding jungle. The air was clean and warm. There was no odor of decay in the jungle, only life. He listened to the sound of the breeze as it passed through the living forest, and he marveled at the unusual sounds of the night creatures.

Strange that I'm not nervous now. I guess these guys are rubbing off on me; they never seem to be concerned about anything. All day long, I've been trying to figure out if it's because they're totally oblivious or because they just accept everything that happens with some kind of unshakable faith. I guess that's what trust is all about.

Drowsiness soon overtook him as the jungle and exotic sounds of his friends' voices lured him toward sleep. His heavy eyelids resisted, and while they opened and closed, visions played out in front of him like changing scenes in a theater show.

His eyes closed. *My body is so light and relaxed.* His eyes opened. Tammah and Uio were reclining on the mat across from him. Eyes closed. *They're cute as a couple. They should get together.* Eyes opened. He glanced at Eah. Her lips were moving, but he could not interpret her words. Eyes closed. *I smell flowers on her skin...like perfume. She's so....* Eyes opened. Eah had guided his bobbing head to rest in her lap, and she was stroking his hair. *So tired, but I don't want to miss anything. Exhausted. This day was so long...more like two days. Eah...what is she doing? She's perfect. I have to tell her something. Can't pick my head up. Don't want to move.*

While Jay let himself fade in and out of sleep, Eah shifted her body to make her lap more comfortable. Across from them, Tammah and Uio reclined together, staring at the lantern plant's hypnotizing light show.

Jay woke when they began to sing. Though there were only three voices, they blended them to sound like a chorus. The beauty of it was inspiring. Jay even hummed along while he felt the vibration of Eah's voice through her body. Never had he been so close to another human being. He tried to stay awake and listen. There were some words he recognized. One was repeated often: *Ahey.* He also heard the names of his Earth companions: April, Paul, Ellis, Perry, and Yori. Eah sang Jay's name over and over. Had he not been so pacified and groggy from fatigue and the sedating fruit, he would have been embarrassed. Instead, the sound of Eah's sweet voice singing his name further intoxicated him with something that he could no longer deny.

Is this love? Am I falling for this alien girl? He closed his eyes for the last time that night.

The songs drifted on through his weary mind before sleep claimed him. Eah moved out from under him, placed something soft under his head, and kissed his cheek. The last thing he felt was her warm body against his as she lay next to him. The last thing he heard was Eah whispering his name, spoken with a deep sigh of affection. "Jay."

CHAPTER 22

Extended Family

EARLY MORNING: DAY 2 ON HOUROU

"Good morning."

April heard Paul's voice at the edge of her consciousness, even as she slept. It was too soon to wake up, though. She had to stay asleep so she could see what would happen next. In her dream, their two small boys were playing under an enormous tree. They laughed and called her to join their games, but when she tried to go, she could not move; glowing vines had fastened her feet to the ground. The scene faded into darkness. When it resumed, she was looking at the same tree through a thick mist. Her sons were still there, but time had passed and they had grown to be teenagers.

They're older...tall and strong, she observed. *There's something else different, too. What is it? I can't see through the mist.* She fought to stay in the dream, refusing to open her eyes until she could find the answer. *Wait. I have to see more.*

"Good morning, sleepyhead. You getting up?"

It's Paul. I have to go...have to wake up now. Her body stirred, threatening to pull her consciousness back into reality. *Show me what this means!* The mist cleared at her command, and the dream faded. With a jolt of surprise, April awoke. But she held a last remnant of the vision in her mind: the bare bodies of her sons were an iridescent white.

"Paul?"

"Sorry. You were kicking around. I figured you were awake."

April forced her eyes to open and saw Paul lying nearby and propped up on one arm. Behind him were things she did not recognize. *Trees. A jungle. A bed of moss. Strange smells and sounds. It's not a dream. I'm still on Hourou.*

"You okay?" Paul asked.

"Huh? Oh...yeah. Fine. Just reorienting. I was having a weird dream."

"Sorry."

She leaned over, kissed him, and then turned around to view their camp. The lighted plant they slept beside was still glowing, but the morning light had diminished the effect. On the other side of it, Keah and Ahee were sleeping, spooned in an intimate cuddle. To April, they no longer seemed so alien. She was even thinking of them as a sort of extended family.

"They're not up yet," she said in a whisper.

"No. They were up late. You, though, passed out pretty quick."

"Up late doing what?" she asked, turning back toward Paul.

He sat up a bit and peered at the sleeping couple. "Well, we talked for a little while, then I got tired. Just before I fell asleep, though, I heard them singing."

"Singing?"

"Yeah. Sounded nice. Their voices were like musical instruments."

"Then what?"

"I don't know. At some point I saw them cuddling together." He stood up and scanned the immediate area. "I have to find a potty plant. Will you be alright?"

"Potty plant?" April giggled softly. "Oh, I like that one."

"Well...that's what they are, right?"

"Don't get lost."

"I won't. I remember from last night that there's a patch of them here somewhere."

Paul tiptoed away, and April turned back toward Keah and Ahee again. Their white skin and hair contrasted against the many colors of their moss bed. Ahee's body was curled into a fetal ball with Keah pressed against her from behind, his arms wrapped around her in a protective embrace. April could not help gazing at their beautiful bodies and faces. Sometimes, they seemed so otherworldly, but at that moment, they could not have looked more human.

As she lay there, April wondered what it would be like living on a perfect planet. So far, she had only experienced a jungle on Hourou. A day's journey through the wilderness, though, had shown her nature was not an adversary here. Neither was it neutral in relation to its residents. Instead, everything that lived on Hourou was there to benefit, sustain, and even safeguard human life. It certainly was not a place like Earth. It was a sanctuary made for a special people.

Keah stirred and rolled onto his back.

Do all the other men here look like Keah? April wondered as she studied his body. *His sons have similar features.* Embarrassed at letting her eyes linger on him, she switched to observing Ahee. *She's a porcelain doll...and Eah is the same. Like mother, like daughter, I guess.* She ran her hand across her own face and down her chest. *What a figure. How could she have so many babies and stay in such great shape? I should ask her. Might as well get everything I can out of this trip.*

Paul returned and sat down next to her.

"You found it?" she asked, pushing herself up.

"Down the main path. Make a left at the big lighted plant. Walk on the blue moss for about fifty feet and it ends in a grove. You can't get lost."

April stood and straightened her wrinkled clothes. "If I'm not back in a bit, come and find me."

"Okay."

Paul took her place and observed Keah and Ahee. Both of them had rolled onto their backs and stretched out across the moss mat that was their bed. Paul stared at them for a while, but then felt guilty for doing so. Even after spending so much time with them, their nakedness still flustered him. *I really need to get over this.*

He guessed about ten minutes had passed, so he rose and left the camp to check on April. She was just returning from the grove when he met her along the path. "Such a strange place, huh?" he said, plucking pieces of moss out of her hair.

"Yeah. But it's so beautiful." She pulled him close in a big hug and buried her head in his chest.

"It sure is." Paul wrapped his arms around her and considered the surrounding trees. Beams of morning sunlight forced their way through the high branches, creating thousands of spotlights that illuminated the colorful flora. "I can hardly believe what we've been seeing."

"Me, too. Some of it is so like home, but other parts..."

Paul stroked April's hair, glad for some time alone with her. The tranquility of the woods, the exotic smells of the surrounding plants, and the soft morning light caused a romantic reaction deep within them both. "Do you feel...safe here?"

"Yes." There was no hesitation in her answer. "I can't explain it, but I feel completely safe."

"Good."

April reached up and stroked his cheek, which was now covered with the stubble of an encroaching beard. "What about you?"

"I'm fine, too. Sorry we missed the marriage conference and the mountains, Babes, but I guess this'll have to do."

April giggled and pushed her body into his. She had not thought about their weekend trip since being taken aboard the spacecraft. Now, after what she and Paul had been through, her plans seemed distant and irrelevant. The rekindling of certain parts of their relationship was still important to her, but she was coming to realize it was being accomplished anyway, only in a much stranger environment and among very different people. Through the bizarre experiences, potential dangers, and raw adventure of it all, she felt closer to Paul than she had in a long time, and she sensed it was the same for him. As for romance, at the moment, if she was not on her guard, she could have even allowed for a quick, intimate encounter within the enchanting and sensual embrace of that protective, alien jungle.

Am I in a trance? she wondered. She took a deep breath and marveled at the heady fragrances of the surrounding flora. *Is it the flowers? How could I consider this right now? But...at the same time...I don't care.*

"You okay?" Paul asked. "You went silent on me."

"I was just thinking about the conference."

"Oh." Paul prepared himself for the start of a conversation he was sure would spoil the moment.

"And about how we don't even need it."

Paul showed her the irresistible, boyish grin that always melted her heart. She closed her eyes and kissed him passionately, indifferent to her surroundings and only wanting to be closer to him.

Both allowed themselves to enjoy each other with no hesitation. Hands searched and caressed while their bodies rubbed together and swooned within affectionate embraces. Alone and unafraid, they became oblivious to all else but their connection at that moment. Then, before the jungle's enchantment threatened to unleash deeper passions, they broke their long kiss and stood still in each other's arms.

"I love you, Babes," Paul said, taking in a deep breath to calm himself.

April could tell that ending their fleeting tryst was the last thing he wanted to do. "And I love you...no matter what planet we're on."

Paul hugged her and laughed, trying hard to shake himself back into reality and cool his inner urges.

April kissed him again and gazed into his eyes with longing. "I wish we were back home."

"Me, too," Paul said with a wink. "But...I do like an adventure."

April raised a curious eyebrow.

"That is...well...oh, you know what I mean."

"It's okay," April said with a chuckle. "I've been wondering for a while now how many plants on this planet are aphrodisiacs."

"Maybe that's why Keah and Ahee are always so happy."

April playfully slapped his chest. "I meant how they affect *us.* We're the aliens here, remember?"

"I get it. Some fruits we've eaten definitely have a stimulating effect. I thought it was just me."

April smiled. "No...not just you."

"Does eating it do that to *them,* though?"

"I don't think so. They might be immune to it since they live here."

Paul shrugged and nodded toward their campsite. "Come on. Let's go back before they think we got lost. Maybe they can get us a plant that makes coffee."

When they returned, they found Keah and Ahee awake and waiting for them. Keah was gnawing on a broken stick while Ahee sat nearby, grooming her long, white mane with something that looked like a pine cone. She reached out her hand and beckoned for April to sit in front of her. April complied, and as she dropped herself onto the matted moss, Ahee scooted close and brushed her hair. Her touch was delicate and attentive, as if she had much experience in caring for the physical needs of others.

Paul seated himself near Keah, who handed him a stick and showed how to peel the bark, split it down the middle, and chew the inside meat. Paul followed his example and marveled at the sweet, nutty taste of the pulp.

"Do all women on Earth shorten their *usu?*" Ahee asked April while brushing and admiring her hair.

"You mean hair?"

"Hay-er," Ahee repeated.

"No. Not all women. Some like to keep it short, but others like to keep it long. I guess I prefer something in the middle. You know...shoulder length."

"I understand."

"What about women on Hourou?" April asked. "Do all women here let their hair—their usu—grow so long?"

Ahee stopped brushing and considered her own hair. "Long? Yes...usu is our *iao.*"

"What is iao?"

"I do not know your word, but iao is honor...displayed on the head of us. Do you understand?"

"I think so. We would probably say crown. A crown is a...symbol...of honor placed on the head."

"Yes," Ahee agreed. "Iao is like the crown of us, then."

"Does it just stop growing when it gets to a certain length?"

"Yes."

April turned around to face Ahee and gestured toward the brush. "May I?"

Ahee smiled and handed it to her.

"Well," April said as she began brushing, "your hair is very beautiful, Ahee."

"The usu of April is iao. It is bee-you-tee-full as well."

"Thanks. It's still nothing like yours, though."

Paul stood and chuckled.

"What's so funny?" April demanded.

"Girl stuff. I think Keah and I should go golfing or something while you two ladies chat."

"Yeah, yeah," April replied in jest. "Do that. We'll go shopping when we're done here and have a nice lunch."

At first, the banter confused Keah and Ahee, but then they realized their new friends were just having fun with each other. Keah rose and offered a handful of his sticks to the women before turning to Paul and motioning for him to follow toward the moss path.

"Come, Paul. We will look ahead."

"Good idea," Paul replied. "So, where do we go today? Are we still far from the others?"

"No, not far."

"How long will it be until we reach them?"

"Long?"

"How much time?"

"Time is the passing of moments."

"Okay, then. How many *passing moments* will there be until we meet up with them?" Paul tried not to sound frustrated, but sometimes Keah's way of saying things exasperated him.

Keah sensed his annoyance. "We are not understanding each other again, are we?"

"Sorry, Keah. I didn't mean it to come out so grumpy. We both obviously have different ways of thinking about certain things."

"On Hourou," Keah explained, "we measure time by the light of our suns. Light comes, and a day begins. Light goes, and a day ends."

"Yes, we do that on Earth, too. We measure time by the rotation of the planet."

"Yes, the rotation. Good. For some planets it is different, but on Earth and Hourou, it is the same, then."

"You've been to *other* planets?"

"Yes. Many."

"Are they...? Never mind. I think I should just stick to learning about *your*s for now."

"Hourou is much larger than your Earth; it is almost twice the size and rotates slower. So, what you call a day is longer on Hourou. There are other differences as well, but explaining them in your words would be...comp-lee-cated?"

"Complicated," Paul corrected. "It's funny how you can use and pronounce some big words and others you struggle with. Our language must be hard for you."

"Funny?" Keah asked.

"Interesting...in a humorous way."

"Oh. Yes, your language is funny to us."

"Now you're getting it," Paul said with a laugh. "Anyway, it's been easy enough for me to figure out that days are much longer on Hourou than on Earth."

"Yes. You asked about how much time it will take to join the others. The answer is one more Hourou day."

"Okay. But how do you know where to meet them?"

"All the Ways on Hourou are easy to follow," Keah replied. "Also...we will light the sky as a sign."

Paul assumed he was talking in riddles again, and he was not in the mood to guess or ask for another explanation. As they continued on together, Paul realized that the ground was sloping, as if they were entering an area of small hills. It was the first time during their journey that they walked on unleveled paths.

Soon, they came to the top of a treeless hill that marked the edge of the jungle. On the other side were cliffs leading down to a valley surrounded by mountains. There, rivers of gold and purple snaked through rolling foothills of green, and colorful trees dotted the landscape and covered the mountaintops.

Paul could also see giant animals roaming across open, grassy plains and congregating near the waters. "I didn't realize how high we were," he said, taking in the view. "The jungle seemed so flat."

"We will now enter the *tsayooorua*—the val-eee."

"The valley? Oh, right."

As if on cue, April and Ahee appeared from behind.

"What a view!" April exclaimed as she joined Paul. "Is that where we're headed?"

Keah took Ahee's hand and pulled her close to his side as the four surveyed the inspiring scenery. "Yes, we will enter the valley and travel in the open now."

April marveled at the scene below. "It looks so beautiful from up here. I'm ready for a new day of exploring."

Paul nodded as he considered the valley. "Me, too."

While Keah and Ahee stepped aside for a talk, April moved closer to the edge of the hill and peered down at the cliffs below. "Well...this ought to be an enjoyable challenge."

* * *

Keah decided against scaling down the cliffs to reach the valley. Instead, he suggested they continue following the jungle's edge to make a gradual descent. That disappointed April. She and Paul had done some rock climbing in recent years, and she had confidence in their abilities. With the addition of increased muscular strength on this planet, she was curious about how they would perform. Despite their insistence that they could handle it, though, Keah resolved to take the easier route.

As they walked, their guides were ahead and just out of earshot, so April asked Paul about something they had not yet discussed. "What do you think about the other people we've seen—the Dah-Ahey?"

"Well," Paul answered, "I know from our time on their ship that there was a rift between the bronze-skinned ones and Keah's family."

"Yeah, but it's hard for me to accept that Ahee and Keah would have a problem with *anyone*. They're so open and genuine."

Paul jumped over a deep gap in the rocky ground, and April did likewise. It amazed both of them how light their bodies were during the leap.

"I bet you could jump twice as far as that," Paul said.

"I won't try it up here...just in case. But maybe in the valley."

"Anyway," Paul continued, "I agree with you; I can't imagine Keah having enemies. The Dah-Ahey on the spaceship were nothing like him and Ahee, though. They were shifty and unpredictable...ready for a fight."

"Yeah. I sensed a lot of hostility."

"They were also wearing something."

"Were they? I guess I was too shocked to notice."

"Each of them had on a type of loincloth."

"Oh, yeah. Now I remember. I wonder what *that* means."

Paul shrugged. "I don't know, but it seems significant."

"Symbolic somehow?"

"Possibly. Clothing is a social thing. It might represent a totally different culture here."

"Their skin color was different, too."

"Yes, it was. And we've seen how people foolishly divide over things like that."

"But that's on *our own* planet," April objected. "And Keah doesn't strike me as being so shallow."

"True. So maybe it's a one-sided thing…from the Dah-Ahey."

April looked down the steep hills and saw the glowing white bodies of Ahee and Keah navigating paths between crags and crevices. "Ahee doesn't like talking about them."

"Neither does Keah."

"Then whatever is going on with the Dah-Ahey, it's big enough to cause discomfort in these really nice people."

"I'm sure we'll find out about it eventually," Paul said. "If there are more people on this planet, that is." He gestured toward their guides. "Come on. Let's catch up to those two. I don't want us getting lost."

As they hurried along, Paul took April's hand and led her down to the mysterious lowlands below.

* * *

Several animals, which Ahee called *mahtee,* followed the party during their descent from the jungle to the valley. Paul and April had already seen them during the previous day, but the creatures still fascinated them. To Paul, they had the body of a flying squirrel but the limbs of a tiny monkey. Flaps of skin under long arms enabled them to glide through the trees when they were not running across branches or swinging on vines. The mahtees' heads resembled that of a red panda: little black eyes, a stubby snout, a toothy mouth, and rounded ears. Short fur, striped with vivid colors, covered their bodies and their long, flat tails ended in tufts of bright hues.

One mahtee took a liking to April and rode on her shoulder while she walked. Sometimes, it would leap into a tree and return with small nuts, which it then fed to her. Ahee said it was not uncommon for the animals to adopt a human family and live with or near them. Since mahtee could learn many tasks, she explained, they were very helpful to have around.

During the long hike, April's little friend would stay with her for a while and then get bored and disappear into the trees to travel with other mahtee. When they reached the edge of the jungle, however, it stopped returning to her. Keah said it must have belonged to a group that lived there. If not, April would have had a hard time sending it away, for the mahtee were both clingy and loyal.

As they continued their journey through the hills, they encountered a variety of wildlife. Some were giant and reptilian, like dinosaurs. Others were of different sizes, from as large as elephants to as small as mice, and they, too, resembled animals from Earth. There were also creatures that were bizarre and alien, incomparable to anything Paul and April had ever seen. At all times, the beasts of Hourou were docile and fearless of humans. Some would even become curious and approach them. When they did, Keah stopped the trek long enough to allow his guests to pet and play with the smaller ones.

A great forest was on the far side of the hill country. When they reached its edge, Keah said they would travel into the woods for a little while and then rest. The trees there were shorter, so it was easier to see the sky through the canopy. Some of the vegetation resembled that of the jungle, but much of it was quite different. Instead of soft colorful mosses, a fine carpet of short green grass covered the ground. To Paul, it was like walking on the well-manicured fairway of a top-rated golf course.

"I've never been good at identifying trees," Paul said to April, gesturing toward some Earth-like saplings. "But those look like maple."

"Let's see." April examined a dangling leaf. At her touch, its light green color changed to patterns of reds, oranges, and yellows. "Wow!" she exclaimed. "Instant fall colors!"

Ahee came alongside and swept both of her hands through a mass of the leaves, creating a trail of color. "When the *oen*—the wind—blows, the trees show their colors."

April repeated Ahee's action, and the effect dazzled her. "It's beautiful! It reminds me of some of our trees back home, but they only change color in autumn—I mean, when the season changes. They turn color like this before they fall off."

"Fall off, and then grow again?" Ahee asked.

"Yes. After winter—the cold season—they grow back again."

"Are there seasons on Hourou?" Paul asked.

"Seasons," Ahee repeated. "Changes—as in temperature?"

"Yes, but outside," Paul said, motioning toward the surrounding forest. "Hot to cold, or warm to cool, and then back again."

"I understand. No, on Hourou, the temperature is almost constant. There are only minor variations."

"Sounds like paradise." April continued playing with the leaves, creating patterns with her hands.

"Imagine what it looks like from a distance when the wind blows through the trees," Paul said to her. "It must be breathtaking."

"Yeah. There's so much beauty here."

"The beauty of Ahey fills Hourou," Ahee declared with pride, "and it is for all people to enjoy. I am happy that you find it so. As you have seen, there is nothing to fear on Hourou."

April smiled, but tears formed in her eyes. "Your planet is perfect, Ahee. Hourou is so pure."

"Yet there is still something that troubles the inside of you."

April let go of the leaves and pushed her hair behind her shoulders to communicate her openness. "I guess I'm just worried about getting back home...and about my children."

"I understand. The children of Ahee are far away as well. But I know they are safe. And the ones of April are also safe. Come!" Ahee took April's hand and motioned for her to follow. "Let us talk of them as we walk."

Paul patted April's shoulder to show his support. "Ahee is right, Babes. They're fine. You two talk. I'm going to catch up to Keah." With that, he trotted away.

"Come," Ahee repeated. She kept hold of April's hand as they followed behind Keah and Paul. At first, the gesture made April a little uncomfortable. It seemed childish for two grown women to be walking together holding hands. Just as quickly as the discomfort came upon her, however, Ahee's innocent smile drove it away.

Why should I be so weirded out? April wondered. *Everything she does is from good intentions. I'm the one who attaches weirdness to it. Why does the first thing I think of have to be so...*

Ahee gave April's hand a little squeeze, and April smiled back at her.

It's like walking with my sister, April decided. *One that I never had. We're like two sisters spending time together.*

They walked hand in hand for a while before either of the women spoke, enjoying their feminine bonding and the forest's peacefulness. Even without words, April knew they were communicating, for every so often she would feel a surge of emotion through Ahee's grip. From Ahee, it was always positive—peace, happiness, joy, acceptance, and love. April tried to reciprocate by thinking of the same emotions and sending them back through their touch, but something always seemed to block her attempts. Eventually, she understood that her inner boundaries were acting like a one-way valve; her insecurities allowed her to receive but prevented her from giving. When she lowered those boundaries, she was rewarded with a beautiful sharing of emotions. It was then April understood how important physical contact was to Ahee and her people, and how they used it to communicate their feelings.

Concerned she might misuse this new skill, April broke the silence and returned to using words. "Ahee, tell me about your children."

"What would you like to know?"

"Are all the others who were on the spaceship really yours?"

"We do not say *your*, or *my*, children, as in possession. We say that they are *from* Ahee and Keah."

"*From*...is to give birth, then?"

"Yes."

"So you gave birth to all of them?"

"Yes. All but Uio...and there are many others on Hourou who are from Ahee and Keah."

"Wow. What about the three on the ship who were different? The three Dah-Ahey that were brought aboard?"

"No. The Dah-Ahey are not from Ahee."

Steep hills were in front of them now, so Ahee released April's hand. One incline was sharp enough that the two had to use hands and feet to climb.

"How many children are from April?" Ahee asked as they climbed together.

"Two," April replied through a few grunts. "Two boys—males. The oldest, Dex, is six years old and Vince is four."

"Earth years. They are small, then?" she guessed.

"Yes. I don't know how to explain their ages to you, though, since that must be different here."

"You have weaned them from the breast?"

"Yes."

"And they need always watching from you?"

"Oh, yes."

"In your years, they are still very young, then."

"That's it," April agreed. "Not babies, but small children."

"Yes, yes. I understand better why you are so concerned. Still, you must trust they are safe."

"I appreciate your encouragement, Ahee. I miss them a lot."

"Yes...I know what it means to miss. Most of the children of Ahee and Keah live away from us...in other parts of Hourou."

"Tell me about the ones who are still with you—the ones I've seen."

Ahee draped her hair around her neck so that it would not encumber her climbing. "Well, let's see," she said in a very Earth-like way. "The first you met was Eah."

"Yes. She is so beautiful...and smart."

"Eah is the firstborn of those you have seen. You would say she is the—oldest—daughter."

"How old is Eah?"

"To us, she is still young, but she is at the age of dyad."

"Dyad?"

"Of pairing—mating."

"Oh. We'd say she's a young adult, then. To me, she looks to be about twenty years old—no more than twenty-five."

"In your years," Ahee said, "Eah is around two hundred years old."

April stopped walking and stared at Ahee for a moment. "Two hundred?"

"Yes."

"Ahee, you only look maybe thirty in our years. Yet Eah seems very close to your age. Actually...*all* of your children look that way. How old *are* you and Keah?"

Ahee hesitated, as if she was doing some complicated internal computations. "In your years, Keah is perhaps six hundred and twenty-five and I am six hundred and twenty."

April gawked at her in disbelief. Clearly, the aging process and life spans were much different here. "Ahee, that's incredible," she said, resuming their climb.

"In your eyes, it must be...strange?"

"Yes, but not in a bad way. I mean, you're all so young and healthy and beautiful."

"And April and Paul are also young and healthy and beautiful," Ahee said. "Is there so much difference?"

"Well, no," April admitted, "and yes."

Ahee grinned as she scaled another steep hill behind April. "These are the wonders of Ahey and of Hourou. There is so much for you to learn."

"That's for sure. So, tell me more about Eah and her brothers and sisters, then."

"Eah studies words and other ways of communication. She has been helpful in our travels, being able to understand others quickly."

"I've seen that, yes. She seems so curious and open and honest."

"Yes. Eah is like that...even more as she enters the age of dyad."

"What happens to her during this time?" April asked, assuming it was the equivalent of adolescence on Earth.

"Eah burns with the desire for dyad," Ahee replied. "But it has been difficult for her."

"Why is that? It seems to me any male would fall for her."

"Fall?"

"Sorry. I mean, any male would want to dyad with her."

"Yes. Yet the dyad must be well-matched, and Eah prefers those who are different."

"Not just any man will do," April deduced.

"Yes. Eah is especially...choosy, you would say. She burns, but she makes it difficult for herself to find dyad. She will learn, though."

"I think I know how she feels. It took a long time for me to realize that Paul and I were meant for each other, even after growing up together. I was stubborn...or my hormones blinded me."

"Your words are a little confusing, but I understand," Ahee said. "It seems much the same for Eah."

"Tell me about the others in your family."

"Tammah is second born of the ones you have seen—the oldest son, born soon after Eah. He is a builder and a crafter of useful things. Tammah is also skillful in games and is strong. He now seeks dyad and will be a wonderful father."

"Yes, I remember Tammah," April recalled.

"Tammah seeks dyad with Uio."

"Really? But isn't Uio from you and Keah?"

"Uio is from another Two—you would say *couple*—who live in another part of Hourou. She is with us to learn more about ahea...about space."

"I understand. So Tammah and Uio are trying to be a couple."

"Yes, they pursue each other. Eah says they are too much alike...always competing. But I see in them a strong dyad. Keah hopes they will learn this from us, so I teach them what I can."

April smiled. It amused her that relationships were complicated even on distant planets. "So that's Eah, Tammah, and Uio," she said. "What about the others?"

"Ua is a son who is also a crafter. He studies how things work and improves them. Then, there is Aai. He is adventurous—an explorer. Even for being so young, Aai has already visited many worlds with us."

"Visited *many worlds?*"

"Yes. Keah and Ahee—we are explorers. We visit other places and bring knowledge back to Hourou. On many travels, we take the youngest that I birthed. Aai has been on almost all of our journeys."

"That's amazing."

At the top of the steep hill they had been climbing, both women stopped and surveyed the area ahead. Spotting Keah and Paul, they resumed walking along a grassy trail that was level.

"There are also youngest daughters, Mahah and Maiha," Ahee continued. "Mahah is caring. She desires to be a mother of many, and she will be a strong birther. Mahah's womb is already warming and her body is being prepared to fulfill her desire. I will be happy when she finds dyad."

"And Maiha?" April asked.

"Maiha is wise. She is quiet and always thinking. She enjoys learning and remembers everything. Though she is the youngest daughter, her knowledge and memory are equal to Eah, who is the eldest. Maiha is also deeply connected to Hourou."

Ahee stopped talking, so April assumed she had reached the end of the list of her children.

"You have a large family, Ahee."

"All is family, and family is all," Ahee corrected. "But I understand your meaning."

"I couldn't handle so many."

"*Handle,* in this use, means to raise?"

"Sorry, yes," April replied. "Just raising two little boys is a lot for me. I can't imagine having more. Sometimes...I think I'd like to try, though."

Ahee stopped walking and considered April's body.

"What is it?" April asked.

She moved closer and placed her hands on April's hips, as if measuring the width of them. Then, to April's great shock, Ahee lifted the front of her t-shirt, exposing her belly and breasts.

"Is your body unable to birth more children?" Ahee asked, placing a hand on April's abdomen.

"No. Uh...it's not like that."

Ahee's unabashed action stunned April, but she also knew by now that Ahee's people did not seem to understand the concepts of personal boundaries or space. Their innocence of thought abolished any need for such social conventions.

Ahee examined April's bare torso like a medical doctor, palpating and looking for signs of something. When she noticed April's uneasiness, she pulled down the shirt and backed away.

April tried her best to brush off any lingering embarrassment. "Um...so..."

"You have the body of a great-mother," Ahee said. "You can birth many children, April, but you *tsawee*—you hold back. Why do this? Do not fear being what you are."

Ahee's ability to discern her desires was amazing. It was true April dreamed of having a large family, but her worries about things like money and social perceptions kept her from sharing that desire with Paul and pursuing it. "Thank you, Ahee," she said. "My body feels built for it. But raising a big family is more complicated where I come from."

"No. Such com-plee-cay-shun comes from inside." She placed her hand first over April's heart and then onto the side of her head. "From here and here. And fear comes from not being. You must *be*, April. Then, fear will cease. This is true no matter what world you call home." She brushed April's hair back and looked deep into her eyes. "We are much alike, April. Learn from your visit to Hourou. Here, you will see yourself more clearly...as you are. And you will see Ahey more clearly as well."

"What is Ahey?" April asked. "You've mentioned that before."

Ahee studied April's eyes for a moment. "This you already know." Backing away, she gestured for April to follow. "Come."

April hesitated, perplexed by her answer. *So much mystery, and yet such wisdom.*

Ahead of her, Ahee unwrapped her hair from around her neck as she walked. A light breeze caught the long white mane and blew it aside like a sail on a tall ship.

We have the same hips, April thought. *Maybe she's right and we are a lot alike. But can I still do the things she does? Maybe this Ahey is a fresh way of thinking...or a way of living.*

Ahee turned and waited for April to catch up, her hair falling back down and framing her majestic figure. April allowed herself to continue her own examination, but found herself even more awed by Ahee's confidence and total lack of self-consciousness.

Whatever this Ahey is, I want more of it.

* * *

From the position of Hourou's primary sun, Paul assumed half of the day had passed during their journey out of the jungle and across the plains and forested foothills. It surprised him that although he had walked for many miles, his legs still felt strong and his bare feet remained uninjured.

Keah only slowed their pace when he encountered a natural obstacle he was unsure if Paul and April could manage. On every occasion, however, the Earth couple welcomed the challenge and impressed their hosts with their determination and agility. Paul was glad he had kept himself in good shape over the years, and the way April was rediscovering her athletic giftedness made him proud.

While they traveled, the two couples often split up. Keah took Paul with him to scout the terrain, leaving April and Ahee alone to stroll together and talk. This gave the women much time to work on their budding friendship. Paul and Keah, likewise, experienced an evolving comfort with each other, and Paul supposed they were becoming friends despite their many differences.

Paul genuinely enjoyed Keah's company, but he still found it awkward conversing with him. Topics like work, sports, and politics, which were common for men to discuss on Earth, were foreign to the people of Hourou. Keah did not have a job, yet Paul learned he was an expert in space travel. For Keah, it was not an occupation; it was simply what he did. As a child, he had wanderlust and an aptitude for science, so his parents educated him in space science and technology. Then he just went off and started exploring.

The concept of money was also unknown to Keah. Paul discovered the citizens of Hourou shared all the necessities of life. The only items they seemed to own were works of art and things of sentimental value. Otherwise, all else was available to everyone, and people took good care of everything.

As for sports, whereas Paul was a fan of many back home, Keah had a hard time understanding the concept of watching sporting events for entertainment, supporting a favorite team, or of people being paid athletes. To Keah, athletic activity was about participation, not just observation. On Hourou, he said, both children and adults played games. For them, though, it was for exercise, fun, and bonding. Paul agreed and tried to show the similarities with sports on Earth, but he could not make Keah understand.

The same was true when Paul tried to talk about politics and government. This time, Keah's explanation of civics on Hourou was almost impossible for Paul to follow. He surmised that Keah's people had developed a strange Utopian society where everyone just got along and things worked out fine. A religion was also involved—like some sort of theocracy—but Paul decided not to pursue that subject. It was not because he was averse to it. He and April both came from families with a strong religious affiliation, and they both remained faithful to it. The problem for Paul was what to do with a faith that was now challenged by the monumental discovery of intelligent people on another planet. His religion had always assumed life on Earth was singular in the universe, and that humans were the pinnacle of creation. Now, he had encountered beings from another world, and he was even visiting their home. To reconcile this was going to be difficult.

April was convinced Keah and his people were human, just of a different kind. If that was true, Paul supposed he could make a few concessions. Perhaps his worldview just needed a modification. And if they turned out not to be human, he was still in the same dilemma anyway and would have to rethink his beliefs about several things. The more time he spent with Keah and Ahee, though, it was easier to accept that they were either really human or nearly so. Some doubt was there, and Paul recognized the source: it was their perfection. There were no flaws in them—physical, psychological, or emotional.

The bodies of Keah and Ahee looked to Paul like a collection of all the best traits, the most attractive qualities, and the most desirable abilities imaginable. If they were human, they were the ultimate humans. Their shape, proportion, and symmetry were unrivaled by anyone he had ever seen. Muscle tone, body fat, hair—all of it was apportioned to perfection. Their forms resembled professional dancers and athletes, moving with grace, agility, ease, and strength.

Paul found their physical superiority the most unnerving; just looking at them reminded him of his own bodily limitations and flaws. Next to such masterpieces of flesh, he felt quite mediocre. Their bodies inspired awe and demanded appreciation. Paul could not even enjoy viewing them sensually. Such purity compelled him to rise above such thinking. This was especially true of Ahee. Here was a perfected human woman, radiating incomparable beauty with nothing to cover or hide it, and yet Paul only regarded her with admiration and respect. She was captivating in the most idealized, feminine ways, but Paul dared not think of her as a body to be objectified for his or anyone else's pleasure. She was too perfect to receive the shallow and unrestrained lusts from typical men he represented back on Earth. Paul understood that only an honorable man could be worthy of knowing and uniting with her. Keah was that man.

Curiously, being around Ahee warmed Paul's heart ever more toward April. Instead of comparing Ahee and her flawless, female features to those of his wife, Paul found a new appreciation for April's womanly complexity. April was not inferior to Ahee; she had the same excellence and beauty inside her. The difference was that Ahee's body radiated its perfection while in April much of it remained hidden, as if behind a cloudy image. The realization taught Paul that perfection, like beauty, was inherent in every human being. There were remnants of it in all people. Here on Hourou, bodies were still close to the original design. On Earth, something had gone very wrong, leaving behind only an image of what once was.

Most of Paul's conversations with Keah were short, so he had a lot of time to ruminate on such observations. Sometimes, he wanted to join April and talk to her about the things he was learning, but when he looked back at her and Ahee, they were always deep in conversation. Rather than interrupting, he kept prodding Keah for answers about his planet, his people, and about how the Earth humans were going to return home.

"So," Paul said after one of their many awkward periods of silence, "though I don't see any signs of regular use, this path we're on feels like a major route to...well, somewhere."

"Yes."

Frustrated by yet another quick answer, Paul decided this time he would just keep talking until Keah came out of his shell. "And?"

"And what?"

"Can you tell me a little more?"

"I have not been enjoyable for communication...have I, Paul? My thoughts have been busy—preoccupied—with many things, especially with the meaning of all that has happened to you and to us."

"I understand. I guess I forgot how all of this is just as much of a shock to you and Ahee as it is for us."

Keah smiled, pleased with Paul's amiableness.

"I almost hesitate to ask this," Paul continued, "but are we the *first* people you've encountered outside of Hourou?"

"No. We have explored many worlds, and on some we have met other humans."

"That's hard for me to believe."

"It was wonderful to discover. We bring back knowledge from those planets because we enjoy learning. That is our purpose for traveling."

"I appreciate the search for knowledge."

"Each planet is different, but the people are very seem-ee-ler to us."

"Similar," Paul corrected.

"Yes, similar."

"And now you've encountered people from Earth. Do you see us as being similar, too? Similar to you? To those other humans?"

"All are from the Two, and the Two are from Ahey."

"That sounds like another one of your mysterious sayings, Keah. I don't understand it, unless you mean that we're all related somehow."

Keah chuckled. "There is still much mystery in *your* words as well, Paul. But, yes, you have indeed understood. As you say, all humans are related."

"But do you see us—the people of Earth—as being like any of the others? Or are we different from those you have encountered?"

Keah stopped walking and glanced at Paul. "You are a problem for us, Paul...like the Dah-Ahey."

"Are you saying we're like the Dah-Ahey?" Paul was confused. From what he had experienced so far, being compared to them was not necessarily a compliment.

"That is the mystery," Keah admitted, "for we see two peoples in you."

"So...we're somewhat like you, but also like them?"

Keah turned away and resumed their hike. "You and April seem more like Ah-Ahey, Paul. And Eah has told us she sees the same in Jay."

"That's interesting...and I'm glad, Keah."

"Meeting you—meeting people from Blue—has been fascinating. There is nothing in my travels that can compare to it. You are human, like us, and yet so different. You amaze us. Ahee and I have enjoyed getting to know you and April."

"The same goes for us."

"That makes the mystery deeper," Keah said in reflection. "Why have the Ways of Ahey banned your world from us? Why did the Dah-Ahey take a wa-ah-ahea and go there against our Ways? What has changed in them?"

"Those are good questions, Keah, and only *you* can answer them. But I have one as well: why would the Dah-Ahey want to visit a planet that none of you know anything about?"

"The Dah-Ahey have learned about life on other worlds," Keah explained. "The people on those worlds still follow the Ways of Ahey, so going to those planets would not *benefit* the Dah-Ahey. They must have been looking for something different, and your world was unknown to all of us. Earth and its mysteries, despite what Mister Carlson has called 'the travel ban,' would be an attraction to the Dah-Ahey, since it seems they no longer wish to abide by *any* of the Ways. That is why they took the wa-ah-ahea and defied the ban. This is all so difficult for the Ah-Ahey to comprehend."

"Unfortunately, it's easier for *my* people to comprehend—theft, defiance, evasion, forbidden fruit." Paul could tell by Keah's expression that he did not understand those words. "Nevermind all that, Keah," he said, changing his tone to redirect Keah's thoughts. "Can you tell me who the Dah-Ahey *are?*"

"The word means *those without Ahey.*"

"And what is Ahey?"

"I think you already know that, Paul, so why do you ask?"

"Well, that sounds either mysterious or evasive."

"If you really do not know the answer...and recognize Ahey...then you must con-tim-plate what is already inside you and...heed...what it will further reveal to you. Search the inside of you, and watch my people, the Ah-Ahey."

"Alright, I will. So...at least I understand about how the Dah-Ahey broke the rules now."

"Yes. To take the wa-ah-ahea and then travel to Blue despite being forbidden is a new situation for us. The Dah-Ahey have never done such a thing. Care of the wa-ah-ahea was our responsibility. We had no choice but to follow and bring them back. What happens next...who can tell?"

"What do you mean?"

"I *will* get you home, Paul. I must also ensure there was nothing left behind of the other wa-ah-ahea. But the Dah-Ahey have broken the barrier between our worlds."

"Why are you so concerned about the wrecked wa-ah-ahea?"

"It is enough that so many of your people saw us and our activity there," Keah answered, "and you will have much to tell them when you return. The technology we use, though..."

"It's way beyond us," Paul admitted. "Would it be dangerous?"

"Dangerous means the potential to cause harm, yes?" Keah looked perplexed. "I have no way of knowing this. Are people on Earth...could people there...?"

Keah's unbelievable naivety again stupefied Paul. "Are you asking me if there are dangerous people on my planet?"

"Yes."

"I'm surprised you haven't figured that out already, Keah. Our fear should have shown you how much danger we're used to on our planet. Unlike on Hourou, there is much danger there...and, yes, there are people who are dangerous and cause harm."

At this revelation, Keah stopped walking and stared hard at Paul.

"Sorry, Keah. I don't mean to offend you. I know life is very different on this planet."

"No, Paul," Keah said, "life is very different on *your* planet." With that, he resumed walking and became silent.

Paul followed, but he decided not to engage in conversation again for a while. Something had upset Keah. Behind him, he heard April and Ahee laughing like two young girls. *Maybe I should have been hanging out with the ladies,* he thought. *So much for the guy talk.*

After a while, Keah stopped on the edge of a deep ravine and waited for Paul to catch up.

I guess I should give the male bonding one more try, Paul thought. He hastened down the side of a hill and came alongside Keah as he stared down into the gorge.

"Well...this looks interesting," Paul said.

Keah chuckled and smiled in his usual way, all traces of tension gone. "So much is interesting right now," he said. "Paul, while you are with us on Hourou, think hard about what you see and learn."

"I will, Keah."

"When you seek...then you will find."

Those familiar words startled Paul. Sometimes, it seemed Keah knew more about Earth and its cultures than he admitted. Yet how, if other humans had never visited there? Paul wondered if there already was a connection between their two worlds that neither of them recognized.

Another mystery to be solved, he thought. *I'll seek, but I hope I don't regret what I find.*

* * *

Keah and Paul continued at a brisk pace, leaving Ahee and April to follow at their leisure.

"Are you sure they won't lose us?" Paul asked, concerned about getting too far ahead and being out of sight.

"Ahee sees the path. In your words, they will be *fine.*"

Paul looked back but could discern no marked trail. "Does Ahee know this place, then?"

"No. But she will know where to walk." He hopped over a giant, exposed tree root and gestured at Paul to do the same. "Come!"

The decline became steeper, and their descent into the ravine was quick. When they reached the bottom, Paul stopped for a moment to enjoy the beauty of the sight before him. They were standing in a gorge at the edge of a shallow stone channel with smooth, curved sides. To him, it resembled a cement waterslide in an amusement park more than a natural river, yet it showed no sign of being artificial. Emerald green water flowed through it at a brisk pace, splashing out where the watercourse looped around trees and huge rocks.

"This is incredible!" Paul exclaimed. "I've never seen water of this color."

Keah knelt at the edge, scooped some with his hands, and drank. "There is a mineral in the rock that makes it appear that way. Are you thirsty?"

"I sure am." Paul joined him and followed his example, finding the tepid water just cool enough to be refreshing. "It's pure...tasteless."

"Come. There is more to see."

The two men followed the river upstream, and soon Paul heard the distinct sound of falling water ahead. After navigating around a few bends, they came to a deep pool beneath a magnificent waterfall. The sight of it caused Paul to pause and gape in awe.

"I can't even find words for this," he said. "*Amazing* doesn't even begin to describe it."

Keah waded into the water. "Come, Paul. Bathe and rest." He then immersed himself and swam underwater toward the waterfall. When he reached the other side of the pool, he clambered up some smooth rocks and stood under a falling stream. "Come!"

Paul scanned the immediate area. Other than Keah and a few animals and birds nearby, he was alone for the moment, so he removed what little clothing he wore, placed it on a big rock, and slipped into the water. Like the river, it was tepid and clean. He felt large grains of soft sand under his feet as he waded deeper.

While Keah showered under the falls, Paul swam around and explored the pool. The waterfall fascinated him, so he moved closer to get a better look at it. Unlike the typical ones he had seen on Earth, this was not a river pouring down the side of a cliff. Instead, water flowed from the top of a giant mass of mosses and plants that were growing on the face of a rock wall.

"Where does the water come from?" Paul asked Keah, trying to be heard above the roar of the falls.

"The *waiehheh* is alive," Keah replied, pointing upward. "It brings water from within the rock to feed the *yeh-heh-yeh*—the forest."

Keah then pointed to thick vines that connected the mass of living plants to the wall behind it. They were smooth, resembling massive pipes. Paul inferred they must have been drawing water from an underground source like a pump. They then used it to nourish themselves and create rivers to irrigate the surrounding forest.

"It's awesome!" Paul exclaimed.

"What's awesome?" a voice asked from behind him.

Startled, he spun around and came face to face with April. "Where...where did *you* come from?"

"You didn't even see us, huh?" She giggled at the stunned look on his face.

Paul looked back at Keah and saw Ahee climbing out of the pool to join him under the waterfall. "Very sneaky," he said. "Where'd you put your stuff?"

"Right by yours, on the rock."

"I guess I should keep an eye on them...in case a little monkey creature shows up and tries to steal them."

April laughed and motioned for Paul to swim with her to a shallower section of the pool. "For one," she said, "mahtee *give* stuff more than they take it."

"Uh-huh."

"Two, there's not much left to take, anyway."

"Wow. This doesn't sound like the same girl who was desperate to find her shoes and clothes a few days ago."

April located a spot in the pool where it was shallow enough to sit. "It hasn't been a few days," she corrected. "We've only been here since yesterday."

"I know." Paul paddled up to her in the shallows. "Time is so strange on this planet."

"One day on Hourou is like two of ours, I guess."

Paul nodded. "That's what Keah told me. Hey, you're pronouncing *Hourou* like a native."

April smiled at the compliment and toyed with her wet hair.

"In fact," Paul continued, gazing at her with appreciation, "you're *looking* like one, too."

April considered her nakedness and then splashed water at Paul. "Oh, stop! Anyway, there's nobody else around, so why not?"

"What about *them?*" Paul asked, nodding toward Keah and Ahee.

"Obviously, they don't care. But how about *you?* You were in the water first, Mister Tarzan of Hourou."

Paul reclined and floated a bit, enjoying how natural everything felt on the unusual planet. "Well, it isn't the *first* time we did this either, you know. Remember back in high school, on your mom's farm?"

"So?"

"Such a scandal!" Paul feigned embarrassment. "I mean, the *whole swim team?* Skinny dipping in the pond!"

"It was just innocent fun," April said. "There was nothing wrong about it...just like now."

"You're right. It *was* fun. Until your mom stumbled onto the scene."

"Oh, she didn't care. I think she got a bigger kick out of scaring everyone."

"It worked on *me*. To this day, I'm still paranoid that someone's going to steal my clothes."

April chuckled, remembering how her mother hid the youths' clothing while they were playing in the water. It was amazing how fast April's friends learned to make coverings out of pond reeds, leaves, and grass. They later found their clothes neatly folded and placed on a nearby bench that overlooked the pond. Her mother never admitted that she did the deed, but the way she laughed when April told her about it gave her away.

"Those were some good times," April said with fondness.

"Look at us now. After being scared out of our wits, we're having a pretty good time here, too."

"You're right. I'm feeling a lot more comfortable."

"You should. There hasn't been one danger since we crashed. The place is perfect."

April agreed. "Yeah. Look at those two over there. They know how to have fun, and they don't have *any* hang-ups about showing it, just like when we were kids back at the pond."

Paul watched as the native couple played under the waterfall, washing each other, laughing, splashing, and embracing. He envied their freshness and simplicity. They could be the wisest of adults when necessary, but in an instant, they could become innocent youth. "I would love to be more like that," he said.

"Me, too."

Paul stood, offering her his hand. "So...let's go join them, then."

April smiled and allowed him to pull her to her feet. Somehow, his body was different in the soft light of Hourou's suns. He looked leaner and more muscular than she remembered. Maybe, though, it had just been a while since she stopped to admire him. Now that they were so exposed to each other, she also noted other physical aspects that she had neglected to appreciate enough. Had this place changed Paul somehow? Perhaps it was she who was changing. Either way, having this new perspective warmed her inside.

Paul noticed April's open appraisal of him, and it made him smile. With her simple act of admiration, he no longer cared about comparing his body with Keah's perfect one. His wife was loving him with her eyes, and at that moment, their bond strengthened him in a way he had not felt in a long time.

* * *

Paul enjoyed frolicking under the waterfall, exploring the natural pool, and sunning on the rocks with Keah and Ahee. He and April felt like kids again, carefree and unhurried by schedules, deadlines, or demands. Soon, though, his thoughts returned to getting home, and he wondered when Keah was going to resume their journey.

As if sensing Paul's concern, Keah sat up on the sun-warmed rock where he had been reclining and said something to Ahee. She responded by rising and walking into the woods. When she returned, she was carrying gourds, some very large leaves, and wads of long, stringy fibers that resembled balls of string.

The gourds were for eating. Keah showed his Earth friends how to crack one open and scoop out the fruit. While they ate, Ahee crafted a knapsack from the leaves and plant fibers she found.

"Is that for carrying more fruit?" Paul asked.

"We must travel through water now," Ahee answered. "This *aophu* will keep your coverings dry." She motioned for April to fetch their clothes and place them inside.

April reluctantly complied. "Are you sure we need to do this?" she asked Ahee before stuffing their scant wardrobe into the sack. "I mean, we can wear wet clothes, and they would probably dry on us quick, anyway."

Ahee just smiled, pushed the clothing into the bag, and tied it shut. She then took some skins from the gourd and rubbed them on the bag's seams. "This makes the leaves close tighter," she said. "No water will enter the aophu now." When she was done, she handed it to Paul.

"You're quite crafty, Ahee," he said after examining the design. "You even included straps." He donned the aophu like a backpack and then posed for April. "I guess we travel native-style."

April frowned, despite Paul's flamboyance. "Sure. When in Rome…"

Keah had already slipped back into the pool and was waving for them to join him.

"You will be fine," Ahee said to April in a very Earth-like way. "Come." With that, she dove into the water.

Paul and April followed, and they all swam toward the waterfall until Keah led them to a stone channel. The current there was strong, making it easy to swim downstream. Paul soon discovered that he could float and the stream would carry him. April laughed with delight when he showed her the discovery, and for a while, the four swimmers just let the water move them. Eventually, though, the smooth-sided channel turned into a typical river, requiring more careful navigation. In some places, it became shallow, and they had to walk through knee-deep water until Keah located a different branch where they could float or swim again. Sometimes, they had to hike through the woods before Keah found a stream that suited him.

As the long journey and the slow afternoon of Hourou progressed, the cozy channels and small streams led them to open lands and a much larger river that wound through majestic hills and valleys. It was near the conflux that Keah stopped for a brief rest. Floating into a tributary, he pointed toward a sandy bank and gestured for them to exit the water there. While Paul and April slogged onto the tiny beach, he and Ahee disappeared into the surrounding trees.

"My body feels so heavy," Paul said.

April trudged across the sand and plunked herself on a large, flat rock. Its surface was smooth and warm, a splendid spot for drying off in the sunshine. "We've been in the water for a long time," she said. "Look at your hands."

Paul examined his palms, which were quite wrinkled. "I'm a prune!" he exclaimed. "All over!"

"Relax, wrinkle boy," April teased. "Put the pack down and sit over here."

Paul removed the makeshift backpack and dropped it in the sand.

"Are you cold?" he asked, noticing a slight shiver in himself as a breeze caressed his unclad skin. "Want your clothes?"

April leaned back on the rock and absorbed its warmth. Already the sunlight and the wind were drying her body. "Not yet." She closed her eyes and stretched herself out. "I'm fine."

Paul watched her for a moment, taking in her beauty and the alluring scene before him. *If we were only alone,* he thought. *We need more times like this together. Why does it take an alien encounter and a trip to a different planet to teach us this?*

"What are you doing over there?" April asked.

"Nothing. Just thinking."

April gazed at him through half-closed eyes, noting his amorous stare and nascent arousal. "I bet you were. Come over here and rest."

Paul trudged over to the rock and dropped next to her. "This is the first time I'm feeling worn out," he noted with a sigh.

"Same here. Maybe it was all that time in the water."

"I wonder where *they* went off to."

April turned her head and squinted toward the woods. "Probably to get food or something."

"In your conversations with Ahee, did she say how much closer we are to our destination?"

"No, but from things I picked up throughout the day, it sounds like we'll be there by nightfall."

"Good. I need a long sleep after today."

April took Paul's hand in hers while enjoying their brief rest. "I wonder if the others are making out alright."

"Hopefully, they're together and with Keah's kids," Paul said. "If so, they'll be fine."

"Think they've all gone native like us?"

Paul chuckled at the thought. "Jay might; he seems like the outdoorsman type. Maybe Yori and Ellis would, but I doubt it. Carlson...definitely not."

"It's funny. We don't even know them, but we can tell things about them right away. Why couldn't we do that with Eah, Ahee, and Keah when we first met them?"

"Probably because they were so different," Paul said. "We make a lot of assumptions based on appearance. Jay is handsome and rugged, so I assume he's an outdoorsy guy. Yori's a brainy student, and Ellis is a professor. I figure them as being more stuffy. Carlson? With that suit and attitude, he's the stereotypical politician. But how are we supposed to react to a naked alien with glowing white skin, big green eyes, and a perfect human body?"

"I guess I felt threatened and scared," April admitted, "even though they did nothing to make me feel that way."

"Other than sucking us into their spaceship," Paul reminded.

"Yeah. That'll do it."

At that moment, Keah and Ahee returned from the woods, pulling a giant leaf filled with long sticks, vines, gourds, and some fruit. They dragged it to the small beach and dumped its contents onto the sand.

"Are we staying here?" Paul asked. "Is that for a shelter or something?" The leaf was large enough to cover all four of them, so Paul thought they wanted to use it as a makeshift tent.

"It is for travel," Keah replied, gesturing toward the river.

"You're going to make a boat out of it," April guessed.

"We say *fahee*," Ahee explained. "Fahee is a vessel for traveling on the surface of the water."

"Can we help?" Paul asked.

Keah chuckled. "As you would say...we've got this. You and April should rest."

"Eat some keer-eh-peee," Ahee suggested, pointing to the fruit. "It will calm the body."

While they ate, Keah and Ahee worked on constructing the boat. Tying flexible, bamboo-like rods together with vines, they quickly crafted a simple frame that fit easily into the concave shape of the leaf. With that in place, they then used sharpened sticks to poke holes through the tough skin, and they tied the frame to its hull with more vines. When it was secure, they turned the little boat upside down and rubbed its entire surface with the gourds they had found. As with the backpack Ahee had made, the gourd's juices caused the leaf to shrink and tighten, closing any cracks or holes and making it waterproof.

Paul guessed the entire process only took Keah and Ahee about an hour to complete. "That is amazing!" he praised after examining the canoe-like vessel. "I see you both know a lot about wilderness living."

"Wild-er-niss?" Keah questioned.

"Wild nature," April explained. "Places outside of civilization."

"Civee-lee-za-ton es tay-oh-eee," Ahee said to Keah. "Ey eeeee o sah uhu es oya sah ee hey."

"Oh, yes. I understand," Keah said. "To you, Hourou must look like this wild nature—or wilderness. But *here*..." He waved his arms at the surrounding forest. "There are no separated places."

"So you have no cities?" Paul asked.

"We have built-places—what you call cities," Ahee answered. "But they are mostly for gathering. There, we meet and do many together-things. What you think of as civilization, though, is everywhere on Hourou."

"Oh. Okay."

"We must leave now," Keah said. He stood and dragged the leaf boat to the water. "Soon we will be where we can join the others. After that, we go to one of our built-places."

"I'm looking forward to seeing it," April said.

Keah motioned for Paul to get into the boat while he kept it stable. Paul obliged. Climbing aboard with care, he seated himself at the bow and stowed his backpack. April got in next, followed by Ahee. Then, in one smooth motion, Keah pushed the craft off the sandy bank and leapt inside, taking a seat in the stern. The boat barely accommodated four adult bodies, so they all had to scoot close and straddle each another.

"Seems to be a little crowded," Paul said to April over his shoulder. He was glad it was her naked body pressing against him and not Ahee or Keah.

April giggled as she hugged him from behind. "I'm thinking of it as *intimate*. That sounds friendlier."

"So," Paul said to Keah, "we're floating, but how do we steer? Is the current just—"

Before he could finish his question, Keah and Ahee both grabbed sticks from the floor of the boat, dipped them about a foot into the water, and then brought them back out. In seconds, the wet ends split apart and opened wide, revealing a thick, fan-like membrane. By tying a small piece of vine around the base of the fan, Keah prevented it from splitting further up the shaft.

"Instant paddles," Paul noted. "Everything on this planet seems to be designed for a special use."

Ahee handed one to Paul so he and Keah could paddle until the leaf boat entered the larger river. Then, they allowed the current to move them for a while, steering away from banks, submerged rocks, and aquatic vegetation. April and Ahee sat quietly, taking in the full beauty of the environment and enjoying the sounds of the water as it splashed along the sides of the natural hull.

They traveled well into the early evening, stopping only long enough to refresh themselves and stretch their legs. Their course took them through wondrous lands of lush, colorful vegetation, different from the woodlands and jungle they had already experienced, but just as fantastic.

There were fields of thin, colored crystals that grew like wheat and made music when a breeze blew through them. There were also hilly spaces where massive mounds of plants moved under their own power, reshaping the landscape before their eyes. Sometimes, the boat passed through small groves where Paul saw trees resembling oak, maple, and ash. Others looked alien to him, especially the ones that could uproot themselves and move. Keah explained those kinds processed certain minerals and fed other plants through their roots. When the minerals became sparse, the trees migrated until they found fresh deposits. Often, Keah said, these types of trees would travel together over long distances—a moving forest.

* * *

Hourou's secondary sun was nearing the horizon by the time Keah steered the leaf-canoe into a small inlet and ran it onto a sandy bank. While Paul, April, and Ahee stretched their legs, Keah dragged the boat to the edge of the nearby tree line and abandoned it there.

"Is this where we wait for the others?" Paul asked.

"No, but we are near," Keah replied. "Can you both walk a short distance?"

"I'm fine," April answered, stretching her stiff muscles. "How 'bout you, Hon?"

Paul grunted as he rubbed his legs. "I can go for a while longer."

"Beyond this forest is a great, open space," Keah explained. "There, we will rest, eat, sleep, and wait for the others."

"Sounds good to me." Paul grabbed his backpack and offered it to April, wondering if she wanted anything from inside of it.

"I'm fine," she said, waving off his unasked question. After spending most of the day exploring the wilds of Hourou unclothed, neither of them was self-conscious anymore. Likewise, they had experienced no physical discomfort that would require covering themselves.

Paul donned the pack and watched April finish stretching. Had she grown more muscular since being on Hourou? He noted outlines on her arms and legs that suggested as much. He glanced down at his abdomen and was happy to see the faint shadow of a returning six-pack in place of his desk-job paunch. In only a few days, their bodies were already adapting to Hourou's ideal. He imagined what might happen if they never left, then brushed off the idea when April's pregnancy scar reminded him of those they would be leaving behind.

When everyone was ready, Keah guided the foursome to a wooded trail marked by glowing plants. This they followed for quite some time before arriving at a wide field of white, knee-high grass dotted with giant rock formations. Keah pointed to the closest one, and the four travelers continued through the field until they reached some massive boulders.

"This is the place for resting and waiting," Ahee said to Paul and April. After searching through the grass, she presented a round, basketball-sized stone to Keah. Pleased with her find, he climbed atop a boulder and motioned for her to toss the stone up to him. She did it so easily that Paul guessed either the thing was deceptively light or Ahee had the muscles of a bodybuilder.

Keah caught the stone and slammed it against the boulder, cracking it open like an enormous egg. As he placed the two halves on the top of the boulder, light radiated from them with the intensity of floodlights. Flecks of color danced in the beams of white like billions of diamonds.

"It's like two bowls of glittery light shooting up into the sky!" April exclaimed.

"Natural searchlights," Paul guessed. "Is it a beacon?" he asked Keah after he had climbed down. "A signal so the others can find us?"

"Yes. This will lead them here."

Ahee flattened the grass at the base of the boulder with her feet. "Rest now. We will bring food and lights from the forest. Sit now, and rest."

Paul and April complied while Keah and Ahee walked toward the woods and disappeared into the trees.

"So, here we wait," Paul said, surveying the immediate area. "I guess the others will see this beacon and follow it. I wonder how far away they are right now."

April reached over Paul's lap and grabbed the backpack. Turning it over in her hands, she searched for a seam that would show where to open it.

"Getting chilled?" Paul asked, assuming the reason for April's sudden desire to clothe herself.

"Not really." She continued to fumble with the pack. "I just want to look decent when the others get here."

"Interesting…"

"What?"

"I agree with you," Paul said, "but I think it's sort of funny."

"It's funny what I said, or funny that I can't get this darn bag open?"

Paul took the backpack from her and examined it, probing for a weak spot.

"Funny what you said…and funny how we feel."

"I'm not following you, Hon."

"We spent all day going native like Keah and Ahee and haven't felt strange about it at all. But as soon as we know the others will be here, we want to cover up."

"So?"

"Why do you think that is?"

April considered her uncovered form and then his. For an answer, she gave a heavy sigh, communicating that she was not in the mood for a philosophical discussion. "Can you just get it open?"

Paul located a seam. The leaves were hard to separate, but with some effort, he pried them apart. He then took out their balled-up clothing and handed April her shirt and shorts. She frowned at their condition while contritely dressing herself.

Paul also donned his tattered attire, wishing he could remain like Keah and Ahee, who even now were returning from the woods and looking perfectly respectful in their uncovered state. As they approached, Ahee glanced at Paul. He thought he noted a hint of disappointment in her eyes. Keah, too, regarded Paul and April quizzically for a moment, but then turned his attention to laying out the items he brought back from the forest. There was a variety of fruit and four melons filled with sloshing liquid. Keah also had a glowing plant that cast as much light as a small campfire. This he placed in the center of the area where Ahee had flattened the grass.

Ahee handed some fruit to Paul and April. "Eat and rest. If you have need, there is a place of refreshing beyond those trees," she said, pointing.

Keah sat next to her, and then they both reclined on their bed of grass. "We have traveled a very long way," Keah noted, fatigue heavy in his voice. "The children of Keah and Ahee, and the others from Blue, will find us here. When they arrive, we will all travel on together."

April lay back, as did Paul, both of them gazing up at the stars in the dark purple sky. Despite all the strange things they had experienced since being taken aboard the alien spacecraft, Paul trusted his new friends. He still had many questions, and much about them remained a mystery, but he believed they were doing their best to take care of their guests from Earth.

"Do you think the others have remained safe?" Paul asked Keah.

Keah closed his eyes and let out a deep, satisfied sigh.

Paul waited for an answer, but when none came, he returned his attention to the sky. *Either he's tired of my worrying, or he fell asleep,* he thought. *I guess I'll find out...eventually.* He felt for April's hand, squeezed it, and she squeezed back. *At least April and I have made it this far. We're safe, and with more luck...we'll soon be on our way home.*

"They are all safe," Keah said, startling Paul from his thoughts.

"I trust your instincts, Keah. You haven't been wrong about any-thing yet."

"Sleep, Paul," he said in a whisper. "There is no fear or danger on Hourou."

After hearing those words, Paul drifted into a deep and peaceful sleep where his dreams were a sanctuary of freedom and contentedness.

CHAPTER 23

The Darkness of Hourou

NIGHT: DAY 2 ON HOUROU

"Ellis, wake up!"

Ellis woke from his deep slumber and squinted at Yori. Shadows, cast by their campsite's glow plant, partially hid her face. "W-what is it?" he asked. "What's the problem?"

"Shh. Keep your voice down."

He rubbed the sleep from his eyes and inadvertently poked her in the side with his elbow. "Sorry," he whispered. *Why is she laying so close, anyway?* When their party bedded down for the night, he and Yori had chosen spots opposite one another. Yet she was now lying right next to him, propped up and shaking him to wakefulness.

"Shh," she repeated, placing a warm hand over his mouth. "Listen. Ellis, are you awake? Carlson snuck off."

Not this again. He brushed her hand away and glanced toward the empty bed of moss where Perry should have been. "So?" he said with indifference. "Maybe he just went to the loo."

"Ellis, you told me to wake you up if anything strange happened, or if Carlson disappeared again. Remember?"

He grunted his acknowledgment as he pushed himself up and forced his body to stand. While surveying their campsite, he noted that the four alien youths were still sleeping, heaped together in a mass of white bodies like a cute litter of kittens. He stepped to where Perry had been lying and felt the moss. It was a little warm, suggesting that Perry had left only a short time ago. *Alright, Carlson, let's see where you're off to now.*

"Are you going after him, then?" Yori whispered, watching him button his shirt and tighten his trousers.

"Yes. You stay here and watch after the young ones. I'm sure I won't be long."

Yori jumped up and brushed debris from her clothes. "Oh, no. You are not leaving me behind this time. I'm not a babysitter, and these four don't need a chaperone. I go with you, like it or not."

"That's not a good idea. One of us should always be with them in case something happens to the other."

"And for two days, you and Carlson have been able to go off on your own while I watched the kids. Isn't that just a bit parochial?"

"It's been to keep you safe, Yori."

"I appreciate the sentiment, but I can take care of myself."

"Yori..." Ellis wanted to press the point, but he held back. Yori was right; she could see to her own safety. She had proven it during their two-day trek across Hourou's hinterlands. He frowned, but acquiesced to her resoluteness. "Fine. Let's get after him, then."

They tiptoed away from the campsite, careful not to wake the sleeping youths.

"What direction?" Yori asked. "Where do you think he would go?"

"There's only one easy path." Ellis pointed toward a moss-covered trail that was demarcated by short, glowing plants. "I doubt he'd backtrack. So, we'll try this way."

Yori followed Ellis, hurrying along the dimly lit moss yet being careful where she placed her bare feet, even though it was as soft and safe as all the other paths they had encountered. The surrounding forest was dark, and it echoed with the strange sounds of nocturnal animal life. Every so often, an eerie shape would scurry across their route, causing a sudden stop from Ellis and eliciting a startled yelp from Yori.

"Do try to keep quiet," Ellis pleaded.

"I'm sorry, okay? Things jumping out from of the darkness tend to startle me."

Startled at every bend in the trail and at every little shadow, Ellis thought. *Why couldn't she have stayed with the kids?* He sighed and turned to face her. She was shaking, and her almond-shaped eyes, filled with fear, were darting between him and the shadowy trees. *Alright, Ellis, take it easy on her. It has been a rough trip.*

"I understand your jitters, Yori," he said with as much gentleness as he could muster, "but we don't want Carlson to hear us."

"I know. But I—" She yelped again before covering her mouth.

Ellis raised a finger and was about to chide her, but stopped when he realized she was seeing something behind him. Goose bumps formed on his skin just before he felt a touch on his shoulder.

"Ellis!" Yori screeched.

He glanced to the side and saw a little furry hand. Another was on his opposite shoulder, and two more were pressing against the small of his back. Craning his neck, he glimpsed a tiny smiling face. "It's alright," he said, relieved. "Just one of those monkey things. What did they call it? A mahtee, that's it."

Yori lowered her hand from her mouth and giggled when the mahtee finished climbing up Ellis's back and seated itself on his shoulder. A shaft of moonlight highlighted the permanent smile on its little face and reflected from its wide, curious eyes.

"Well, it looks as though we have another member on our night-time expedition," Ellis said, scratching the creature's head. "Shall we continue?"

Not waiting for an answer, he turned and resumed their hike along the path, allowing the mahtee to enjoy the ride. He would not have been able to shoo the creature away. When they encountered them the day before, Maiha had told him they were stubborn animals. "Stuck to me like a Japanese graduate student," Ellis said to his new companion.

"I heard that."

"Alright, little guy," he whispered to the mahtee, "perhaps you'll come in handy on this outing."

The path soon took a sharp turn, and the forest canopy opened enough to expose the sky. In the moonlight, Ellis could see the cliffs they had descended earlier that evening, which gave him a rough idea of where he was heading. As long as their route followed along the cliff base, he was certain he would not become lost.

Beyond the edge of the woods, they found an open area strewn with rocks and boulders. Yori came up alongside Ellis, her eyes searching for the path while the mahtee reached over and groped her hair. "Should we go back and get a glow plant?" she asked, batting away the creature's probing hands.

"No. I don't know how to uproot one without damaging it. We have the moonlight, though, and I think I can make out the trail ahead." He continued walking for a few yards, carefully testing the ground under his bare feet. "The moss continues in this direction. I see...sparkles in it. Can you?"

"Yes," Yori replied, examining the moss. "Yes, I see it. Like glitter. That should help."

"Let's keep going, then."

"Wait. We found a path, but we still don't even know if Carlson came this way."

"That's true enough. But I'm no trail guide, Yori. I suppose we could look for signs of his passing, though."

"Like footprints?"

"That would certainly be helpful."

"Like the footprints right over there?"

Ellis' eyes followed Yori's pointing finger to a part of the path where he could indeed make out indentations in the moss. The sparkling effect was darker in them, and they had the unmistakable shape of human feet. "Well done!" he exclaimed. "The prints must be very fresh. Otherwise, the moss would have sprung back up by now."

"It shows that Carlson's smart enough to follow the soft trail," Yori observed.

"Let's do likewise...and before we lose the footprints."

They followed the spoor between crags and boulders and over rocky hills until they arrived at the bank of a narrow brook. On the other side, the mossy path continued. Perry's impressions were still visible, but they looked different. Ellis stepped gingerly over the running water, then stooped down to inspect the trail. "Are you seeing this, Yori?"

Yori bent down beside him and studied the imprints. "There are two sets of prints now," she confirmed.

"Either Carlson's being followed, or someone joined him here."

Yori looked at the surrounding hillocks. Then she scanned the cliff and the distant forest. "Let's go back, Ellis," she said, nervous. "We probably shouldn't be out here alone."

Ellis rose and walked along the path a little further, examining the prints. "They're parallel—side by side—walking together. Carlson met a friend out here."

"Who?" Yori asked. "Who else would be out here? If there were more of the native people around, the kids would have known, don't you think?"

"We can only theorize. But I plan to find out. If Carlson has been sneaking off and meeting with someone, we need to know about it."

Yori let out a sigh. "You're right."

"So let's move before we lose the prints." Ellis adjusted the mahtee on his shoulder and waited for Yori to catch up. "Stay close now, Yori," he urged. "We don't know who or what else is out here."

* * *

After rushing along the trail for quite some time, Ellis abruptly halted and held up a warning hand for Yori to do the same.

"What's happening?" she asked in a whisper. "Do you see something?"

There was nothing up ahead but a dimly lit path of moss, huge boulders, and brush. Still, Ellis was nervous, and the mahtee on his shoulder was fidgety. Yori's intuition convinced her that something was about to change, and probably not for the good.

Ellis scanned the rocky landscape without answering her. The mahtee mimicked his movements, or perhaps it was he who was mimicking the animal.

"What's wrong with *him?*" Yori asked.

"He's been acting this way for a while now. He keeps looking around as if—"

"Ellis," Yori interrupted, "did you hear that?"

Ellis cocked his head. "Hear what? I was talking."

A second eerie growl rumbled through the quiet night air. The mahtee stood upright on Ellis' shoulder. The way it stared into the rock-strewn field alarmed Yori.

"What...*was* that?"

"I don't know, and I certainly don't like it."

"Ellis, let's go back now. Who knows what lives out here? I didn't make it all this way for a dinosaur to squash or eat me."

Ellis understood she was referring to some of the giant creatures they had already encountered on their journey. Though every animal had been a docile herbivore, Ellis was sure there must be carnivores around as well. He believed that nature always provided a food chain to maintain balance. Unless Hourou was quite different, which he doubted, there had to be predators to thin herds of other animals and uphold the natural order.

"Stay still, Yori," Ellis warned. He strained to see in the dim moonlight. There was another growl, this time closer. Frantically, he searched for a place to hide or a route of escape. Behind them were some tall boulders. Without hesitation, he grabbed Yori's hand and pulled her toward them. The next sound was much louder, like a lion's roar, and heavy footsteps, crunching and scattering fragile rocks, accompanied it.

"Climb!" Ellis ordered, pushing Yori against the tallest boulder. "Get to the top! Quick!"

Yori needed no prodding. In seconds, she was already halfway up, pulling herself along the rough surface, using whatever crevices she could find. Ellis was right behind her. The top was wide and slanted, so it accommodated both of them and even offered some concealment from the approaching beast. Ellis crawled alongside Yori, ensuring she was secure by helping her to position her feet and hands. She held on to the boulder in a death grip, eyes filled with terror.

"Ellis," Yori whispered.

"Shh!" he warned. "Not a sound! Maybe it will pass by us."

Ellis risked a peek over the edge and flinched when an enormous shape appeared from within the shadows of the rock field. It was standing right where he and Yori had been moments ago. The mahtee, still on Ellis' shoulder, craned to get a better view. "Please...don't...move," Ellis muttered under his breath.

Yori smothered a gasp with her hand, sure that the mahtee would expose them. But the little animal just slunk down Ellis' back in silence and disappeared into the darkness.

Ellis continued watching the larger beast as it became visible in the moonlight. Four-legged and feline, it was as big as an adult elephant. The head resembled that of a mountain lion, as did the rear legs and tail, but the front limbs were smaller and ended in grasping hands. Short fur covered its body, striped like a tiger in indiscernible colors.

The beast sniffed at the boulder that hid Ellis and Yori. Before it noticed him, Ellis ducked his head, looked at Yori, and raised a single finger to his lips, signaling for her to remain quiet. She nodded and closed her eyes, as if praying. He held his breath and did likewise.

Seconds later, Ellis felt a rush of air as the creature lifted him from the rock. Held high in the grasp of a massive fist, he could only watch in helplessness while the beast also grabbed Yori and sniffed at her with its giant nose. She screamed once, and then her body went limp, dangling lifelessly while the hunter examined its prey.

Ellis squirmed against the beast's restraint, but it only made the thing tighten its grip. "Ow! Put me down!" he yelled.

Of course, the monster ignored his command. Holding the two captives close to its furry chest, it looked toward the cliffs and then carried them into the dark wilderness.

Ellis was now close enough to see Yori's face. She was still in a faint. "Yori! Are you alright? Yori! Answer me!"

She stirred and slowly opened her eyes.

"Yori!" he called again. "Can you hear me? Look at me, Yori!"

As she recovered from her blackout, she realized where she was and struggled to free herself. "No! Ellis!"

"Don't struggle! It only makes the beast tighten its grip!"

Yori kept trying to get loose, but she soon found that Ellis was correct. "Ellis! What's happening to us?"

"Save your energy," he instructed. "Make your body go limp."

"Where is it taking us? Why are we even still alive?"

"I don't know. It doesn't seem to be interested in eating us...at least not for the moment."

"Look! There's a rope on its neck."

"So there is." Ellis examined that with interest. "Perhaps the beast is domesticated." He also noticed that his other traveling companion— the mahtee—was now riding on the creature's shoulder. "And there's our little friend."

Yori twisted around to get a clearer view. "He's not afraid," she noted. "And this—whatever it is—doesn't seem to care about him."

"That's a good sign, Yori," Ellis said, gladdened by the strength in her voice. "If it's not a carnivore," he said under his breath, "perhaps we'll only be play things and not a late-night snack."

"What did you say?"

"Nothing. But I'm thinking that we're safe for the time being. If it meant us harm, we—"

"I get the point," Yori interrupted.

"Are you injured at all?"

"No, but if this animal keeps tightening its grip, I'll be going down a dress size."

Ellis frowned, wondering if she would survive to wear a dress again. To the beast, the mahtee was just a little nuisance. The two humans, however, could provide it with a few satisfying meals.

"Don't squirm, Yori," he demanded. "Go limp. If it thinks we're dead, it might get careless and give us an opportunity to escape."

"Okay," Yori agreed. "I hope you're right."

* * *

The cat-beast carried its two human prizes through the shadows of the high cliffs, but soon changed direction to enter the nearby woodlands. Ellis squirmed in the animal's grasp and turned his body forward so he could see where it was going. Yori did the same. Then both of them went limp, hoping the creature would lose interest and release them.

The forest ahead differed from the ones Ellis experienced during his two days on Hourou. Gargantuan trees resembling the great baobabs of Madagascar grew far apart between rocky hillocks, colorful scrub, and moss-laden paths. They had wide, smooth trunks that were at least two hundred feet tall and topped by stubby branches with enormous, flat leaves.

"Yori, are you seeing all of this?" Ellis whispered.

"Yes. I'd say it looks pretty, especially in the moonlight, but I'm thinking of other things."

"As am I."

"It's taken us quite a distance, Ellis. If we can even get away, how are we going to find our way back?"

"We'll think of something. Now that we're in a forest, keep your eyes open for something to use as a weapon...like long sticks for spears."

"I'm not much good in a fight."

"Most of us aren't...until faced with fighting for our lives."

"I was hoping it would've dropped us by now. Why go so far? Animals don't normally behave like this."

"Have you seen *anything* normal since we crashed on this world?"

"No," Yori admitted. "But it's been a beautiful and safe place."

"Maybe you have something there."

"What do you mean?"

"I've been expecting to end up as this creature's dinner—"

"That's reassuring. Thanks."

"Let me finish. We might suppose the worst only because we're comparing this planet to our own—to how things happen there. Why are we afraid when nothing has happened during our visit here to warrant such fear? No danger has threatened us—not one."

"Until now."

"Yes. Until now."

"So what does that do for your hypothesizing?"

Ellis glanced up at the face of their captor. The creature ignored them, huffing and sniffing as it ran through the forest. He noted the beast was acting more like a dog that was fetching something for its master than a monster looking for a private place to have a meal.

"As strange as it is to say it, I think it's taking us somewhere," Ellis said.

"Not to a den where it will feed us to its cubs, I hope."

"A distinct possibility," Ellis admitted. "That's why we have to be diligent in getting free and defending ourselves."

"Why not fight it now, before—"

"And be crushed?" Ellis interrupted.

Yori considered the ground beneath her dangling feet, wondering what she would do if the creature dropped her. Running would not get her far. The animal could take two steps to her ten with its enormous stride. Ellis was right. The only chances they had were in fighting or out-thinking it.

Soon, the forest thickened and a dark canopy blocked much of the moonlight. Glowing plants marked trails that led deeper into the woods. The cat-beast chose a path as if by memory and quickened its pace, clenching its prey tighter while navigating around odd-shaped vegetation and unseen obstacles. It was heading for a well-lit intersection of pathways. When they arrived there, they encountered a crowd of bronze-skinned natives. The creature slowed a little, allowing them to view what it carried, but it did not stop. Nor did the people make any attempt to free the two captives. Instead, they just watched with curiosity while the animal passed by, straining to get a better look at the strange humans trapped within its fists.

"Ellis! They're the same as the brown-skinned ones we saw on the spaceship!" Yori exclaimed as she gawked back at her audience.

"Indeed. But this doesn't seem to be our stop."

"Why are they just staring at us?"

"I don't know. Perhaps to them this is a normal sight."

The aliens were certainly similar to those Ellis had encountered on the alien craft. Their skin was a mix of bronze and brown and some of them painted lines on their bodies that followed the natural contours of their muscles and bones. The women all had knee-length, black hair, while the men wore it only to their shoulders or tied back in a ponytail. All were naked save for their tiny loincloths, like the wild jungle tribes of Earth.

As the beast passed through the middle of the gathering, Ellis wanted to call out to the natives. He stopped himself when he remembered they would not understand his language. Yori tried anyway, but her shrill voice became lost in the surrounding commotion and thumping of the animal's giant feet.

The crowd of bronzes thinned further down the trail, but Ellis could make out encampments scattered throughout the forest. Hundreds of people huddled in groups around glow plants, slept on moss beds, and strolled between campsites.

"We seem to have entered a settlement," Ellis said. "Perhaps it's a village. If so, there might yet be hope for us."

"Unless they're cannibals," Yori quipped.

"Now you're sounding like Carlson. How about expressing a little optimism, Yori? After all, I warned you to stay behind."

"I was wondering when you were going to bring that up."

"Observe everything. We may find a way out of this."

Because the trail was well-marked by glowing plants, Ellis could see a small glade just ahead of them. Natives gathered at the entrance, and by their imposing stances, they appeared to be guarding it. The cat-beast slowed to a walk and growled as it approached the formidable looking group.

"Be ready, Yori," Ellis whispered. "I think we may have arrived at our destination."

"Okay. I'm with you."

When the creature reached the guardians of the glade, it did not pass through them. Instead, it paced along the entrance, huffing and sniffing at them like it was expecting something to happen. One of the male guards hurried away. The others, as well as a growing group of onlookers, did nothing more than watch the cat-beast and try to get a better view of the captives.

"Now what?" Yori asked. "Some sort of standoff?"

"Look at the clearing," Ellis suggested. "It's lit up."

Yori twisted her body around. The glade was indeed glowing and bathed in pastel colors.

"Must be lots of glow plants in there," she noted. "I think I see stone structures, too."

"Maybe this is the entrance to a village, then."

After a few tense moments, the guard who rushed away reappeared. A female with a lighter skin tone than the others accompanied him. Unfazed by the cat-beast's menacing growls and defiant stomping, she strode up to it, pushed her hair behind her body, and spoke in soothing tones. The calming effects of her actions were immediate. The creature stopped pacing, bent down, and sniffed her with affection.

"A pet, then?" Ellis wondered out loud.

Yori squirmed and tested its grip again. "I hope so."

The female reached out, petted the beast's nose, and continued to speak to it. This elicited a deep purring sound Ellis could feel rumble through his own body.

"I beg your pardon," he called out from under the creature's chest, "but since this beast is clearly friendly toward you, would it be too much to ask for us to be set free?"

The woman regarded him while she scratched the animal's furry cheeks. Then she said something that made it loosen its grip. Ellis promptly pushed at its fingers, which gave him just enough room to slide out of its hand. After dropping to the ground, he looked up at Yori and waited for her to do the same. She wiggled her body and let out a little yelp when the cat-beast willingly released her and she fell.

"Are you alright?" Ellis asked, pulling her to her feet.

Yori hurried to readjust her disheveled clothing. "Yes," she replied. "So...now what?"

Ellis glanced at the natives. "Can anyone here understand me?"

They responded only with curious and quizzical stares.

"Well, at least they're not poking at us with spears," Yori said.

Ellis turned his attention back to the female native, who was now right in front of him. "Can *you* understand me?" he asked her as he reached for Yori's hand.

The woman stopped playing with her pet and waved as if warning them to move out from under its hulking body. Ellis understood the action and pulled Yori away from the creature. While doing so, his eyes searched for an escape route and for something he might use as a weapon.

"Don't do anything yet, Ellis," Yori cautioned, feeling the anxiousness in his hand's tightening grip.

"Get ready," he whispered.

"No. There's nowhere to run."

"This could be our only chance."

"No, Ellis. We're surrounded. Trust my intuition this once."

"Then what do you suggest?"

"Observe...like you told me. She got the monster to let us go. Let's see what she does next."

"You've picked a bloody good time to become brave and analytical."

"Well, am I right?"

"Of course."

The bronze woman reached for the big cat's rope leash and gave it a tug, bringing the beast to rest on all fours and causing its mahtee rider to jump off. The mahtee considered the girl for a moment, but rather than choosing her for a new companion, it darted into the surrounding woods. She followed it with her eyes and smirked. Then she gestured for the other natives to step aside to allow Ellis and Yori to enter the glade.

"Us?" Ellis asked her. "Go...in there?"

She did not answer. Turning away, she led her giant pet back toward the path and disappeared into the darkness.

"Looks like she wants us to go in alone," Ellis said to Yori.

"What tipped you off?"

"Funny. Well...let's not disappoint her."

Towering trees and two stone pillars marked the glade's entrance. Inside, a walkway made of glowing cobblestones crossed a grassy field and ended at a high wall. Behind that was a formation of enormous monoliths. Ellis and Yori followed the path until they reached a four-foot-wide gap that split the wall from top to bottom.

"The only entrance," Yori observed.

Ellis examined the gap and noted that the walkway continued through and then turned to the left and right. "Looks safe enough," he said, "and well-traveled. It reminds me of—"

"Ellis, we have an audience."

He glanced over his shoulder and noticed a group of curious natives gathering just inside the glade's inner partial portico. "No surprise there."

"It's like they're waiting for us to go in."

"Well, now that they've blocked our way out, I suppose we'll have to oblige." He stepped into the gap and beckoned Yori to follow him. On the other side, they faced another wall where the path split off to the left and right. High above, they could see the starry night sky.

"Giant hallways with no roof," Yori said. "At least we have light. What do you think makes the rocks glow?"

"No idea. They're not painted. Probably fluorescent minerals inside." He considered each direction and shrugged. "Let's go right."

"Good. I was hoping you wouldn't say: 'Let's split up. You take the left, and I'll take the right.'"

"That only happens in bad movies. Everyone knows the survivors are the ones who stick together."

The path followed the curves of the walls on either side, continuing in a circular pattern even when they had to change direction. After many twists and turns, Ellis deduced they were walking in a stone labyrinth. It did not take long to reach the center. Once there, they discovered a large amphitheater that filled a natural depression. Rows of short, glowing stones ringed the structure, presumably to provide seating. Ellis estimated it could accommodate several thousand people.

"Incredible!" he exclaimed, taking in the sight from the uppermost row of seats. "This is the first architecture we've encountered on this planet, Yori."

Yori was just as awestruck. "It looks ancient. Everything glows. It must have been beautiful once."

"It's actually not that old!"

The voice startled them, but both immediately recognized it as their wayward politician. Ellis spun around, his eyes peering into every shadow as he searched for him. "Carlson!"

* * *

"Down here!"

"There he is, Ellis." Yori pointed to a dais that occupied the central space of the amphitheater.

Sitting on a throne-like seat made of glowing rock, Perry waved for them to join him. "Come on! Come on!"

"What the devil..." Ellis said. While he and Yori descended along the steps, they saw that at least a dozen of the bronze-skinned natives was sitting at Perry's feet and attending to him with food and drink. The strange scene resembled a fictional royal court—the magnate on his throne and his subjects doting on him.

"Well, well, well," Perry called out as his visitors passed the last rows of seating. "Look what the cat dragged in!"

Ellis and Yori exchanged confused glances.

"What is going on here, Carlson?" Ellis demanded.

Perry put up his hand, signaling for them to stop in front of the dais. Ellis threatened to advance, but Yori grabbed his arm and pulled him back.

"Careful," Yori whispered. "We don't know what he's up to yet."

Ellis held back, but not before showing Perry a disapproving scowl.

"Now, now, my Earth friends," Perry said, noting Ellis' defiance. "There's no need for hostility here." He rose, waved off his attendants, and strode toward Ellis and Yori with royal pomp.

Yori smiled at him, but only to keep the peace. "Listen, Perry. We're glad we found you, but why—?"

"Patience, Miss Shimizu," he interrupted. "I will explain everything." He had been simpering with the arrogance of a supreme dictator, but when he stepped even closer and put his hands on their shoulders, his countenance darkened with urgent dread. "Listen to me carefully, both of you," he said, desperation in his voice. "If you follow my lead and play along, we just might get out of this."

"Get out of what?" Ellis asked, alarmed by Perry's sudden trepidation. He glanced at the natives. They were studying him, like overachieving students expecting a climactic end to an important lesson.

"I can't explain right now," Perry whispered. "Everything depends on you playing along. Can you do that? Or would you rather be cat food?"

"We can do that," Yori replied, giving Ellis a pleading glance.

Ellis rolled his eyes and scowled again at Perry. "I swear, Carlson, if you're—"

"Good!" Perry patted their shoulders and backed away, resuming his loud and pompous act. "It makes me happy to have your cooperation." As he swaggered back to his seat, he made a gesture toward one of the female natives. "Offer some food and drink to our guests," he commanded.

The girl rose, pushed her hair behind her body, and held out a bowl of fruit.

"Come closer," Perry said to Ellis and Yori. "They won't bite."

Yori walked across the dais and accepted some of the fruit. Ellis followed, eying Perry with growing suspicion.

"Do the thing with the hair," Perry instructed Yori. "It seems to make them happy."

Yori complied. With shaky fingers, she combed through her hair and pulled some behind her ears. In response, the female native bowed with reverence.

"Careful with the gestures, Yori," Ellis warned.

"Quite so, Minister," Perry agreed. "Body language means a lot to them."

"But they don't know what we're saying?" Yori asked through a bite of fruit.

"I do."

The voice came from behind the hulking throne. All heads turned toward the spot, just as another female native appeared. She looked similar to the other girls that were there with Perry, but her skin was a lighter bronze. A black mane of hair reached down to her knees, flowing over a sheer white gown that did nothing to conceal the shapely body underneath. Ellis recognized her as the same girl who had controlled the cat-beast outside of the glade. Yet, there was something else familiar about her as well. While he studied her face, she bored into him with a powerful gaze and seated herself at Perry's feet.

"Ah, the queen has returned," Perry said, mocking in his voice. "My friends, this is Ria—at least that's the easier version of her name. She's tried and tried to get me to pronounce it right, but, alas, I can't make heads or tails of their unusual language with all of its ohs, ahs, and uhs."

Stupefied, Ellis looked back and forth between Perry and Ria, unable to decide which of his many questions to ask first.

Yori broke the awkward silence by doing what made sense to her feminine nature. "It's a pleasure to meet you, Ria," she said, trying to hide the tremble in her voice. "Is it true that you're a queen—a leader of these people?"

Ria blushed and covered herself with her hair, embarrassed by Yori's question. Oddly, she looked up at Perry for an answer.

"*Queen* is a figure of speech," Perry explained. "We must use many figures of speech around here. It makes our Earth conversations much more intimate. Are you catching the bone I'm throwing?"

Yori gave Ellis a questioning glance, but he was just gawking at Perry and Ria.

"I see you're wrestling with an identity crisis," Perry said. "Yes, you recognize the woman, Minister. She's the same one you saw on the spaceship. The white angels beamed her up—her and her two cohorts in crime, that is—right after us. You remember the story."

"But—"

"Let me finish, Minister. So here is Ria. She and her male friends have been tailing us since the crash. That stopped when we traveled near the lands where many of her people live, and she reunited with them."

"Why are *you* here, Carlson?" Ellis demanded.

"Me? Well, I'm what you'd call a lab rat."

Yori looked sideways at him, her eyes squinting with suspicion. "What are you talking about?"

"Ria contacted me during our journey, wisely discerning that I am the smartest of our group, and—"

"Of course, you seem to have set her straight regarding that mistake," Ellis quipped.

"And," Perry continued, ignoring the swipe, "she reached out to me for help."

"Help with what?" Yori asked.

"Help with being her study partner."

"You're not making much sense," Ellis chided.

"And I told you already that it must be that way. Honestly, Minister, can't you just read between the lines? I'm telling you important headlines from today's paper."

"I think I'm following you," Yori said. "Let me guess about the rest of the story. The girl hooked you like a fish after a worm and she reeled you all the way here."

"Right! The feminine analysis scores against the male bravado!" Perry joked.

"Hilarious," Ellis rebuked.

"Now," Yori continued, "she wants to examine you; you're a lab specimen."

"Right again, Miss Shimizu."

"Because you're so concerned about being in this fish tank," Ellis added, catching on to the cloaked conversation, "I assume you expect a frying pan if the fish don't cooperate."

"Yes, Minister," Perry said with sincere appreciation. "Now there are *three* little fishes in the tank, since two of them couldn't resist following the lead fish upstream."

Yori put her hands on her hips and took a step toward Perry. "Well, the big tuna wouldn't be in this tank if—"

"You will tell us of Blue!"

Startled by Ria's sudden and loud demand, the Earth humans gaped as she rose from her place at Perry's feet and addressed them.

"Yo woo-eds have no meee-ning," she said, trying to form words they would understand. "Ria mus learn. You will tell the Dah-Ahey of Blue."

"Now Ria," Perry said in his best pompous style, "you know we made an agreement."

"Agreement?" Ellis asked.

Perry rose and began pacing between Ria and the Earth visitors.

"Nothing formal, of course," he said with a chuckle. "Ria wants to learn everything about Earth. It fascinates her for some reason, almost to the point of being an obsession."

Ria looked at Perry through desperate eyes. "You mus take—"

"I know, little honey pot. I'm getting to that part."

Yori cringed at Perry's blatant disrespect. He was playing the role of a belligerent despot when he should have been acting like a respectful ambassador. She wanted to intervene for Ria but hoped Perry was exaggerating his act for a good reason.

"So," Perry continued, "I agreed to tell Ria all about Earth if she would explain to me all about her people and their relationship with the other inhabitants of this planet."

"The Ah-Ahey," Ria added with contempt.

"My little Ria! How well you follow along now! Thank you!"

Ria beamed at Perry's false praise, unaware he was mocking her.

"See, Minister, how quickly they pick up our language?"

"Yes," Ellis replied, "but I still object to the contemptuous delivery of your comments. *We're* the visitors here...the guests."

"We'll get back to that point in a moment," Perry rebuked. "As I was saying, I agreed to a simple exchange of information. Unfortunately, Ria is reluctant to tell me *anything* about the Ah-Ahey—that would be the white aliens—and her people, the Dah-Ahey. I've not been able to discern why, but the subject seems to be very distasteful to Ria."

"Then it sounds like your *agreement* is useless," Yori noted.

"Not quite, Yori. Ria came up with an alternative, being a shrewd negotiator—something I respect so very much." Perry smirked at Ria. "Why don't *you* tell them about your proposal, my dear?"

Ria reached behind Perry's seat and retrieved a bundle wrapped in large leaves. As she unrolled it, Ellis recognized remnants of clothing the Earth visitors had stored aboard the alien spacecraft. Ria dropped her robe and examined Ellis and Yori for a moment. Then she clothed herself with the tattered items.

"Ellis, that's my lab coat," Yori whispered, "or what's left of it, anyway."

"Yes, and she also found Mrs. Theele's shoes, unless those are yours as well."

"Don't interrupt," Perry warned. "This is where it all gets very serious."

Ria was unsure how to wear the clothes the correct way, but she was proud of her efforts. Convinced that she had dressed herself like an Earth human, she paraded along the dais like a fashion model. Behind the bewildered visitors, a large crowd of Dah-Ahey had entered the amphitheater unnoticed, providing Ria with a sizable audience. They watched her in silence, amazed at how she was flaunting her new costume.

To Ellis, she resembled a hung-over college student who could not dress herself after a long night of revelry. She had discerned the use of some purple panties, wearing them over her diminutive loincloth, but had stretched someone's socks over her breasts and had placed April's shoes on the wrong feet. Yori's lab coat, which Ria had draped over her shoulders, resembled a bolero jacket after its previous alteration.

Ellis held back a snicker when Ria presented herself to the three Earth visitors. She twirled before each of them, beaming and expecting praise. Speechless, Yori nodded and offered her an awkward smile. Ellis did the same, but Perry just sneered at her, keeping up his act of an unimpressed tyrant.

"You will take us to Blue," she said, bowing to Ellis and Yori. "Carlson said he will thee-ink about it. You are here now, too. There is control in the three. You are complete. So you can take us to Blue." She rose and stood before Perry. "Carlson, there is no more thinking. You are three and can now do this. You must take us back to Blue."

Perry looked at Ellis and Yori with raised eyebrows, wondering if they now understood their predicament. For a long, awkward moment, no one said anything. Then Perry rose from his seat, picked up Ria's robe, and handed it to her.

"This is much more your style, kitten," he said with heavy sarcasm. "If you go to Earth, you must learn about life there *first*. I told you before, we dress to impress, and what you're doing makes you more like a...well...like a clown."

Ria took her robe from Perry and considered her half-dressed state. "Cah-low-en?"

"*Clown,* my young doll face," Perry corrected. "Dressing yourself is only *one* of the many lessons you have to learn. Otherwise, you would never fit in there. That's what you really want, right? To go back to Earth...and stay?"

Ria's eyes widened with surprise.

"You see, my little peach princess? I'm pretty good at the guessing game, too. Thank you for verifying something important."

Ria ignored his comment as she changed back into her robe, unfazed by his rude manner.

"Look here, Carlson," Ellis demanded. "I've had enough of you disrespecting this girl. Some of your actions here I understand, but I won't stand by any longer and watch you treat her like this!"

"I'm actually being quite kind, Minister," Perry said as he watched Ria finish changing. "That's better, my dear. Now, I must talk to my friends here in private. That means away from other people. Would you mind asking everyone to leave?"

Ria nodded and offered Ellis and Yori a genial smile. With a slight flick of her wrist, she commanded the entire crowd of Dah-Ahey, including the ones on the dais, to exit the amphitheater. When all of them had left, she picked up the Earth clothing and held it to her chest like a cherished gift.

"Of course," Perry said to her with mock kindness. "You can keep those. I don't think Minister or Miss Shimizu here will mind."

"Uh, sure," Yori said. "Please do."

Ria bowed to her again before strutting out of the amphitheater.

"Alone at last," Perry said with relief, "but probably not for long."

"Why don't you start from the beginning, Carlson?" Ellis suggested. "How did you get here in the first place? Why have you been sneaking off with that girl? Just what—"

"We don't have time for all that," Perry interrupted. "I told you already. The girl sought *me* out. I played along so I could learn something about her people. You should both understand and appreciate *learning*."

"Alright," Yori said, trying to stay calm. Like Ellis, she was quite angry, but knew it would gain nothing to fight with each other. "Why all the subterfuge? Why the act? These people have put you on a pedestal and you're treating them like...like—"

"Will you two at least give me the benefit of the doubt? I'm not enjoying this. What kind of person do you think I am?" Perry dropped himself onto the throne in a huff, frustrated by their accusations.

Yori softened, but was still dubious. "Okay. So what is *really* going on here, then?"

"Look," Perry answered, "you've both seen how these people learn language so quickly. They pick up on little things we don't even realize we're saying or doing. I'd think they were mind readers if I didn't know better. What throws them off, though, are figures of speech, sarcasm, and odd descriptions. Derisive words and doublespeak also throw them off; it goes over their heads."

"Well, I'm glad you didn't mean all that," Yori said. "It was difficult to watch."

"Of course I don't mean it!" Perry chided. "It's the only way I've been able to prevent them from figuring me out."

"Alright, we get it," Ellis said, relieved. "What about all this talk of agreements? What do these people want? Are we in danger here?"

"I told you. They want to know all about Earth."

"What specifically?" Ellis asked.

"Everything! How we live, communicate, dress. What we eat, what we do. Everything."

"Why?" Yori asked.

Perry hesitated. "Ria wants to go back with us. She hasn't said why. I'm assuming she might wish to stay there, but who knows? She just asks questions. When I ask them to her, she dodges them—expertly, too, I must admit."

"Do you think she's hiding something?" Ellis asked.

"Obviously."

Ellis studied Perry's face, wondering if he was holding back some information. "Interesting."

"Yeah, but it gets us nowhere," Perry said.

"What do you mean?" Yori asked.

"I mean that we're not going anywhere until we get past the stalemate."

"So we're prisoners?"

Perry shrugged and threw his hands in the air. "That's not how *they* see it, but here we are, and my acting will not impress them very much longer. Ria's a shrewd one. She must know I'm stalling now."

"Why not tell them we're leaving?" Yori asked. "We say 'Thanks, but no thanks,' and we walk out of here."

"Not going to happen," Perry said.

"Why not?"

"For one thing, I have no idea how to get back to where we came from, do you?"

"No."

Perry glanced at their bare feet. "How *did* you two find your way here, anyway?"

"Completely against our will," Ellis answered. "We followed your trail for a while. When we reached the base of the cliffs, a cat-like beast accosted us. Then it brought us here straightaway."

Perry stood and looked them both over. "Are you hurt?"

"No," Ellis said, surprised by Perry's concern. "It's strange, but the animal was mostly gentle."

"That was Fluffy."

"Who?" Yori asked.

"The big cat. It's Ria's pet...and the second reason we can't just walk out of here."

"You mean it would attack us?" Ellis asked.

"I wouldn't want to find out."

"All it did was carry us here," Yori noted. "It might be like all the other animals—"

"We're in a different environment here, Miss Shimizu." Perry interrupted. "The people are unfamiliar, and the animals are, too...at least the giant cat ones. Anyway, we don't know how they've trained them or how many more they keep around here as pets. So I'm not willing to just go running into the woods. At worst, they'd unleash the beasts and let them hunt us down and eat us. At best, they'd just grab us and bring us right back here."

"What do you suggest, then?" Ellis asked.

"I don't know. I suppose we'll have to *talk* our way out. They've been treating me like royalty. I can keep using that as leverage."

"To what end?" Ellis wondered out loud.

"To get them to let us go," Perry answered. "We'll stall for time. Keep them guessing. Maybe we can confuse them enough to think we're of no good use to them."

"That could backfire and get us killed," Ellis proposed.

"Killed?" Yori snapped. "I doubt the people of this planet are *capable* of violence."

"That might be true of our angelic friends with the snow-white skin," Perry said, "but these are the Dah-Ahey. We know nothing about *them*. Frankly, their mysterious ways concern me. They're *very* different from the Ah-Ahey. Don't let Ria's cute-little-girl act fool you."

"Well, she seems to fancy *you*, Carlson," Ellis jeered. "You must have charmed her well during your little trysts."

"Don't be ridiculous!" Perry rebuked. "It takes a lot more than a pretty naked girl to distract me from what I want."

"What *do* you want?"

"Only information. I've uncovered a dark side to this *Planet of Eden*. There's much more going on here than the Ah-Ahey have let us know, Minister. If we are indeed ambassadors from Earth, then we'd better have all the facts."

A long silence followed Perry's revelation. Ellis walked to the far end of the dais to gather his thoughts.

"So," Perry said to Yori, "what do *you* think?"

"I agree. We have to be very careful here. I'm just not sure that keeping them confused is the right way."

Perry smirked and shrugged his shoulders. "Let me know when you come up with something better."

Annoyed by Perry's smugness, Yori was about to assail him with a well-deserved rebuke when Ellis returned to them.

"Look, Carlson," Ellis said. "I'm sorry for doubting you. I mostly deal with physics problems, not people problems. This is *your* realm— negotiations, secrets, politics. You keep taking the lead here. Perhaps we'll soon figure a way out of this mess."

Perry ignored Yori's glare of disagreement and smiled at Ellis' sudden show of respect. "The three of us are in this together now," he said. "Ria thinks there is ultimate strength in three. She seems to think we can do anything."

"I wonder if that includes escaping," Yori quipped.

Before Perry could answer, a deep growling sound interrupted their conversation. Ellis and Yori recognized it right away. The cat-beast was loose inside the amphitheater. Ellis grabbed Yori's hand and pulled her behind the throne, using it for cover. Perry scanned the area, standing his ground with defiance.

"Perry, be careful!" Yori shouted.

"Shh! Don't be so loud," he demanded. "Ria, my little lovely, are you there?"

Ria appeared through one of the high entrances, now clothed in only her scanty loincloth and Yori's lab coat bolero. Flanked by two impressive Dah-Ahey males, she strode with authority toward the dais. Among the moonlight and glowing stones, she looked alluring and frightening at the same time.

"Ah, there you are," Perry called out. "And where is Fluffy?"

Ria made a slight gesture with her hand and the beast stepped out from the shadows behind the dais. Another signal from Ria brought two more of the beasts into view, each on opposite sides of the amphitheater.

"Surrounded," Ellis said.

"Come out into the open," Perry whispered to Ellis and Yori. "Don't show fear of any kind. Remember that."

"Sure," Yori mumbled. "Three giant cats and a vexed woman with a small army behind her. Nothing to fear here."

Perry ignored her comment while he assessed the situation. Ria's facial expressions seemed different. No longer playing the part of a naive and infatuated young girl, she was now mimicking Perry's role as an arrogant autocrat. As she climbed the dais, she motioned for the two males to wait on the bottom steps. She then sashayed past Perry, pausing to stroke his cheek, and flopped herself onto the throne.

Perry refused to show that he was stunned. "My little doll-face returns at last," he said, eying her with mock appreciation. "The jacket adds a pleasant touch, sexy, but I think I like the robe on you better."

Ria sneered at him with an expression that was unbecoming for her beautiful face.

"She's copying you, Carlson," Ellis warned. "Please be careful what you teach her."

"Quite right, my good man. She's a fine actress indeed. I almost wish—"

"Perry," Yori interrupted, "How about if you use what little authority you have left and tell her we're leaving before this situation deteriorates?"

"Leee-ving?" Ria questioned, staring at Perry. "There is no leaving, *my good man.*"

As if on cue, the cat creature just behind Ria's throne growled, emphasizing to Perry that he was losing the upper hand. To maintain some control, he sat with smugness on the arm of the seat and leaned in close to Ria. Before he spoke, he glanced at the amphitheater and saw an audience of Ria's people seating themselves.

"My little cupcake," he said in a whisper, "we have to rejoin the others." Ria stiffened, but Perry kept talking to her in soothing tones. "We have to get back to them, Ria—to the others from Blue. We can't leave Hourou without them."

Ria grinned, resuming her act of innocent young girl. "Blue? Yes! You will take us to Blue!"

"It would be better for you to learn first. You remember how confusing it was when you were there? It frightened you. You're only excited now because you're back on Hourou. On my planet, there is much to fear, Ria."

Ria's head dropped and her lips formed a pout. Before she could switch back to her arrogant act, Perry touched her chin and gently turned her face toward him.

"I could teach you right *now,* Ria. I *want* to do that. But there are some things that you have to teach *me,* too. I'm a visitor here...like you were there. I've met two types of people on Hourou. Are there any more?"

His soothing tone captivated her. "No," she said, staring into his eyes. "There are only the two—the Dah-Ahey...and the *others.* Perry

Carlson, you must teach me about Blue. No more words without meaning. Do not play games with me. Please."

"No games. I will honor our agreement...*all* of it. I like you, Ria, and the Dah-Ahey. You're a lot like the people of Earth." Ria smiled, taking that as a compliment. "The Ah-Ahey aren't like us at all, though. Is that why you don't like them? If I knew more, maybe I could help both—"

"Yes, *help* me, Perry Carlson. The Dah-Ahey are free. We do not want the Ways of Ahey as the others do. We are like *you*...free...not like—" She stiffened again, pain showing in her eyes as she realized Perry was exploiting her infatuation to learn what he wanted to know. "How good you are at the games, Perry Carlson," she said with false appreciation, resuming the role of a spoiled princess. "You have learned a little, but I have also learned a little."

"And what have you learned, my dear one?" Perry asked, trying to hide his concern.

She smiled at him while she slowly rose from the throne. "How much alike the Dah-Ahey and the people of Earth are...my bird-brained little boy-toy."

* * *

Perry felt his jaw drop.

"You are fun, Perry Carlson," Ria said. "I like games with you. And you *will* teach me everything about Blue. When I have learned enough, you and Ellis Minister and Yori Shimizu here will take me with you to Blue. What happens to the other Blues on Hourou...I do not care. They are probably just like the Ah-Ahey. But they will see, Perry Carlson. They will see how the Ah-Ahey are not like them...and they will lose their freedom, too, and—"

A sudden gust of wind interrupted her. Before she could brace herself, a second blast caused everyone on the dais to tumble onto its hard stones.

Ellis rose onto hands and knees and glanced over his shoulder into the night sky. Directly above him, four massive shapes descended toward the amphitheater. More blasts of wind caused the Dah-Ahey spectators to panic. With shouts and screams, they rushed from their seats to find cover.

"Are they spaceships?" Perry asked Ellis, trying to be heard above the surrounding noise.

Ellis strained to see in the dim light. "No! They're...creatures!"

"Flying dinosaurs," Yori yelled.

An enormous, bird-like animal hovered over the dais, creating a tempest with its wings, while three others did the same above the rest of the amphitheater.

"Yori, it's going to land! Move!" Ellis warned.

Yori scrambled out of the way just before the beast above her landed. "I...can't believe it," she muttered. "A Quetzi?"

The creature set its feet on the stone platform and folded its wings to stand on all fours. With the height of a full-grown giraffe and a wingspan of at least forty feet, it was no wonder the giant bird could create small wind storms. Colorful feathers covered its sleek body, and a pelican-like head bobbed atop its long neck.

"It looks like a Quetzi!" Yori exclaimed after crawling closer to Ellis.

"A what?"

"A Quetzalcoatlus. It was the largest flying dinosaur on Earth."

Her knowledge of prehistoric animals impressed Ellis, but the thing he most wanted to know was what such birds liked to eat. He hoped it was an herbivore, like Hourou's other inhabitants. The thought caused him to remember the cat-beast. "Where's Fluffy and his mates?" he asked Perry.

"Fluffy is still here," Perry answered, gesturing toward the feline as it paced behind the dais. It looked bored and unimpressed by its avian equal. "His friends ran off." He eyed the giant cat and bird with caution while rising to a crouch and making his way to Ellis and Yori.

Ria jumped to her feet and straightened her loincloth and jacket. Then she glared with defiance at the bird-beast and yelled at it. "Ooooh-eee-et-sah!"

Behind her, the amphitheater had cleared and the three other birds were landing in the seating area. Although the light on the dais was dim, the glowing stones along its perimeter illuminated the underside of the landed bird enough for Ellis to see a rope dangling from its neck. A few moments after Ria's command, a white body climbed down and into view. It was Ua, the young Ah-Ahey male who had been leading Ellis, Yori, and Perry through the wilderness. Ellis scanned the amphitheater and noticed each of the birds also had a rider. He assumed they were Ua's siblings—Aai, Mahah, and Maiha.

"Ooo-oh-yee, Ria," Ua said after dismounting. He was polite yet wary.

Ria frowned at him and flicked her hand in a downward motion to communicate disapproval. With reluctance, she accepted his formal greeting by pushing her hair behind her body and smiling. Ua did likewise, still eying her with open suspicion.

"Ah-ya Ooo-oh-yee, Ria," he said. "Tsa eeeee-oy suisa ah Blue."

"Ehe!" Ria responded in refusal. "Suisa ah Blue ewe Dah-Ahey!"

The Earth humans looked on while Ria and Ua approached each other and engaged in a heated verbal argument. Ellis studied them, hoping to understand at least a few of their words. After a few moments, though, he became frustrated with his lack of interpretive skills.

"Yori, Carlson," he said, "are you getting any of this? I heard 'Blue.' Are they arguing about *us?*"

After receiving no response, he turned to find that Yori and Perry were being led away from the dais by Aai and Mahah.

"Where are—"

A pair of white hands grabbed his arm and pulled him toward the empty amphitheater. It was Maiha. She was grinning at him, but he could tell she was anxious.

"Maiha? What are you doing?"

"Come, Ellis Meeen-eh-ster," she said with a hushed voice. "We leave now."

"Leave? How? On one of *those* things?" He shuffled along with hesitation while she guided him beneath her giant avian mount. The bird stood motionless and quiet, tilting its massive head and examining him with curiosity.

"Climb up now," Maiha instructed, handing Ellis the rope that hung from the bird's neck.

He looked back at the dais and noted that Ua was distracting Ria by drawing her deeper into their dispute. The two were standing toe-to-toe, bickering in their language and trying to intimidate each other with unbroken eye contact. A quick glance toward the other birds in the amphitheater revealed that Yori and Perry had already climbed up and were waving at him to do the same.

"Go!" Maiha said, giving him a shove.

"I get the idea." The rope had large knots that he used as hand and foot holds. After pulling himself up and sitting behind the bird's neck, he reached down to help Maiha. "Come on up, then."

Instead of accepting his hand, Maiha motioned for him to lean forward. Then, in one nimble action, she leapt onto the rope, swung herself up, and landed in a straddling position right behind him.

Ellis cringed when she pressed her body against his while grabbing for the reins. He was not sure what embarrassed him more—Maiha's superior climbing skills, being sandwiched between the bird's neck and her unclad figure, or being rescued by a young girl.

Maiha waved to her brother and sister across the amphitheater and pointed up at the night sky, signaling that she was ready to take flight. In unison, the three birds stood on their hind legs, lurched up, and flapped their great wings to get airborne.

The noise of their departure drew Ria's attention from Ua. "Ehe!" she yelled as the winged creatures rose. From behind, she felt a blast of wind when Ua's bird also took flight. Spinning around, she realized too late that while she was watching the escape of the Earth humans, Ua had leapt to his mount and made his retreat as well. Helpless and frustrated, she stood alone on the dais, staring forlornly at the bird that was taking Perry away from her.

Ellis craned to see what was happening below and smiled at the cleverness of Ua's extraction plan when he noted the boy's mount whooshing upward. He could also make out Ria, gawking up at Perry.

From her expression, he assumed she was crying, and before he was too high, he saw her quivering lips form the name of Carlson.

Carlson, you fool. What have you gotten us into now?

* * *

With the amphitheater and its bizarre spectacle behind them, the flying giants carried their riders far above dark forests and moonlit fields, lakes, and rivers. Warm wind buffeted Ellis' face. The ride was frightening, but his thoughts were on worse things. Ria had been more than a match for Perry's toying and manipulation; she was not as gullible and innocent as he had assumed. Now she was also heartbroken and angry. It was clear Perry had created mistrust between the Dah-Ahey and the Earth visitors. But what about the Dah-Ahey and the peaceful Ah-Ahey? Perry probably caused further damage to that already shaky relationship.

"Maiha," he asked the girl, "how did you find us?"

"Finding was easy," she answered. "But first we had to get the *yarae*. That is where we were all going—to their resting place—before you left us."

"The yarae? You mean this bird?"

"Buh-erd? Bird? Yes, yarae is like a bird...I suppose."

"Your use of our language is improving, Maiha."

"Yes. I learn." Maiha pulled on the rope, directing their mount to climb higher. "When we woke," she continued, "we found you were all gone, so we searched for you. It was my idea to search from above, so we went to the yarae. Then, it was easy to find the meeting place of the Dah-Ahey."

By the excitement in her voice, Ellis could tell she was enjoying her little adventure. She had no fear of being hundreds of feet above the ground, rushing through the night on the back of a giant flying dinosaur. She was like a carefree child in the body of a young woman.

"So you just assumed we would be with the Dah-Ahey? Why?"

"Because that is where Ria would be."

"How did you know *she* was involved?"

"A mahtee told me."

"A mahtee? You mean they can talk?"

"To me, yes. But not with words."

"So...my little friend was useful," Ellis said under his breath.

"Friend?"

"Nevermind. Who *is* Ria? Is she a leader among her people?"

"Ria is Ria. Lee-deh? I do not know this word. Ria is Dah-Ahey."

"And who are these Dah-Ahey? Are they your enemies?"

"There are still many of your words I do not understand, Ellis Meeen-eh-ster. The Dah-Ahey—they are not like the Ah-Ahey. You can see this, yes? They are *Dah*-Ahey. It is better for you to...stick together...with the Ah-Ahey."

"What's so wrong with them?"

"*Wong?* I do not understand. Ria is Dah-Ahey. The Dah-Ahey are *Dah*-Ahey."

"I'm clearly missing something here," Ellis said in defeat.

"Keah and Ahee will es-plain all to you. Look there, Ellis Meeen-eh-ster. They have made light to show us the way."

Ellis looked in the direction Maiha was pointing. In the distance, two radiant beams stood like bright towers in the night sky.

"Are those beacons?" he asked, wondering why he had not noticed them earlier.

For an answer, Maiha directed her mount toward the lights. Her siblings did likewise, so Ellis assumed it was their destination.

"So...Keah and the others are *there?*"

"Yes, it is Keah and Ahee's light. It will draw the children of them there...if they were sep-ah-rated...like us. Now we will all be together again, Ellis Meeen-eh-ster. Does that make you happy?"

Ellis starred at the lights and nodded. "Very much so, my dear. Very happy, indeed."

CHAPTER 24

Reunions

EARLY MORNING: DAY 3 ON HOUROU

Hourou's secondary sun, Tameen, peeked over the horizon and spread its orange glow into the star-filled sky, announcing the planet's first dawn. To Jay, it would have been a typical sunrise if he was back on Earth. On Hourou, however, the lesser sun created magical color patterns across the landscape. At certain angles, it looked as though Tameen was shining through a giant prism. He wondered if the watery upper atmosphere had anything to do with the light distortions.

A loud squawk and the sound of distant voices jolted Jay from his brief reverie. The noise came from the airborne yarae that was carrying him and Eah on its back. Eah had drafted two of the birds the night before for faster travel as they sought to reunite with her family and his companions from Earth. The voices were those of Tammah and Uio, who rode together on their own yarae, soaring above Eah and Jay and shouting to them in their native language.

Jay hugged the giant bird's feathery neck and tried not to look down too much as it skimmed the treetops. Eah sat close behind him with one arm wrapped around his waist and her free hand working the reins of their mount. Like Tammah and Uio, she enjoyed the flight, laughing with delight and flipping her hair in the wind.

Tammah yelled something down to her and signaled for her to climb. While she guided the yarae upward, Jay noticed two towers of sparkling light in the distance, shooting into the sky from a rocky plain still shrouded in shadows.

"There, Jay! Do you see?" Eah said as she tugged on the reins to alter the yarae's course.

"What is it?"

"The light of Keah and Ahee!"

"A signal? Then they're fine, just like you said."

"Yes. Just like I said."

Jay smiled at her mimicry of his tone. Whenever she spoke now, she was trying to sound more like him. "Smarty," he said to himself.

"Smarty," she repeated, giving him a quick body squeeze.

He had forgotten again; her sense of hearing was far more sensitive than his own.

"Do you see?" she asked, pointing to the lights. "Other yarae are there."

Eah's vision was also uncanny. Their yarae was already much closer to the beams, but Jay still could not discern details on the ground.

"I can't see anything yet," he admitted, "but I'll take your word for it. I wonder—" The sound of Tammah and Uio whooping and laughing from above drew his attention to the underside of their bird. "Those two haven't stopped goofing off since we got into the air."

"Goofing?" Eah said.

"Playing."

"Yes! They are having fun with the yarae. Tammah would like to race with us, but I will let him go first. We should not startle the others that are already on the ground."

Eah pulled her arm from around Jay so she could wave off her whimsical sibling. Upon seeing her signal, Tammah directed his avian beast to pick up speed. With a few mighty flaps of its wings, it shot ahead and began a quick descent toward the towers of light.

Soon, the skyscraping beams were right in front of Jay and Eah, and she was directing their mount to circle while they waited for Tammah and Uio to land. Jay watched with fascination as Tammah guided his bird to perch itself on a wide boulder near an encampment. Now that he was closer, Jay could make out six other yarae perched on boulders or walking the perimeter of the camp. He grinned when he recognized familiar figures jumping up and down and waving at him from below.

"I see them!" he said, excited. "It's April, Paul...and your parents!"

Eah snuggled up behind him as their yarae made one last circle around the beams. "Do you see more people, too?" she asked while she concentrated on working the reins.

"I think so. Your other brothers and sisters, yes. They're hard to miss." Jay counted the white, glowing bodies below. "Six, including your parents."

"Ah," Eah said with relief. "Then they are all here. And those from Blue?"

"Yes, there they are! Ellis and Yori. And Mister Carlson is with them, too."

"Hold on, Jay." Eah dropped the reins and wrapped both arms around him. "The yarae will take us down to them now."

Jay gripped the yarae's neck-rope just as it tilted its body and swooped down toward the encampment. "Take us in, big guy!" Behind him, Eah whooped and laughed, clearly pleased that he was enjoying the ride.

The drop was quick. To slow its approach, the bird extended its rear legs and then flapped forward. After alighting on the soft grass, it folded its wings and steadied itself on all fours while waiting for the two riders to dismount.

"Nice landing," Jay said to his feathered carrier.

Eah unwrapped the neck-rope, slid from behind Jay, and climbed down.

Jay followed, glad to have something solid under his feet again. "That was fun, but we must have been on that bird for hours." He wanted to stretch his cramped leg muscles, but Eah was already grabbing his hand and pulling him toward the encampment.

"Come on, Jay," she said, beaming with excitement.

April was the first to welcome them when they entered the campsite. "I'm so glad you're alright!" she said, drawing Jay into a hug.

"Same here. It's been an incredible couple of days."

April released him and turned to Eah. With a polite bow, she pushed her hair behind her ears to signify a formal female greeting.

Eah did likewise, but then she unexpectedly embraced April, imitating her hug with Jay. "My sister, April."

"I'm happy to see you, too, Eah." The gesture surprised but delighted April. She pulled away and gazed into Eah's eyes, opening an empathic bond so they could communicate their feelings without restraint. Eah's joy was almost overwhelming, and within it, April sensed the excitement and confusion of newfound love. "I understand you, Eah," she said with a nod. "If there's anything you want to know about how this works on Earth...just ask me, okay?"

"Okay," Eah agreed.

During their quick exchange, April noticed something different about Eah's emotions. In their past connections, Eah's feelings were melodious, like fine-tuned instruments in an orchestra. Now, however, they were inharmonious—pleasant sounds, yet distinct and competing. Unsure what else to say, April did her best to communicate awareness and acceptance through their bond and then broke it off.

Eah nodded her thanks and sidled closer to Jay, studying his face.

"What?" Jay asked. "If you're wondering about me understanding anything from your private conversation, I didn't."

"You could tell what we were doing, though," April praised. "I'm impressed, Jay. You've learned a lot in two days."

Eah smiled and poked him in the ribs.

"Ow! Not nearly enough, I'm sure," he said with a chuckle.

When Eah saw her parents approaching, her eyes grew wide with happiness, and she hurried away to meet them. The rest of her siblings did the same, enclosing Keah and Ahee behind a curtain of white bodies.

Their reunion touched Jay deeply. It also brought back feelings he thought he had buried long ago—a profound loneliness and longing for the closeness of a family.

"Are you okay?" April asked, noting a change in his expression.

"Huh? Me? Yeah, fine. I'm just tired..."

"Well, there he is!" Paul's approaching voice helped to snap Jay out of his brief pensiveness. "And you're still in one piece, too."

"Yeah. I survived. Actually, survival isn't something you have to worry about on this planet, though, is it?"

"That's true," Paul said, gripping Jay's hand. "But it's great to be together again."

Jay nodded. "It feels as if weeks have gone by, but also like I just saw you guys yesterday."

"We know what you mean," April said. "Hourou is on its own timetable."

"I'm sure we'll have some stories to swap," Paul suggested.

"You've got *that* right," Jay agreed, looking past Paul toward Eah and her family reunion.

Paul followed his gaze. "You and Eah hit it off pretty well?" he guessed.

"Yeah. I'm still trying to figure all of that out—"

"Mister Harrison!" Ellis appeared from behind and gave Jay a friendly slap on the back. "The last intrepid explorer to return. How are you, young man?"

Yori was right behind him, grinning with happiness at seeing Jay.

"Hello, Ellis. Yori."

Yori gave him a big hug. "How have you been, Jay?"

"Just fine. We walked a lot. Ate off the land. Saw some crazy things. But Eah, Tammah, Uio—they were never worried, so it was more like a long and interesting hiking trip."

"Same for us," Yori said, "but we—"

"There are still more *interesting* experiences ahead of us, I'm sure," Perry said, entering the huddle of Earth humans. "I'm glad you're well, Jay. You, too, Mister and Missus Theele."

"Thank you, Mister Carlson," Paul said.

"Perry. Please."

"Of course. And it's Paul and April."

"Carlson here has a story that warrants an immediate hearing," Ellis said with blatant peevishness. "Right, Carlson?"

After exchanging curious glances, all the others in the Earth party turned to Perry.

"What's going on?" Paul asked him.

Perry shifted on his feet. He was smiling, but his nervousness was obvious.

"What happened to you guys?" April asked Yori. She knew Yori and Ellis were both holding back.

"Let's not spoil our reunions," Perry said. "Yes, there are some important developments I have to tell you all, but it can wait for a better time."

"Is it something serious?" Jay asked.

"I don't know yet," Perry answered, pondering the question.

No one pressed him for details. They knew Perry would only deflect further inquiries, and none of them wanted to ruin the otherwise cheerful atmosphere.

"Does anyone know where we're going from here?" Jay asked, breaking a short, awkward silence.

"Keah said he's taking us to one of their cities," April answered.

"And that should be most interesting for everyone," Ellis said.

Yori brushed a piece of moss from her shoulder. "I'm just hoping for a hot bath."

"Don't get too excited," Paul warned. "A city here probably won't be what we expect."

"Nothing here has been," Ellis retorted, "and I think I'm getting used to the unexpected."

* * *

Keah waited for Hourou's primary sun, Tahah, to rise before announcing that the group should prepare to leave for the city. The

Earth humans were glad to hear it. They had enjoyed the time between sunrises, sharing stories from their adventures, but they were eager to experience civilization on Hourou.

Preparations for the next part of their journey were minimal; there was no need to pack supplies since the trip would be short. Keah explained they were going to a place called *Atsaahwua,* which was the most spectacular and well-known of Hourou's cities.

"There are many wonders in Atsaahwua," he said. "During your visit, you will discover more about Hourou and about life here. Our people built Atsaahwua for learning."

"A city filled with academics," Perry quipped. "I'll either die of loneliness or finally get some answers."

"Maybe you'll find a book there about improving communication skills," Ellis shot back.

April stepped between the two men to interrupt their gibing. "Will you be staying with us?" she asked Keah.

"We will all remain in Atsaahwua with you, yes." With that, he ushered the company away from their encampment and toward an area of the surrounding field where eight yarae waited, prepared for flight.

"Looks like we'll be flying *Air Yarae,*" Jay joked.

"In the dark, I could handle it," Yori said. "But now..."

April draped an arm over Yori's bare shoulders. "Just think of it as a giant, feathered friend."

"It's not them. I love the yarae. It's the height."

"I know," Jay agreed. "For me, it helped to keep looking ahead and not down."

"Right. Look ahead...not down."

Mahah gestured to Yori from underneath a bird. "You wee-ell ride wit me again, Yori!"

"How did she hear us from way over there?" Yori asked.

"You haven't figured out their super-hearing yet?" Jay teased.

"Super-*everything*, it seems."

While Keah's family assisted their Earth guests with mounting the yarae, Keah ran back to the boulder in the center of the camp, climbed to the top, and dropped the two halves of the light emitting stone onto the soft ground below.

"No need for a beacon now, I suppose," Ellis said, watching Keah with interest.

After climbing down, Keah placed the halves back together and returned to mount his yarae.

"Will it burn itself out?" Ellis asked Keah.

"The stone? No, it will heal."

"Heal? Is it alive?" Ellis asked.

"Part of it, yes."

"Amazing!" He took a last look before accepting a rope from Maiha. Then he clambered up and sat behind their yarae's neck. "Looks like it's you and me again, Maiha. Take it easy on me up there, will you?"

Maiha giggled, positioned their mount for flight, and signaled to Keah they were ready.

The seating arrangements were the same as they had been during the multiple arrivals to Keah's camp: Ellis rode with Maiha, Perry with Aai, Yori with Mahah, Jay with Eah, and Uio with Tammah, while Keah was with Paul, April with Ahee, and Ua flew alone atop a smaller mount. One by one, the yarae took flight into the morning sky, climbing higher and circling the field below until every bird was in the air. Then, they formed a triangular pattern behind Keah's yarae and their riders drove them to great speeds.

"What's the hurry?" Jay yelled over his shoulder to Eah, amazed at how fast she was coaxing the yarae to fly.

"What is *hurry,* Jay?"

"Why are we rushing? Why fly so fast?"

"Oh. We go fast, yes! Keah must arrive at Atsaahwua soon."

"Okay. One more question."

Eah laughed as the strong wind pulled her hair from around her body, causing it to trail behind her head like a long, black veil. Jay sat in front of her, so he could not see what she found so humorous.

"Sorry. I guess I ask a lot of questions."

"I am happy to answer them, Jay."

"So, why do you call Keah by his name if he's your father?"

"His name is Keah."

"I know, but don't you have special words you use for special relationships?"

"Special ree-lay-shun-ships? Oh, I understand. Connections—bonds—between people. You have said this word before."

"Yes. So, where I come from, we have special names for those close to us. A father might be called daddy or papa..."

"I understand. Yes, when I talk to Keah, I sometimes call him *Aha*, which is a word like *father* yet filled with deeper meaning. But when I speak about him to others, it is always Keah—his name—because in a name is honor."

"Okay. Now I get it."

Both of them listened to the passing wind for a while before Eah spoke again.

"Jay, one more question," she said, trying to imitate him.

"Sure. Go ahead."

"Do *you* have a special name for *me?*"

Jay felt a slight drop in the pit of his stomach that had nothing to do with flying. "Uh...what do you mean?"

"Don't you have special words you use for special relationships?" she teased.

"You're sure quick at picking up on things," he said with a chuckle.

"So? What special name would you have for Eah...for *me?*" She was clearly not going to let him wiggle out of the conversation, and being hundreds of feet above the ground offered him no physical escape route.

"Well...uh...it takes time to come up with one."

"Oh."

Jay could not see the sly smile on Eah's face, so he assumed the awkward silence that followed was from disappointment. "I'm, uh, sure I'll think of something by...later today."

Eah chuckled and slid closer behind him. As she tightened one arm around his waist, she flicked the reins with her free hand, directing their yarae to pick up its speed.

If she could make the day go by faster now, Jay thought, *I bet she would.* He patted the yarae's feathered neck and then moved his hand downward to rub out some stiffness in his thigh. Startled, he realized too late that it was Eah's leg he was touching. She did not flinch or express any discomfort. Still, after a few strokes, he removed his hand. *Where is this leading?* he wondered. *Am I avoiding something...or encouraging it?*

CHAPTER 25

Beautiful

MORNING: DAY 3 ON HOUROU

The yarae carried their human riders over miles of expansive plains and colorful forests. Far ahead, a mountain range along the horizon connected green lands with a cloudless, lavender sky. When rolling foothills appeared below, the birds slowed their speed and descended toward a valley where three rivers combined to form one. On a peninsula between two of the rivers, Jay saw tall, glimmering spires reaching skyward like giant crystals. Rainbow beams bathed the surrounding forest in prismatic colors as the pinnacles reflected the light of Hourou's twin suns.

"Is that the city?" Jay asked Eah through the whoosh of passing wind.

"Yes. Atsaahwua."

"It's amazing!"

"Does it make you happy?"

When its other structures came into view, Jay could not form words to describe how he felt gazing upon Atsaahwua's magnificence. He was in awe at the sight of it. "Happy? I'm blown away." A slight tingle ran through his body as Eah moved her hand up from his waist to his chest and rested it over his heart.

"I feel your *blown away*," she said with a laugh, "and your happiness. Shall we go down now?"

"Yes!"

Eah yelled something to her father. Jay assumed it was a signal she was going to break formation because she then prompted her yarae to dive. Jay gripped the bird's neck-rope just before it folded its wings back and shot like a missile toward the trees. Above him, he heard the excited voices of some of Eah's brothers and sisters yelling at Eah and laughing.

"They think we're racing them?"

"Yes," Eah replied with a wide grin. "So we will race!"

With a nervous laugh, Jay tightened his grip and stared ahead. Their yarae was already in the lead, so all Eah had to do was ensure the others would not pass them. With a series of tugs on the reins, she directed their mount to swoop erratically during the quick plunge, forcing the other yarae to avoid a collision. Just above the treetops, she made the bird level off while she searched for a suitable opening in the forest canopy.

"Eye-aye-hah!" she said. "There!"

The yarae seemed to notice the spot as well. Satisfied that the gap between trees would accommodate its bulk, the great bird lurched back and batted the air with its massive wings to slow their descent. Sticking out its legs, it then issued a shrill cry to warn of an imminent landing and touched down gently in a mossy clearing.

"Let's go, Jay!" Eah said, lowering her climbing rope and slithering to the ground.

Jay followed, and as soon as his feet met the turf, the yarae lowered its head and waited for Eah to remove the rope from around its neck. She slid it off, petted and praised the bird, and then gave it a playful slap to send it away. With a loud squawk, the beast took to the air and disappeared past the forest canopy. Seconds later, another yarae landed in the same place.

"Eh-ioy-ooooh-eeeee-tsa, Eah!" Tammah cheered as he and Uio dropped from their mount. Both of them were laughing, so Jay assumed they must have been congratulating Eah for winning the race.

"Ahhh-iiiiii-eh-yo," Eah replied. "Tammah says we raced well."

"Mo-tee-vay-ted, Jay," Tammah said, joining them with Uio. "When Eah is motivated, she will not be stopped."

Jay winked at Eah. "So you have some of Tammah's competitive streak in you, huh?"

She considered his words for a moment and then gave him a smirk when she understood his meaning. While they waited, the other yarae landed one by one in the clearing, depositing their riders and departing in haste to make room for the next arrival.

When everyone in Keah's company was present, he guided them to a path that led into the surrounding woods. A carpet of soft, multi-colored moss reminded the visitors of other parts of Hourou they had seen, yet the forest was much different. The trees and other vegetation sparkled as if coated with glitter, and it all resembled giant versions of undersea plants back on Earth.

Soon, they left the splendor of the woodlands and Atsaahwua stood before them. From the air, it had been a dazzling mystery; up close, it was a wonder that confounded the senses. A white, waist-high wall marked the city border and seemed to go on for miles. In front of it, an aquamarine river hovered above the ground with twisting currents. Its splashes created dreamy musical sounds under a colorful, otherworldly mist. Colossal spires dominated the skyline and gravity-defying ribbons of moving water twisted around many of them, flowing upward with no apparent end.

Just outside of Atsaahwua, thousands of people traversed the arteries leading in—wide avenues that passed over and under the encircling, floating river. Ornate arches marked the city's entrances, each covered with sparkling gems and wrapped in bright green vines. Everywhere, the bodies of native travelers created a flow of white along the vivid colors of the roadways. There were animals as well, of all types and sizes, roaming within the crowds.

Keah's chosen path ran parallel to the river and wall, ending at one of the cobblestone highways that would take his party into the city. A thin layer of soft moss, embedded with red and silver glitter, blanketed the avenue. The moss emitted light when tread upon, creating brilliant patterns underfoot. Before leaving their trail, the Earth visitors stopped to appreciate what lay ahead.

"I have no words to describe this, or what I'm feeling right now," April said.

Ellis came alongside her. "I would say *fantastic,* but the word is quite inadequate. This defies description."

"Absolutely amazing," Paul offered. "It takes my breath away."

"This pleases you?" Ahee asked from behind them.

Yori beamed as she answered. "Oh, yes! It's the most beautiful thing I've ever seen."

"*Beautiful* is its name," Aai said, appreciating Yori's fascination. "Say Atsaahwua, Yori."

"Ots-aah-woo-ah."

"Very good! You sound more like one from Hourou."

"Uh...thanks." Yori glanced at the young man, surprised by his sudden expressiveness. "You...and Ua, Mahah, Maiha—all of you have been excellent teachers."

Aai studied her face and nodded. "I will teach you more in Atsaah-wua...if that would make you happy."

"Um...sure. Yes, that would be nice."

He smiled and turned away, allowing Yori to take a longer appraising glance. Until then, Aai had remained in the background, quiet and distant. She presumed he was just shy, which to her was an endearing quality, since she was an unassuming person herself. She tried not to ogle him, but her eyes lingered a little too long.

"You are a...stoo-dent of the body, right? Bi-ah-lo-gee?" he asked.

"What? Um...student?" She was also surprised by his use of English and imitation of her inflections. He had been studying her speech. "Yes. Oh, biology...yes, human anatomy and physiology. I've been learning about cellular processes, especially those that affect the immune—"

"Don't get her rambling about her classes again, Aai," Ellis warned.

"But...I have enjoyed hearing Yori speak."

"I know. For two long days, though, she's analyzed and described the physiological reactions of the human body to alien stimuli."

Yori gave Ellis a playful jab with her elbow. "Sorry...*professor.*"

Their camaraderie and joking amused Aai, but Yori sensed something more in his unsubtle glances, and it was not the first time.

"Aai appreciates *my* lessons, Doctor Minister," she chided. "Right, Aai?"

Aai grinned, and his face seemed to swirl with pastel colors, quick and almost imperceptible. In a flash, his skin returned to normal.

Yori wondered if this was how he blushed. Since flirting was not one of her specialties, she changed the subject. "You've told us Hourou is populated," she said to him, "but seeing so many of your people together is incredible."

"They will welcome you. We always have visitors in Atsaahwua."

"From other parts of Hourou?" Yori asked.

"Yes. But also from other *weeuao*—other...plan-nits."

Yori shook her head. "It's so hard to believe. There are people on other planets? Like you?"

"Like *us*," Keah corrected, gesturing toward the entire group, "and all are welcome to visit here."

"Well, we should fit right in then," Perry said. "That is...if they're all *human.*"

Keah raised a questioning eyebrow.

"What are you expecting, Perry?" Paul asked. "Blobs and tentacles?"

Perry shrugged, feigning innocence. "I don't know. *He's* the space traveler."

"Carlson..." Ellis warned.

April cleared her throat as a distraction. "Keah, I think Perry is wondering if we'll blend in...since we're from Earth, and our planet is unknown to anyone."

"*Blend in* means to fit in," Eah explained to Keah. "It means to look like everyone else—to *ceeee-ih-oa-ye-eh-oh.*"

Keah nodded and questioned Eah in their native tongue. While answering, she reached toward Jay and took hold of his shirt.

"What's *this* all about?" Paul asked April in a hush.

Keah studied his guests' tatters while he and Eah engaged in a brief conversation.

"Something about our clothes, I guess," April replied.

Paul rolled his eyes. "Uh oh."

When she finished talking, Eah turned to the group of visitors. "We do not have words in the language of Hourou for some Earth things," she said, apologetic.

"I was asking Eah how to say words about your...coverings," Keah explained. "Blending in will be difficult with those. Very few cover their bodies in Atsaahwua."

The Earth guests shuffled nervously as each regarded their state of dress.

"Um...I'm not sure I'm...ready to just—" April said, stammering.

"Me neither," Yori agreed.

"This won't be a problem, will it?" Paul asked Keah.

Ahee reached toward April and ran her fingers along her t-shirt. "You may choose to remain covered," she said. "To see those who are a little different is not so unusual here."

"Good," Perry announced. "Let's go with that, then."

Paul chuckled. "With the way these rags are falling apart, it might not matter pretty soon, anyway."

"Paul," April warned, "let everyone be comfortable."

"Just making a joke to calm the nerves, Babes."

"You will be very welcome here," Keah reminded. "Atsaahwua will make you comfortable."

"That takes care of fashion concerns, but what about us being from Earth?" Perry asked. "Since our planet is off limits for travel, how do we explain being here?"

Keah pondered his question for a moment. "The meeting of our two worlds affects everyone. As on your planet, there will be consequences on Hourou...and beyond."

"Maybe we shouldn't mingle," Yori said. "You could keep us hidden until we leave."

"The sky cannot hide the birth of a new star. And the direction of a river's flow cannot be mistaken."

"That sounds good in a fortune cookie," Perry said to his group, "but there are really only two choices: we tell people where we're from, or we don't tell them."

Jay stepped closer and raised a finger toward Perry. "I think we should—"

"Keah's right," Perry continued, ignoring him. "We can't hide what's happened. The people in that city are going to be curious. The Dah-Ahey we met were *quite* interested in where we are from, and as an ambassador—"

"As an ambassador, you must respect the customs and methods of your hosts," Ellis reminded. "There is a striking difference between the Dah-Ahey and the Ah-Ahey, Carlson. By now, you should appreciate the value of using caution on this planet."

"Wait. What *happened* with you and the Dah-Ahey?" Paul asked Perry. "Keah, do you know about this?"

"Yes," Keah replied. "Ua told us of the meeting."

"That's all irrelevant right now," Perry said. "We're talking about blending in."

Ahee stepped in, raised her hand, and gestured toward the city. "As you have heard, there are many visitors in Atsaahwua. Your presence will be more welcomed than questioned."

"We understand," April said. "Right everyone?"

Besides Perry, all the Earth visitors nodded in agreement.

"I'm sure the people will soon find out about us anyway," Perry said.

Keah forced a smile as he spoke. "Yes, but it must happen according to the Ways of Ahey, and I will explain it all to them after you have returned to your home."

"Observe and learn, Carlson," Ellis warned. "Think about last night. What did negotiating while outside of your element get you then?"

"There's a lot more to that than you know," Perry shot back.

"I'm sure. Meanwhile, take a fresh approach here. Look around. We're standing at the edge of a wonder of wonders and you're still concerned about all the politics. Go with the flow, Carlson."

Perry smiled, but it was the sort of smile one uses when he knows the futility of continuing an argument. "Fine. We'll go slow," he said to Keah, "but at some point, the two of us are going to talk about some things."

"We will talk, yes," Keah agreed, his eyes boring into Perry, "about *many* things."

* * *

There were no vehicles in Atsaahwua, but many animals meandered along the roads and walkways within the bustling masses of people. They did not seem to be for riding or hauling. Rather, people either took no notice of them or treated the creatures as beloved pets.

In contrast to Earth cities, travelers in Atsaahwua did not rush to get anywhere. Everyone went about their business peacefully, greeting one another with a friendly word or a pleasant smile. There was no rudeness or pushing through the crowds since space was never lacking in the thoroughfares, no matter how many moving bodies filled them. Instead, the streets and walkways slowly widened or contracted to accommodate the changing number of pedestrians.

By now, the members of the Earth party had accepted the natural state of their host family. Clothing was unnecessary on a paradise-like planet and for people who followed an uncorrupted moral philosophy. Being in Atsaahwua, however, compounded any discomfort with undress that still may have lingered. Here, the visitors were surrounded by scores of others who lived as naturally as Keah and his clan.

After passing through an arched entrance and entering Atsaahwua on one of its major thoroughfares, Jay considered his own group and wondered if they felt out of place. Paul and April did not seem to care about the masses of undressed bodies around them; they were too busy examining the architecture of the buildings. Likewise, Ellis and Yori were like two science students studying subjects in a lab. Only Perry seemed as uncomfortable as Jay. He kept eye contact and smiled at everyone, but Jay could tell he was nervous.

The people in the city looked similar to Eah and her family. Though there were some variances in color, most of the women had the same flawless, iridescent skin and either black or white knee-length hair. The men, too, resembled Keah and his sons; almost all of them had the same build and tone. Some, however, presented themselves in black or in different solid colors, and a few had patterns that resembled Polynesian tattoos.

"At first," Jay said to Eah, "I thought everyone looked pretty much the same, but I'm seeing their differences now."

Eah smiled and toyed with her hair as they walked. "In Ahey, everyone is the same, yet different. We are each special."

"I'm not even sure I know what Ahey is."

"Yes, you do."

"No, I don't."

Eah stopped, turned him toward her, and stared into his eyes.

"What?" Jay asked. The idea of one of their strange moments happening in a public place discomforted him. "Maybe we shouldn't—"

"Yes," Eah said, searching. "I see Ahey in you."

"In me? What is it?"

"Is!" she corrected. "Not what, or it...*is!*"

"Ahey *is?*"

"Yes! Now you see. *Is,* Jay. Ahey *is,* and Ahey is in you...as I have said." With that, she released him and trotted away toward the others.

Jay shrugged off Eah's strange comment, accepting it as yet another mystery. The reverent insistence in her tone, however, supported his suspicion that Ahey was not a philosophy or vague religious belief, but in fact her people's deity. If so, it was going to make for some interesting discussions later among the members of his own party. As he caught back up with the group, he stayed near Paul and hoped for an opportunity to ask for his opinion.

Paul was in the middle of questioning their hosts about the city. "So, who built all this?"

"All people build," Ua replied. "All who wish to contribute do so, and Atsaahwua creates some of its own designs as well."

"Your use of our language is excellent now, Ua," Paul praised.

"We have all been learning from you. Mahah is the only one who remains quiet."

Mahah gave him a shove for teasing her. "And Ua will probably *run off at the mouth* whenever he can show off his *vast knowledge*."

"Without a doubt," he said, shoving her back in jest.

Eah stepped in to distract their play. "There is always something new to see in Atsaahwua when you visit," she said to the Earth party.

"The craftsmanship here is brilliant," Ellis noted, "and the variety is amazing. The entire city is a giant work of art."

Keah stopped the group in front of one of the great spires and ran his hand along its ornate surface. "Each generation, and every family, adds their own creativity. Here, with their hands, they share visions, tell stories, celebrate life. It is how we use these places."

"So no one *lives* in Atsaahwua, then?" Jay asked.

"I do not understand," Keah replied. "*Lives* means to be alive, yes?"

"Sorry. I mean, does anyone make their home here in Atsaahwua?"

"Home. Home is where one is from."

"Yes, but it also means a place where someone, uh, sleeps and keeps their personal things, and spends a lot of their time."

"Families on Earth build structures we call homes...or houses," Ellis said, trying to assist Jay with an explanation. "They are special places meant only for that family and their closest friends. That is where we eat, sleep, and spend much of our time together. We build them inside and outside of cities."

"I understand," Keah said, "but there is no such way on Hourou. Our home is everywhere."

"I think what Keah means is that people come and go as they please and stay wherever they want to stay," Yori explained. "It doesn't seem that property ownership is a big deal here."

Ellis scratched his head and considered the surrounding structures. "Interesting. So, are there any temporary lodging facilities here in Atsaahwua? Places for people to rest while they're visiting?"

"Yes," Ahee answered. "There are many resting places. Anyone can use them for as long as they have need. Do you require one now?"

"No, no," Ellis said with a laugh. "We're just trying to understand the purposes of your city, I think."

"Atsaahwua is a built-place—a city—that has become a center for learning," Keah explained. "People come here from all over Hourou to learn."

Ellis gestured toward the crowds in the streets. "That would account for all the kids here as well."

Until that moment, the others in the Earth party had somehow overlooked all the children within the throngs.

"Oh, they're beautiful!" April gushed. "How did we not notice them?"

"There are too many wonders for us to take in all at once," Ellis answered.

Like miniature versions of their parents, the littlest residents of Hourou were everywhere. Adults chaperoned most of them, but some of the older children ran around in groups or walked along by themselves.

April spotted two small boys that reminded her of her sons back home.

"So cute," she muttered, eyes welling up with tears.

"Just like ours," Paul said. He took April's hand while they watched the youngsters at play. "Nearly the same ages, too."

"Not quite, though. The way Ahee explained it to me, those kids could be near a hundred years old...in our time."

"That's, uh...wow. You'll have to tell me more about that later, Babes."

The swarms of people passing by fascinated the Earth guests, so Keah allowed them to observe while they paused under the shadow of the spire. Perry was the only one who seemed eager to keep going, fidgeting next to Ellis and agitated about something.

"What's wrong, Carlson?" Ellis asked in a hush. "You seem very nervous."

"Look back in the direction where we entered the city."

Ellis turned around and considered the scene behind them. "What am I looking for?"

"Keep looking."

Ellis scanned the crowds, but nothing stood out to him. He was just about to dismiss Perry when he glimpsed a familiar skin color. "Are those—are those Dah-Ahey?"

There was no need for Perry to answer. Their appearance was unmistakable. Bronze bodies and loincloths made a stark contrast against the surrounding Ah-Ahey people. A group of about twenty of them worked its way through the crowds, searching the streets with penetrating eyes.

"What are *they* doing here?" Ellis asked with agitated concern.

Perry shrugged his response. When one of the female Dah-Ahey looked in his direction, he ducked behind Ellis.

"Relax, Carlson. I doubt they're the same ones we encountered. I don't think they're following us, either."

Paul was standing nearby. He followed their stares until he saw the Dah-Ahey. "Keah, are Dah-Ahey allowed to be here, too?"

Everyone in Keah's party turned around just before the multitudes hid the bronze-skinned standouts again.

"All are welcome," Keah replied. "Also the Dah-Ahey."

"It is good to see them here," Ahee added. "We always hope they will one day return to the Ways of Ahey and become reunited with the Ah-Ahey."

"Still," Keah said, "for them to visit Atsaahwua while you are also here is...interesting."

Keah and Ahee continued to stare into the crowd, even after the Dah-Ahey had disappeared from sight. With a slight twitch of her head,

Eah communicated something to Keah that snapped him out of his pensiveness.

"It is time for us to separate," he said with sudden resolution. "We will meet again when night comes. We hope you enjoy Atsaahwua. This visit will provide answers to many of your questions." He smiled and bowed to the Earth guests. "Ooo-oh-yee." With that, he took Ahee's hand and motioned for the rest of his family to follow. One by one, they stepped into the passing crowds and disappeared into the mass of bodies.

Eah, Tammah, and Uio stayed behind to be escorts. Aside from Jay, the visitors felt apprehensive about being left in a strange city with only three spirited youths as their guides. After a brief argument about how to form groups, they decided Paul, April, and Jay would go with Eah to learn more about Hourou's culture, while Ellis, Yori, and Perry would travel with Tammah and Uio to the science and technology districts.

Perry was not pleased about his assignment. He would have preferred to mingle among the residents and learn something about the differences between the planet's two people groups. Eah objected, reminding Perry of Keah's desire to keep things low-keyed. In the end, Perry relented and agreed to go along with Tammah and Uio as long as they promised to teach him about customs and relationships.

"I like science," he told them, "but my business is with people."

"Why don't you come with us, then?" Paul asked.

"Thanks, but no. I'd feel like a third wheel. I'll take my chances with the science club."

With a decision made, the two groups parted ways and headed for different sections of the city. While they traveled through the streets, no one spotted the three bronze-skinned bodies weaving in and out of the crowds behind them—no one except Perry. Careful not to alert his party, he strained to glimpse the Dah-Ahey observers. There were two males and one female. They were good at staying hidden within the throngs, but the female showed herself while crossing an intersection. Perry felt a drop in the pit of his stomach when he recognized her.

"Ria."

CHAPTER 26

Laura's Dilemma

Alex blew into the sipping hole of his travel cup's thin plastic lid, wondering if he really should have brought hot coffee aboard a military helicopter. After taking a sip, he stared hard at Laura. "So, what do you think the word *Ria* means?"

"I don't know," she answered, looking up from her tablet, "but somehow we're going to find out."

The aircraft hit light turbulence, causing Alex to shift his weight as he stood near a window. "Day four," he mumbled.

"What?"

"It's the fourth day since the abductions."

"Oh."

"Have you watched the news at all?"

Laura put down her tablet and sipped her own coffee, grimacing at the strength of the military brew. "Not much."

"The sightings and abductions are all they're talking about...across the globe."

"Everything else is insignificant. People no longer have to wonder about extraterrestrial life, and from what I've read, most are believing it."

"Haines helped with that," Alex noted. "He's loving the spotlight right now."

"Let him."

"I'm not sure that's a good thing, though."

"Why? It keeps him out of *our* way."

"Not Haines. I mean...people believing it."

Laura shot him a look. "You don't want people to believe in extraterrestrial life?"

"I don't really care *what* they believe. My concern is about how fast they're having to digest it. Did you see the reports about the rioting?"

"People riot all the time nowadays."

"You're right, but this is just the lead-up."

"To what, Alex? They're finally getting the truth. What's wrong with that?"

"Sometimes, the truth makes things worse before they get better."

"I agree. But maybe the President's speech will calm it down. Silence from our government hasn't helped us or the rest of the world."

"I'm glad he postponed it until later this morning. Waiting on us, I suppose."

Laura smirked. "Like everyone else."

As the helicopter banked and circled the crash site, Alex grasped his cup and leaned against the window to get a better view of the ground. "They've been doing a lot of digging since Friday," he noted. "They exposed the whole remnant now." He studied the black shape, imagining how it must have fit as a corner of the triangular spacecraft. "It looks sheared off. I'd bet the visitors don't even know it's still here."

"Maybe they couldn't finish their recovery."

"Why? Why stop taking it...or destroying it?"

"Because something important was *inside*."

Alex gestured toward Laura's tablet. "Did you read the whole briefing?"

"I've been skimming it. There's not much. I wish we would've been told and sent out earlier."

"You could've gained an hour or more if you came by yourself."

"I wanted my DD with me this time."

"Show of force?"

"Not really. Honestly, it's personal. If what they found is for real…"

"I know. Our grandkids will always remember the story of when Grammy and Grandpa made history by being the first—"

"No…I just wanted you with me, Alex."

Unsure how to respond, Alex returned to his jump seat and both of them prepared for the landing. As soon as the helicopter touched down, a soldier riding with them opened the side door and they hopped out. Then, two soldiers on the ground escorted them toward a security checkpoint in front of a small, prefabricated building.

Colonel Richter was waiting for them. "Good morning, Director Turgis."

"Good morning, Colonel. This is Alex Vaughn from the Agency. He's my deputy director and has top level authorization. Alex, this is Colonel Richter."

"Good morning, sir," Alex said, shaking the Colonel's hand.

"Nice to meet you, Mister Vaughn." Richter motioned toward the security gate. "This way please."

Two checkpoints kept the building secure from unauthorized entry. At the second, guards scanned their bodies and handed each of them a sealed package of protective clothing. After entering the prefab, a man in a lab coat escorted them to a changing room and showed them how to put on their suits and facemasks. When they returned to the main hallway, they saw Colonel Richter talking to a woman in similar safety gear. She looked nervous.

"Do what you can," he was saying. "We don't have a choice."

Laura and Alex approached, so Richter made introductions. "Doctor Tannish, this is Director Laura Turgis and Deputy Director Alex Vaughn from the Agency." The three exchanged nods. "I'll meet you both outside when you're done with Doctor Tannish."

"Since time is of the essence," Tannish said to Laura, "we have to forgo some protocols."

"We understand."

"I should check your seals before we proceed to the examination room."

"Go right ahead."

Tannish walked around them and inspected the seals in their suits. "I assume you've been briefed?"

"I have the report from the engineers," Laura answered, "but I'd also like to know what happened between their discovery and my arrival."

"Not much...as you'll see. Well, you've done good with the seals. Please follow me." She led them down a side passageway that ended at a windowless steel door. "Once we're inside, please stay at the back of the room until I've prepared the subject for your examination...and don't make any sudden movements."

Laura took a long, centering breath while Tannish opened the door. "Well...here I go," she whispered to herself. "Making history again."

Tannish hurried them into a spacious room that was replete with medical equipment. After securing the exit, she continued further in, but then stopped short when she heard a commotion. "Wait here," she said to Laura.

In an examination area, three technicians in protective suits were in pursuit of a young, naked boy who expertly dodged their every attempt to apprehend him.

"What is happening here!" Tannish demanded.

At the sound of her shrill voice, the boy stopped running and sat in a corner between two large pieces of equipment. Calm and motionless, he glared at his pursuers while they assessed their next move.

Laura stepped closer to get an unobstructed view of the alien visitor. His unclad body looked human, but with an otherworldly bronze glow. Otherwise, he resembled a ten-year-old male. Long, black hair flowed down to his shoulders, framing a russet face and bright green eyes.

"Ria!" he shouted at his captors. "Eeee-ay-ah-ooooo-tsa-eh-hah! Ria!"

"What's happened?" Tannish asked her team members.

One replied through huffing breaths. "He won't cooperate, Doctor. We tried everything, but can't get near him. He's as slippery as an eel."

"Eeee-ay-ah-ooooo-tsa-eh-hah! Ria!" the boy repeated. His words were forceful, but softened by a strange, exotic accent.

"He keeps saying the same thing over and over."

"Okay," Tannish said. "Give him a rest. Wait outside." She guarded the door while the three exited the room. "As you can see," she said to Laura, "our visitor doesn't want to be touched. We coaxed him out of the remnant and ushered him here, but we haven't been able to lay a hand on him for a physical inspection."

"Why wasn't I consulted about this?" Laura demanded. "Who authorized an examination?"

"A thorough examination is essential for determining if this is a hoax."

"Someone still thinks this is all a *hoax?*"

"I follow orders. My opinions are irrelevant."

"You're a *military* doctor, then?" Alex asked.

Tannish crossed her arms. "Please get on with your work, so we can do ours."

"Oh, I will, thank you," Laura shot back. With caution, she approached the alien boy and crouched so she could make level eye contact. "We...are here...to help you," she said. "Do you understand?"

His eyes bored into hers. If he was afraid, he hid it well, for she could sense no fear in his gaze. After a long moment, he glanced past her shoulder at Tannish.

Somehow, Laura inferred he wanted the nervous doctor out of the room. She rose and spun around. "We want to be alone, Doctor."

"I can't do that, Ma'am."

"Okay, then..." Laura unzipped a pocket in her suit and pulled out a large, color-coded card attached to a lanyard. "*This* says you can...and you *will.*"

Tannish recognized the privileged ID immediately. "I...I apologize, Ma'am. Had I known—"

"With this level of authority, do you understand how important it is that I'm here?"

"Yes."

"Good. And the sooner we're done here, the sooner we'll be out of your way."

"I'll be right outside should you require anything."

While Tannish exited the room, Alex moved next to Laura. "I need one of those cards," he said, never taking his eyes off the alien boy. "So now what?"

"Now...we examine our visitor," she answered, crouching again and gazing at the boy's face. "Who are you? Do you have a name? Can you understand me?"

"Woo-eds," he replied, pointing at her facemask.

Through his intense stare, she could sense his answer. "I...I understand. You need to see my mouth. Is that it?"

"What?" Alex asked.

"He wants to see our mouths."

"How did you infer that?"

"Intuition."

"Taking off these masks is not a good idea, Laura. We could—"

"It might help," she interrupted, reaching behind her head and feeling for the seal of the suit's hood. "If he's trying to understand our language, he needs to watch our lips moving."

"What about contamination? You're about to take an enormous risk."

Laura hesitated. "Like I did in their spaceship, I know. But policies, procedures, and protocols will *not* get us quick answers, and we have little time here."

Alex shook his head.

"If you disagree, as my DD, this is where you can threaten to override me and take over the investigation."

"Just...hurry before Tannish gets back."

"In this together?" She could not tell if Alex was smiling or frowning behind his mask, but she saw encouragement in his eyes.

"Of course we are, Laura."

"Lah-rah?" the boy said, mimicking Alex.

Surprised, Laura pushed back her masked hood. "Yes...Laura. I am Laura." She pointed to herself and then at him. "You? You are?"

"Eeee-ay-ah-ooooo-tsa-eh-hah! Ria!"

"There's that word *Ria* again," Alex noted. "The one he kept repeating when they found him."

"Yes," Laura affirmed. "What is Ria?" she asked the boy.

At the sound of the word, he jumped to his feet. "Ria! Eeee-ay-ah-ooooo-tsa-eh-hah! Ria!"

"Be careful," Alex cautioned.

Laura stood and backed away, unsure what the little alien would do next. "Ria? Are you Ria?"

"Ehe," he replied, frowning at her misunderstanding. "Woo-eds." He pointed at his mouth. "Ay woo-eds."

"Is he hungry or something?" Alex asked.

"I...uh...look, we don't have much time here. Do you understand me? Can you tell me who you are? Where do you come from? Who are your people?"

The boy studied her lips as she spoke. "Sah."

"What? What is Sah?"

He closed his eyes and repeated the word. "Sah."

"Interesting," Alex noted.

"What?"

"That he's been inside the remnant all this time. Why didn't someone find him until now?"

"He was in some sort of little room. An interior wall opened up during the excavation and he came tumbling out."

"So, he was hiding, or a stowaway. Well...he looks human. Other than his skin and hair, he'd pass for a typical Earth kid."

"Almost."

"The way he's watching you speak does make it look as if he's trying to learn our language."

"I wish we had time to work with him," Laura said, shaking her head. "Here we are making first contact with an intelligent being from another planet and we're being rushed by schedules and agendas."

"I'm not defending it, but there *is* a countdown, Laura. The rest of the world is waiting for answers, and our bosses need us to deliver a quick assessment of...of him. So, what's our game plan here?"

Laura considered her frustrating dilemma. Alex was correct. People in high places were counting on her to bring back information before they committed to actions that would have global consequences. An alien visitor was still on Earth, and he was sitting right in front of her. The world had its answer about other intelligent life in the universe. But Laura needed other answers, too: would someone return for him, and when? Only the boy could tell her, and to do that, he would have to learn a new language.

"I'll have to stall for time," she said. "We'll suggest to the committee that the President should hold off on making any announcement until we can communicate with our visitor."

"It might work," Alex replied, "or they could decide to keep him a secret and go on with their plans, which is what I predict."

"You're probably right...as usual."

"Sorry. But think about how they've handled it so far. By giving you only a few hours to investigate this—"

"I know, Alex. They're pressured for time, too. I get it."

Alex took a few careful steps forward. The boy watched his movement but otherwise did not react. With his next step, Alex added a slight lurch to see if he would flinch. He responded with a simple, knowing smirk.

"What are you doing?" Laura asked.

"He's reading us—studying our body language. He knows I'm messing with him."

Laura smiled, and the boy returned it. As she looked into his eyes, she somehow sensed he wanted to trust them both. "He's also able to project feelings."

"What? How can you tell?"

"Take off the mask and make good eye contact. But first, think about being friendly. Put it into your mind that you don't want to scare him or cause him any harm and try to project that."

Alex stepped backward, unfastening and removing his suit's hood. He then looked into the boy's eyes and waited. After a few moments, he sensed gratitude.

"Unbelievable!" he exclaimed. "Is he able to read our minds?"

"I don't think so. It's more of an emotional connection—like between two people intimately familiar with each other."

"That's not the case here, though."

"No. It's an analogy. But it does feel...relational..."

"Next you'll be saying his kind are distant relatives."

"See? You just did it."

"Did what?"

"You knew what I was thinking."

"I took a guess."

"Yes. A very good guess. You know me well, Alex, but you also read my facial expressions and sensed the energy of my emotions."

"I see. And that's what *he's* doing?"

"Something like it, I'm guessing."

"Well, I suppose it's a start to solving our communication problem."

"This is *huge,* Alex. Make eye contact with him again and tell me what you feel."

Alex complied, clearing his mind of concerns. When their eyes met, he allowed the boy to draw him deep into his gaze. A long moment passed. Then, with a shudder, Alex backed away.

"What's wrong?" Laura asked, alarmed.

"I...I'm fine. Just a little light-headed."

Laura grabbed his arm to help steady him. "What happened?"

"It was a...flood. He let me feel his raw emotions. But it was like someone venting all their problems until you end up feeling rotten yourself."

"So, what you felt from him was bad? Negative?"

"Not necessarily. That's just the way I'm describing it. Sharing feelings."

"Empathy," Laura noted, "Empathic communication."

"You studied that a while back, didn't you?"

"Yes. I saw it in action, but it never really convinced me."

"How about now?"

The boy stood and crept toward the exam table. Laura and Alex backed up to give him space. He eyed them both, wary but fascinated by their conversation.

"Alex, what exactly did he communicate?"

"It's hard to say. On the receiving end, it was a jumble."

"Did anything stand out?"

Alex thought for a moment. "Concern."

"Like being afraid? Fear? Of us? Of being left behind?"

"No, not fear. Concern about...someone." Alex considered the boy again, pensive. "He misses someone—a girl."

"What? How did you figure *that* out?"

"Guy stuff."

"Not funny."

"An impression then. Let me try asking him something." Laura released his arm, and he took a few steps toward the table. "The girl is Ria, right?" he asked the boy. "Girl? Ria?"

The boy's eyes widened with a mix of surprise and appreciation. "Dah gur-el es Ria," he repeated.

Laura gasped. "Imitating the words," she noted in a whisper.

"You are afraid for her?" Alex suggested.

The boy shook his head, confused. "Ehe. Mo woo-eds."

"Alex," Laura said to the boy while pointing at Alex. "His name is Alex. I am Laura."

"A-yek, Lah-rah, Sah."

"I can tell you're trying to understand us," Laura said. "We want to know about Ria. Is she coming back for you? Is that what you were showing Alex?"

By his facial expressions, Laura could tell he was comprehending some of her words.

"Um...look," Alex said to the boy. "We need to know if she is coming back for you. It's really important." He pointed to his eyes. "Send me another message, buddy. Is Ria coming back?"

The boy mimicked Alex's mouth movements and then brightened with excitement. "Ria es comee back!" he exclaimed. "Yes! Ria es comee back foh me! You mus hep Ria! Hep the Dah-Ahey. When Ria comes back—"

The sound of Tannish opening the door interrupted him. "Are you finished with your examination, Director Turgis?" she called from the rear of the room. "Did you make any headway?" She waited to approach, craning to see what Laura and Alex were doing.

Laura cursed under her breath. "We're finished, yes."

The boy hopped on the exam table and questioned Alex with his eyes.

"Yes," Alex said to him in a hush. "We understood you. Will you let them examine you now?"

The boy nodded. "Yes."

"Is everything alright?" Tannish asked.

"Fine, Doctor," Laura replied. "You can come over here. I think you'll find our visitor a little more compliant."

Tannish rushed to join them in the examination area. "You've removed your masks. There are quarantine regulations that—"

"Do I have to show you my Get Out of Quarantine Free pass, Doctor? We're leaving. You'll be receiving orders to release everything your lab cameras have recorded over the past thirty minutes. Unless you want an immediate change of duty station and a new career in oblivion, I suggest you don't view the recordings...or copy them."

Laura did not wait for a response. After a last glance at the boy, she motioned for Alex to join her in leaving the room. Both of them were silent as they removed their protective suits and exited the building. As promised, Colonel Richter was waiting for them outside.

"So, what do you think?" Richter asked Laura.

"This changes everything, Colonel. We have to get to a briefing now. Can you set us up with another fast ride?"

"Already taken care of," he said, pointing to the helicopter that had brought them to the site. "And I'll be joining you."

"Before we leave, I need you to take possession of the camera recordings from the examination room—everything from when we entered to when we left. There can be no copies, and it wouldn't be a good idea for anyone to view them before doing this."

"You two get aboard," Richter instructed. "Give me a few minutes while I see to it myself."

Laura climbed in and dropped herself into one of the jump seats. "Are you okay?" she asked Alex. "Any weird side effects?"

"You mean from the empathic stuff? No. But I *am* concerned about contamination. We could have contaminated ourselves...or him."

"Maybe it was stupid, but we got our answers."

"We sure did. The kid is for real—a real alien being...isn't he?"

"I'm convinced. Aren't you?"

"Yeah. But he's so human-like. I wonder how close he is to us."

"Tannish will examine him now. She'll find out for us. I can hardly grasp what just happened in there, Alex. We were actually *communicating*."

"Well, we know they're coming back. You have your evidence, but we still don't know the *when*."

"I don't think it will be long."

"How can you be sure?"

The helicopter pilots and two other soldiers climbed aboard, motioning for them to get buckled into their seats. Laura answered Alex while she slid into the straps. "If the visitors are anything like us, they're going to notice the kid missing and want him back. They'll return alright...and soon. It's not just a chunk of the broken spaceship they'll be after. They left a child behind."

"Unless he was left behind on purpose," Alex noted.

"I hadn't thought of that."

"He seems innocent enough, but my gut tells me there's more to him being here than just an accident."

As the aircraft came to life, Laura peeked out the side window and saw the Colonel carrying a briefcase and heading back to join them. "Be sure to tell that to Richter," she said with heavy sarcasm.

"I only share my deepest fears with you."

Laura smirked. "Alex, you have an incredible way of keeping me on my toes."

"That's my job. But let's hope our bosses stay on theirs. This whole thing could get real messy now."

Colonel Richter hopped on board, motioned for the pilots to get the craft airborne, and dropped himself into an empty jump seat. With a genial smile, Laura leaned toward the window for a final look at the alien remnant and the prefab where the child was probably undergoing an intense medical examination. "Messy?" she said to herself. "We're already there."

CHAPTER 27

A City's Heartbeat

EVENING OF DAY 3 ON HOUROU

The living city of Atsaahwua displayed its nocturnal splendor after both suns of Hourou disappeared below the horizon and the sky became dark and filled with stars. Towering crystal spires now glowed with pastel colors, wrapped in floating rivers that pulsed to the rhythm of the city's heartbeat. On the streets and walkways below, white bodies reflected the colorful light of the surrounding structures, creating a moving rainbow as the people socialized, explored, and enjoyed the nighttime metropolis.

The Earth visitors reunited late in the evening, weary from their day of exploring. At Eah's insistence, they let her take them to a place where they could lodge for the night. Anyone visiting Atsaahwua, she explained, could locate an unoccupied apartment and make it their home for as long as they needed it. Accommodations, like everything else in the city, were free to use and furnished with every imaginable luxury.

Eah, Tammah, and Uio located an abode of suitable size, ushered the group inside, and then pointed out all of its features and provisions. The place was expansive, yet its design conveyed comfort and coziness. There were many rooms within its homey depths. Some were small and simple, while others were spacious and palatial. Everywhere, there were works of art, ornately designed furniture, and beautiful, tropical-like plants.

When Eah was satisfied that her guests were comfortable, she left with Tammah and Uio to find the rest of their family. Meanwhile, the Earth visitors gathered together in the great room.

"This place is beyond words," April said as she plopped herself onto a soft divan that resembled a huge bean bag chair. "How can you even describe it?"

Yori reclined on a type of futon across from her. "This house, or the city?"

"Both."

"Everything looks and feels so alive," Yori said. "The city is just like the jungle in a lot of ways."

"It seems the builders used the jungles for inspiration," Jay suggested. "They've imitated it in their designs."

"Well noted, Jay," Ellis complimented, examining the carved patterns in a nearby wall. "The city is a giant work of art, fashioned from the various forms of life found on this planet. Very little is inorganic. They built almost everything by using living organisms."

Across the room, Paul studied a high, arched doorway, marveling at its construction. "You wouldn't know it looking at some structures," he said, running his fingers along its grooves. "Most of them look and feel like rock, marble, or other building materials. We even walked on a path that could have been solid gold."

"We saw gemstones everywhere, too," April added. "They reminded me of versions of rubies, diamonds, emeralds, sapphires, and others from Earth."

"Most of them are organic as well," Ellis said. "At least, that's how our guides explained it. Somehow, the artists among the people can coax the shapes and colors out of the living rocks."

"This entire day has been more overwhelming than anything I've experienced since they took me up in their spaceship," Yori declared.

Ellis nodded. "It certainly has. I've been curious about your personal tour, Yori."

"*Personal* tour?" Paul asked her.

"We ran into Eah's brother, Aai, later in the day," Ellis answered for her, "and he invited her to observe medical treatments, so we split up. What did you learn about the alien physiology, Yori?"

"Well, I—"

"*We're* the aliens here, Ellis," April corrected.

"Quite right. You'll have to excuse an occasional use of the word, my dear. As Yori has stated, much of what I've learned here today defies explanation. *Alien* is often the first term that comes to mind."

"I know," April agreed. "Sorry, Yori. Tell us what you saw."

"Well, it's a question we've all wanted an answer to ever since we met Keah and his people: Are they *human?*" Yori paused, struggling to describe what she had seen.

"And?" Perry prompted, clearly impatient.

"Regarding their physiology, that's where the word *alien* stops."

"You're saying they're human, then?" Perry asked.

"Oh, they're human alright. *Perfectly* human."

Ellis crossed the room and sat on a lounge next to her. "Please explain."

"They're *perfect humans.* Their bodies are almost just like ours, but they function with no observable defects. From what they showed me, at the cellular level, there's no degeneration and no sign of genetic mutation."

"How can that be?" Paul asked.

"I don't know. But what I observed was the total biological perfection of the human organism. At least...it's perfect compared to our own physiology."

"You said *almost,*" Perry noted. "You said their bodies are almost just like ours. What are the differences?"

"Good question, Carlson," Ellis said. "Perhaps, Yori, you could start with what makes them different."

Yori nodded in agreement. "Well...in one of their medical buildings, Aai showed me an exam room with a huge black plant growing in the middle of the floor. Some of its leaves were big enough to cover a human body. Aai stood behind one and touched it in certain spots, like he was pushing buttons. He was talking to me the whole time—probably explaining—even though I couldn't understand much of what he was saying. After a few seconds, the leaf sort of lit up from inside. When it did, I could see right through it...and into his body."

"So, like an X-ray?" Perry asked.

"No. It was in real time—a color display of what was happening inside. Aai even stroked the plant in different ways to make it magnify what I was seeing."

"I'm not surprised," April said. "On our tour, we watched people using plants to do amazing things, too. They work with them like we would with machines."

"Yes," Yori agreed. "Most of their technology comes from what grows on this planet. Here, nature does the task better."

"Quite so," Ellis said. "While Yori was away, Carlson and I were treated to a tour of a communications facility. From there, Tammah said people could talk with others all over the planet. Instead of using cable lines or satellites, however, they send data through a vast network of flora that does it naturally."

"How?" Paul asked.

"That is where our own communication broke down," Ellis admitted. "Like Aai, Tammah still has limited use of our language, so I couldn't make sense of his explanations."

"Let's get back to the *human* thing," Perry suggested. "Yori, you said their bodies were almost biologically perfect. Did anyone explain how this is possible? Are you convinced they're natural, or could these people have manufactured them somehow?"

"I never took you for the science fiction type, Carlson," Paul quipped.

"We need to establish if they are really human," Perry shot back. "I think it's rather important."

"Their bodies are human," Yori answered. "There are only minor differences. The positions of a few organs are a little off. They also have a few small muscles we don't have. But these things exist in our bodies, too. What stood out the most is the lack of genetic mutations...and their ability to change their skin pigmentation. Otherwise, they're perfect human bodies. How they got that way—and how they remain so unflawed—is what I'd still like to know."

"They also don't seem to age after a certain point in their development," Ellis added.

"That's correct," Yori affirmed. "Their bodies go through the same early developmental phases as ours until the young adult stage. Then...they stop aging."

"That accounts for the lack of elderly people among them," April noted.

"Yes," Yori agreed. "To us, their seniors are only in their thirties...but they could be hundreds of years old."

Perry smirked, doubting. "*Hundreds* of years?"

"Well, it's difficult to compare, since they measure time differently on this planet. Plus, with no physical signs of degeneration, you can't even estimate age."

"Ahee told me that...in Earth years...Keah would be six hundred and twenty-five and she would be about six hundred and twenty," April informed.

Yori shook her head. "That's amazing. To me, neither look over thirty."

"The strangest thing is how the older children appear to be the same age as the parents," Ellis said.

"Well, if you consider how they stop aging after their physical development stops, it makes sense," Yori explained. "As adults, they all seem very close in age, yet they're hundreds of years apart."

From across the room, Jay stared out a window and listened to the conversation, picturing Eah in his mind. She appeared to be the same age as him. Was she really ten times older? "What about...um...the rest of Keah's family?" he asked Yori.

"Good question, Jay," Perry said. "It sounds like you've fallen for an older woman."

April shot Perry a warning scowl. "Don't tease him. We've established that we're all human, and humans do what humans do."

"Uh-huh."

Jay could not tell if Perry was ridiculing or chiding him. Likewise, though he appreciated April's defense, she was also making public assumptions about Jay's relationship with Eah. Jay was the youngest of the group, but that did not mean they should treat him like a teenager. He spun from the window and glared, ready to reprove them all.

Yori, noticing Jay's annoyance, caught his attention and motioned for him to go easy. "Let's all stay on topic," she suggested to everyone. "Jay asked about the ages of Keah and Ahee's *children*."

"Ahee didn't tell me all their ages," April said to Jay, "but she mentioned that—in our measurement—Eah would be about two hundred years old."

Jay hid his surprise by turning back to the window. The streets outside were empty, giving him an excellent view of the surrounding buildings. Like Eah, they appeared to be young—no weathering, no decay. Yet, they were ancient.

"As far as development goes, Jay," Yori said, "Eah is a young woman in her early twenties. So, don't let the difference in years trip you up."

"The age of my friends doesn't bother me," he said. "I treat everyone the same."

Jay's implication brought a sudden stop to the conversation.

"So," Perry said, breaking the uncomfortable silence, "how long do the people here live, then?"

Yori shrugged. "I don't know. Death was hard to discuss with them. From what I understood, though, their bodies sort of shut off when they reach about one thousand years old. Then, they talk about some kind of *transition* to a different state of being. That part sounded more religious than scientific."

"You're saying they live to be a thousand years old?" Perry asked.

"Sounds like it, yes."

"How do they stay so healthy?" Paul asked.

"Their immune systems are impervious to any pathogens." Yori explained. "That's how they can travel to other worlds and not have to worry about germs, viruses, or other infectious organisms. Plus, as far as their own planet goes, the environment has ways of destroying dangerous microorganisms brought *here* from other places."

"Which is why they haven't been concerned about being infected by us," Ellis postulated. "They have a double protection. They can't catch anything, and nature here automatically immobilizes any organism that might cause harm to the planet. It's extraordinary."

The room became quiet again while everyone considered Yori's new information. April stretched and yawned. "So...is anyone hungry?"

"We've been eating all day," Ellis replied. "Everywhere we explored, food was abundant...and free."

"Same with us," April said. "It grows all over. I'm going to fix a drink, though. Someone showed me how to mix a few fruit juices together to make a tasty smoothie. Any takers?"

Everyone agreed to try one, so April left the room and headed down a long corridor toward what Eah had described as a kitchen. Yori followed, offering to help.

"So," Yori said, as they both collected containers and the correct fruits. "I've been wanting to get another female's perspective on our day of learning."

"Me, too," April admitted.

"You, Paul, and Jay studied the culture here. What kinds of things did *you* learn?"

"Well..." April thought for a moment while she peeled some of the fruit. "It's overwhelming. I don't even know where to begin."

"Be general," Yori encouraged. "Tell me your observations about their society."

"I really like the way of life here."

"Why?"

"I guess because everyone is equal."

"How so?"

"The men and women treat each other as complete equals. There's no rivalry and no feeling of having to compete. They respect everybody."

"I noticed the same thing," Yori agreed. "People everywhere were polite."

"Exactly. And it was genuine, not forced or fake."

"Did you notice how males take the lead more, though?"

"I guess so."

"What did you think of *that?*"

April could tell Yori was probing, as if she wanted confirmation of something that was bothering her. "To me, men here are more chivalrous than controlling. It's not about power. They have a deep respect for women. And the women treat men the same way."

"But there's still a patriarchal bias in their society, isn't there?"

"What do you mean?"

"The men have the final say about things. In the end, they take the lead."

April found a utensil suitable for mashing and used it to squeeze juice out of the fruit she placed in a bowl. A purple liquid squirted out, and both women giggled as they dodged the spray.

"I know what you're getting at, Yori," April said, "but you can't compare this place to our cultures back home. From everything I've learned, and from my conversations with Ahee, society here is based on complete harmony. If they don't agree on something, they won't do it. Unity is in the male and female relationships, in their family interactions, and in how they all get along together."

"I can see that, too," Yori admitted.

"It may seem like men have the final say-so, but when men and women do everything in unity, that can't really be the case, right?"

"It seems contradictory, yes."

April pointed at herself with the dripping utensil. "I grew up in a home where my father was the head of the family, but my mom always had an equal say. That sounds old fashioned to most people today, and a lot of women would claim it's patriarchal and controlling, but they've had a wonderful marriage for thirty-five years."

"My family was that way, too," Yori said. "But my mother was pretty strong-willed. She's the one who pushed me to pursue medicine."

"I can be like that, too. But Paul and I still always work together. He gets my advice on almost everything, which is good because I'm right most of the time."

Yori laughed as she dropped more peeled fruit into April's bowl.

"Seriously, though," April continued, "we have our share of disagreements and spats, but we find solutions as a team. I let him make the final decisions on things, but only after we've agreed as a couple. There's a similar relationship between the men and women here, only it seems to work much better on *this* planet."

"Seems to," Yori admitted.

"There aren't any power struggles," April stated. "I guess that's what I like. We try to act equal back home, but these people have perfected it. They could teach us a lot."

"They already have," Yori confirmed. "The things I saw today are almost too fantastic to believe. Their technology might look primitive, but it's so far advanced compared to our own..."

"I love how they use what's natural," April said. "They work *with* nature instead of against it."

"Yeah, that's a great way to explain it." Yori dipped a finger and tasted the juice. "Tastes good. So...don't let me go into a science lesson here. What else about the culture sticks out to you?"

Pleased with how her colorful beverage was turning out, April lined up some cup-like vessels and filled them while Yori wiped up their mess. "There's a deep appreciation for life," April answered. "All life. They cherish being alive. You see it in their relationships, and it's also in their art and music. It's beautiful."

"They don't have a problem with *creating* life either," Yori joked. "There are kids everywhere. In some places, they outnumber the adults."

"I can barely keep up with two boys."

"Imagine being fertile for several hundred years, April. And they obviously don't use birth control."

"Ahee said she and Keah have had a lot of children."

Yori raised an eyebrow. "Other than those we've met?"

"Yeah. She said they live on other parts of Hourou."

"Did she say how many?"

"No. But since they have such long lifespans, they must have plenty out there."

"One of their doctors told me the women continue having babies until their bodies simply stop. They don't have a menopausal stage. And they can keep giving birth way past Keah and Ahee's ages."

"Well," April mused, "they're certainly not as limited as us."

"Still, that's a long time to be having kids."

April shrugged. "Finding a mate must be weird when everyone looks the same age. How do they know who's younger and who's older?"

"Good question."

Both women worked in silence for a few moments, pondering what they had discussed.

"Nothing here is very private," April eventually said. "I wonder how they handle their, uh, couple-time."

Yori chuckled. "Thinking about lovemaking, even on an alien planet? You must have gotten comfortable here already."

"I'm just *wondering*," April retorted. "Don't act like the thought hasn't crossed *your* mind, too."

"Maybe. Anyway, *Jay* seems to be doing fine with interpersonal relations."

"At least you confirmed that Eah's human. The rest is up to him, I guess."

"Physical compatibility shouldn't be a problem."

"Really?"

"I asked a lot of questions about mating."

"To Aai?" April asked, surprised.

"He appreciated my curiosity. Plus...I wanted to see if I could make him blush. His skin did an amazing thing when I talked about certain subjects."

"Oh my gosh, Yori."

"He translated for me when I asked the medical people about reproduction."

April blushed a bit, but she was clearly curious. "And?"

"It's very...interesting," Yori said with a laugh. "As you say, they're not private about very much."

"What did you find out?"

"Sex is very special to them. Unlike for us, it's not a recreation. They treat making love like an intimate ritual. And they make plenty of time for it...plenty."

"Did they tell you...I mean...most of them live in the woods," April noted. "So they do it right out in the open? What if someone's out walking and stumbles onto them?"

Yori shrugged. "There's no shame, embarrassment, or perversion in them. They'd probably just smile and move on. But it doesn't sound like intrusions happen. They go to secluded places—not to hide, but to get rid of distractions. They treat it as a ceremony...of love. It's a sacred thing to them."

"I see."

"They have only monogamous relationships here, too. Imagine being married to the same man for a thousand years."

April offered a sly smirk. "Well, if he's a good man..."

"He'd better be. Good at *everything*."

"Yori!"

"What? I'm just saying."

"I think all the naked men walking around are getting to you."

"Please. I'm a med student, remember? I've seen hundreds of bare bodies."

"True. So have I...*now*."

"And?"

"It's not a big deal anymore," April admitted.

"Good."

"Actually, it's freeing—not having to think in a sexual way just because you see a nude body."

"Exactly."

"Can I ask you something personal, Yori?"

"Sure."

"Does any of this *attract* you? I mean...the men. Perfect looks. Perfect bodies. Highly masculine..."

"Of course. But it would be pretty sad if I had to come all the way to an alien planet to find a mate."

April smiled and motioned toward the hallway.

"Jay *is* getting along fine with Eah. Maybe you just have to be more...unconventional—whether here or back home."

"I need to work on that, yes. My culture tends to be endogamous. So does my family."

"Remind me what that word means."

"Endogamous? Marrying within one's own group."

"Oh, yeah. Well, it might be up to you to break that tradition, Yori. There's a purpose for everything. You could be on this journey to discover new ways of thinking."

Yori considered April's suggestion and shrugged. "It's possible, I guess. Since being here, I've felt...different. They've challenged a lot of the things I used to believe. But that's not all. The beauty of this place...of the people, the peacefulness, the cooperation—love—it shows you how life *should* be."

"I know. There's something holding it all together, though...bigger and beyond just the culture or society."

"They all talk about the Ways of Ahey. Do you think it refers to—?"

"I came to check on those drinks," Ellis interrupted, appearing in the doorway.

"Just finished them," April said. "Now that you're here, you can help carry."

Ellis approached the work table and took two cups. "Eah's back," he said, sniffing at the contents.

"Only Eah?" April asked.

"She said the rest of the family is on its way."

Yori considered the bowl of leftover juice while she sipped from her cup. "We have plenty extra if we need it. Let's take these for now."

When they returned to the great room, April and Yori passed out the drinks. Jay shared his with Eah, and her eyes lit up with surprise when she took a sip. "Aiey-oooooh! Eey-uh-sah, April!" she praised. "You have learned to mix well."

"Thanks."

Eah talked a little about the flavors of various fruits, but April could tell something was distracting her. When separate conversations began among the group, she also noticed Eah's subtle gestures toward the main entrance, as if she was asking Jay to leave with her.

After a few moments, Jay put down his drink and cleared his throat. "Um, I'm going to step out for a few minutes," he announced to whoever was listening.

"Have fun," Yori said, grinning.

Eah grabbed Jay's hand and everyone watched them exit the apartment.

"Is anyone else here concerned about those two?" Perry asked.

Yori shot him a knowing grin. Paul and Ellis just shrugged.

"Hold on." April went to the main entrance to ensure Jay and Eah were not within earshot. Satisfied, she returned to the seating area and sat next to Paul. "Okay. What's the problem, Perry?"

"Yeah. Seems pretty natural to me," Paul remarked.

Perry shot Paul a perplexed look. "Are you *serious?*"

"Come on, Perry," Paul said with a laugh. "Jay's a boy. Eah's a girl. They're young..."

"You *are* serious."

"Yes! There's nothing wrong with it."

"Paul's right, Carlson," Ellis agreed. "So Eah took a liking to Jay. He's an attractive, budding man, after all, and quite the gentleman."

"And according to Yori, she's old enough to be his great, great, great grandmother," Perry noted.

"Only when using our Earth measurements," Yori reminded. "Developmentally, they're close enough."

"Let them be young," Paul entreated. "What right do we have to interfere, anyway? They're both adults. It's not all just from Eah either. Jay's attracted to her, too."

"Sure he is. Young. Perfect body. Walks around naked…"

"Oh, come on, Carlson!" Paul shot back. "I can't believe—"

"Can I say something here, please?" April interrupted.

Paul shook his head and took a long drink from his cup.

"I have a few concerns about Jay and Eah, too," April admitted, "but we shouldn't judge their relationship according to our own standards and prejudices. We're in unknown territory here."

"Exactly!" Perry agreed. "So let's not take this lightly either."

"I'm not," Paul stated. "I just prefer to let nature run its course, that's all."

"I think they make a rather cute couple," Yori admitted.

"Me, too," Ellis said. "They remind me of another *unusual* pairing I've seen recently."

Perry shot out of his seat and sneered at Ellis. "That has *nothing* to do with *this!*"

"Sure it does," Ellis said, placing his empty cup on a nearby table. "If we're going to be analyzing intimate relationships, we should be fair across the board."

"What are you talking about, Ellis?" Paul asked.

"I think it's time you told us all a bit more about Ria, Carlson," Ellis suggested.

Perry dropped back into his seat and finished his drink, wishing it was something stronger. "I will," he said. "But first we finish *this* topic. I'm concerned about Jay. If he falls for Eah, which has probably already happened, he's likely to make some poor decisions. How are you going to deal with their cute relationship when it comes time for us to return home? What will you do when he says he doesn't want to go back?"

"He won't," Paul answered. "Jay's a smart guy, and he's more mature than a lot of older adults I've met. If it would make you feel better, I'll talk to Jay. But I will not interfere in his life any more than I would in yours."

"I've aired my concern," Perry said. "What happens will be on your conscience, not mine. I've got bigger issues to deal with than a foolish crush."

CHAPTER 28

Crush

EVENING OF DAY 3 ON HOUROU

Eah led Jay away from his group's temporary abode toward one of the city's towering spires. All around them, people still wandered the streets and walkways, but their numbers had diminished since the suns dropped below the horizon. As in Earth cities, Atsaahwua was transitioning from daytime business to nighttime leisure.

Jay heard distant music and smelled aromas in the light breezes, bringing to mind cafes, restaurants, and nightclubs. He scanned the streets with interest and wondered if Eah's people built such places. Exploring the city's nightlife would have to wait, though, because Eah clearly had other plans. Blithesome and excited, she trotted at a quick pace until they reached a ramp that connected the street to spiraling walkways along the outside of the tower.

"Where are we going?" Jay asked.

She gestured for him to follow as she began the climb. "Come! You will see!"

Jay smiled and followed a few paces behind, captivated by the adorable way she scampered onto the hanging sidewalks. Her every action displayed the excitement of a young girl under careful submission to the grace of an elegant woman, and it fascinated him. She never seemed to mind his stares, so he openly admired her body while she strolled ahead. A slight breeze on the higher levels played through her hair, causing its mysterious blue speckles to glitter in the surrounding light. The effect, combined with the glow of her skin under the changing pastel lights, made her look quite otherworldly. Yet Jay also noted the womanliness in her movements—a dainty misstep and stumble, her delicate grip on a railing when she crossed a narrow catwalk, and the rhythmic sway of her hips as she walked.

The barrage of sensory stimuli around him was both wonderful and mind-boggling. Jay especially liked the sensations of his bare feet treading across the walkways, so he slowed his pace. A rubbery material, soft but also a little gummy, coated the surfaces of every footpath. He assumed the adhesiveness was for traction and safety. With caution, he stepped closer to the edge of the ramp and peered downward at At-saahwua's many levels of floating rivers and suspended streets. Already, they had climbed at least half-way to the top of the spire, which was no doubt where Eah was taking him.

Jay enjoyed the view for a moment before trotting to catch up with Eah. He found her on the next level, standing near a wall and speaking to someone concealed in shadow. "Eah?" He approached her but then stopped short, surprised to discover she was talking to no one. "Eah? What are you...doing?"

She motioned for him to come closer. "Jay, this is Yee. He has been asking me about Mahah. I told him she will soon be in the resting place with our guests."

Jay's eyes scanned the darkness, but he only saw the marble-patterned wall.

"Okay. Uh, Eah, I don't see..."

As he spoke, something shifted in the shadows and came into view. The shape was of a young Ah-Ahey male, camouflaged with the same colors and patterns of the surface behind him. As he stepped closer to Eah and Jay, his bare skin changed to a milky gray. Seconds later, it matched Eah's iridescent white.

"Ooo-oh-yee," Yee said to Jay with a slight bow.

"Oh. Sorry. I didn't see you standing there."

Yee smiled while examining Jay, and his green expressive eyes widened a little. Turning to Eah, he asked her something in their native tongue. Jay only recognized the word *Dah-Ahey*.

"Ehe," Eah responded flatly. She continued speaking to him, but also used a few sharp gestures to emphasize certain words.

By now, Jay knew enough about how Eah and her people communicated to recognize when she was being defensive. Yee was not arguing with her or teasing, but it still looked and sounded as if she was defending Jay.

Yee pointed at Jay's pants and made another inquiry. Again, Eah replied with a denial. To add emphasis, she reached over and opened Jay's unbuttoned shirt, rubbing his chest while she spoke. Jay blushed and thought perhaps he should speak on his own behalf, but Yee seemed to accept what Eah said to him. With an ambiguous grin, he nodded and walked away from them, heading toward the down-ramp.

"What was *that* all about?" Jay asked after Yee disappeared from sight.

Eah shrugged. "Yee was...curious about you," she answered. "He asked if you are Dah-Ahey."

"Why would he ask *that?*"

She examined a button on Jay's shirt and rolled it between her fingers. "Because of your coverings."

"Oh...yeah."

"Do all the people on Blue cover their bodies?"

Jay shuffled and looked around to see if anyone else was nearby. Somehow, the subject of clothing kept finding its way into their conversations. He supposed it was inevitable when the rest of the population found no need for adornment. "Well...yes."

"Why?"

"Lots of reasons."

"Reasons?"

"It's protection. Earth isn't like Hourou. We have different weather there—hot, cold, wet. We have to protect our bodies from all that."

"But you are all on Hourou now," Eah objected. "Such *pro-tech-shin* is of no use here."

Jay pushed away from her and leaned against a railing, feigning a desire to look at the scenery. There were fewer people at this level, but after what Jay saw of Yee's ability to camouflage himself, he doubted he could ever be sure someone was not nearby and merely unseen.

"I guess we use clothing—coverings—to hide, too," he said, pensive.

"Hide?"

"Like Yee."

"Yee was not hiding."

"Blending in to the environment, then."

"I do not understand."

"It's a way of fitting in—looking like everyone else. It must sound crazy to you, but dressing in certain ways does that for us. Some people want to stand out, though, so they dress to look different. What you wear communicates things to others...about how you see yourself. It's complicated."

"Hide, not hide. Stand out, not stand out. I do not get it. I understand protection. Sometimes, we must shield our bodies, but this happens outside of Hourou only, on other worlds that are still developing."

"I guess that's sort of what I mean," Jay conceded. "Like I said, it's complicated, Eah. Your world is so different...so innocent."

"What is inn-oh-cint?"

"Innocent," Jay corrected. He was eager to change the subject. "Hey, are we going to the top of this place or what?"

Eah flashed a very Earth-like smirk. She was getting better at mimicking his expressions. Pushing away from the railing, she grabbed his hand and led him to another ramp. After ascending several more walkways, they arrived at the top of the spire and stepped onto a wide rotating deck that was covered with soft, living grass. A transparent, waist-high wall surrounded the entire area to provide unobstructed viewing.

Eah located a spot away from the people already there and gestured for Jay to sit. He complied, marveling at his bird's-eye view of the city and landscape.

"This is incredible, Eah."

She gave him a moment to appreciate the breathtaking panorama. "Have you been...enjoying Atsaahwua?"

"Very much. I understand why its name is *Beautiful*."

Eah smiled, pushed her hair back, and scooted closer to him until their hips were touching.

Jay considered putting his arm around her, and his heartbeat quickened. *What am I doing?* he thought. *Am I about to flirt with an alien girl?* He glanced at her and felt a familiar yearning, but inside he argued with himself. *Slow down, dude. For one, she's human and not some weird alien. Two, you've already been flirting with her; you just don't want to admit it. Three, it's been Eah who's been doing all the touching and has acted so...inviting from the start.*

A waft of air blew some of Eah's hair across Jay's lap. He admired the length and color of it while continuing his internal debate.

Actually, Eah's incapable of being suggestive, he reasoned. *I'm confusing her openness with flirting. All this time, she's just been comfortable admitting and expressing her interest while I'm the one who's been hiding it.*

Jay could no longer deny his intense attraction to her. It was hard to resist falling for someone so captivating and mysterious. Still, a war raged within him. When he was not battling against sensual feelings, he was doubting how a man as imperfect as him could have a relationship with a girl as perfect as her. Besides being from vastly different planets, they also represented disparate societies with contradictory viewpoints and morals. Would Eah accept him if she realized how opposite he was from her?

I guess it's possible that we're not as incompatible as I feel, he guessed. *She can read me like a book, so she must have figured out a lot about me by now. If so, it hasn't turned her off.*

Eah drew in a slow, deep breath and released it under a soft, feminine moan. The sensuous sound conveyed serenity, but it also titillated Jay's senses. He scanned their section of the rotating observatory and noted that it afforded some privacy, which made their setting even more romantic. It reminded him of a date during his teen years when he had taken a girl to the county fair. They spent all day there but saved the giant Ferris wheel for last. During its gradual rotation, the ride malfunctioned, stranding them at the top of it for an hour. Nothing much happened up there. Jay had wanted to express some kind of affection, but he feared the girl's reaction. She seemed receptive, but awkwardness held him back. It was the same now. The amorousness of the evening enthralled him, but he was not sure if Eah shared the sentiment.

"What's...uh...beyond the forest down there?" he asked, trying to distract himself from his mixed-up feelings.

"In that direction is what you would call the *mountains*," she answered softly. "That is where Keah will find the material for building a new wa-ah-ahea."

"How long does it take to build a spaceship like that?"

"Long?"

"Sorry. How many days?"

Eah pulled her knees to her chest and hugged them, sighing as she replied.

"Few. One or two days."

"Wow. That's all?"

"As explorers, we have made many wa-ah-ahea."

"I see."

Feeling more confident, Jay reached for Eah's hand and felt a rush of excitement as he gently caressed her fingers. A breeze moved the grass, tickling his bare legs. For a long moment, they both just stared at the scenery passing before them.

"Eah," Jay said, breaking the silence. "I can tell you're curious about Earth and about why we live like we do there. If you ever want to ask me something, I'll always do my best to give you answers."

"I know this, Jay. I will ask you more when Keah allows it."

"What do you mean? You're not *allowed* to ask me about my planet?"

"Very little," Eah admitted, "until we understand how and why we have been connected to Blue...and why now. Until this is revealed, Keah decided it is better not to learn too much about life there."

"Is he afraid of something?"

"Afraid?"

"Does he fear something about it?"

"There is no fear in the Ways of Ahey."

"But we're here now...on Hourou...and you *have* been learning about us."

"Yes."

"And he's allowed you to hang around me. Isn't he worried about that?"

"Worried? Hang?"

"Isn't he concerned about the two of us spending so much time together? Uh...getting close?"

"Ehe. No. I asked Keah about that earlier, after I left you in the resting place."

"You did? About what, exactly?"

"About...getting close."

"Oh. And...uh...what did he say?"

Eah smiled at his obvious discomfort. "He and Ahee accept what is happening, even though it is...unusual."

"Great. So they think I'm *weird?*"

"No," Eah replied with a chuckle. "Unusual is the word I chose. In our language, the closest is *ee-yauhou.* To them, the idea of you and I getting close is ee-yauhou...strange, but acceptable because of who you are."

"Who I am?"

"I told them you are of Ahey and that I have seen the Ways in you."

The remark stunned him. How could she make such a claim when she knew nothing about his personal beliefs?

"There might be a better word than ee-yauhou, though," she continued. "It means *strange, but acceptable.* The strange part I understand, but not the acceptable part."

"What do you mean?"

"According to our Ways, we should have never met."

Again, her bluntness astounded him. *So does she want to get close or not? Have I been misreading her all this time?* He stole a glance and noted a distracted pensiveness in her eyes, as if what she said confused her as well. It was the first time he saw such uncertainty in Eah, which did nothing to help his lack of confidence in their new relationship.

"Well," he said, "I'm glad we met, even if it is a little *ee-yauhou*."

His use of her word elicited a soft giggle. She squeezed his hand. "I am, too."

"So, if I'm understanding you correctly, you're saying Keah doesn't want you to learn a lot about life on Earth, but that learning about each other is okay?"

"Something like that. Keah said the Ways of Ahey only mention travel to the blue planet. They do not guide us about what to do if the people from there were to visit Hourou."

"That could never happen without help," Jay noted. "We don't have the technology for space travel beyond our own moon. Definitely not past the next closest planet."

"That is why meeting someone from Blue has never been a concern."

"I see," Jay said. "No one from the other inhabited worlds thought we would ever leave."

"Not for...as you would say...a long time."

"That means someone out there has been watching us then," Jay reasoned.

"There are...observers," Eah said. "They can watch planets from afar."

Jay shook his head. "Wow. It's so hard to take all this in sometimes. But I understand how you and your family must feel. By coming to Earth, you did something against your law—the Ways—even though you had no other choice. Then you had to bring some of us back with you."

"Yes. Now you see. It should not have happened. Still, I am sure there is a purpose in all of it."

"I agree. I don't believe in chance or in coincidence or in accidents. There are reasons behind everything."

Eah nodded. "Yes. That is also the Way of Ahey."

"So...through Ahey, Keah will figure out why all this has happened?"

"We *all* will learn the why."

"But Keah is sort of like a leader, right? He decides?"

"Leader?"

"He's in charge. An overseer of the people. He tells others what to do?"

"Keah is the father of me, and he dyads with Ahee, who is the mother of me."

"Yes, but is he above everyone else?"

"I do not understand."

"One person, or a small group of people, have all the authority."

"Oh. No, Jay. People live in *Ahey,* and they are *one.* Authority belongs to all, not one or a few. That seems more like the ways of the Dah-Ahey."

"I see." Jay let go of her hand and fidgeted a bit. Had she been comparing him to the Dah-Ahey? It was not the first time he wondered about that. He considered asking her, but did not want to ruin the evening. "Well, things are much more complicated on my planet," he admitted. "So are the people there. In fact, I like it a lot better on Hourou."

"I like you better on Hourou, too," Eah said, laying back and stretching herself across the grass.

Her sweet smile and the mystery in her voice warmed Jay's heart again. He gazed at her while the night breeze slowly peeled away the long mane of hair that covered her body. Mindful of his inner urges, he still allowed his eyes to appraise her. She was radiant in the light of Hourou's moon, glowing like the soft white orb itself.

She's so perfect, Jay thought. *How could she ever love me?* A sudden compulsion to touch her overcame him, so he moved his leg until it rested against hers. The contrast of their two skin colors symbolized how he felt about their improbable romance. No matter what either of them wanted, and despite how close they were becoming, they were still worlds apart.

As he always did, Jay sought escape from such hopelessness by losing himself in the moment. He rubbed his leg against hers a bit, curious about its smoothness. While he did so, he spotted a patch of her skin changing color. He gasped, which made Eah flinch and sit up. Both of them watched as her entire knee turned to a shade of tan that matched Jay's own skin tone. Surprise filled Eah's eyes, but not fear. She rubbed the spot, and it slowly returned to its original state.

"This pleases you?" she asked, studying his expressions.

Jay could tell she was searching for his approval. "Well...it's, uh...it's pretty cool, yes."

"That means it pleases you?"

"I'm not sure I understand. *Pleases* me?"

Eah touched his face. When he did not react, she sighed and turned back to observing the scenery.

Did I just miss something here? he wondered. *What am I supposed to say? I think a tan looks good on you?*

Deflated yet unwilling to allow his ignorance to ruin what could have been a delightful moment, Jay draped his arm over her shoulders. "Can you tell me why it happens?"

"What are you asking, Jay?"

"Why does your skin change color?"

"The changing is natural among the people of Hourou."

"So...*anyone* can do it?"

"Yes. But not always."

"What do you mean?"

"It begins when the body becomes more mature. At first, when you are younger, it happens only sometimes. Later, we learn to control the changing and can change at will."

"Ah. So you sort of grow into it."

"Yes. Grow and learn."

"When you're an adult, can you *always* control it?"

"Mostly. But sometimes emotions can still cause the changing."

"Like being nervous or upset?"

"I do not understand those words."

"Scared? Afraid?"

Eah hesitated before answering, and Jay sensed she was a little embarrassed.

"Your word *excited* describes one emotion," she explained.

Jay blushed. Although the idea pleased him, he never considered that he could excite a girl.

"I...uh," he stammered. "Well...*excited* can have a few meanings."

"Excited," Eah repeated. "Like when—"

"It's okay," he interrupted. "I get it. Certain intense emotions can still trigger the changing." Flustered, he looked away from her. *It's a good thing* my *skin can't change color. I'd probably look like a rainbow right now.*

"This makes you...uncomfortable?"

"No! No! I'm trying to understand better, that's all." He felt her shift under his arm. "I hope my questions aren't too...uh...personal."

"Personal?"

"Where I'm from, it's impolite to talk about other people's bodies."

"What does im-pole-lite mean?"

"There are just some subjects you don't bring up among...strangers."

"Strangers."

"Well...not that we're strangers, but there are so many differences in the ways—"

"Jay," Eah interrupted, "I can see you want to know more. Ask me."

"Okay. When I first saw you on your ship—on your wa-ah-ahea—your skin was black. The only ones who were white were your parents."

"Black?"

"Black is a color. It means, uh, very dark." He pointed at the star-filled sky. "The sky at night is black, but the stars are white."

"Oh, I understand," Eah said. "Yes, in the wa-ah-ahea, we allowed our bodies to take on the black of what surrounded us. Keah and Ahee willed to remain white."

"So white is the color you stay most of the time?"

Eah thought for a moment while considering her body. "There are many colors, and people enjoy them all. The white and the black are colors we most often return to, though. It makes it easier to find each other, so you will see most people that way."

"What about the others? The Dah-Ahey? They look different from the rest of you."

A slight frown on her face made Jay wonder if talking too much about the Dah-Ahey was considered a social taboo. Still, he waited for her to answer.

"They are not like the Ah-Ahey," she said.

"So...they can't change color?"

"Very few can, and they cannot control it."

"But they used to do it...like the Ah-Ahey?"

"Yes, when *they* were Ah-Ahey. But when they turned from the Ways of Ahey, most lost the changing."

"So all the Dah-Ahey are that bronze color?"

"Bur-ons?"

"Sorry. Bronze. It's another color. What I mean is...are *they* all the same color?"

"Yes. They are all the same."

Eah's troubled expression reminded Jay that she did not enjoy talking about the Dah-Ahey.

"Um...I haven't seen your parents change. Does it stop when you get older?"

"No. Changing is simply a choice."

"What is the purpose? I mean, for what reasons do you change—other than for emotional reasons?"

"It is a gift to us from Ahey. Changing is...fun. We like to change sometimes and feel even more connected to what is around us."

"And you can choose the colors you change into?"

"Yes. Our eyes must first see. Then, we can will the change."

"Wow! That's really cool, Eah. So, if I asked you to turn the color of this grass, you could make your skin match it?"

"Maybe."

"Maybe?"

"I am still…learning the control of the changing. You do not wish me to try it, do you?"

She stiffened a bit, suggesting to Jay that she was nervous about the idea.

"No, not at all. I actually like you how you are."

The way Eah searched his eyes revealed a deep yearning for his acceptance.

"You do?"

"Yes…I really do."

Jay returned her gaze, trying hard to convey honesty while fighting with himself over backing off or finally kissing her. Eah's longing stare through half-closed eyes seemed to beg for his decision. Once again, he fell into her mysterious trance. Lost in their combined stream of emotions, he did not notice her complexion changing until the skin around her eyes had turned to a light brown.

"Am I changing now, Jay?" she asked, noting a sudden surprise in his gaze. "What are you seeing?"

"Your, um…" He shook himself from the trance. "It's okay. Don't worry about it."

In seconds, her entire face was only a shade lighter than his. He wanted it to continue, curious to see what she might look like as an Earth girl.

Eah pulled some of her hair forward as a covering. "Now you see how emotions can cause the changing."

"It's amazing, Eah." Jay brushed the hair aside and stroked her soft cheek, marveling as it returned to its original white color. "You should never be embarrassed about it. You're beautiful."

Eah grinned with appreciation, and Jay could tell she was relaxing again.

"What did I look like?"

"Your face was changing. Your skin almost matched mine."

She chuckled. "Like you?"

"Almost, yeah."

"Did it please you?"

"It was...interesting. But like I said, Eah, I like you the way you are."

"I like you the way you are, too, Jay."

The two sat in silence for a while. Each could feel the other's heart pounding with expectation and desire, but neither had the courage to attempt physical expression. It was Eah who finally broke the stalemate. With a heavy sigh, she scooted out from under Jay's arm and stood. "We should return to the resting place," she said with an apologetic tone. "Keah and Ahee are there now."

"How do you know?" Jay asked.

"It is the knowing...inside," she answered, pointing to her chest.

Jay rose and straightened his clothes, wondering if she also could tell how much he hated the idea of ending their intimate interlude. "I wish we could stay a little longer."

"Me, too. But...we should go."

She sounded frustrated. Jay assumed it was because she shared his disappointment, but he sensed there was more.

"I can tell something else is bothering you, Eah. What is it?"

"Bothering? No. But I am wondering..."

"About what?"

"You know *much* about me, Jay, but I have learned little about *you*."

"You're right. I spent all day learning about your culture. You showed us art, the city's architecture, how people live, told more about your family, but it was all one-sided."

Eah grabbed his hand and led him off the platform. "I wish to know more about you, Jay."

"Oh." He took one last look at the cityscape below before they stepped onto the ramp and began their descent. *Too bad I can't take a picture of this,* he thought. *Then again, who would I show it to? Few people even care I'm gone.*

"Jay?" Eah prompted, confused by his sudden sullenness.

"Talk about *me*? Okay, but there's not much to tell. What do you want to know?"

She released his hand and trotted toward a narrow footbridge formed by living vines. Specks of glowing material within the bark lit a safe path across and created a green glow on her white feet. "What dyad are you from?" she asked, beckoning him to join her on the bridge. "I mean...who are the people in your family?"

"That's an easy one," Jay replied. "I don't *have* a family."

"I don't understand."

"My parents—my dyad—died when I was young."

"*Died* means...the body finishes?"

"That's one way of putting it, yes."

"How did this happen?"

"I'm not sure. Once, I was told they were missionaries, but they didn't die doing that. Someone else said they picked up a strange disease. One time, some government people came to visit the ranch and asked about me. I was still young, so I created this fantasy that I was the child of secret agents. Anyway, I never could get straight answers out of foster parents or counselors. So...I gave up asking."

"I do not understand many of those words. Mish-ah-nary?"

"It has to do with religion."

"Ree-lige-in?"

"Wow. How do I explain *that?* For us, it's like God, churches, symbols, sacred writings, things you believe, and how you live your life. We have a lot of religions back home. A religion is a set of beliefs that guides your life, I guess."

"This sounds like the Ways of Ahey," Eah noted.

"I've wondered about that, too," Jay acknowledged. "I mean, I wondered if Ahey was like a religion."

"Ahey *is,*" she insisted. "Ahey is not *religion.*"

"I'm probably not explaining it very well. Let's change the subject."

"What is *God?*"

As they continued toward another ramp, Jay looked at her in amazement. "You're asking me some tough questions here, Eah," he said with a chuckle. "God? Well, to us, God is the creator of everything. He existed before everything, made everything, and oversees it all. From there, people have very different ideas of what he is and how to relate to him."

Eah nodded, smiling. Jay wondered if it meant she was understanding or if she thought the idea was amusing. He hoped it made sense to her. If Ahey was God to her and her people, it would be one more area of compatibility between them. He needed that, despite its potential consequences for religious beliefs back on Earth. Aliens believing in God? It created too many new questions.

"Does any of this make sense to you?" he asked.

"Maybe."

"You like using that word."

"Maybe," she teased.

"Ask me something else," Jay implored. "Something easier."

She guided him down a wide ramp that led to the lower walkways. Fewer people used them now. Jay was glad; he wanted their conversation to be candid, but also private.

"With no dyad, you have been always alone?" she asked.

Jay rolled his eyes and frowned.

"This question also displeases you?"

"No. But you're picking some tough subjects."

"Tough is difficult?"

"Yes. Very much," Jay chided.

"Oh."

"It's okay. I've just never had to talk much about things like this."

"But we talk well together, don't we?"

"Yes, Eah, and your use of our language is getting better and better after every conversation."

"Tell me more, before we get back to the resting place."

"Alright. What was the question?"

"With no dyad, you have been always alone?" she repeated.

"No. Other families—dyads—took care of me. We call them foster parents. I lived with a few different families for a while. When I got older, I went to live at a youth ranch—a place for young adults to work and study. I made a few friends, I guess. It was hard because kids came and went a lot. So...I mostly kept to myself."

"Who is a friend of Jay?"

"Well, there's a kid named Cody that likes to hang around me. You'd get a kick out of Cody. He's a pretty funny guy."

"Kick?"

"He would entertain you."

"Is this Cody like you?"

"Like me? Oh, no. Cody is...well...Cody is a very different sort."

"Would Cody like *me?*"

Jay laughed. "Seeing you would scare the wits out of him. His face—you should have seen it when the ship crashed and—"

"You saw the other wa-ah-ahea?" Eah asked, surprised.

"Well...yeah. I mean, Cody and I were chasing it through a field and heard it crash twice. The second time, four people came out and—" He paused, and his eyes opened wide from a sudden revelation.

"*Four* people, Jay? *Four?*" Eah asked.

"Y-yeah. Let me think. Yes, there *were* four. It was dark...and hard to see. I was shocked by everything that was happening, but..."

"Four," Eah repeated, pensive.

"This is the first time I thought about it since everything happened," Jay admitted.

"But you are certain? Four people?"

Jay closed his eyes and revisited the scene in his memory. "Yes. I can still see it in my mind. There were four people that came out of that ship." He opened his eyes and stared hard at her. "Eah, that means—"

"Yes, Jay. We only brought back *three* of them."

"So...a Dah-Ahey remains on Earth."

Both of them pondered that for a moment before Eah spoke. "We knew of only three leaving Hourou," she said, her eyes distant and reflective.

"And I was thinking of only three because that was how many you grabbed. I didn't remember the fourth until just now."

Eah nodded. "Ria did not tell us of the other when we questioned her."

"Who's Ria?"

"In your words, it is a long story. Ria is one of the Dah-Ahey we brought back to Hourou."

"The female one? Where is she now?"

"Among the Dah-Ahey again."

"Along with the other two? How can you be certain they survived our crash?"

"They did."

"Wow. I forgot all about them."

"Please remember, Jay," Eah pleaded. "Were you following three or four before we brought you aboard the wa-ah-ahea?"

Jay strained to recall the chase through the nature preserve. The more he thought about it, though, the more convinced he became there were three figures in front of him during the pursuit.

"We were following three," he said after a long pause. "Now that I'm remembering, I'm sure it was only three."

"A fourth Dah-Ahey remains on Blue," Eah said to herself.

"The fourth one must not have left the crashed ship. Either that or he went off alone."

"The fourth would not *choose* to remain alone on a strange and forbidden planet," Eah said. "It is possible Ria *hid* the other from us."

"That means she left someone behind on purpose. But why?"

"We were close to catching her," Eah recalled, "but we hesitated when she tried to land her wa-ah-ahea. We lost sight of it, and that is when it crashed."

"Why did you hesitate?"

"It had been damaged—worse than ours—and we needed one to remain intact so we could all return to Hourou."

"Makes sense."

"Ria hoped they could all hide from us on Blue. But when she realized how close we were to finding her, she must have hid one Dah-Ahey before running away with the two others."

"If that's how it happened, she has a bigger plan."

"Plan?"

"She knew that even if you caught her and brought her back to Hourou, you'd still have to return to Earth and find him," Jay explained.

"Yes, and that might, as you would say, *give her another shot* at returning as well."

"We call that insurance."

Eah grabbed his hand and picked up their pace. "Jay, we must tell this to Keah and Ahee...now."

* * *

When they returned to the apartment, Jay and Eah found her family already there, as she predicted. In the great room, Keah was pacing back and forth while everyone else sat watching him. No one spoke and there was an air of seriousness, leading Jay to believe that he and Eah had arrived at the end of an important conversation. They entered the room quietly and slid into a long, soft settee next to Paul and April.

"Welcome back," Paul said to Jay in a whisper.

"What'd I miss?"

"Plenty. But I'll get you caught up later. How was your date?"

Jay felt himself blush, and he frowned at Paul's joke. "We were just talking," he insisted.

"Fine by me."

"I'm serious."

"Make sure you know what you're doing," Paul cautioned.

"I do."

"And consider all the consequences, Jay."

"I am."

April nudged Paul as a signal to keep quiet, so he leaned closer to Jay. "We'll talk later?"

"Sure." On the other side of Jay, Eah was fidgeting. He placed a reassuring hand on hers and whispered to her. "When are you going to tell Keah?"

"Let us listen first."

As if on cue, Keah stopped pacing and returned to the center of the room.

"There is something I do not understand," he said to the group.

"What is it?" Perry asked. "I've told you as much as I can."

"Why did Ria choose now to visit Atsaahwua?"

"She followed us," Perry answered.

"But why?" Yori pressed. "Something's still missing from your story."

"What else can I say?" Perry asked. "Do *you* know her, Keah?"

"Yes. I know Ria."

"Well," Perry asked, "why do *you* think she would come? She's allowed to be here. I assume she has been here in the past."

"Not so fast," Ellis demanded. "That's a nice deflection, Carlson, but Keah asked you first."

"I told you—"

"What was the *real* agreement you made with Ria before we found you with her?" Ellis interrupted.

"Real agreement?"

"Yes," Yori said. "You've conveniently left something out."

"Yori," Perry warned, "remember what I said about leaving the politics to me?"

"Ria desires to return to Blue," Keah surmised. "Perry Carlson, did you agree to help her with this?"

"Agree?" Perry shifted in his seat.

"Keah can read you like a book, Perry," April reminded, "so you might as well tell him everything."

"I'm not sure *what* her plans are," Perry insisted. "We both agreed to an exchange of information. I wanted to know more about the Dah-Ahey, and she wanted to know about life on Earth. In our.... negotiations...she may have inferred I could get her back there."

"May have inferred?" Paul asked. "Does she think that or not?"

Perry hesitated, then shrugged.

"The people here don't play games with words, Perry," April reminded.

"You haven't met the Dah-Ahey."

April gave a questioning glance to Yori and Ellis.

"Unfortunately," Ellis explained, "Carlson taught Ria some lessons in rhetoric. She caught on quick. Still, she struck me as very gullible."

"Then if Perry even insinuated he could, or would, help her, she would likely believe it," Paul guessed.

"Yes," Ellis affirmed. "Nice going, Carlson."

"Well, that explains it," Yori said. "It explains why she's here, right?"

Keah was about to say something but turned to Eah as if she had spoken to him. Only Jay and April noticed the series of minute gestures that passed between the two. As if having just received permission to speak, Eah stood and addressed the room.

"There is more," she said. "Jay told me there were *four* Dah-Ahey in the wa-ah-ahea that traveled to Blue. One of the Dah-Ahey is still there."

Eah's revelation stunned everyone.

"Jay," Paul said, "are you sure? You're the only person here who witnessed the crash."

"Yes. I'm sure. Cody and I saw four people come out of the crashed ship."

"What about when you were following them through the woods?" April asked.

"We thought we were chasing all of them, but it was dark out there. Now that I've had time to think about it, though, I remember only three leaving the crash site."

"I only saw three figures ahead of us when we were running through the pasture," Paul noted.

"We only knew of *three* Dah-Ahey," Keah said. "And we tracked only those."

"It didn't hit me until Eah and I were talking a little while ago. Everything happened so fast; then I was aboard the ship. I'm sorry for not figuring it out sooner."

"No one is blaming you, Jay," April said. "In fact, you may have given Keah the last piece of the puzzle. It explains why this Ria person is so set on getting back to Earth."

"I had no knowledge of this," Perry declared. "Ria never mentioned it during our conversations. It's news to me. However, that's not the only reason she wants to return so badly."

"Oh, please don't tell us there's more, Perry," Yori pleaded.

Ahee rose and joined Keah in his pacing. "Go on, Perry Carlson," she urged.

"As I told you earlier," Perry said, "Earth fascinates Ria. She's *obsessed* with it. My guess is that she wants to take up residence there—her and all the Dah-Ahey."

"That can never be," Keah said. "Ria knows it is forbidden."

"Well, she stole one of your ships and got herself there, didn't she?" Perry reminded. "She probably feels your rules don't apply to her or to her people anymore."

"It is the Way of Ahey," Ahee asserted. "It applies to everyone...even to the Dah-Ahey."

"That's all fine and good," Perry said, "but now Ria has even more incentive to go back...unless she doesn't care about the one left behind."

"She cares," Keah insisted. "She hid the other for a purpose."

"It's also possible the fourth one wanted to stay with the crashed ship," Jay offered.

"Ehe—no," Ahee said. "If the missing one remained in the other wa-ah-ahea, we would have brought him, or her, into ours when we retrieved the...reek-ige?"

"Wreckage," Jay corrected. "Then he or she must have gone off alone."

"We can't know any of that for sure," Perry said, standing to draw everyone's attention. "Keah, why is there a rift between the Ah-Ahey and the Dah-Ahey? This is what I was trying to learn from Ria."

"Riff?

"Rift. A division. Disunity and disharmony."

Keah nodded. "You see it clearly," he stated. "You can see the difference."

"Of course," Perry replied. "But what caused it?"

Keah glanced at Ahee and indicated that they should sit. After sliding into a settee, he reached for a cup on a nearby table, sipped from it, and passed it to his wife, all the while studying Perry. "Ria and the others like her no longer live according to the Ways of Ahey," he said. "They are *Dah*-Ahey."

Beside him, Ahee covered herself with her white mane, expressing discomfort. "Their ways are now *koyoyi*," she added. "In your language, that means *turned against*, but koyoyi implies a stronger opposition."

"Their koyoyi happened generations ago," Keah explained. "We do not understand how or why. The Ah-Ahey of Hourou have always desired to live according to the Ways of Ahey. Then, like a great wave, the koyoyi overtook some of our people. They turned from Ahey and left to be apart from the Ah-Ahey. This is the great division."

"I think I understand," Perry said. "We have many such factions on our planet, and plenty of disagreements. Too often, it leads to terrible things."

"We have seen the Dah-Ahey turn back to Ahey," Ahee said. "Some become Ah-Ahey again. Many, though, do not."

"It seems to me that Ria found an alternative solution," Perry noted.

"What is that?" Ahee asked.

"Leaving Hourou."

"We will not allow that to happen, Perry Carlson," Keah said.

"Why? Why not move them somewhere else? If not Earth, let them find a better planet. Then your people don't have to worry about them anymore. They just want to live free."

"Is this the freedom that exists on Blue?" Keah asked, suspicious.

"No," Paul answered, clearly agitated by Perry's attempted meddling. "Freedom doesn't mean being able to do anything you desire. That's being *enslaved* to your own selfish passions. Real freedom includes choosing *not* to do certain things for the sake of protecting the common good."

"You speak with much wisdom, Paul," Keah complimented. "What you said is according to the Ways of Ahey."

"Being forced to live according to ways that one does not accept is not freedom either," Perry rebuked.

"Nobody on Hourou is forced to do anything," Paul corrected. "Am I right, Keah?"

"What do you mean by *forced?*" Keah asked.

"See? They don't even understand the concept."

"He doesn't know the *word*," Perry asserted. "Keah, forced means to compel someone to do something against their own will."

"No one could do this," Keah said, incredulous. "Your will is your own, and only you can change it...from inside. For someone to attempt such a thing would bring divisions that could—I cannot imagine the consequences."

"That is true on Earth as well," Paul said, trying to calm Keah's growing agitation.

"Though many have tried anyway," Perry added with heavy sarcasm.

Paul glared at Perry as a warning. "Sometimes, Perry, sharing ideas isn't the best thing. Let's not pollute this pristine culture. In fact, I think the sooner we leave this planet, the better."

"I have to agree with Paul," Ellis said. "Our presence here has not been all good for your people, Keah, and I am sorry for that. Obviously, our ways are as foreign to you as yours are to us. We don't want to meddle in your affairs by imposing our own beliefs and practices on you. Right, Carlson?"

"On my planet, part of my job is to be a negotiator," Perry said to the host couple. "If I can help to heal the division that exists between you and the Dah-Ahey in the time I have left here, I'm available to you."

Keah and Ahee looked confused. After studying Perry for a few moments, they whispered to each other and seemed to come to some sort of decision.

"We only recognize some of your words," Keah said to Perry, "but we understand enough. You are kind in your offer of help, Perry Carlson, but for the Dah-Ahey there is no healing apart from Ahey, and they will not once again unify with the Ah-Ahey until they first seek unity with

Ahey." He stood and made his next statement to the entire group. "And the Dah-Ahey will *not* leave Hourou."

After letting his command sink in, Keah turned toward Ahee and offered his hand to her. She took it and they both rose.

"Let us speak no more of this," Ahee suggested. "Your day in Atsaahwua has been overwhelming, and you are all tired. Become refreshed in this place. Stay and rest, for when the suns of Hourou next meet, you will experience more wondrous things at the mountain."

"Thank you, Ahee," April said. "It has been a very exciting day. We appreciate you letting Eah and the others guide and teach us about your culture."

Ahee pushed her hair behind her body and smiled brightly at April. Then, with a nod, she indicated to her family that it was time to leave. "This staying place is for you," she said to her guests while her children filed through the main entry portal. "We will sleep in the next one. If you have need of anything in the night, come to us."

"Keah," Ellis said, stopping him at the entryway. "Earlier, before Jay and Eah returned, you said the material to make a new spacecraft was deep under a mountain."

"Yes."

"Won't it take a long time to dig it out? Do you have mining equipment there already?"

"Nothing is there already," Keah replied.

"Then how will you be extracting it?"

Keah smiled. "You will see, and it will amaze you. Tomorrow, Ellis Minister, we will be moving mountains."

CHAPTER 29

Moving Mountains

MORNING: DAY 4 ON HOUROU

Ellis felt warmth on his face, and it roused him from sleep. Through one lazy eye, he peeked at the ceiling and saw orange sunlight beaming into the room through a small skylight. On Hourou, orange meant it was first sunrise. For Ellis, it also signified the start of his fourth day on the alien planet. The soft divan he had chosen for a bed conformed to his body like a snug embrace, making him want to stay in it a little longer. He needed to get up, though. With reluctance, he pulled himself from the bed's grip and scanned his surroundings. The other lounges where Jay and the Theeles had slept were empty, but Yori and Perry were still there, sleeping on settees.

Careful not to wake them, Ellis rose and sought the lavatory, cringing at the idea of using an alien plant to relieve himself again. With no alternative, he took care of business in haste before heading to the nearby bathing chamber. It was unoccupied, which he appreciated since the cavernous space provided little privacy. He crept to the edge of the enormous, sunken pool that filled the center of the room. A fine mist clung to the water's surface—radiant, magical, and swirling in pastel colors. All around him were luxurious furnishings and beautiful works of art, bringing to mind royal palaces and noble people.

Although the decor fascinated him, Ellis wasted no time shedding his clothes and sliding into the warm, flower-scented water. He swam the length of the pool and discovered the other side had a recess with underwater benches and jets, similar to the whirlpool bath he used at his fitness club. He paddled in and reclined on a bench, closing his eyes while the massaging streams soothed his body.

"I see it even has a hot tub!"

The voice startled Ellis from his reverie. Through the mist, he spotted Yori on the other side of the pool, undressing.

"They thought of everything!" she yelled to him. "I could never afford to visit a spa like this back home!"

Terrified at the sight of Yori stripping and preparing to join him, Ellis diverted his eyes by frantically searching the room for another exit. "I was about to leave!" he called out. "Give me a minute to dress and you can have it all to yourself! Do you see towels anywhere?"

His only answer was the sound of a large splash. When he glanced over, all he saw was a pile of clothing where Yori had been standing and ripples from her dive into the water.

Just stay under, he pleaded as he stood to exit the pool. Before he could jump out and run for his clothes, Yori's head resurfaced, and she swam toward him.

Ellis dunked himself back down and cursed his slow response. "Stay there!" he yelled to her. "I'll, uh...slip out and give you some privacy!"

"What?" she asked, trying to hear him over her splashing.

Before he could do or say anything further, Yori was at the recess, positioning herself in front of the strong jets. Ellis could only hope the bubbling water would hide his exposure and embarrassment.

"This is wonderful, Ellis!" Yori exclaimed, floating onto a bench. "Just what the body needs."

"Yes...uh...q-quite nice," he stammered. "Uh. Look, I was about to get out and find something for breakfast. If you, um..."

"Ellis Minister," she interrupted, "I believe you're actually embarrassed."

"Don't be silly," he countered. "I'm merely thinking of your privacy."

"I love the way you say *prih-vih-sea*," she joked. "Sounds so much nicer than *pry-vah-sea*."

"Well, I—"

"Oh, stop it, Ellis! You've been here long enough to realize there's no need for *prih-vih-sea* in this culture."

"That is *profoundly* evident," Ellis admitted, "but it is not *my* culture. We don't have communal bathing where I come from."

"Sure we do," Yori corrected. "You don't get out of the classroom enough."

"Yori, I really would like—"

"Okay, okay. Sit for a few minutes and enjoy the hot tub. I'll have a swim and stay on the other side of the pool till you're done. Seriously, you'd think—"

"Wow! You two are fitting right in!"

Ellis snapped his head around and saw Perry in the entryway, staring at them with a sly grin on his face and standing with hands on hips like an over-attentive chaperon.

"Next, I suppose you'll be painting yourselves with tribal colors!" Perry quipped. "Or maybe just white?"

"Push off, Carlson!" Ellis barked. "Don't spoil a pleasant morning!"

Yori waved her hand in dismissal. "He's just joking, Ellis. Ignore him."

"You're too touchy, Ellis Minister!" Perry yelled back. "Better spend more time in there and relax! Don't worry, I'll leave you two skinny-dippers alone! I only came here to wash up and tell you I'm taking a walk!" He strode to the edge of the pool and tested the water.

Ellis stood, forgetting Yori's proximity to him. "Where are you going?" he asked Perry.

"For a walk!"

"You'd better not try to rendezvous with that Ria girl!" Ellis warned. "And don't pretend you forgot she's wandering around the city some-where!"

"Give me a break, Minister!" Perry said as he splashed water onto his face. "I'm going to check on our young friend, Jay, who nobody else here seems to care about."

"Paul said *he* would speak to Jay about Eah. Why don't you stay out of it?"

"Paul and April Theele have gone as native as you two. Since I'm the only one of our party who still has his head, I feel inclined to warn Jay myself."

"Ellis," Yori entreated. "There's no use trying to convince him. Jay can handle himself. Now sit down and relax before you, uh...catch a draft."

Ellis glanced at Yori and noted she was struggling not to look at his full exposure. He cursed to himself and splashed back down into the water.

"Do what you like, Carlson!" he yelled. "But be in the park—down the street—before the suns meet! That's what Keah told us!"

"I don't remember him saying that!"

"The Theeles left a note before they went out this morning! Go read it!"

"Fine!" Perry agreed with a laugh. "You two have fun!"

With that, Perry exited the room and Ellis inwardly scolded himself for not asking him to first bring over his clothes.

"You're not thinking of following him again, are you?" Yori asked, noting his yearning stare toward his discarded coverings.

"Not until you just suggested it."

"Let him go, Ellis."

Ellis sighed and leaned on his bench. "You're right, of course."

"Keah knows the entire story now. He'll handle Perry and Ria. Let's enjoy what we have here." She closed her eyes and lay back, floating and enjoying the sensations of the fragrant and soothing water.

Ellis diverted his stare and frowned. *Well, there's no escaping this,* he thought. *I guess I'll stay here and soak for a while. If Carlson gets himself into trouble again...he's on his own.*

* * *

The deserted streets of Atsaahwua's lodging sector surprised Perry, but the quietness pleased him. He needed solitude while deciding on his next move. There was so much to consider, and it was hard to deliberate amidst the myriad distractions of this alien planet. A casual walk through an urban neighborhood, even one as foreign as this, would help clear his mind.

To avoid getting lost, Perry restricted his stroll to a few familiar roads with distinct landmarks. He required little time for his musing, and after circling the long city block that surrounded his temporary home, he was ready to search for the rest of his party. According to the sloppy note Paul left near the refreshing room, they would be in a nearby park-like area. Perry knew he could locate the place, despite Paul's sketchy directions. What puzzled him, though, was how the man found something with which to write. From what Perry had learned, writing on Hourou was unnecessary. Since all the people had an exceptional memory, they mainly relied on unwritten communication and oral tradition. Perry also witnessed how his host family had an uncanny ability to communicate with each other from great distances through a strange sixth sense. Combined with an infallible intuition and the use of plants and animals to send messages anywhere across the globe, written words were indeed superfluous.

He climbed a ramp to the next level and noticed a contained forest several blocks away. A winding, elevated footpath led there, so he followed it, using the treetops as a landmark. In a short time, he arrived at a down-ramp, descended to the ground, and found himself in front of a giant arch that marked the park's entrance. He studied the structure as he strolled underneath. The surface was smooth like marble, but it was warm to the touch and pulsated as if alive. At its peak, there were familiar etched symbols. Two resembled sunbursts, presumably representing Hourou's twin suns. Others could have been the towering spires of the city. Perry guessed they were telling the story of the city's founding. A line of people figures was walking in front of two larger ones that were stepping out of a round portal. On the other side of the portal was an enormous, blue circle with a small white one orbiting it. Further from those were symbols of stars, clouds, and the unmistakable shape of a human hand.

Perry decided not to waste too much time trying to analyze the unusual engravings. His goal was to find young Jay Harrison and talk to him about his problematic relationship with Eah. Somehow, he would show Jay the folly of pursuing his obvious and silly crush on the white-skinned, alien girl.

Jay is a smart kid, he thought as he entered the grounds. *He'll come to his senses. He has to. I need someone else on my side.*

Beautiful, tree-lined paths led to different parts of the park. In the center was an expansive, open area carpeted by short, pink grass, and that is where Perry spotted Jay and the Theeles. He stopped at the edge and watched yet another bizarre scene play out in front of him. Keah's children, along with Jay, were bolting after Paul and April while they ran across the field. Evidently, it was some sort of game. Perry smiled, not because he appreciated their fun, but from the humorous sight of the Earth humans being chased through a pink meadow by white, naked natives.

I really think I am the only one in this bunch who has not lost his mind, he thought in defeat. *This planet has intoxicated them all. Paul Theele was right. The sooner we get home, the better.*

Perry waited for Paul to notice him standing there, then signaled he wanted to talk to him.

"Hang on!" Paul yelled in response. After saying something to April, he hurried over to meet Perry. "Ready for some exercise?" he joked, trying to catch his breath.

"Is that what it is? Looks more like playing tag to me."

"April and I came here to jog. The kids followed us. We tried to explain jogging to them, but they turned it into a game."

"What about *our* kid? Have you talked to Jay yet?"

Paul glanced back at the field just as Jay was tripping and tumbling into the grass. In seconds, three white bodies collided with him and fell into a heap. Paul smiled at their laughter. "No," he said to Perry. "I haven't been able to get him alone."

"I see. Well, maybe you can find some time after you finish your games?"

"Honestly, Carlson, you're making too much of this whole thing. What are you so worried about, anyway? You think Jay is going to upset the delicate balance of intergalactic relations between Earth and Hourou?"

Perry glared at Paul and clenched his fists. "Clearly, I'm the only one taking anything seriously. Enjoy yourself, Paul." With that, he turned to walk back toward the tree line.

"Perry, wait!" Paul pleaded. "I'm sorry, okay? I feel you're blowing it all out of proportion, though. Have you considered the possibility that all this was meant to happen?"

"I'm a practical thinker, Paul, and I don't get philosophical when I'm in stormy waters."

"What stormy waters? We're standing in a paradise, for goodness' sake!"

"You haven't seen the other side of this paradise yet. I have."

"What's that supposed to mean?"

"You'll find out before we leave, I'm sure," Perry answered. "You won't listen to me, anyway. To all of you, I'm just an untrustworthy politician. So, learn for yourself." He headed toward the forest but yelled out a final warning from over his shoulder. "Better talk to Jay before I do! I won't be as soft! The boy is heading for a heartbreak, and you know it!"

* * *

Paul kept watching Perry until he disappeared into the trees. From behind, he heard April's voice calling out as she rushed to join him.

"Paul?" She studied his expression when he turned and acknowledged her, then she grimaced. "Uh, oh. What happened?"

"Just Perry being Perry," Paul replied.

"Oh."

"He's still going on about Jay."

April sighed and glanced at Jay romping in the field with Eah and her siblings. "What do *you* think we should do?"

"About Jay? I don't know. I'm more concerned about Perry."

"Why?"

"According to him, we've all lost our minds."

"Trying to get something good out of this weird experience doesn't mean we've gone insane."

"I know," Paul agreed. "I'm not worried about being crazy, but this place and these people...they *have* had a seductive effect on us."

"Yeah, it's called being in paradise. We're enjoying it a little before we lose it. That makes us sane, not crazy."

"You're right, Babes." Paul smiled, took her hand, and they both started walking back into the field. "I only wish Perry could see things the same way."

April gestured toward the scene before them as if presenting it to Paul. "Paradise comes with a choice."

* * *

While Perry walked the paths that encircled the park, he pondered how he could talk with Jay in private. *The kid is never alone,* he thought. *If it's not the Eah girl, someone else is always around him. I guess I'll have to see what happens when we get to the mountain.*

Back home, he was famous for being able to manipulate circumstances and people to meet his needs. Here on Hourou, it was more difficult to use those skills. He had some success with Ria until Ellis and Yori showed up and ruined it. Keah and Ahee were even harder to manage than Ria, though. They always seemed to be a few steps ahead of him, despite acting ignorant. Jay was the obvious target from among his own group. Perry just needed a few uninterrupted moments with the lad to get things started.

At a nearby intersection of dirt paths, he noticed Ellis and Yori heading toward the center of the park. Yori's hair was still wet from her swim. *She looks cute.* Perry immediately chastised himself for the thought. *Come on, old man. Don't let your guard down.* He had no desire to meet up with either of them again, so he hid himself behind a tree until they passed. Glad to be unnoticed, he waited until they were gone before continuing his stroll.

We're all here now, he noted. *Gathered like a group of obedient tourists waiting to be picked up by our tour bus. Well, I hope Keah doesn't expect us to hike to the mountain. These people really need to invent some better transportation.*

When Ellis and Yori were out of sight, he stepped back onto the path, wondering if he should join them and stop being such a loner. He was not averse to light conversation or being drawn into the strange games of the alien kids. Rather, he wanted a little more time to think. From the paths, he could watch for Keah's arrival. A short distance away were benches that surrounded a pool and an ornate fountain, so he waited there. With a sigh, he plopped himself onto a soft cushion of moss and stared at the trickling water, contemplating his impending talk with Jay.

Lost in his thoughts, Perry did not notice a lithe, feminine form dropping from thick tree branches overhead and gliding silently onto the bench next to him.

"Why did you let them take you, Perry Carlson?"

The voice was soft, but it startled Perry. He tried not to show surprise. "I knew you would eventually find me, my little fluff muffin," he said in a flippant tone, still staring at the fountain.

"More games with words, Perry Carlson?" she asked, feigning disappointment. "Is this how *all* of your people talk, or just you?"

"I'm better at it than most," he said with a chuckle. "Why are you here, Ria?"

Perry turned to face her, but then diverted his gaze. She had doffed her loincloth and was using only her long hair to cover herself.

"I'm here for *you,*" she answered, draping an arm over his shoulders.

Perry shrugged her off and stood facing the fountain. "For *me*? What are you talking about? And why the sudden lack of modesty?"

"Always you use words I do not know in your game playing," she said with a sigh. "But I have been learning more of them, Perry Carlson."

"Oh, yes? And how, without me as a teacher?"

"You have not seen me, but I have been with you," she said, giggling while her fingers caressed her body. "Not even the Ah-Ahey have seen me."

"That's where you're wrong, buttercup. We all saw you come in to the city."

"Come in...and disappear."

Perry spun around and stared into her eyes. "You figured it out, then?" he asked, excitement in his voice. "You can still do it?"

Ria stood to give him a demonstration, pushing her hair aside as she strode toward a wide tree trunk. While she walked, her skin changed until it matched the same colors and patterns of what was behind her.

Witnessing the rapid change dumbfounded Perry. *Completely camouflaged.*

"I have re-found my changing, honey boy," Ria teased. "Now it will be easy for you to take me to Blue."

Perry stared hard at the spot where Ria was standing, but his eyes could not separate her body from the trunk of the tree. Not even her hair was visible. "I can't see you."

Ria tiptoed away from the tree and came up behind him, changing her skin to match her surroundings with every movement. Perry flinched when he felt her hands reach around his waist and her warm breath on his neck and ear.

"You will keep your promise, Perry Carlson?" she asked in a whisper.

Perry glanced downward and noticed her fingers returning to their original bronze color. "My promise?"

"Yes," she said, salaciously pressing her body against his back, "your promise." She giggled and pushed away, letting her fingertips drag slow along his waist.

Perry refused to fall prey to her attempted flirtations. "They know about the other one," he warned, spinning around to face her.

Surprised and distracted, she feigned ignorance. "What...other one?"

"The other Dah-Ahey you left on my planet."

Rather than answering, she toyed with her hair and pretended to be examining her skin for signs of remaining color differences. Perry could tell she was stalling and struggling to form a response. Her sudden insecurity pleased him.

"I know about it, too, dumpling," he said. "What else have you been keeping from me?"

Ria spun away from him in a pout. "Nothing!"

"Trust is very important on Blue," Perry said. "And you need someone *you* can trust. So, you'd better tell me all of it, Love, or this conversation ends right now."

"If you deny me, Carlson," she warned, "I will still find a way into the new wa-ah-ahea. No one will see me. I *shall* return to Blue...with or without your help." She turned back to face him, and her expression changed from the pout of a young girl to the lustful gaze of a desirable woman. "But you *will* help me, Perry Carlson," she pleaded. "Because you promised."

Perry returned to the bench and sat down hard. "Cover yourself and come here," he said, patting the spot next to him. "We have some planning to do."

* * *

In the grassy field, Paul, April, and Jay continued their morning games with Eah and her siblings. Ellis and Yori sat together in the grass and talked, occasionally coaching or cheering for the players. During one unusual match, they had to scoot out of the way when Uio tackled her brother Ua to the ground and covered his face with her hair while she pinned him down.

"Don't let her get away with that move!" Ellis shouted to Ua.

"On the boys' side, then?" Yori asked.

"She clearly caught him off guard," Ellis complained. "He's being too soft with his sisters."

"Uh-huh."

Ellis laughed and poked Yori with his elbow. "Why don't *you* go out there and join them?" he dared. "You told me the other day that you'd played university volleyball. You're still in great shape."

Yori blushed and toyed with her hair. "I just got cleaned up. Plus, I didn't bring my workout clothes."

"Obviously, you don't need—"

The sound of rushing wind interrupted him. Everyone in the field looked to the sky just as a small, black, triangular craft crossed over the tree line and landed nearby.

"Did they make a new ship already?" Yori asked, jumping to her feet.

"No," Ellis replied, studying the air ship. "This is something different."

The curious aircraft was much smaller than the spaceship that brought them to Hourou. It was also flat, carrying its passengers and cargo atop a single deck. Ellis counted two white bodies on the craft, a male and a female. Guessing they were Keah and Ahee, he motioned for Yori to follow and trotted after the others toward the landing site.

"The *wa-hah-ho-yee-ho* will take us to the mountain," Keah explained, gesturing for them to board what was ostensibly a people ferry.

He and Ahee sat at a control station in the craft's bow. While Paul, April, Jay, and Eah claimed four seats behind them, everyone else plopped down in outward-facing benches. The middle of the deck was an open space meant to store cargo, as evidenced by the stack of crate-like containers there. At the stern was a control terminal and a single seat, which Tammah occupied.

"Where's Mister Carlson?" Jay asked as he leaned over one of the aircraft's wide gunwales and scanned the empty field.

"He went back into the park," Paul answered. "I was hoping he wouldn't get too far away."

Ellis stood and studied the tree line. "He'd better not be causing any trouble."

"Like how?" April asked.

"I don't know," Ellis admitted, "but I can't help feeling like he's up to something."

"You really don't care for politicians, do you?" Yori asked with a chuckle.

"It's not that. He's actually a very smart man, and I know he cares about causes and people. But when it turns into meddling in the affairs of others—"

"Here he comes!" Jay hollered. "Come on, Mister Carlson! Time to go!"

Perry climbed aboard the humming airship and dropped himself into a seat next to Ellis, smiling.

Ellis interpreted his grin as pretense. "You're in a good mood, Carlson," he chaffed.

"Shouldn't I be? We're one step closer to going home."

Ellis nodded and gripped his seat as the sky ferry began a slow, vertical rise. When it reached the treetops, Ahee spun around and motioned for everyone to hold on while Keah turned the craft's nose toward the distant mountains. With a whoosh of air, it then sped off, leaving the pink field of grass far behind and a blur of passing buildings below.

The trip was short and uneventful. It was hard to have conversations through the rushing wind, so the passengers relaxed and enjoyed the scenery. When the ferry reached the foothills, Keah slowed its speed and circled a natural clearing where hundreds of Ah-Ahey were working around what appeared to be a giant cannon.

"What in heaven's name is that?" Ellis asked.

"It is the *ah-ey-ai*," Keah explained. "It is our tool. With the ah-ey-ai, we expose the materials needed for building the wa-ah-ahea.

"Looks like a giant gun to me," Perry noted. "Are you going to blast away at the mountain?"

"Blast means destroy?" Keah asked.

"More like to explode something," Perry answered.

"No, Perry Carlson, we will not explode the mountain. We will *move* the mountain."

Keah set the ferry down at the edge of the clearing and instructed his guests to disembark and wait nearby while his children unloaded the cargo. "Ahee and I must speak to others about the progress here," he explained, "but...as you say...we will be right back."

"Would you mind if I came with you for a closer look—to observe?"

"Yes, Ellis Minister," Ahee replied. "Come, and I will explain the workings of the ah-ey-ai."

Paul propped himself against the side of the ferry and watched them leave. "At what point do you think Ellis's head will explode from taking in too much information?" he asked April.

April chuckled and gazed at the nearby activity. Keah's family was busy unloading crates and dodging around Yori while she struggled to make her windblown hair more presentable. April smiled at the funny scene but frowned when she saw Perry and Jay involved in a private and animated conversation. "Uh-oh."

"Uh-oh what?" Paul asked.

"Perry is talking to Jay."

Paul glanced in their direction. "They seem fine. Jay's an adult. He can handle himself."

"I know, but Perry can be intimidating."

"Don't stare. Just let them talk."

"I—wait. They're done. Jay's coming over here now."

Jay walked straight over to Paul and April. He looked sullen.

"Everything okay?" April asked him.

"Do you guys think there's anything wrong with Eah?" Jay blurted.

"Why are you asking that?"

Jay checked that Eah was not within earshot before answering. "Something that Perry said."

"*What* did he say?" Paul pressed.

"He rambled on about how I should be careful about getting too close to her. Evidently, I don't know enough about her, or her people, or their culture. He kept pointing out our differences. It's like he thinks there's something wrong with her."

"And how do *you* feel about her, Jay?" April asked. "That's what is most important."

"Yes," Paul agreed. "Not what Carlson says, or anyone else."

Jay leaned against the side of the ferry and gazed at Eah as she helped her siblings haul some cargo away. "I've never met anyone like her," he said. Even at a distance, she somehow sensed his attention and glanced back at him with a smile. "I know that's pretty obvious," he continued. "What I mean is...well...she's just great. There's nothing bad about her at all."

"You two have gotten close," Paul noted.

"Right now...we're just friends."

Paul showed him an unconvinced smirk. "But you'd like to be *more* than friends."

"Can't hide much from you guys."

"Only because we've been there, Jay," April said. "And it's *your* business, so don't answer if it makes you uncomfortable."

"It's okay. I consider you both to be friends. I appreciate the concern. Mister Carlson's, too. He can be hard to deal with, but he's looking out for all of us."

"In his own way, yes," Paul admitted. "So, what about Eah?"

Jay sighed. He was not used to discussing his feelings, especially those pertaining to girls and relationships, but he needed to talk to someone. "She's perfect," he answered. "I've had a few girlfriends in the past, but it never worked out. Eah is different...and she's the first person to accept me just how I am...unconditionally. She sees my imperfections, and she still..."

"She still wants to be with you," April added.

"Yeah. But regardless of my own feelings, there's still the impossibility of it all. I mean...come on, she's a girl from a different planet. Am I going nuts? Do you guys think she has some kind of magical power over me, or is it something about this place?"

"It sounds like *love* to me," April noted.

"She's practically a...soul mate," Jay said with a chuckle. "At least she *would* be if things headed that way."

"I think they already have," Paul suggested. "Come on, Jay. You're not *that* dense, are you? The girl is infatuated with you."

"Yeah...I guess she is."

"And you?" April asked.

"If you're waiting for me to say I'm falling for her...well, I am."

"And you couldn't pick a better match," Paul complimented. "Besides April here, but she's already taken."

"Thanks," Jay said. "But is it weird? I mean...to fall for an alien girl?"

"She's *human*," April corrected.

"But from a different *race* of humans."

"There is only *one* race, Jay. Every human is related, and she *is* human. You've seen that. Just because she has a different skin color and comes from a different place and culture doesn't mean you can't fall in love with her. If it's the real thing, you'll overcome your differences."

"April's right," Paul added. "There's nothing wrong with you or Eah or with you two getting close. *Everything* has changed now, Jay. We've met fellow human beings from another world. Nothing will be the same for you, or us, or the people here and back home. Like Keah says, all we can do is go where the current leads. You're just lucky enough to have found someone beautiful to enjoy the ride with."

"I wish I could stay here longer," Jay confessed. "I know you guys have kids and family to get back to, and I want that for you. But I don't have any reason to go back right away—no one to go back to, really. It'd be nice to stay and explore more."

"There is still an entire planet we haven't seen," Paul agreed.

"There's also the problem of what happens to Eah and me after Keah takes us all back home."

April placed a reassuring hand on Jay's shoulder. "Take one thing at a time, Jay," she advised. "Enjoy the moment. That's how Eah and all the Ah-Ahey live, and look what it's done for *them*."

"The future will work itself out," Paul added.

"I hope so."

"Whatever happens," April said, "we're here for you. Okay?"

"Thanks. I've never had that before."

April gave him a quick hug and backed away when she noticed Eah heading their way. "Here comes Eah. Show her the same acceptance she's shown you, Jay. A woman needs to see a man's confidence."

"I will."

Eah paused before approaching them, but Paul waved her over.

"How is everything going?" he asked her.

"Tammah is taking the power to the ah-ey-ai. We are going to use it soon."

"Power?" April asked.

"I do not know another word," Eah said. "It is the force of happening. Does that make sense?"

Paul nodded. "I think so. We would say you're fueling it up."

Eah shrugged and motioned for them to follow her. "Come. You will see how the Mouth of Ahey works."

* * *

At the giant ah-ey-ai, the Earth visitors met up with Ellis, who was beside himself with excitement, eagerly pointing out what he had already learned.

"A fantastic design," he said, "made of living materials, like we saw in the city."

The device was broad, tubular, and longer than five buses parked in tandem.

"It's so wide you could drive a car through it," Paul declared, peering into the cavernous cylinder.

"Is the whole thing hollow?" April asked Ellis.

"No. Only about half of it is an actual barrel. The other part houses a special chamber that keeps the reaction contained."

"What reaction?" Perry asked.

"I'm not sure. Possibly a type of nuclear fusion."

Perry's eyes widened with surprise. "Nuclear? Is that what this thing is? They're using a nuclear device to do mining?"

"Well, that would certainly take care of 'moving the mountain,' as Keah puts it," Paul said.

"You're both thinking too much in terms of weaponry," Ellis admonished. "Nuclear reactions produce *energy*."

"I know all about the uses of nuclear technology, Minister," Perry retorted. "Just explain how it works."

"What is this, a congressional hearing? I'm sorry, Congressman, but I can't answer that. I don't speak Ah-Ahey, and I've only been on the site for a short time. Would you like me to request an operation manual for you?"

Perry rolled his eyes and stormed off to find Keah.

"My, he's touchy this morning," Ellis joked.

"Something is troubling him," Yori noted. "He tries to mask his emotions, but I can tell by his expressions."

Ellis stood back and appraised her admiringly. "You're developing the Ah-Ahey way of perception, Yori. I'm impressed."

April gave Yori a high-five.

"Thanks, Ellis," Yori said, "but men aren't hard to read most of the time."

"Anyway," Paul prompted, "about this giant contraption?"

"Yes, is it some sort of cannon?" Yori asked Ellis, running her hands over its smooth, dark surface. "It's too pretty for that. Look at these gold etchings."

"Similar to a cannon," Ellis explained, "but not for launching a projectile. It must shoot something, though. My guess is that a fusion reaction produces a beam of intense energy."

"Like a giant laser weapon?" Paul asked.

"Perhaps."

April noticed the workers moving tools and supplies toward the tree line. "I'm thinking they're getting ready to use it soon." Behind her, Ahee appeared through a mass of white bodies. "Ahee, did all these people come from the city—from Atsaahwua—to help you?"

"Yes."

"There must be hundreds of them," Paul guessed.

"Many more are waiting at the base of the mountain," Ahee explained. "The ones there are called the *Aihanyaah*—the crafters of the wa-ah-ahea."

"I can't wait to see how they do it," Paul said. "How long—I mean, when will they finish building the new wa-ah-ahea?"

"When both suns of Hourou are nearing the horizon, the shape of the wa-ah-ahea will be nearly complete. During the night is the bonding."

"What is the bonding?" April asked.

"The Aihanyaah must...*dream?* No...the word is...*imagine?* They imagine the inside structures and give form to them, filling the wa-ah-ahea with purpose."

"So, they'll finish it by tomorrow morning?" Paul asked.

"At first sunrise, yes. Then, we will be ready to return you to Blue. Does this please you?"

"It pleases me, but it also makes me sad," April answered. "It means our visit to Hourou is nearing an end."

"Yes." For the first time since their meeting, Ahee's eyes expressed sadness. "But let us not talk about leaving right now. This day is for building the new, and Keah would like to show you the powering of the ah-ey-ai."

Keah came up behind her, smiling and motioning for them all to move toward the rear of the cannon. Once there, a lift raised them to a platform on the device's top surface. Four Ah-Ahey workers were already there. Two opened a crate, while the others removed a panel, exposing a small port that was shielded by a glowing blue disk of light.

"The energy is stored here," Keah said, pointing to the container, "but a reaction will release it, and also the will."

"What do you mean by *will?*" Perry asked.

"With the will, we release power, Perry Carlson. The mountain there keeps us from the materials we need to build a new wa-ah-ahea. When the people combine their wills, should the power that is released be used to move...or, as you say, to destroy?"

"It's impossible to move something like that," Perry argued. "At least with the technology *we* have. Destroying it would be the only option."

"On Hourou, we preserve," Keah stated. "And it is not technology that holds the true power, Perry Carlson. It is the will that uses it."

"If you can just *wish* the mountain away, why build a nuclear cannon?" Perry retorted.

"The ah-ey-ai is the mouth that gives action to the will."

Keah reached into the crate and pulled out a black, grapefruit-sized sphere. With a twist, he split it in half. "What is inside?" he asked Perry, showing him the bottom part.

"Nothing. It's empty."

Keah inserted his fingers and with a pinching motion removed a tiny pellet. "Not empty," he corrected. "What appears to be powerful, like the ah-ey-ai below us, is not the power at all." After showing the granule to each of his guests, he held it above the cannon's glowing port. "The true power is here. Like the will, this speck can release aid…or destruction."

The port's protective field flickered when he dropped the pellet through it. Two workers then replaced the concealing panel in haste, and Keah motioned for everyone to return to the lift. By the time they reached the ground, the cannon was humming and a violet glow emanated from its barrel.

"What happens now?" Ellis asked.

Keah answered while he hurried them toward the edge of the clearing. "Now, we watch the Mouth of Ahey and the unified will at work."

All the Ah-Ahey workers stood along the perimeter of the field, watching the cannon with expectancy. Keah's daughter Mahah, and Yee, the young man Jay had met the night before, rode all around the ah-ey-ai on horse-like animals, searching for stragglers. When they were sure everyone was at a safe distance, they signaled to Keah, and he directed a female technician to engage the device.

The woman stepped to a portable work station nearby and waved her hands over its multi-colored buttons. This caused the entire ah-ey-ai to glow with life as the gold etchings on its surfaces became illuminated from within. Any previous resemblance to a weapon disappeared. The massive gun had now become a living piece of art, and the beauty of its design was on full display. The people cheered, and their creation rewarded them with a loud roar.

With nervous expectation, Yori stepped closer to Ellis, and Paul wrapped his arm tight around April's waist. Next to them, Perry gawked at the cannon with appreciation and awe.

"Let's see what you can do," Perry mumbled.

Ellis nodded, wide-eyed and eager. "Quite."

Steps away, Jay joined Eah and her people in their shouts and cheers. Like frenzied fans in a sports arena, everyone whooped and hollered as if inciting the ah-ey-ai to take action. When their noise reached a crescendo, rays of light began emanating from the device's barrel. Seconds later, the rays gathered into a wide beam of energy that shot across several miles toward the closest peak.

Ellis braced himself for a grand explosion, but the mountain only faded and disappeared before his eyes. "It's gone!" he heard himself shout.

"No! Look!" Yori yelled, pointing into the sky.

A translucent image of the mountain hovered above the spot where it once stood, as if projected by the cannon's continual beam.

"What...what just happened?" Perry asked.

"They...literally...moved it," Ellis replied, gaping at the sight.

"Truly I tell you, if you have faith as small as a mustard seed, you can say to this mountain, 'Move from here to there,' and it will move. Nothing will be impossible for you," Paul recited.

"A biblical reference?" Ellis asked. "Science did this, Paul, not religion."

"Good science doesn't reject what's beyond the natural," Paul countered.

"But how did they do it, Minister?" Perry asked.

"At first, I thought they had perfected cold fusion. But now I see it's actually similar to the technology they use for traveling through space—the manipulation of dark matter."

"Is that the mountain up there?" Yori asked, pointing to the floating image.

"Yes, but more like a representation of it."

"What do you mean by *representation?*" Perry asked.

"In layman's terms, they turned matter inside out. The mountain's molecules are now hidden within the dark matter that surrounded them, rendering the object—the entire mountain—nearly immaterial and simple to manipulate or maneuver. Up there is a visual representation of it. I suppose the device maintains a residual image so the people can tell where the molecules are."

"So, they didn't destroy it."

"Correct, Carlson. It is still quite intact. With the particles in this state, they can move them wherever they please. My guess is that they only wanted it out of the way for a short time while they dig for what is underneath it."

"Do you know what they're mining?" Yori asked.

"A special material they need for building their spacecraft."

"So they blast a beam of energy at the mountain, turn it inside out, move it, and then just put it back?"

"It would seem so," Ellis guessed.

"I think I understand why they want to recover that chunk of crashed spaceship so badly," Perry said. "Imagine if someone reverse-engineered this technology and used it as a weapon."

"I cannot even fathom it."

"I do not know the word *weapon*," Eah said.

Every member of the Earth party spun around and stared at her, startled and embarrassed at forgetting she was still with them. Jay's eyes pleaded with the group to change the subject.

"Oh...I'm so sorry, Eah," Perry said. His voice was heavy with sarcasm, which was lost on Eah but obvious to everyone else. "We forgot you were still here, honey. Otherwise, we would use smaller words."

Jay tensed. "That was really—"

"What Mister Carlson means," April interrupted, "is that we sometimes use words that are only understood among ourselves."

"So...*weapon* is something you only use among yourselves?" Eah asked.

The Earth guests looked at one another nervously. The truth of Eah's statement stung.

"Yes, Eah," Yori answered. "That's a word that only has meaning on Earth."

"Thank God," April muttered.

Eah thought about Yori's answer for a moment and seemed satisfied. "Then *weapon* will remain on Earth," she declared.

Everyone nodded and shot each other worried glances, wondering how much Eah truly understood.

"Come," Eah said, gesturing at the sky ferry. "We will show you the mountain up close before returning to Atsaahwua."

As she walked away, Jay glared at Perry and took a few menacing steps toward him. "Never try to confuse her like that again." The threat behind his warning was clear, and Jay allowed it to hang in the air for a moment before turning to follow Eah.

Perry smiled with appreciation as he watched Jay leave.

"That was uncalled for, Carlson," Paul chastised. "You know how he feels about Eah."

"Yes...and now I know just how much."

Ellis scowled at him and raised a warning finger. "When he gives you a black eye, you'll understand even more."

"We'll see." Perry snickered and walked away, pacing himself far behind Jay and Eah.

"If Jay does that," Yori said to Ellis while he ushered her toward the ferry, "I might blacken his *other* eye."

April took Paul's hand, and they followed the others out of earshot. "We really need to get home," April said. "I don't want to see this peaceful place soiled by violence."

"Don't worry, Babes. Soon, we'll be long gone...and will take all of our baggage with us."

CHAPTER 30

The Bonding

NIGHT: DAY 4 ON HOUROU

Jay had calmed down by the time his group was on their way back to Atsaahwua, but he was still angry. Perry had no right to badger him about Eah, and his rudeness toward her was infuriating. It was hard enough for Jay to sort through his feelings about her. The last thing he needed was Perry meddling and causing him to doubt their budding relationship. To make matters worse, Jay tried to hide his emotions from her during their return trip to the city. It was futile, of course. Even through his cloaking and deflection, she sensed his anxiety. Despite Eah's proclivity for openness, though, she did not press him about it. Instead, she sat quiet and contemplative while he fidgeted next to her on the sky ferry, wondering what she must think of him.

The aerial tour of the mountain's floating image and of its crater was amazing, and Jay was glad for the distraction. Keah piloted their aircraft around the entire circumference, even daring to penetrate the apparition's transparent surface to show its immateriality. On the ground below, hundreds of Ah-Ahey streamed into the rocky abyss from the surrounding forest, carrying tools and other equipment. Ahee said that once the digging was complete, they would clear the area of all people and animal life and ease the mountain back down, never to be moved again. To prevent damage to the environment, she explained, they could only conduct such massive disruptions one time. Future mining would have to be done at a different site.

Jay recalled the day's events while he rested alone in an isolated lounging room deep within his temporary city dwelling. *I can't believe Carlson was so stupid as to talk about weapons,* he thought. *Eah's people don't even understand what a weapon is.*

He rose and paced a bit, haunted by his conversation with Perry near the giant cannon. *You must see it, Jay,* he remembered Perry saying. *The Dah-Ahey are the ones who are like us. They've embraced their darker side. They don't ignore that they have one, or try to hide it. The others are living in some sort of religious fantasy world. Does their way of life seem realistic to you? Surely it's obvious who's really the different ones.*

Jay clenched his fists when he recalled his response to Perry, wishing he would have said more. *I totally disagree with that,* he had countered. *The Ah-Ahey don't even know what a 'darker side' is. To them, the Dah-Ahey are complete opposites.*

You do see the difference, then? Perry had asked.

Of course!

And which of the two groups do you identify with more?

With that question, Perry effectively steered the conversation to where he needed it to go, for Jay had to admit people on Earth were more like the Dah-Ahey.

Well?

Okay. So there are more similarities between us and the Dah-Ahey, but—

Then why aren't we spending just as much time with them as we are with the others?

Even now, Jay seethed at how Perry had backed him into a philosophical corner. He had also placed tiny doubts in Jay's mind, which made him more incensed. Not knowing how to answer Perry, Jay stormed away. Paul and April were nearby, so he sought them for consolation.

Do you guys think there's anything wrong with Eah? he had asked. The question still tormented him. Until his chat with Perry, Eah was nothing less than perfect. Perry's implication of the Dah-Ahey being the more believable of the planet's inhabitants, however, forced Jay to admit he did not know enough about her and the Ah-Ahey. She had been so open with him, but whenever he mentioned the Dah-Ahey, he could see great discomfort in her. Was it because Perry was right? Did Jay have more in common with the darker side of Hourou?

Jay stopped pacing and took a deep breath. *I'm going to find Eah and explain what's bothering me,* he decided. To have an honest talk with her about it made the most sense. He did not want her comparing him to the controversial, bronze-skinned natives. Even if what Perry said was true, and the people of Earth were more like the Dah-Ahey, could he not *learn* to become like Eah?

The sound of someone approaching from down the hall interrupted his pondering. Facing the arched entryway, his body tensed when he saw Perry peek into the room.

"Ah. There you are," Perry said. "You could get lost in this place with all of its rooms."

Jay was not pleased to have his peaceful refuge invaded by anyone, especially by Perry. He expressed it with a penetrating glare.

"Then again," Perry continued, "maybe you were trying to *be* lost. Sorry if I'm intruding."

"Whatever," Jay said with a smirk. "I was about to leave, anyway."

Perry raised his hand, signaling Jay to wait. "Give me one minute," he entreated. "I was actually looking for you. I came to, uh…well…to apologize for upsetting you."

Jay was curious, so he waited for Perry to continue.

"I was probably out of line asking you about your relationship with Eah, and I'm sorry for sticking my nose in your business. But please understand, Jay, that I am only watching out for you—for all of us. Even though it seems like we've been on this planet for a long time, we haven't. There's so much more we need to learn about it. I want to make sure we consider all the facts and possibilities, that's all."

Jay was a little suspicious of Perry's disarming manner, but it seemed genuine. He let out a sigh before replying. "I appreciate your concern. But what happens between Eah and me has nothing to do with you."

"I could make an opposing argument—that it will indeed affect everyone back home, as well as the people of Hourou. But I came here to apologize, not to argue."

"Good. Apology accepted." Jay moved as if to leave.

"One more thing, if you'll hear me out."

With a huff, Jay spun and stared at him. "What is it?"

"It might be hard for you to imagine, but I'm a father. In fact, my daughter is only a few years younger than you."

"And?"

"Please accept this next advice as coming from someone who's been around the block a few times. We've only just arrived here, Jay. Eah is beautiful, and she's very nice. But you've got a lot to offer, and you can afford to take your time. There are lots of girls on Hourou, and you don't know what else might be out there. A good-looking, smart guy like you could easily play the field." Perry stepped aside, as if allowing Jay to leave. "That's all I'm going to say. I'll let you get on with your evening."

Jay was about to walk out, but then hesitated.

"Something wrong?" Perry asked, seating himself on a lounge.

"There's one thing you're not considering, Congressman."

"Oh?"

"You've said our people are more like the Dah-Ahey. Even if that's true, we don't have to be."

"What do you mean?"

"I've spent my whole life trying to fit into one imperfect situation after another, surrounded by some very messed up people. When I finally find something good, and people who are so pure, what's wrong with wanting to be like *them*? If there's a better way, shouldn't we try to follow it?"

Perry nodded, but Jay's question clearly stumped him. "Well...we all have interesting choices to make here. I am sure yours will be the right ones."

Jay knew the statement had a hidden meaning behind it, but he did not feel like fencing with Perry. "I know what *I'm* doing. How about you?" With that, he spun and left the room to find Eah.

* * *

Perry leaned back in his seat with a huff, scanning the room with eager eyes. "Well, you see how it is now, don't you?" he asked.

A hint of movement caught his eye just before the outline of a human body appeared against a far wall. Perry gaped as he watched the feminine form change its color and become separated from its surroundings. In seconds, a familiar bronzed-skin woman stood before him, smiling weakly and quivering with exhaustion.

"Ria?" Perry jumped up and rushed over just as her knees buckled and she began dropping to the floor. "What's the matter? Are you alright?"

Ria could only moan while she fell into his embrace.

"You'd better rest for a bit," he said, leading her to a lounge. After she laid down, he decorously blanketed her body with her hair. "I'll check the hall. If someone comes, you'll have to change again. Ria? Are you listening?"

She groaned and nodded, so Perry backed away and checked the hallway to ensure nobody was nearby. When he returned, he found Ria propped up on one arm, checking her skin for discoloration.

"What happened?" he asked. "Are you alright?"

"Yes. I...am unable to...hold the changing...for long." Her voice was shaky.

"It drains you—drains your energy," Perry surmised.

"Yes. Drains."

"You can rest for a bit, but I have to get you out of here. Will you be able to change again?"

Ria pushed herself up and looked around. The only way out of the room was through the single doorway. "No. No more changing. We must think of something else."

"We'll wait until everyone has gone to sleep. Don't worry about it right now. You're exhausted. Can I get you anything? Water? Food?"

"Why are you...staring at me like that?"

"You look ill."

"Ill?"

"Sick. Unhealthy."

"Stop using Earth words, Perry Carlson. What are you saying?"

"Never mind." Perry reached over, gathered her cascading hair from the floor, and moved it over some exposed skin. "Well, at least we learned a few things tonight, didn't we?"

"Learned? What?"

"First, that your changing is far from perfect. Second...well, you heard Jay. I told you he's infatuated with the girl. He won't even consider another—whatever you call it—dyad."

"I listened to your words, yes, but I do not understand enough of them. How can I know you really tried?"

"This is *my* area of expertise, darling. I used doubt, and I offered alternatives. He's infatuated with the girl, and when it's that bad, you can't talk a man out of anything. This plan of yours won't work."

"I will make myself as Eah for him!" Ria barked, her voice and usual tone returning.

"What are you talking about? Tricking him into thinking you're Eah? You can change your color, sweetie, but you can't change the rest of you."

"Our bodies are the same," Ria reminded.

Perry had not considered it until then, but Ria was correct. Other than the difference in skin color, the bodies of the Ah-Ahey and the Dah-Ahey were nearly identical, as if poured from the same mold. "It will never work. People from Earth are not that gullible."

"Always the Earth words. What is gill-uh-bull?"

"*Gullible.* It means being easily tricked. Fooled. Anyway, Jay would know right away. You should have told me this was your idea. I would have saved us both the trouble of sneaking you in here."

"Then sneak me out," Ria huffed in defeat. "I must return to my people. There is only one way left now."

"And what's that, Cupcake?"

Ria stood to test her wobbly legs. "You will see, my hero. You will see."

* * *

Jay wandered through the hallways of the palatial house, peeking into each room and hoping the first person he found would be Eah. The sounds of splashing lured him to the bathing chamber. He entered just as a white body dove into the pool and disappeared under mist and ripples of water. Wondering if it was her, he knelt at the water's edge and peered through wisps of vapor. Two female bodies were way out in the middle, heads bobbing as they treaded water and conversed. Their nude skin was too beige for either to be Eah. It was Yori and April.

"Come on, April!" Yori said, loud and playful. "Don't tell me you haven't noticed!"

"What? They all look the same to me."

"I'm not talking about the whole body! Don't you think it's interesting that all the males are *circumcised?*"

"Yori! Really!"

Jay wondered why Yori's question would embarrass April, since the two ladies were not in mixed company. As he scanned the enormous room, he counted only four other females there. They were on the far side of the pool, shrouded in pearlescent mist, but their sparkling black manes were easily distinguishable.

"Fine. Don't admit to looking," Yori teased. "Seriously though, April, think about it. Circumcision is a cultural practice. Actually, it's mostly been a religious rite where *we* come from."

"So?"

"This intoxicating water is going to your head, girl. Isn't it fascinating that the same practice occurs way out here on another planet populated by humans?"

Before April could answer, both women noticed Jay backing away from the pool.

"Hi, Jay!" Yori yelled out to him.

April yelped and hid behind her. "Oh, gosh!"

"What? It's only Jay," Yori teased. Enjoying April's embarrassment, she motioned for Jay to join them. "Come on in!"

"Yori! Stop!" April demanded. "It's *ladies'* swim."

"Oops! Sorry, Jay! Ladies only right now! You'll have to come back later!"

"Yeah," Jay said. "I was, uh, actually just looking for Eah."

"She's on the far end," Yori informed with a sly smile. "Why don't you go over and get her?"

"Uh—"

"Yori!" April rebuked.

"Oh, alright," Yori said with a pout. "I think he's blushing enough. Hey, Jay! We'll send her out to you, okay?"

"Thanks!" Jay glanced across the pool just as Eah climbed out and waved at him. He waved back, but headed for the hallway to wait for her there.

"Such a gentleman," Yori said to April. "I'm impressed."

The two women turned toward Eah and watched as she entered a small alcove. Air buffeted her body as soon as she stepped in, which she used to dry herself.

"I wondered why there weren't any towels," April said.

"Pretty efficient," Yori noted.

"Efficient? Wow, Yori. You're sounding like Ellis."

Yori responded to April's teasing by splashing at her, which started a friendly water fight between them. From the alcove, Eah laughed at their antics while she finished drying herself. Then she stepped out and rushed toward the outside corridor, giving them both a polite smile as she passed by.

Yori swam to the edge of the pool and watched Eah leave. "Isn't young love the best?"

"Come on, Yori," April said, joining her. "You're not that much older than Jay."

"I'm not twenty-two anymore, though."

"No boyfriend back home, then?"

"I've been too busy studying. In fact, this trip to Hourou has been my first break in a real long time."

"Too much work and not enough play," April warned.

"I know. I envy Eah and her people. You don't see *them* stressing about exams or careers."

April nodded in agreement. "They don't stress about *anything.*"

When Eah disappeared behind the mist, both women pushed away from the pool's edge and resumed their swim, talking and giggling like teenagers, while the potent waters lulled them into relaxation.

* * *

"What does 'ladies swim' mean?" Eah asked after meeting Jay outside of the bathing chamber.

"Huh? Oh. It means *women only.* On Earth, women like to get together and do things without men being around sometimes. It goes both ways. Men often do activities without women, too. I guess they tire of being together."

Eah considered his explanation while she tidied her damp hair. "It is different on Hourou. Women and men always want to be together. We do *everything* as one."

"I've noticed that," Jay said with a chuckle.

A knowing smile parted her pink, iridescent lips. She was learning. Subtle humor and jests used by him and the other Earth visitors were less confusing to her now. The look she gave Jay conveyed understanding, but also playfulness. On a girl from his planet, it would have been suggestive. But Eah wore the expression with elegance.

Jay propped himself against a wall and waited for her to finish primping. He was glad she never confused his curious gazes with leering. He did not intend to ogle, although at that moment she looked especially sexy to him, with her wet hair and sparkling skin. The way she leaned over and used her fingers to comb away tangles in her damp mane was alluringly feminine.

When her appearance satisfied her, Eah took hold of Jay's hand and led him down the main hallway toward the exit.

"Where are we going?" he asked.

"Come. There is something I want to show you."

Once outside, Eah stopped to scan the night sky. Beyond the glowing city spires, stars filled the black void, and Hourou's nearby nebula swirled with pastel colors.

Jay heard laughter and music in the surrounding neighborhood. "What's happening tonight?"

"The people are celebrating the building of a new wa-ah-ahea...and the bonding."

"Oh. What are you looking for?"

Eah did not answer; she was too preoccupied with searching the sky.

Maybe now's a good time to suggest finding somewhere private where we can talk, he thought. "Eah, do you think we could—?" He paused when a glint of light caught his eye, emanating from something large and round in the shadow of one of the spires. It was gone in an instant, like the sudden flash of a camera.

"There!" Eah exclaimed. "Come!" She grabbed Jay's hand again and led him to a ramp.

Behind another spire, he saw the same light burst. "What is that?"

"Come!"

After ascending to higher levels, Eah took him across several suspended bridges and narrow walkways until they reached an observation platform on the outer edge of the city. Jay scanned the horizon and recognized the mountain range where they had been earlier that day. The peak that the Ah-Ahey moved was now back in its place, silhouetted against the starry sky.

Eah continued to search the darkness above them. Then she cupped her hands around her mouth and sang out a long, loud, high-pitched note. After a few moments, soft, pink light bathed the platform and Jay finally saw what Eah had been tracking. To him, it looked like a giant ball with hundreds of ropes hanging underneath its bulk. At first, he thought it was a type of hot-air balloon, but its purposeful movements showed it was actually a living creature.

"Um...what is that?" Jay asked.

"It is *ahoonu!* Watch!"

Pastel pink light blinked from within its round body as it hovered above them.

"It lights up like a giant firefly," Jay said, awestruck by its size.

"There are such animals on Blue?"

"No. Not these. But there are tiny flying insects—animals—that glow at night in a similar way."

Eah sang out again and the balloon-like beast responded by flashing and dropping toward them. "Ahoonu are gentle," she said to Jay, noting his uneasiness. "They see by hearing and touching. In that, they are much like us."

"You can communicate with them, then?"

"Eeee-saah. Of course."

The creature continued to descend until its luminous appendages enshrouded the entire platform. Jay stood still, dazed by its tameness, while Eah twirled and danced within its glowing curtains. After spending a few moments enjoying her attention, the ahoonu shifted and many of its arms curled upward.

"We must climb now, before he rises," Eah said.

Jay met her excited expression with a dubious stare. "Climb?"

"Yes, like this." She took hold of an appendage while placing her foot in the crook of another. With a gentle tug, the strange animal then pulled her off the platform and into its mass of tentacles.

Jay followed her example, laughing nervously while the creature raised him up and placed him on some crisscrossed appendages that formed a seat. Eah climbed over and sat next to him.

"What now?" Jay asked.

"The ahoonu will carry us." Eah signaled their readiness by tugging on one of the creature's tentacles. Slowly and silently, it rose off the platform and joined more of its kind in the air.

"Where will it go?" Jay asked, glancing at the dark trees under his dangling feet.

Eah grasped his shoulder, causing a surge of exhilaration in his body as she communicated excitement through her touch. "Would you like to see the new wah-ah-ahea?"

"Um...sure. But how do you steer this thing?"

"You can direct ahoonu this way," Eah replied, taking an appendage in each hand. When she pulled gently on each one, the creature banked left or right in response.

"Okay," Jay said, "but what about stopping?"

Eah pulled on both appendages at the same time and it slowed to a stop, hovering above the treetops and waiting for her next command. She then made a whipping motion, and the ahoonu continued on its course toward the mountains, following the others.

"We will go and see the bonding," she said. "Then..."

When her voice trailed off, Jay guessed she was undecided about what to do afterwards or unsure how to tell him.

"Then?" he pressed.

"Then...I will let *you* decide what happens."

A tremble in Jay's gut signaled nervous excitement. What was she up to? He reached over and brushed some hair from covering her face. "Alright. Let's go."

It did not take long for the small pod of ahoonu to reach the place where the new wah-ah-ahea was being built. Jay looked down through the mass of glowing tentacles and could see the grassy clearing where the giant cannon still stood. Beside it, the spacecraft appeared as a blurry triangle of blackness. The sight brought to memory two very confused campers, standing in a field on Earth and staring up at the same type of object.

It also reminded him that his stay on Hourou was coming to a quick end. Soon, he would be aboard that spaceship, returning to his own planet. The thought of leaving caused a sinking in his gut. He glanced at Eah and noticed the hint of a frown on her delicate lips.

Words were unnecessary. Both sensed what the other was thinking, especially when their eyes met. Jay reached out and offered Eah his hand. She smiled and took it, fingers entwining with his in a tight grip that expressed what she could not say—she did not want him to leave. He nodded his understanding. At that moment, all doubt disappeared. Eah was a part of his destiny. Though it seemed to be an unlikely meeting between two people who were literally worlds apart, their connection was a preordained bond that each of them had only to discover and accept. Jay loved Eah, and he could tell she loved him, too. The only thing left for them to do was to stop hiding it.

Eah guided the ahoonu to circle the clearing a few times so they could examine the work being done on the new wa-ah-ahea. Many Ah-Ahey surrounded the craft, molding its soft hull and coaxing it to hold its triangular shape. Others carried tools and crates in and out of the ship. When some of them saw the pink light of the creatures overhead, they stopped and waved.

"They're certainly happy," Jay noted.

"Yes," Eah agreed. "For them, the wa-ah-ahea means a fresh beginning."

Although the scene fascinated him, Jay wanted to get away from there. To him, the spaceship represented an ending, not a new birth. He gazed at Eah until she sensed his eyes upon her and turned to face him.

"What is it?" she asked. A trace of nervousness hid within her tone.

"Can we...go someplace and talk?"

Still holding his hand, her thumb caressed his as she answered. "Do you...desire to return to Atsaahwua?"

"Not necessarily. Just...somewhere away from everyone."

Eah's eyes lit up as an idea came to her. "Yes. I know a place like that." She pulled on an appendage and the ahoonu floated back toward the city. "In the forest outside of Atsaahwua, there is a spot where dyads go..."

"Dyads? Are we allowed, then?"

"Allowed?

"Can we go there, too?"

"Eeee-saah. And if no one is there...well...it is isolated."

Jay tried not to expect anything other than talking. This would be the first time they would truly be alone together. He did not want to spend what could be a romantic evening fighting off his sensual appetites. He needed to tell her how he felt about her and hear just how serious she was about him.

Eah directed the ahoonu to halt and lower them to the ground outside of the city's natural border. After watching the creature rise again and leave to rejoin its companions, she trotted onto a mossy path and motioned for Jay to follow. Small, glowing plants marked the edges of the trail as it wound around enormous trees and took them past trickling brooks and shallow ponds. When they were deep inside the forest, Eah chose a smaller footpath that ended at a narrow glade.

"This is the place," she said in a whisper. "Come."

It was a secluded dell, filled with white, fibrous plants that resembled feathers floating above the mossy ground. When Jay and Eah strode into their midst, the fibers moved away to create an opening. Then they surrounded them like a curtain.

"What is this?" he whispered, taking Eah's hand.

"It is called *aho*...a plant that lives in the air. Aho is only visible at night."

Jay reached out to touch one of the hovering plumes, but it avoided his fingers. "It reacts to movement," he noted.

"Come deeper," Eah urged.

At the center of the glade, Eah stopped and sat down, gracefully covering herself with her hair and beckoning for Jay to join her. As he did, the aho massed and concealed them even more.

"Just when I think I've seen the most amazing thing on Hourou," Jay said, "you show me something else fantastic."

Eah gazed at him while she toyed with her hair. "I thought I had seen the most amazing things on Hourou, too."

"Really?" Jay blushed at her implied compliment.

"Do you...do you like the...aho?" she asked, unable to hide the nervousness in her voice.

"Yeah. Makes it romantic out here."

"R-romantic?"

"Uh...romantic...yes. It means the environment is—that it brings out special feelings of...you know."

"I know what?"

Jay smiled and shifted on the soft moss. *So much for dropping hints,* he thought. *What am I supposed to use as a lead-up: Gee, it's nice out here, and by the way, I'm in love with you?*

Eah kept gazing at him from behind the veil of her sparkling hair.

"Romance..." Jay continued. "Special feelings between two people who...are close."

"Special feelings?"

Jay sensed her nervousness growing. It helped to know she felt as awkward as he did, but only a little. "Special as in, uh..." he stammered. "Feelings meant for only one person. Like...love."

"And *love* means what?"

Intense interest filled her questioning eyes, which made Jay wonder if she was testing him. Did she already know?

"Um...well...I guess love is a deep affection that people have for each other."

"Like...friendship?"

"You can love a friend, yes, and your family. That's one kind of love. There's also *romantic* love, like...um...between a man and a woman who...uh—"

"Who are more than friends?"

Excitement surged through Jay's body. "Yes...more than friends."

"And on your planet, what is *that* love like?"

"Well, when a...man and woman...love each other that way, they don't—they don't want anyone else. They give themselves to each other completely...and...would do anything to stay together. Does that make sense?"

"Yes."

"I think two people who love each other like that—they've found their perfect match. They...become one."

Eah nodded and brushed away a tear. "I know of this love, Jay," she said, her voice soft and dreamy. "On Hourou, we call it *oha*."

"Oha," Jay repeated. "I like that. It sounds exotic."

While he gazed into Eah's eyes, Jay allowed her to draw him into an empathic bond. Time seemed to stand still as he waded into the ocean of their combined emotions. Probing for her thoughts, he sensed she was trying to ask him a question. Within her chaotic waves of feelings, though, he could not interpret it. He needed to hear her words.

Eah's lips parted as if to speak, but she hesitated.

Ask me...so I can tell you, Jay said to her through their psychic bond.

"Jay," she finally asked, "do you oha—do you...love...*me?*"

Jay did not hesitate to answer her. "Yes. I love you, Eah."

When their lips met, heat shot through Jay's body like an uncontrollable fire. Eah's passionate kiss conveyed her love for him, but he still needed to hear her say it.

"Eah," he said, breaking away. "Do you—?"

"Yes, Jay. I love you. *Ah-oha-nee.*"

They kissed again, this time with more fervor. Through their bond, each sensed the storm of conflicting emotions in the other give way to calmness and clarity. Resolution and joy replaced uncertainty and fear. Love had been expressed at last.

Though he did not want to hold back—did not want the kiss to stop—Jay gently pulled away and opened his eyes. "I can feel everything you're feeling," he said in a whisper. "I never thought two people could connect this way."

"We are bonding, Jay," Eah said through a bright smile, "as a dyad. Ah-oha-nee, eh dyah."

"What does that mean?"

"I love you, *my dyad.*"

Jay kissed her again, euphoric at the idea of them becoming a dyad. He wanted badly to touch her—to remind himself she was real—so he pulled her close and caressed her face, neck, and hair. As he did, Eah moved her hands down from his shoulders and began trying to unfasten his shirt buttons. Jay flinched, so Eah slowly broke off their kiss.

"What has frightened you?" she asked.

Jay fidgeted, but did not pull away from her. "I...uh...well, I guess I'm just worried about...moving too fast."

"We are not moving," Eah said with a chuckle. "You are only experiencing our oha—our love—moving us on the inside."

"I know. That's, um, not quite what I meant by moving, though."

Eah looked perplexed. "Then...what?"

"I just don't want you to get the wrong idea," Jay explained. "I mean...it's not that I don't...you know...want to be with you, but—"

"Take off the covering of you, Jay," Eah interrupted. "I wish to see you fully."

Jay's eyes opened wide with surprise. "Um...you want me to undress?"

"You are frightened because you are hiding from me," Eah stated with tenderness. "Ah-oha-nee, Jay. There is no need for you to hide. *Uncover.*"

Before he knew he was doing it, Jay stood up and undressed as quickly and modestly as he could. Eah watched with respectful impassivity. When he finished and sat down again, she smiled supportively but said nothing.

"Actually," he said, breaking an awkward silence, "sitting here in the buff isn't all that bad."

"I do not know *bad*."

"Of course you don't," Jay agreed. "Ah-oha-nee, eh dyah."

Eah scooted closer and peppered his lips with tender kisses. "Ah-oha-nee."

With his eyes closed, Jay succumbed to her delicate attentions, permitting his entire body to enjoy sensations that were intensified by their empathic bond. Eah's kisses were sweet rewards for his courage. He sensed admiration in them, but also her desire to express more. When her fingertips began tracing the contours of his muscles, he immediately recognized the intrusion of his lust and its eagerness to intervene in the innocent exploration of their newfound love. Giving in only a little, he toyed with her hair and allowed his hands to stroke down the sides of her warm body, wondering what she would think if he went further. She already saw his passion, but he was not sure how far she wanted to take it.

"So...what do we do now?" he asked between kisses.

"What do you desire, Jay?" Her voice was soft and innocent, not seductive.

Careful, Jay, he thought. *You're a gentleman, remember?* He slid his hands down to her hips. *Yeah, but we're a dyad now.* Eah kept kissing him tenderly, indifferent to his touch. *You don't even know what that means here.* His hands traveled upward again, tracing her abdomen but hesitating to rise higher. *You should back off and cool down. Don't mess this up.* Heeding the inner warning, he drew back to answer her question.

"On Earth," he explained, "when a guy and girl get together—when they decide to be a dyad—they...well, they...get intimate. I guess it seals the bond or something. It shows the depth of their love. At least that's what people say."

Eah reached out and placed her hand on Jay's chest, feeling his pounding heartbeat while she surveyed the rest of his body. Jay squirmed and tried to block her view of certain parts of his anatomy. She ignored the futile action and the tenderness of her expressions showed that his excitement did not offend her.

"I do not understand such a custom," she said. "A mating comes before the true bonding?"

"I don't know how to explain it," Jay admitted. "Many of the customs on Earth make little sense to me, too. Most have never seemed quite right."

"And the bonding custom?"

"I was always taught you waited until marriage—that means dyad— to be intimate...to mate. I guess that's why I've been nervous around you. Even though most people where I come from probably don't believe in waiting, I still do. But there's also a strong desire to...well, to do more than I should. Does that make sense?"

Eah felt his heartbeat again and looked him over as if studying all the parts of his body.

"Yes. It makes sense, and I can see your conflict, Jay. What...pain this must cause for you and the people of Blue."

"You have no idea."

Eah smiled and kissed him. "On Hourou, *first* is the bonding. The *Ai*—the mating—comes later...after the dyad has been tested and declared openly."

"Tested?"

"Yes. The dyad must be proved so everyone can see it is meant to be."

"I already know." Jay returned the kisses, matching Eah's intensity while inwardly fighting with himself over whether to give in to his desires or get them under control before it was too late.

"Do you...desire the Ai—the mating—now?" she asked.

Jay pulled away and gazed into her eyes. "Part of me does," he admitted. "I love you, Eah. I want—I want the dyad with you. But it has to be right, and for me that means honoring what I believe...and honoring you." *No matter how painful this is for me to do.*

"I am filled with joy at hearing this, Jay," Eah said, trying to get her own passions back under control. "Perhaps this is the first test for us."

"What do you mean?"

"This was the thing between us—the barrier—when we were on the wah-ah-ahea."

"Barrier?"

Eah nodded. "Remember? We tried to connect...to bond."

"Yeah," Jay recalled. "It was an epic fail on my part."

"I sensed honor in you then, but also...overwhelming desire."

Jay squirmed a little. "Uh-huh."

"But now you have shown that your honor can control your desire. This is the Way of Ahey, Jay!"

"Sounds good, but...where does that leave *us* now?"

"Leave us?"

"Our relationship. Are we, uh, okay?"

Eah took his hand and placed it on her chest. "According to the Ways of Ahey, do you desire to dyad with Eah?" she asked, placing her own hand over his racing heart.

Jay guessed she was performing a type of ceremony. He looked deep into her eyes, searching for that place where he could lose himself in her love. "Yes. According to the Ways of Ahey, I desire to dyad with Eah."

"Ask *me,* Jay," she urged.

"According to the Ways of Ahey, do you desire to dyad with Jay?"

"Yes," she answered, holding back a sob. "According to the Ways of Ahey, I desire to dyad with Jay."

A sudden puff of air blew down on them, stirring up the floating aho and causing it to dance in flashes of fiery red and gold.

So let it be.

Jay heard the ethereal voice within the depths of his mind, and could tell by Eah's rapturous expression that she did, too. As the aho settled and formed a shielding curtain around them once again, Eah melted into Jay's arms. He pulled her close, unsure what the dance of the aho meant but confident that the One who spoke into their minds and hearts had accepted their commitment to each other.

I've never seen Eah or her people pray, he thought, *but now I understand why.* He stroked Eah's hair while she snuggled in his embrace. *Their connection to you,* he said to the Voice, *is constant. They don't have to stop and pray, because they're always praying.* He smiled at the tickling sensation of Eah's joyful tears dropping into his lap. The idea of sending a prayer from a distant galaxy, though baffling, seemed right, and it was the only thing he could think of to do next. *I know you're there,* he continued, *even on this planet. I love this girl...and I want to be with her. How that can work...well...I'll just have to leave it up to you.*

Eah hugged him, and they remained tightly entwined for a long time, expressing their love through affectionate caresses and kisses until Eah finally pulled away, rose, and offered her hand to him. No longer self-conscious in front of her, Jay chuckled while he stood and bent to retrieve his clothing. Something had indeed changed inside of him.

With his passions under control, he was free to be with Eah on a level far surpassing anything he had ever experienced. He had persevered through an important trial—one that had instantly matured him beyond his mere twenty-two years. As he walked out of that mystical glade with Eah, he was now a true man, for his honor had been tested, and he had stayed strong.

* * *

As was typical on Hourou, time passed slowly and the night was long. Jay and Eah hiked back to Atsaahwua and dined together in a public eating place that resembled a quaint street-side café. Eah introduced him to new foods and drinks, giggling at his funny faces when he sampled dishes that confused his sense of taste. After dinner, she took him to another lounge—like a nightclub, he thought—where musicians and singers performed a variety of mystifying compositions. One particular piece reminded Jay of a favorite rock ballad, so he pulled Eah from her seat and taught her how to slow-dance. Minutes later, other Ah-Ahey couples joined them, laughing as they mimicked the intimate swaying.

They were the quintessential young couple, deeply in love and not afraid to show it. Eah made Jay feel like he had been among her people all his life, and it did not take long for him to forget all about leaving Hourou. Soon, however, he became tired, so Eah took him to the house where his friends were already fast asleep. Standing at the entryway, they continued their light talk; neither wanted to part and end their blissful evening. When Jay could fend off sleep no longer, though, he pulled Eah close for a final goodnight kiss. She then tore herself away and strode down the empty street, looking back every so often for another glimpse of Jay before she disappeared into the darkness.

Jay took a deep breath and gazed up at the stars with gratitude bursting from his heart. It had been a perfect evening with a perfect girl. Eah would fill his dreams that night. Maybe they would dream together. At that moment, anything seemed possible. He looked down at the threadbare rags in his hand—a deteriorating costume he no longer needed. Even Hourou did not like what they symbolized, evidenced by the dismantling microbes that worked to sterilize the molecules. As if loath to do so, he slowly dressed himself in the tatters before entering his temporary dwelling. Once inside, he located an empty sleeping room and collapsed onto a soft settee. Just before sleep overtook him, he heard once more from that strong yet peaceful voice.

You've done well. Rest. Believe.

CHAPTER 31

Mixed Reactions

L aura picked at the cold dinner on her plate and shifted uncomfortably under Alex's gaze.

"It tasted better when it was warm," he remarked. "Want me to order you something else?"

"No, it's not the food."

"Well, I can't do anything about your company. I'm still on the clock, so where you go, I go."

"It's not you either."

Alex waved at their waiter and pointed toward the empty glasses on the table. In silent swiftness, two attendants cleared the dishes, poured wine and coffee, and presented a dessert menu. Their prompt attention was indicative of the outstanding, five-star service that made his favorite restaurant famous throughout the capital.

"This whole thing is spiraling out of control," Alex said, after taking a sip of wine and sliding Laura's glass closer to her hand. "The entire world is going crazy now."

Laura sipped, but just stared at the tabletop. Silver glitter in its smooth, black surface twinkled in the candlelight, resembling a nighttime sky filled with stars. She smirked when she considered the name of the restaurant: The Starfield. Everything was reminding her of the alien visitation. Alex was correct, too. People everywhere were having mixed reactions to the news of the UFO sightings, the abductions, the crashed spaceship, and the official response from her government.

"You were right again," Laura whispered.

"What?"

"You were right again," she repeated louder. "You said the committee wouldn't wait for our report, and you were right."

"They probably believe it's too much for people to handle," Alex guessed. "Or they're afraid of what we're dealing with now."

"But they could have waited. Instead, they had their plans made ahead of time. In fact, it seems like they sent us to the site just to get us out of the way."

"They most likely did. But you're still leading the investigation. Haines must be furious."

"He has the crash site," Laura reminded.

"Yeah, but you have the kid."

Laura flashed a half-smile. "Well, I guess that's something."

It still made her angry that the committee had already decided against telling the world about the stranded alien before they sent Laura and Alex to examine him. Then, at their debriefing, the chairman ordered them both to keep the boy's existence a secret. His reason was that people needed more time to assimilate the discovery of other intelligent life in the universe. Likewise, her government required more time to study the remnant and the child.

Laura disagreed and pointed out how some nations were already in a panic. Too much secrecy, she warned, could further damage shaky international relationships.

We need to keep the peace at all costs, the chairman had told her, *even if it means withholding some information for now.*

What about their return? Laura had asked. *The alien boy said they would come back for him. We won't be able to cover that up when it happens.*

There is no cover-up, Laura, the chairman insisted. *You, more than anyone, should realize that's not how we operate. All we need to create total chaos is for the fanatics to think we're running another Area 51 here.*

This thing is bigger than all of us. You see what it's already doing all over the world. When you shatter people's beliefs, it creates a vacuum. We dare not allow it to be filled with distrust and hate. We must take one small step at a time.

Laura took a few gulps of her wine while she recalled the rest of her earlier conversation with the committee chairman.

I understand all of that, sir, she had told him. *We're taking every precaution to keep the boy's existence a secret. But I believe a return of the visitors, probably to reclaim the boy, is imminent. For all we know, they could be here now, watching us. How we handle our first contact with them—*

We've already considered all of that, Laura. Obviously, we don't want any misunderstandings. But they've taken some of our people, and we've got one of theirs. What we would like to see during the first contact is a trade to show mutual good will. And I can think of no one better suited to handle that than you. That's why the committee is taking you off of the crash and abduction investigations and giving you the lead on Operation Fair Trade. You have whatever you need at your disposal, but other than protecting the alien boy, you do nothing without consulting me. I must have your word of full cooperation on that.

You have it, sir, and thank you.

After their meeting, Laura and Alex began planning how to move the child to a safer place. They would do it as soon as Doctor Tannish's team decided he was protected from biological risks and posed no threat to anyone. Laura hoped it would be unnecessary to transport him in some sort of protective bubble, which would make his existence much more difficult to conceal. It was true they had already taken many chances exposing the boy and themselves to potential contamination. With the best science and technology available, humans still often made reckless decisions in the name of expediency. Laura realized she was at fault for doing this, too. Even now, as she sat with Alex and they discussed how to proceed with their new mandate, she wanted to abandon all protocol and whisk the little visitor away to a safe house so she could spend some productive time communicating with him.

Laura drained the remaining wine from her glass and cringed at the thought of Tannish treating the poor kid like a lab specimen.

"Okay," Alex said, "I recognize that look. You're getting fired up about something. What is it?"

"I was just thinking of the debriefing and our next moves," she answered.

"And?"

"First, we have to ensure Haines doesn't remove the remnant from the crash site."

"Why? Wouldn't it be safer somewhere else?"

"Probably, but that's the most logical spot for the boy's people to come back to. If they think like us, they'll want to revisit the places where they've already been. The crash site should be our staging area for their return."

"Makes sense. So we tell Haines to leave it there. I love the idea of bossing him around. Then what?"

"We need a safe place for the boy—somewhere close to the site, but protected."

"There's nothing out there. We'd have to set up a prefab and a bivouac for—"

"No military. Not at *our* site. Maybe a few, but any more than that would draw attention."

"That's going to be hard for the committee to accept," Alex reasoned. "They'll want the kid under constant guard. And I'm inclined to agree, Laura. Not just for our benefit, but for his, too."

"We'll figure that out once we know a destination."

"Okay. What about the site? How should we prepare it? I can oversee that if you like."

Laura showed him a sly smile. The wine was lightening her mood, but she also appreciated his enthusiasm. "You're just dying to get one up on Haines, aren't you?" she asked with a chuckle.

"Not for myself...for *you*. He thinks he's in charge over there. Wait until he finds out the Agency can still direct him. He'll blow a gasket."

"He *is* in charge at the site, Alex," Laura reminded. "True, our mandate supersedes his, but he'll stall us and throw roadblocks in our way if he feels left out. So you finesse it, okay?"

"Alright. You know I wouldn't do anything indecorous. I'll just—"

"Indec...what? Is the wine getting to you, Lover?"

"Indecorous. Wait. *Lover?* I thought we were still on the clock."

"We always are, *Lover.*"

"You mean I get paid to—?"

"Enough of that, young man," Laura teased.

Alex laughed and searched his jacket for a pen with which to sign the restaurant bill. "I'm charging this dinner to *your* account," he announced, "since this is your work meeting."

"Fair enough. Just remember what I said. I'm being serious about Haines. He's happy because he'll be in the history books, but he still has a chip on his shoulder, make no mistake."

"I will handle him with the utmost tact," Alex promised with a sly grin. "I paid the bill. Now what? Head to your place?"

"Very funny."

"A guy has to try. Let me guess, we're going back to the site tonight."

"That's right, mister."

"Are you fit to drive? I'm not."

Laura pulled out a colorful badge from beneath her blazer and waved it in front of Alex.

"A new one?" Alex asked.

"This is yours," she said as she handed it to him. "I've got my own."

"Thanks."

"Since you have one now, you can fetch a ride. Call and find us a fast flight to the site."

"You're rhyming," Alex laughed. "Sure you don't want to go home for an hour and...rest?"

"Get moving, buddy," she retorted. "We still have lots of work to do tonight."

* * *

Getting to the helicopter that would transport them back to the crash site was harder than Alex expected. He decided they would walk, since the nearest government building with a helipad was only four city blocks away. When they left the restaurant, however, they discovered teeming sidewalks and traffic gridlock. People were everywhere, and they did not resemble the usual evening tourist or work crowd.

Panicky assemblies quickly turned into protests after the government's official response to the alien visitation earlier in the day. The nation's president had called for understanding and patience while the investigation continued. He even offered to allow foreign scientists and leaders to tour the crash sites and examine the remnant. Unfortunately, many people misinterpreted his carefully chosen words as political spin and proof of a cover-up. The immediate results were disruption of business and civil unrest. Rallies and marches blocked access to buildings, overwhelming the capital's police forces. Soon, the military showed up to help maintain order.

On their way to the closest helipad, Alex and Laura suffered more than a few bruises as they pushed through the crowds. Alex even had to drag Laura through a group of UFO enthusiasts who were turning their rally into a rowdy celebration. Alex might have enjoyed the impromptu street party if, aside from being fueled by spirits, it was not also being inflamed by anger. He chuckled to himself when he encountered a parade of signs reading We Told You So, but the protest was far from funny. Laura nearly lost her handbag to thieves, and groping hands came at her from all directions. Alex caught one man just as his lecherous hand was reaching for Laura's blouse. Without thinking, Alex stopped the pervert's act by administering a quick jab to his face. Laura saw the man slump to the hard asphalt while holding his bleeding nose, and she glimpsed Alex rubbing his knuckles. Because of the surrounding chaos, though, she did not stop to question Alex and did her best to remain close to him.

"What a mess!" Alex exclaimed after they were aboard their helicopter and looking down at the city streets from the air. "What is wrong with people? Is it so hard to stay calm and just get on with your life? This has gotten crazier with every passing hour!"

"I don't approve of rioting and violence," Laura replied while she tidied up her clothing and hair. "Speaking of which...how's your hand?"

Alex rubbed his red knuckles and smirked. "I don't approve of perverts."

"It's too bad things have to get out of control," Laura remarked. "People have a right to make their voices heard, but there's no reason to be uncivil."

"Some of them down there are just using this as an excuse for their own factionalism."

"I agree. But think about the others, Alex. We're asking them to trust us with what is the most significant event in human history. They aren't protesting high taxes or some social agenda. I'm surprised it's not a lot worse."

Alex considered the streets under the speeding helicopter. Traffic was at a standstill on most of them. On the outskirts of the city, there were clear signs of rioting. Smoke billowed up from several buildings on the riverfront and small car fires lit up darkened neighborhoods. "Someone had better do something before this devolves into—"

"Your phone is blinking," Laura said, pointing to the device on a nearby seat.

Alex retrieved it and answered. "This is Alex," he said, straining to hear through the ambient noise. "Yeah. Go ahead. Yes. Okay. Slow down, I—"

Laura watched the expression on Alex's face turn from anger to shock and then to outrage as he listened to what must have been bad news. She braced herself, wishing now she had ordered one more glass of wine before leaving the restaurant.

"Why weren't we informed *hours* ago?" Alex demanded, clenching his fist and gazing at the darkness on the other side of the helicopter's window. Pause. "I don't care! I don't care! Someone should have immediately notified Director Turgis!" Pause. "Well, why—?" Pause.

"Alex, what is it? Laura questioned.

Alex held up a finger, signaling her to wait for a moment. "Go on," he said to the caller. Pause. He cursed and stomped his foot. "Okay. We're en route now. Hold it all together, Jacobs. Use agency protocol, but cooperate with Colonel Richter. Right. See you in about...thirty minutes."

Alex cut off the call and looked at Laura. He tried his best to show her a tiny smile, but his eyes betrayed a profound concern.

"What happened now?" Laura asked.

"The kid's gone missing."

"What? How? When?"

Laura's seat restraints prevented her from jumping up and pacing, adding to her growing frustration.

"Jacobs says that Tannish was about to get a blood sample and the kid vanished. It was about two hours ago."

"Two hours? Why hasn't someone told us?"

"I don't know. Confusion at the site. Disrupted communications. We were at our debriefing. Jacobs has done her best to assert Agency control, but Richter made it a security issue...and rightly so."

"What do you mean?"

"We'll have to get the details when we land, but Jacobs said the kid literally vanished before Tannish's eyes."

"Vanished?"

"Yeah. Completely disappeared. Jacobs said it was pretty chaotic there, so I cut her off. I hope you don't mind."

Laura minded a little, but it was Alex's job to be the liaison between her as the agency director and the field staff. "It's alright. Sounds like we're walking out of one mess right into another, though."

"What a day," Alex said in a huff.

"They've *got* to find him, Alex!" Laura demanded. "Everything depends on that boy now."

"I know," Alex agreed. "They locked down the entire site right away and have been doing a thorough search. Jacobs said no one can get in or out. They'll find the kid."

"Two hours ago," Laura considered, "and they haven't found him yet. That doesn't make me feel very secure."

* * *

At the crash site, Laura and Alex met with Colonel Richter and Doctor Haines to review video recordings of what had transpired when the alien visitor disappeared. Laura stared hard at the computer monitor in front of her, studying the movements of Doctor Tannish's team and the boy's reactions.

The child was mostly compliant during the basic physical examination. He stayed on the exam table and allowed Doctor Tannish and her assistants to do many visual and non-invasive tests on him. When they directed him to lie down and Doctor Tannish reached for a syringe, however, the boy's facial expression showed a determined resistance. Tannish kept looking over her shoulder at him while she prepared her other instruments, but she did not seem to notice the mischievous grin on his face. Then, like a fading image, the boy's body slowly took on the appearance of its surroundings until he became invisible.

"He's like a chameleon," Alex said, pointing at the empty exam table on the screen. "You can't see him at all." He turned to address Richter and Haines, who were watching the recording from behind them. "Was it the same way up close?"

"Yes," Colonel Richter answered. "Even standing just a few feet away, Doctor Tannish said she couldn't tell if he was still lying there."

"We can get Tannish in here if you want to interview her," Haines offered.

"Yes," Laura said. "Please send her in."

Haines exited the room, unfazed by Laura's commanding tone.

"Colonel, security here is *your* job," Laura said with careful respect. "What's been done to find our visitor so far? Have there been any signs of him?"

"We tracked him for a while," Richter said, "mostly through the cameras, which are all over the crash site. Doctor Tannish and her staff made a thorough search of the examination room, which you can see her doing there in the recording. What you can't see is one staffer exiting to inform my people. It was then that the...boy...slipped out. Down the hall, he must have waited at the exit door until someone opened it. We know he left the building because a soldier felt an invisible shove while he was entering. A small bare footprint in the dirt just outside confirmed it."

"Anything after that?" Laura asked.

"We had no visual sightings, but the cameras recorded some strange events: an object floating by, probably carried by the camouflaged boy; changes in the background, most likely him passing across patterns he couldn't duplicate; and a few blurs from him running back and forth in front of a camera. We could tell he was in the immediate vicinity of this building and in a panic. It also looked like he was trying to get past the barrier around the remnant, but we already had that locked down good and tight, so he wasn't—and isn't—going to access that."

"So you've been able to contain him in the area just outside, but no one can see or capture him?" Laura asked, trying not to sound incredulous.

"You saw how slippery he was with Tannish's people," Richter answered. "With an ability to camouflage himself, a cunning intelligence, and fear for his own life, he's proved to be a tough little bugger to catch. We'll get him, though. He can't keep it up for much longer."

"What makes you so sure?" Alex asked.

"Trust me, we'll have him."

"What else is out there besides people and cameras?" Laura asked.

"We already had ground sensors around the outside perimeter of the site. There are now over a hundred more out there, strategically placed throughout the interior. All personnel are wearing body cameras with live feeds. I'm telling you...it's only a matter of time."

"I don't have to tell you how important he is," Laura noted. "Finding him is the highest priority—not just for one agency, but for *all* of us."

"My superiors made that clear to me, too, Miss Turgis. We all know what's at stake here."

"And Haines?"

"He's been fine...content to be focusing on the remnant." Richter stepped forward and placed a reassuring hand on Laura's shoulder. She flinched a little, but only because it had been bruised during her dash through the streets of the capital. "This is *our* show out here—yours and mine. You tell me what you need, and I'll tell you what I need. But...when, and if, it comes to the security of the people here and the interests of—"

"I get it, Colonel," Laura interrupted. "I have no intention of overstepping my mandate, but I *will* do whatever it takes to recover that boy."

"And I'll help you as much as I can."

Haines returned moments later with Doctor Tannish close behind. She looked haggard and dejected.

"Hello again, Doctor Tannish," Laura said. "I only have a few questions to ask you. First, when the boy disappeared, did it look to you like he became immaterial, or did his body simply camouflage itself?"

"Are you asking me if he was still physically in the room?" Tannish asked in a derisive way. "Of course he was still in the room."

"How did you know this?"

"I heard him climb off the table and his footsteps on the bare tiles."

"And you couldn't grab him?"

"You can see the recording there. He was completely camouflaged. We couldn't tell where he was."

"He must have been constantly changing to adapt to whatever was around him," Laura surmised.

"That was my impression, yes."

"Were you able to retrieve any physical samples left behind in the examination room? Any hair follicles? Any fluids or skin cells we could use to examine his DNA?"

"No," Tannish admitted. "We did a thorough search for all of that —and more—and we found nothing. Evidently, he doesn't slough off cells as easily as we do. The room contained no biological artifacts or contamination of any kind."

"Thank you, Doctor Tannish," Laura said, trying hard to hold back her frustration. "I'll read your report on the examination. That's all I need to know right now."

Tannish left in a hurry, and Haines stepped toward the door to follow her.

"Doctor Haines," Laura called out.

Haines spun around to face her. "Yes?"

"The work on the remnant—I'm assuming it has stopped?"

"Of course," Haines replied. "We postponed all operations while the search has been underway."

"Do you feel confident you prevented the boy from getting back to it before the extra security measures were—"

"Yes," Haines interrupted. "There was no way for him to get to it. That area already had been tightly secured...to prepare for—"

"For moving the remnant," Laura finished. "But that will not happen now. The remnant must stay put. Until we find the boy, that's all we have left."

Her assertive tone clearly bothered Haines. Heavy fatigue and tension were causing politeness and professional courtesy to falter. Laura glanced at Alex and he looked up from checking his phone messages with an expression that suggested caution.

"The committee has already informed me that you're in charge of our *visitor*," Haines said coolly. "The remnant is being prepared for transport to a military installation where I have been tasked with—"

"I'm afraid I have to side with Miss Turgis on this, Doctor Haines," Richter said, interceding. "Nothing—and no one—leaves this site until we find the boy. After that, you can both take it up with your superiors." Richter seated himself behind his desk and shuffled through a stack of folders. "Now, if you don't mind, I have to report back to *mine*."

"Of course, Colonel," Laura said. "Alex and I will need to meet with Agent Jacobs. Is there a private room where we can—?"

"Doctor Haines," Richter said, "can you take them to a secure room?"

The power play was clear. Colonel Richter was subtly reminding both Haines and Laura that he was ultimately in charge at the site. Haines was being pigeonholed by the Colonel and by Laura, and he knew it. Laura would use her connections to override them both if either of them hindered her from finding the boy. Alex was the only one who seemed complacent.

"Thank you, Colonel," Alex said. He rose, crossed the room, and opened the office door for Haines and Laura. Two Marines waited in the hall, meant as escorts for the civilians.

"Please don't leave the building by yourselves," Richter called out as they exited. "Since you arrived, we've laid more ground sensors. You'll need an escort if you want to go outside."

"Understood, Colonel," Laura said. "Thank you."

Laura noted a brief smile on Richter's face just before the door closed.

This is our *show out here—yours and mine.*

Laura considered the words from her private conversation with Richter and hoped he was being genuine. With everything now at stake, she did not want a continuing power struggle. All that mattered to her at the moment was finding the boy.

As if reading her thoughts, Alex leaned in close and whispered. "Don't worry, they'll find him. He couldn't have gotten far."

* * *

Several miles from the crash site, moonlight silhouetted the figure of a young boy as he foraged in a well-tended garden behind a farmhouse. The plants he found were bitter and hard to chew, but he knew his body needed nourishment to continue the changing. Maintaining the colors, patterns, and constant shifts had taken all of his strength and concentration. Now, he was weak, unable to change again, and barely able to stand on his own bare feet.

Bare. The people of Blue covered their bodies, so he decided he should cover his, too. Perhaps he could find some coverings in the ugly, boxy structure on the hill. First, though, he needed more food. Unlike

Hourou, the vegetation here seemed to have few nutrients. It was not satisfying. His body craved more, so he grabbed at whatever looked and tasted palatable and ravenously chomped and swallowed, hoping he would soon feel satiated.

As he surveyed his surroundings, his thoughts turned to Ria. *Wah-ya-so eeee oh, ahe. Why did you leave me?*

He no longer sensed her presence and instinctively knew she had left the planet. Looking upward, he wondered where she went. The night sky was strange to his eyes. There was no color, and the stars were few. Ominous, billowy, white things floated through the air. Could they be alive? Some of them were thin enough to see through.

When he had his fill of the distasteful plants, he wandered closer to the boxy structure and studied its form. It must have been some sort of building, he guessed, like the one near the wrecked wa-ah-ahea where those people had temporarily trapped him. On Hourou, buildings were different—not sharp and linear, but round and natural. The people of Blue were harsh with their designs. Maybe they were just mimicking what was around them. The nearby forest felt fierce. Even the ground was unforgiving. In fact, walking was becoming painful. He searched for a soft path but then remembered how people there wore special, foot-shaped coverings on their feet.

They craft their coverings for specific functions, he reasoned. *I will not find these in the outside. I must look for them on the inside.*

He crept away from his hiding place and across short wet grass toward the building, cringing with every step now that he had become more aware of the pain in his feet. There was a low window, so he approached and peeked through it. All was dark and quiet, and he sensed no people inside. Satisfied, he sat down to rest and winced as his bare buttocks touched the hard, pebbly ground.

I will get in and find coverings, he thought. *This is Blue, and I must be Blue-like.* He considered his body and frowned at the idea of hiding it. *Ria said we must learn the ways of the people here. So, I will study them. Then I will know for myself if Blue is for the Dah-Ahey.*

Determined and unafraid, the boy stood and stumbled under the pull of a foreign gravity. He was not as strong as he had been on Hourou and would have to adjust to that. He would overcome anything this world threw at him—do whatever was necessary to complete Ria's mission in her place. No longer concerned about her leaving, he resolved to succeed where she had failed. He would learn the ways of this planet and make a suitable new home for his people.

CHAPTER 32

The Dah-Ahey Interruption

MORNING: DAY 5 ON HOUROU

"Time to get up, sleepyhead."

Paul's voice sounded far away. But even while she slept, April knew he was somewhere nearby, gently trying to wake her. On most mornings, it would have been easy. Unlike Paul, she was a morning person, preferring to rise with the sun. Their visit to Hourou had changed that a bit, though. Besides confusing her internal clock, it introduced her to a new pace of life where there was rarely a need to rush.

"Come on, Babes. You have to get ready."

Ready? Not yet.

April wanted to finish her dream first. In it, she was soaring through the sky like a human airplane with outstretched arms for wings. A fantastic world, filled with color and life, dazzled her from below. Rivers of golden light, twisting through pastel forests and fields of sparkling crystals, beckoned her to follow them to a faraway mountain range. Like a bullet, she shot toward the closest peak and reached it in an instant. Green moss carpeted its rocky top, which she nearly touched while gliding past. Then she swooped down close to ridges and cliffs, all the while laughing with glee at her daring aerial acrobatics.

The mountaintops were so peaceful. April slowed her speed to glide among them for a while, and it was then that Paul appeared, flying next to her. She wondered how he had caught up since she had always been the faster flier. With a playful grin, she darted away and hoped to lure him into a chase. When she glanced back, though, Paul was just circling above a deep canyon and gesturing for her to look down. While she returned to his side, she scanned the valley floor and noticed a black void in the shape of a triangle. Where had she seen this before? It seemed familiar. As she and Paul studied it from above, an avalanche of brown mud began rolling down a mountain toward the massive hole. This upset her, but she did not understand why.

Paul took hold of April's hand and pulled her into a floating embrace. "Come on, Babes," he whispered into her ear. "Time to get up."

"I don't want to." With a pout, she closed her eyes and snuggled against his chest.

"Wake up. We have to fly."

"But I *am* flying!" As she forced her eyelids to open again, her dream vanished. Paul was now hovering over her, freshly shaved, dressed, and smiling while she lay naked on a soft bed. The setting reminded her of one of their rarer, intimate weekday mornings. "You look good," she said, framing his smooth face in her hands. Still muddled, she gazed at him seductively. "Do you *have* to go to work today?"

"Wake up, Babes," Paul said. "Come back to me. We have to get going."

The firmness in Paul's voice induced a return to reality. April propped herself up on her elbows and looked around the room. They were alone, which was a relief because there were no blankets to use as a covering.

"My clothes..."

Paul stood and presented a neatly folded stack of threadbare rags. "At least they're clean," he said, noting April's disapproving frown.

With a bashful twist, she turned onto her side and curled up while reaching for the clothing.

"Don't worry," Paul said. "Nobody else is around. Anyway, we had this room to ourselves, remember?"

"We did?"

While slipping into her tattered shirt and shorts, April surveyed the empty chamber and tried to recall the evening's events. Coming back to the real world after having such vivid dreams was difficult. As her mental fog lifted, though, she remembered a wonderful dinner with Ahee and Keah, games with their family, a celebration in the city, and several special drinks she and Ahee concocted when they returned to the apartment.

When everyone else had gone to bed, Ahee poured one last potion for the two couples, which they enjoyed together in the pool. It did not take long for Paul and April to get very cuddly after that drink, but neither Ahee nor Keah seemed to mind. To give their Earth friends some privacy, though, they moved to the other side and eventually climbed out of the water to leave.

Before exiting the bathing chamber, Ahee approached Paul and April at the pool's edge, stooped down, and touched them each on the shoulder. "Please," she had said, "enjoy our gift to you."

After finishing their drinks, Paul led April to a small secluded sleeping room in the furthest part of the apartment, where they shared an intimate and exciting evening.

Now that April was fully awake and remembering their special night, she understood what Ahee meant by *gift.* "That last drink was pretty potent," she said to Paul while smoothing out her clothes.

"Really? I don't feel hung over, do you?"

"No. Not that kind of potent. I think it had an aphrodisiac in it."

"Don't blame *me,*" he said with a chuckle. "You and Ahee made them."

April pulled him close for a hug and ended it with a passionate good-morning kiss. "Who's complaining?"

"Hey. If you keep that up, we'll be late."

"Late for what?"

"Keah wants us all to meet in that park again...to go with him to inspect the new spaceship, remember?"

"Oh, yeah. But why so early? It must be only first-sunrise."

Paul shrugged before offering April a bowl of fruit. She chose a few small ones that looked like apricots and stuffed them into the pockets of her shorts, which to her great happiness were fitting more loosely than when she arrived on Hourou. Paul did the same before placing the bowl on a table and hurrying April along.

"What's the rush?" she asked.

"Everyone else has already left."

April stopped in front of a refreshing room. "I'll meet you in the bath to wash up." After giving him a quick peck on the cheek, she stepped in and disappeared behind a curtain of vines.

Paul continued down the hall and waited for her just inside the bathing chamber. The early morning light that was channeled through skylights created a warm glow in the misty air above the pool. "Like something out of a dream," he said to himself.

When April arrived, she stripped off her clothes in haste, dove into the water, and swam underneath all the way to the other side. Paul watched admiringly as she resurfaced and climbed out, marveling at how her athleticism had reawakened since their arrival on Hourou. Through the mist, he could see her blurry form hurry into an alcove where gentle jets of air would dry her body. When finished, she stepped into an adjoining recess made of reflective walls to tidy her damp hair.

"I like the mirrors here," she called out. "They make you look thinner."

"You *are* thinner," Paul yelled back. "We've both dropped some weight...and added some muscle."

April caressed her skin while examining her figure. Paul was right. She lost the flab that had frustrated her for years. Her muscles had also become firmer and defined. It was as if she was regaining some of her youthful shape. Impressed and satisfied, she returned to Paul and picked up her clothes. "How long do you think we've been here?" she asked while she dressed.

"Only a few minutes. But we do have to get going."

"No, I mean *on this planet,*" April clarified.

"Oh. By my count, we're on our fifth day."

"It seems more like a few weeks, though, doesn't it?"

"Sure does. Ready?"

"Ready."

Paul took her hand as they left the pool chamber, and they headed down the hall toward the building's main exit.

"How much time has passed back home, I wonder?" April asked.

"Ellis has two theories: either we've been gone for several weeks in Earth time, or only a few days. I'm hoping for the latter. I don't like to think of the stress on the boys and our families if it's been longer."

"Yeah..."

"It has been amazing, though," Paul added quickly. He did not want to ruin April's mood with thoughts of a long separation. "The entire experience, I mean."

"It sure has," she agreed. "There's a lot I'm going to miss."

"Me, too."

Outside, the streets and walkways were already busy with foot traf-fic. Many Ah-Ahey traversed the levels of suspended bridges and ramps, talking amongst themselves and offering nods and greetings as April and Paul passed by.

"It didn't take long for the people here to get used to us," Paul noted.

April gestured a greeting to a teenage couple passing by and holding hands like her and Paul. "You'd think they'd be more curious about where we're from, though," she said to Paul.

"I know. They've accepted us being here as if visitors from other planets are a common sight."

"Keah said it pretty much is," April reminded.

"Human life on other planets... It's still hard to believe."

April watched a large family emerge from a lodging on the other side of the street, and the scene warmed her heart. A horde of energized children bolted out of the domicile while a pair of sleepy parents tried to corral them. The littlest ones nearly collided with the teen couple as they passed by, but the teens just laughed it off as they helped to control the agile brood.

"When do you think Keah's going to tell them all about us?" April asked.

"That's *his* business," Paul replied. "Who knows, maybe this will lift the travel ban."

April smiled at the idea. "That would be nice. I'd like for us all to come back here one day."

* * *

On their way to the park, April stopped a few times to admire the gravity-defying rivers that wrapped around many of the city's buildings, spires, and suspended bridges. Several had fish and amphibious animals swimming within them, which seemed just as impossible as the idea of floating streams with no borders. The watery works of art delighted April, and she was glad Paul gave her a few moments to wander among them.

The couple caught up to the rest of their party at the enormous arch in front of the park's main entrance. Eah was there with Jay, of course—the two inseparable now. April studied them while she and Paul approached from behind. They were holding hands, as usual, but their body language implied an even more intimate familiarity. From knowing glances and affectionate touches, she deduced that Jay and Eah were no longer keeping their feelings a secret.

April appreciated the young romance, but it still concerned her. Soon, they would all go back home, and so far Keah and Ahee had not invited Jay or any of them to return to Hourou. Nor did they mention future trips to Earth. That meant a breakup was inevitable, unless something changed in the next few days.

Tammah and Uio were also there, examining the arch with their Earth guests and trying to understand what they were saying about it.

"Then the symbols of the suns and the city represent *this* place," Perry said to Eah as April and Paul stepped into the group.

"Yes. It is Atsaahwua...the first built-place of the Ah-Ahey."

"Who are the two giant people?" Yori asked.

"They are the first Ah-Ahey to come to Hourou. We call them the First Dyad."

"So...the original settlers," Yori said. "And they brought animals with them?"

"Yes. Those images with them represent the first animals on Hourou. They came with the First Dyad."

"What about the round doorway?" Ellis asked. "Would that symbolize their spacecraft...their wa-ah-ahea?"

"No," Eah replied. "It is the doorway to Hourou that has been closed. There are no more doorways between worlds. That is why we must build the wa-ah-ahea."

Ellis gasped and looked at Eah with amazement. "So...there were...um—"

"What about the hand?" Perry interrupted. "What does *that* mean?"

"It is the hand of Ahey, guiding the First Dyad through the doorway."

"What planet did they come from?" Ellis asked.

Before Eah could answer, the whoosh of an overhead sky ferry signaled that the rest of her family had arrived. Keah landed the craft in an open area close to the arch and motioned for the group to board.

"History lesson over," Paul quipped. "Time to go."

"But..." Ellis lifted his hand to protest, but everyone was already walking away. After a last look at the symbols, he shrugged in defeat and followed.

"What's wrong?" Paul asked as Ellis caught up.

"There's a mystery back there that may be important."

"I've seen a lot of those on this planet," Paul noted, "and I believe some should *remain* mysteries."

"Why?"

"Because I doubt we could handle the answers."

Ellis frowned in disagreement but said nothing more.

While the group boarded the sky ferry, Keah addressed them from the center of the craft. "We will visit the wa-ah-ahea now. The Aihanyaah have completed their crafting work, but we must ensure it is prepared for travel."

April saw a few surreptitious glances shared between Keah and Eah. Whatever Keah's message was to her during the quick unspoken exchange, it made Eah fidget a bit.

"While Ahee and I inspect the wa-ah-ahea," Keah continued, "Tammah will show you the inside. It is like the one you traveled to Hourou in, but much larger. We have also improved the design so it can withstand the atmosphere of your planet."

"That's a relief," Perry muttered.

April ignored the remark. Beside her, Jay was in a hushed conversation with Eah, and their voices were loud enough for her to overhear.

"So you didn't tell them?" Jay asked.

"Ehe. They were sleeping."

"What about this morning?"

"It was not possible to be alone with them."

"When, then?" Jay pressed.

"Jay...they already know."

A gust of air filled April's ears when the ferry shot forward, preventing her from hearing more of their conversation. Since the noise of the rushing wind also hindered talking, April settled into her seat and practiced interpreting the unspoken communications of Eah's family.

She began with Uio, Mahah, and Maiha, who were facing each other and engaged in a rather animated, non-verbal dialog. It was easy for April to figure out the subject of the girls' conversation by their frequent glances at Eah and Jay and their mischievous grins. More than once, Uio pointed at Jay's clothes, and April could tell she was explaining to her sisters how they kept from falling off his body.

Neither Jay nor Eah concerned themselves with the girls. Jay seemed lost in thought, oblivious to everything around him. As with most Earth men, he was hard to read. Eah, however, was not as skilled at concealing her emotions or feminine signals. April could interpret much in her body language. Quick amorous looks at Jay, fidgeting in her seat, and toying with her hair exposed what was on her mind; she wanted Jay's attention.

As April concentrated on Eah, she could almost feel the girl's confusion. Eah thought she was giving Jay obvious hints, but he was not responding. It made April wish she could tell her that Jay just needed more practice reading unspoken languages. Besides this tension, though, April sensed another dominant emotion in Eah. It was sometimes hard to connect words to Eah's body movements, but when she did, one word kept expressing itself in most of Eah's subtle gestures: love.

So, April thought, *Eah's not just fascinated with Jay, she's head over heels in love with him.* The idea made her smile. *I wonder if her parents know. She's not doing much to hide it.*

Scrutinizing Eah's non-verbal communications soon caused April to feel like she was eavesdropping on an intimate conversation, so she turned her attention to the others on the ferry. Tammah had positioned himself as a sentinel at the rear of the craft and was working its aft control panel. His behavior revealed little, but April noted apprehension whenever he looked ahead at the mountains. The two other boys, Aai and Ua, appeared to be subdued, but she also detected some unusual disquietedness in their body language.

Because Ahee and Keah were at the front of the craft and facing forward, April could not see their faces. In their movements, though, she saw tension. Several times during the flight, they communicated about subjects that included Eah and Jay. April guessed this from Ahee's subtle, anxious glances at the young couple. Before she could interpret more, the ferry slowed and the grassy field where the giant cannon had done its work came into view. The device was no longer there; in its place was an enormous spaceship.

The scene reminded April of running through an open field back on Earth, just before she was snatched up by a similar-looking craft. At the time, she was not able to get a good look at that wa-ah-ahea. All she remembered was that it was huge, black, and triangular. This new one seemed much larger. "It's massive!" she exclaimed to Paul, peering over the gunwale to get a better view. "How do you think the size compares to the one we were in before?"

"I don't know," Paul admitted. "Looks a lot bigger, though."

"It seems three times as big," Jay offered. "I got a good look at the one that crashed—well, *before* it crashed—while it hovered above Cody and me. This must be triple that size."

"I wonder why they made it so much larger," Paul said. "Eah, do you know?"

Eah held her hair from blowing in her face while she leaned over and looked down at the ship. "It has grown. It was not like this when Jay and I saw it in the night."

"Oh. So you came way out *here* last night?" Paul asked Jay with a raised eyebrow and a knowing grin.

Jay ignored his needling. "Eah wanted to show me their progress. You wouldn't believe how we got out here."

"Uh-huh."

"Paul," April warned, "don't embarrass them."

The ferry landed a few moments later. After disembarking, the passengers split into two groups. Tammah and Eah led the Earth party while Keah gathered the rest of his family and went ahead to the new wa-ah-ahea.

As her group approached the massive spacecraft, April noted how it was floating a few inches above the ground. Warm air flowed from underneath, flattening the grass and then curving upward to envelop the entire hull. There was a strange energy all around it, too, like ionization during an Earth thunderstorm. Though the craft was very alien to April, everything about it looked and felt clean and new.

On one side of the vessel, a long ramp extended from a gaping portal that was wide enough to accommodate another smaller ship. April marveled at the size of the opening, wondering why the builders had made it so big. It was then she noticed how few Ah-Ahey remained at the site. Only a small workforce was present, and most of them were rushing around with an unusual sense of urgency.

Keah's family had already disappeared into the bowels of the enormous ship by the time Tammah guided his party up the ramp. Once inside, they found themselves in a cavernous empty hold. Tammah motioned for them to stop when he realized Perry had fallen behind.

While they waited, April puzzled over Perry's deliberate lagging. Ever since they landed at the site, he fretted, dallied, and stared at the surrounding forest. Several times, April saw Ellis and Yori looking back at him and then sharing a knowing glance. Did they suspect him of being up to something?

"Well, at least we didn't have to get *beamed* in," Perry remarked when he caught up to the others inside.

"You've been falling behind, Carlson," Ellis taunted. "Lose something?"

"Yes," Perry replied with unveiled sarcasm. "I seem to have misplaced my giant, mountain-blasting canon. Have you, by chance, seen it lying around anywhere?"

Ellis smiled at the deflection, but he would not let Perry get away with it. "No. I thought you were looking for a smaller toy...bronze colored, curvy—"

"Alright, boys!" Yori broke in with a scolding tone. "Let's be nice, please. Our host is trying to give us a tour, remember? Can we all just act like happy tourists?"

Ignoring Ellis's jab and Yori's rebuke, Perry turned to Tammah and motioned toward the vastness of the hold. "Why the massive, empty room?"

Tammah stepped forward to explain. "The remaining pieces of the wa-ah-ahea that was...I believe your word is—"

"Stolen? The *stolen* one?" Perry asked.

"—crashed," Tammah continued, "will be kept here when we retrieve them."

"Oh. I see," Perry said. "Looks to me like *this* spaceship can accommodate a lot of people. Will you be taking others on the trip back to our planet?"

April cringed at Perry's obvious attempt to extract information from Tammah. "Why not let Tammah explain things as we go along?" she suggested with a hint of firmness.

"Just asking."

Tammah motioned for them to follow him across the soft black floor of the hold toward a nearby ingress and passageway.

"Have you sensed all the tension in the air?" April asked Paul in a low voice.

Paul glanced around to ensure no one was within earshot. "I sure have. What's *with* everyone this morning?"

"It's not just the Earthlings. I've been reading anxiety from Keah, Ahee, and Tammah, too. Even the workers are subdued."

"That might be from working all night," Paul reasoned. "As for Keah and Ahee, they're probably concerned about Eah."

"You read that, too, huh?"

"Well, she and Jay are much closer now. Something must have happened between them last night. You can't hide that from your parents. Remember how it was with us?"

"Yeah, but this is different. Plus, I can tell Jay has really strong scruples. I doubt he would compromise them...or Eah's...especially in this environment."

"How do you know? I mean, Jay may be principled, but he's still a *guy*, and guys—"

"I know because he's a lot like you," April interrupted.

Paul considered that for a moment before continuing. "Thanks, but I wasn't exactly a saint when we were their age. Waiting for marriage was not on my program."

"I was no better. But we didn't have the same values then."

"True," Paul agreed.

"Anyway, we're talking about *now* and about *them*."

"I know. Besides that, though, I don't like the way Carlson is acting. There's something going on with him."

"I've seen it, too, but I can't imagine what," April said. "Maybe all this stress is just the natural lead-up to us leaving."

Paul grinned and nodded, but April could sense his doubt. "We'll see."

* * *

Tammah did his best to explain the purposes of the craft's many rooms and components while he led the group through the wa-ah-ahea's long corridors. Because he wanted to practice speaking in English, he only asked Eah to translate when he could not express certain Hourou words or concepts.

"As you already know," he said when they reached the spacecraft's power plant, "the wa-ah-ahea is partly alive. Here, deep in the—" He turned to Eah. "Eah, Eh-see-ih-hah...oho-ua...sa neh oho-ua?"

"You mean *O-hoo*," Eah replied. "The word is *belly*."

"Yes. O-hoo...the *belly* of the wa-ah-ahea. Here in the belly, power is—"

A loud rumbling sound, strong enough to vibrate the floor and tickle everyone's bare feet, interrupted Tammah's explanation.

"Is that being caused by your power source?" Paul asked.

Tammah and Eah shared apprehensive glances when the living vessel reacted to the rumble by sending a shiver through its surfaces. From a nearby room, they all heard concerned voices yelling out to each other just before the corridor filled with white bodies.

"What's going on?" Ellis demanded. "Are we lifting off?"

Tammah stopped a female worker and questioned her. After explaining to him what was happening, she rushed down the hall with the other Ah-Ahey.

"Tammah," April said. "What is it?"

Tammah nodded at Eah and gently pushed her to leave before turning to address the group. "You must follow Eah now."

"Why? What's happened?" Paul asked.

"The Dah-Ahey," Tammah answered in a solemn tone. "They have arrived."

* * *

Eah took the Earth party directly to the vessel's bridge. There, Keah, Ahee, their family, and a few Ah-Ahey artisans had gathered in front of the forward corner of the triangular room, which was transparent from floor to ceiling. No one noticed the visitors entering, and April understood why when she approached and viewed the scene outside.

Like an avalanche of bronze, hundreds of Dah-Ahey were streaming down from the forested mountainside to amass at the edge of the open field and surround the wa-ah-ahea. Among them were also mighty beasts, most of which April had not yet seen during her visit to the planet. Some were reptilian—colorful dragons with snake-like heads—while others resembled giant bears carrying riders and gear on their backs.

While the Dah-Ahey gathered, Tammah joined a small group of his people who were standing guard in the field. Though outnumbered, the Ah-Ahey looked undaunted by the coming confrontation, holding their ground and just watching as the numbers of their bronze kin grew. No one on either side spoke, which added even more tension to the scene.

On the bridge, there was also silence. From the grave expressions on everyone's faces, April could tell they did not welcome the sudden appearance of the Dah-Ahey.

"It looks like some sort of showdown," Yori finally said. "But why is no one talking?"

After a moment of pensiveness, Eah replied. "They are waiting."

"Waiting for what?" Ellis asked.

Eah nodded toward the scene outside. From amidst the crowd of Dah-Ahey, two hulking catlike creatures broke through the perimeter, entered the field, and slowly approached the Ah-Ahey. Behind the beasts, a young woman wearing strange clothes and flanked by two male Dah-Ahey sashayed across the short distance separating the opposing groups.

"Ria," Perry said in a whisper.

"What?" Yori exclaimed. "Perry, please tell me you didn't know something about this!"

"I didn't exactly—"

"I knew it!" Ellis bellowed. "You've been sneaking off and seeing her, haven't you?"

"No! That is—"

"Something's happening out there," Paul interrupted, drawing everyone's attention back to the glassy wall.

Tammah had stepped away from his group and intercepted Ria and her entourage. He and the girl were now engaged in an animated argument while the others watched them.

"Well, *this* scene certainly looks familiar," Ellis commented. "I wonder if they're arguing about *you*, Carlson."

"What do you mean?" April asked.

"This same thing happened when Ua found us with the Dah-Ahey," Yori said. "Ua and Ria were in a heated debate while the rest of us slipped away."

April wondered if such an escape was also the current plan. If Keah stayed, would Ria and her people try to steal the wa-ah-ahea? Perry had said that Ria obsessed over returning to Earth. Was this her scheme—to take the ship by force? If so, judging by the army of Dah-Ahey with her, she would have no problem doing so.

Ahee stepped to a nearby control panel and pointed at a button. A moment later, the room filled with the sound of Ria's brusque voice as she yelled at Tammah in their native language.

From Ria's gestures, April could tell the girl was frantic and unbalanced. She also recognized something about Ria's clothing. "She's wearing my shoes."

"Looks like she found Yori's lab coat, too," Jay noted. "But why does she have socks on her—"

"I hardly think this is the time for fashion commentary," Ellis admonished.

"No, it's important," April countered. "She's trying to dress like one of *us*."

"Interesting," Paul said, "but why does it matter?"

"Because she thinks she's going to Earth."

Keah nodded in agreement. "April is correct. Ria has come because she believes she is leaving with us."

"Are you going to take her?" Perry asked. "You have plenty of room in this spaceship. You can't take all of them, but you could fit a good many in here."

As Keah turned toward Perry, his eyes expressed deep disappointment. "The Dah-Ahey must *not* leave Hourou."

"Keah," Perry said, "you have an opportunity here to heal this rift between your two peoples. Why not just give them what they want? Take Ria, and as many of the others as you can, and bring them with us. Then come back and pick up the rest."

"You do not—"

"Maybe they would get along better on *our* planet. We could learn from each other. And with the Dah-Ahey gone, you can keep this perfect place all to yourselves. Everybody wins."

"Perry Carlson, you—"

This time, Ria's vixenish voice interrupted Keah's response. "Perry Carlson!" she yelled toward the wa-ah-ahea. "We have an agreement! Do the people of Blue use words that are true? What are you teaching us now, Perry Carlson? You have brought strange knowledge to Hourou! You are teaching us about *untrue!*"

"Blast it, Carlson!" Ellis shouted, trying hard not to curse in front of his hosts. "What have you done now?"

"She—she's obviously taking a lot out of context," Perry answered.

"The context on this planet is perfection!" Ellis exclaimed. "Or close to it! Haven't you figured that out? You've contaminated their culture with...with—"

"Easy, Ellis," Paul warned, stepping between him and Perry. "Let's not make it worse, okay?"

Ellis noticed that Keah's family was staring at him with troubled expressions and realized his anger was contributing to their uneasiness. "I'm sorry. I apologize for that outburst."

Outside, Ria was still shouting toward the wa-ah-ahea, but in her own language.

"What is she saying now?" April asked Eah.

"That the Ah-Ahey must take her to Blue," Eah replied. "She said Perry Carlson promised this to her, and that she will teach the people of Hourou about...*untrue ways*...if we refuse."

"What does she mean by that?" Jay asked.

"I do not understand *untrue*," Eah replied. "Is this somehow related to the word *true?*"

Jay looked to the others for help with an explanation. "Um..."

"Eah," April said, "Some Earth words have no meaning here on Hourou."

"Yes," Eah agreed. "Yet...Ria understands?"

"She's learned," Perry interjected, "but not very much."

"We'll see...Carlson," Ellis said.

Perry did not care for Ellis's peevish tone. "Perhaps the purpose of us being here is to help these people *learn* other ways of thinking," he suggested. "Have you considered *that* in your observations, professor?"

"Enough damage has been done here already," Paul warned. "We'd be wise to do as Keah says."

"And Keah says *what?*" Perry demanded.

April cringed and hid herself behind Paul. The situation inside the spacecraft was getting just as tense as the one outside. Perry had infuriated Ellis and Paul, and both seemed ready to drag him out of the ship and feed him to the giant cat creatures. Yori was trying to remain levelheaded, but she was not about to step between the angry men. Jay looked as worried as April, but more so about the reactions of Eah and her family. April felt a drop in the pit of her stomach when she followed his concerned glances and saw how confused and upset the Ah-Ahey had all become. Somehow, calm had to be restored.

Keah kept his eyes on the activity outside. Despite the mood on both sides of the window, he seemed unshaken. After sending a few unspoken directives to Ahee and Eah, he turned to face Perry. "Perry Carlson, you will come with me. The others of you must remain here."

"Where are we going?" Perry protested. "If I go out *there*, it'll only make matters worse with the girl."

"You will talk to Ria," Keah commanded.

"But—"

"Tell her you spoke about taking her to Blue before understanding the Ways of Ahey on Hourou. Remind her that only those who follow the Ways of Ahey may travel between worlds."

Perry raised his hands in objection. "Keah, I don't even know what *Ahey* is, or what those Ways are!"

"The primary Ways indwell the minds of all people," Keah said, pointing to his head. "I have just told you another: traveling to other planets is only for the Ah-Ahey."

"But why?" Perry demanded. "Why do you have this rule? Maybe this is part of the problem between your two peoples. Ria told me the Dah-Ahey only want their freedom. Making rules like these and preventing her people from doing what you can do is not fair, Keah. Can't you see this?"

"Carlson!" Ellis said through gritted teeth. "I'm warning you for the last time to stop interfering with the culture of this planet. You are not an intergalactic ambassador! If you were, you would keep your nose out of their business. Are you trying to start a war here before we leave? Is that what you want?"

"I'll go with you, Perry," Paul offered. "Let's just get this done."

"Paul, no!" April objected.

Keah turned to Paul, showing a slight smile that conveyed appreciation. "Paul, you must remain on the wa-ah-ahea, but I thank you. It is important for Perry Carlson to show Ria he has acted alone. She will understand this if the rest of you stay here." Turning back to Perry, Keah bored into his eyes with a glare that denied Perry any more objections. "You will come with me...now."

Perry searched the faces of his compatriots for a hint of support. Finding none, he frowned and wagged an angry finger at them. "Stand there and renounce the politician, then! After all, he couldn't possibly be right about anything. Minister, you think I want to start a war here?

Really? Back home, I've talked nations *out* of war more than a few times. It's not *me* who'll begin one here. Just remember that...all of you. Remember I said it when all hell breaks loose down there. Because that's exactly what's about to happen."

With that, Perry stormed off toward the exit portal. Keah followed him, resolute yet bewildered about his rebuke.

"God help us all," Paul whispered after Keah left the bridge.

Everyone else resumed watching the Dah-Ahey interruption. During the dispute with Perry, Ahee had silenced the outside noise, so she reached over to a control panel and raised the volume again.

Ria was still hollering at the wa-ah-ahea while the throng of Dah-Ahey behind her remained silent. After a few moments, Keah and Perry appeared and joined Tammah and the other Ah-Ahey. When Ria saw Perry, she stopped yelling, put her hands on her hips, and smiled at him in triumph.

"Okay then. Let me handle this," Perry said to Keah. Resuming his role of pompous dictator, he left the others and strode across the field toward Ria, all the while glaring at her with an indignant scowl. He halted his march just a few feet in front of her. "You know, my little pumpkin, bribery is not a nice thing to use on me."

"Be my hero, Perry Carlson," Ria demanded. "Take me with you now to Blue so I can learn the ways of your people, and I will teach you things that are...beyond your imagination."

"Next, you'll be telling me we'll rule the Earth together as husband and wife," Perry said with a chuckle, "as the supreme dyad."

Ria tilted her head and squinted, contemplating Perry's sarcastic comment as if it was an intriguing suggestion.

"Let's be serious here, Ria," Perry urged, stepping closer and hoping to distract her from his poorly chosen words.

Ria stuck her hand out as a command to stop. "No. You said this thing before about *ruling,* and I must think. To rule...yes. You are already a ruler on Blue..."

"You misunderstood me, kitten. What I said was—"

"Your explanations only confuse," Ria interrupted. "I know the meaning of *many* of your words, Perry Carlson, including *rule*." She closed the gap between them and her bright green eyes bored into his with intensity. "I know your desires. You want more rule on your planet."

"Ria—"

"Yes. You also want Ria. Take me with you to Blue, Perry Carlson, as you promised. Take me to Blue and you will have more than you can now imagine."

Perry tried to break eye contact and step away from her, but he found it hard to move. "I...I can't—"

On the bridge of the wa-ah-ahea, Eah gasped and reached out toward the scene as if to stop it. "Ehe, Perry Carlson! No!"

"What is it, Eah?" Jay asked. "What's wrong?"

"It is like a bonding. She is—I do not know a word for it—to uncover the *waiooua*...the soul."

"She's enchanting him," Yori said, "and hypnotizing him somehow."

On the ground, Perry swayed under Ria's gaze. "Stop this, Ria," he demanded. "This isn't—this isn't what you said would happen here."

"You have given me so many ideas, Perry Carlson," Ria said in a dreamy voice. "You know other ways that I also want to know. To rule...yes, to rule—"

"Do you want the boy back, or don't you?"

Ria lost her mental hold on him and stumbled backward, gawking. "The *boy?*"

"Yes, the one you left on Earth, cupcake. You haven't forgotten him already, have you? He's the one to whom you promised the dyad...when he comes of age. He's the one for you, not me."

"Sah," Ria mumbled, shaking herself from her own trance.

She kept repeating the name, which angered one of the male Dah-Ahey who had accompanied her into the field.

"Ria, ah ey-hee yah woo, Sah?" the young man demanded after walking up behind her.

Ria spun around to face him, and the two began arguing like youthful lovers having a jealous spat. She addressed him as Wae, which she pronounced *Why-eh*. During their shouting match, Perry interpreted enough to understand that Wae resented Ria's affections toward an outsider. What angered Wae more, though, was the revelation that she had taken Sah—a future love interest—with her to Earth. Evidently, Ria had already promised to bond with Wae.

As the argument became heated, Perry could feel the energy of rage envelop all three of them like a thick fog. Although he could not understand all the words, he knew Wae was hurling insult after insult at Ria. Her bronze face was turning red with anger and embarrassment, but it was not until Perry saw tears in her eyes that his own fury erupted. Before he could stop himself, he advanced upon Wae and slapped him hard across the face.

Each second seemed to pass by in slow motion. Wae stumbled and fell to the ground in shock, holding his face and gawking at Perry. Ria dropped to her knees and stared at Perry with horror in her watery eyes. Perry looked at his hand, still held high in the air after his slap, and then glanced at the nearby crowd of Dah-Ahey. All of them had the same dumbfounded expression on their faces, as if it was the first time they had ever witnessed such an action. Indeed, the very idea of doing it had sent them into a stupefied state, where they were powerless to think or move.

Bewildered and ashamed of his act of violence, Perry quickly dropped his hand and helped Wae to his feet. Behind him, Ria stood, took hold of Perry's arm, and spun him around to face her. He was expecting either a verbal tirade or a slap from her, so it surprised him when she just smiled and stepped past him to approach Wae.

After Ria examined the mark Perry had left on Wae, the two locked eyes and communicated non-verbally. Then, in a blur of motion, Ria slapped Wae's other cheek, smiling as she studied her hand and the redness that was forming on the side of his face. Both of them grinned at each other, and then Ria offered her cheek to Wae, which he slapped in a quick, harsh motion.

Perry recoiled in horror when Ria touched the bruised spot and cackled in delight. She was actually reveling in the power of giving and receiving pain, and Perry immediately regretted having caused it. When she and Wae started slapping each other again, he tried to step between them, but something pulled him backward instead. Keah and Tammah, having approached them all unseen, were yanking him away, despite his struggle to break free and stop the savagery.

It was not until they were halfway back to the wa-ah-ahea that Perry ceased in resisting his rescue. Under crushing despair, he went limp and just allowed himself to be dragged while watching the surrounding scene in a partial daze. From the edges of the forest, white bodies poured into the center of the field and mixed with bronze ones in a bizarre fray. Perry wondered where the legion of Ah-Ahey had come from. Had they been expecting this confrontation with the Dah-Ahey? Ria's plan was ill-conceived and foolish, but how could the Ah-Ahey have predicted it when they knew nothing about strategy? Even when he felt the ship's ramp under his stumbling feet, Perry still strained to get a last glimpse of Ria. What would happen to her now? Though he wanted desperately to see her, she became lost in a sea of clashing bodies.

On the bridge, Ahee was supervising the raising of the ship. While she darted from station to station, she called out commands to her family in a firm voice that redirected their attention from what was happening outside. The flurry of activity helped to rouse the members of the Earth party from their stupor. Ashamed over Perry's actions, they made a sheepish and discreet withdrawal to the back of the busy room.

A distant thud from inside the wa-ah-ahea signaled that someone had retracted the ramp and sealed the service portal. Soon afterward, Perry entered the bridge and hurried to the main viewing window. Keah and Tammah were close behind. With a nod, Keah acknowledged Ahee's unspoken report regarding the ship's readiness, then he plopped into his chair. Tammah joined the rest of the bridge crew, glancing at his siblings but otherwise avoiding their questioning stares. There would be time for explanations and reflection later. Right now, they all had a job to do.

Keah gave the command to raise the ship, and a moment later it was level with the treetops. On the ground below, hundreds of Dah-Ahey slapped and hit each other in an ecstatic frenzy, mimicking what Perry had done but laughing as the ferocity of their blows intensified. With shock and revulsion, the small band of Ah-Ahey that had been guarding the wa-ah-ahea pushed their way into the huge brawl and attempted to stop the bizarre melee. The Dah-Ahey did not turn on them, even when other Ah-Ahey streamed into the field from the woods to help. The discovery of power through physical force—of inflicting pain to control others—was too precious to share. It required practice and mastery first.

Perry slumped to the floor while his tear-filled eyes searched for Ria. Just as the wa-ah-ahea rose over the level of the tallest trees, he glimpsed her partially dressed form in the center of the field, spinning around wildly and slapping whoever approached her. As if sensing Perry's stare, she stopped to watch the rising vessel. He could not see her face, but through their brief psychic contact, he felt a deep and miserable despair. Perry was leaving without her, after promising to take her with him. He broke that promise, which taught her about lying along with violence. Perry's gut wrenched, and he knew sickness would come if he kept watching. Then, as if to save him from further pain, the wa-ah-ahea turned away and shot into the purple sky of Hourou.

"Congratulations, Carlson," Paul said from the rear of the bridge. "You've just introduced sin to the Planet of Eden."

CHAPTER 33

Tensions

Jay sat alone against the rear wall of the bridge, watching Eah work and hoping Perry's impulsive act and the heated arguments of the Earth humans did not doom his future relationship with her. *What must she be thinking?* Her sadness was easy enough to read. He also noted confusion and distraction; she was struggling to concentrate on her duties. He stared hard at her and tried to send a few nonverbal questions—*Are you alright? Is there anything I can do?*—but she did not respond.

He studied Keah and Ahee, who were also preoccupied with raising the ship, and found the same lack of response. *That's strange,* he thought. *They always react, even to the smallest expression, but now they've completely tuned me out.* He wondered if their avoidance was a sign of disapproval regarding him and Eah bonding. Maybe they were worried Jay would end up being like Perry, polluting their perfect society—and their daughter—with ways and ideas contrary to their own. *I would never do that, though.* But how could he be sure? Eah lived a life that modeled perfection—or at least as close as any human could get to it. If they continued their bonding, would he ascend to that ideal, or would he drag her down? *I'm not Carlson,* he reasoned. *I have self-control. When I was alone with Eah, I proved that.* Such mastery over his passions had given him confidence and hope, but could he convince

Eah's parents he would be different? Or was this to be the end of his fleeting romance?

Jay hoped the situation would work itself out once they returned to the city, but the forlorn expressions of his Ah-Ahey friends tormented him with more doubt. He had never seen them show sorrow. On their perfect faces, sadness looked as foreign as he felt at that moment. How fast everything had changed! He had finally experienced the joy of being truly accepted by someone. Then, in a flash, he was back to being an alien again.

His Earth friends must have felt the same way. Jay saw utter anguish in them. April and Yori had broken down and were crying. Paul tried to console them, but he was barely holding himself together. Ellis, too, was struggling to maintain his usual reserved composure. Stunned and morose, he sat nearby with his head in his hands, just staring into the blackness of the floor. Across the bridge, Perry sequestered himself in an isolated spot where he could pace back and forth. Among all of them, he looked the worst. Jay studied his pained expressions and was actually pleased by his genuine show of remorse. If Perry acted any other way, Jay was sure the angry Earth party would never allow him to return home. He imagined the man being exiled on some alien planet, forced to live alone with the memory of his sin like Cain was after he killed Abel.

Despite his resentment toward Perry and his concern for everyone else, Jay's thoughts kept returning to Eah. *Am I that selfish?* he asked himself. *Is something wrong with me?* He glanced at the viewing window, expecting to see a landscape with Atsaahwua in the distance. Instead, all he saw was purple sky. Realization then overwhelmed him like a crashing ocean wave. *We're still rising! Keah's not going to the city; he's taking us back to Earth!*

* * *

With tired eyes, Keah stared at the clear sky beyond the bridge's transparent forward corner. Regardless of whether he wanted to, they were leaving Hourou. The wa-ah-ahea had decided that for him. Before he even gave the command to lift off, it had prepared for a long-distance flight, as if sensing the need to escape from something. He wondered how a semi-living vessel could understand such a concept. Escape? That implied danger, but there was nothing dangerous on Hourou. This, along with many other foreign thoughts, would require much deeper consideration. Such contemplation, however, would have to wait. The needs of the people within the ship were more important.

Behind him, Keah heard the sobs of his Earth friends. He wanted to give them a few more moments to comfort each other before facing them, but he also had to restore calmness on the bridge. His crew—his family—were doing their best to concentrate on piloting the new wa-ah-ahea. They, too, required consolation, and he was having a hard time restraining his own emotions. With much effort, he rose from his command chair, gave a signal to Ahee to join him, and then drifted to the back of the room.

"Keah," Paul said, standing to meet him, "I don't even know...what to say to you." His shaky voice was heavy with shame.

"We, too, are having difficulty expressing our feelings, Paul."

April stood also, and she tried to stammer out something—any-thing—that might relieve her anguish over what they all had witnessed. "Keah, I...I just can't believe what..."

"Words are unnecessary," Keah said. "We perceive your pain."

Ahee glided to Keah's side in her usual graceful way, but dignified movements were not enough to conceal her sorrow. She wrapped her body in a cocoon of white hair while she spoke. "April, you are very perceptive. Among the others from Blue, you have the best understand-ing of our communication."

"Yes...I suppose I do."

"You can see our confusion," Keah stated. "And you feel the grief of the children of us."

"Yes," April agreed. Tears returned to her eyes while Keah and Ahee stared at her, waiting with expectancy for her to interpret more. "We're making it worse, aren't we?" she asked them. "Along with their own emotions, they're experiencing *our* sadness and pain."

"It is overwhelming for us," Ahee said, "and for you."

April detected a subtle request behind Ahee's words. "I understand. It would be better if we went somewhere else so you can work and talk."

"We shall join you soon," Keah said. "Uio will take you all to a resting room where you may care for yourselves."

While Uio approached, Ellis and Yori stood and waited with April and Paul.

"Carlson's the only one who should be getting locked up," Ellis said.

"We're not being *locked up*," April corrected. "Empathy is part of their communication. Our emotions, which are extreme to them, are wreaking havoc in this room."

"Empaths..." Yori nodded with understanding. "Then we're bombarding them with feelings they've never encountered."

"*More* trouble they don't need," Paul said.

"Just like Carlson," Ellis added.

Hearing his name mentioned from across the bridge, Perry stopped pacing and came to join the group. Jay did likewise when he noticed them all gathering near the exit portal.

"What's happening?" Jay asked.

"Uio's going to take us to another room," Paul answered. "We need to give Keah's family some space."

Jay nodded toward Perry. "What do you think they'll do with *him?*"

"I'll tell you what *I'd* like to do with him right now," Ellis said.

Perry paused and waited for Keah and Ahee to finish a brief conversation with Uio. When she walked away to join the Earth party, he sheepishly approached the couple. "Keah...Ahee...I...I'm so sorry for *all* of this." He braced himself for some kind of coldness or rebuke from them.

"This river of events was already flowing well before your arrival," Keah said. "You, Perry Carlson, stepped into it with the rest of us."

"But I *polluted* it," Perry admitted. "Made it dirty."

"Your actions also exposed what has been happening beneath the surface," Keah said. "We were not aware of how far the Dah-Ahey had drifted. Some things are now clear, while others..."

"I understand."

"You all are still our guests—our friends," Ahee said. The warmness in her voice barely hid a hint of uncertainty.

Perry avoided her eyes. "I don't deserve your kindness...or forgiveness."

"It is the Way of Ahey, Perry Carlson," Keah asserted. "We know no other. We *want* no other."

"If Ahey is your religion," Perry said, "it's the only one I've ever encountered that I wouldn't mind learning more about." He looked past them both at the purple sky beyond the viewing window. "I suppose you're taking us back to our own planet now?"

"Yes," Keah admitted, addressing the entire Earth party. "We are leaving Hourou and will return you to your home. Go with Uio. I must explain to the children of us about...the strange things they have seen and do not understand."

"I wish you didn't have to do that, Keah," Paul said.

Keah nodded, and sadness changed his genial smile to a frown. "Yes..."

"Please," Uio said in a soft voice, "come with me now." She then pressed through the exit portal.

One by one, the members of the Earth party followed her until only Jay remained on the bridge. He hesitated to leave, which Keah and Ahee correctly interpreted as a desire to speak with them.

"Keah," Jay said, struggling to find the right words, "there's something—"

"Go with them, Jay," Keah interrupted. "Our journey is long, and we will have many conversations before we reach Blue."

"Okay."

Before leaving, Jay needed one last glimpse of Eah. She was across the room, busy working at a control station, but she turned to face him after sensing his attention. He expected the usual deep connection when their eyes met. In its place, though, he encountered a wall of profound sadness. It broke his heart. He wanted to go to her and offer comfort, but Keah was motioning for him to leave. Conflicted and defeated, he forced a smile and left the bridge.

* * *

Uio guided her guests down a long, winding corridor to one of the ship's many lounges. Once inside, she pointed out the room's principal features and then politely took her leave.

"Is anyone else experiencing déjà vu?" Yori asked while they all explored the space.

"It looks nearly the same as the waiting room in the first spaceship," Ellis observed. "At least we know where everything is."

Jay waved his hand over a small control panel that was embedded in the wall next to a massive opaque viewport. His action activated the port and made it transparent, causing the room to brighten with the purple-tinted light of Hourou's sky.

"How did you do that?" Paul asked him.

"I remembered how Eah turned it on the last time."

Perry, Ellis, and Yori plopped themselves onto soft settees in the room's center, while Paul and April joined Jay in front of the viewport. The wa-ah-ahea was already so far from the ground that details in the landscape below were difficult to discern.

"Our leaving is so sudden," April said. "I've been wanting to return home ever since we left it. Right now, though, I'm wishing I could stay on Hourou for just a few more days."

"Me, too," Jay agreed. "But I wonder if they would even let me after…"

Paul placed a comforting hand on Jay's shoulder. "Try not to worry, Jay. Somehow…things will work out."

The sound of a body passing through the main entry portal drew everyone's attention to the rear of the room. It was Uio again. Rather than joining them, though, she stood just inside the entrance, struggling to force a smile while wiping away tears from her red eyes and wet cheeks.

"We are about to enter the waters," she announced with a shaky voice. "Ahee sent me to remind you. The wa-ah-ahea will shake as it passes through, so sitting would be more comfortable for you."

"Thank you, Uio," April said.

With a slight bow, Uio stepped backward and allowed her body to be swallowed up by the portal, disappearing back into the corridor beyond. Jay, Paul, and April joined the others in the seating area and prepared for the ship to enter Hourou's watery upper atmosphere. Seconds later, a forceful bump jerked the vessel and rattled its occupants. Through the viewport, the scenery changed from clear sky to a swirling pool of colored light.

"Extraordinary!" Ellis exclaimed.

"Like Eah says, it's a floating ocean," Jay noted.

"More properly, layers of water vapor that form a canopy."

Jay shrugged off Ellis's scientific observation and tried to find solace in the changing scene outside. As their vessel passed through the planet's watery shield and shot out the other side, frozen droplets slid across the viewport and fell back into Hourou's atmosphere. When the view cleared, Jay could see the blackness of space and the nearby nebula that gave Hourou its purple sky. It was a beautiful sight, but he could not fully appreciate it; his thoughts kept returning to Eah. Whereas space once suggested the ultimate escape from a troubled existence, it now represented the potential loss of a new life he had finally found.

"Was this all for *nothing?*" Jay asked himself out loud, watching the planet becoming smaller in the viewport.

"There's a purpose in everything, Jay," Paul answered. "Sometimes, we can't see it until much later. Our experience has been no accident. We were all meant to be here for this. What we do with it all *now* is what's really important."

"Well said, Paul," Yori praised.

"Speaking of *purpose,*" Ellis said, looking to Perry, "what was the purpose of hitting the Dah-Ahey boy? What was going through your thick head back there, Carlson?"

Jay cringed at Ellis's bluntness, but Perry seemed to expect a confrontation and he did not retaliate with defensiveness. Instead, he leaned forward in his seat and engaged Ellis with unexpected genuineness.

"I don't know," he replied. "I suppose I was just reacting to what the boy said."

"What did he say?" Paul asked.

"He was insulting Ria—harshly. I guess a sense of chivalry overtook me, and I wanted to defend her."

"Oh. Her knight in shining armor," Ellis taunted. "How do you know he was insulting her? I thought you didn't understand their language."

"I don't," Perry admitted, "but I know an insult when I hear one...in *any* language."

"Even if he insulted her, you hardly needed to take it that far!" Ellis rebuked. "Can you comprehend the magnitude of such an action among people like them?"

Perry sat back hard, and his head dropped. "Yes," he answered. "Unfortunately, I can."

"What's *unfortunate* is the aftermath," Ellis continued. "There could be a full-scale war underway!"

"Ellis!" Yori warned. "Let's not start one here, too! Okay?"

Perry waved off Yori's indirect defense. "Minister is right, Yori, and I deserve his indignation. I don't blame any of you for hating me. I mishandled the situation, and I'm the one who has to live with the guilt. So if you all want to pile it on, now's the time."

Ellis wanted to do just that, but Yori reached over and grabbed his hand as a warning to back off. "What's done is done," she said. "We can't fix it. We're on our way home now, so it's up to Keah and his people to sort it all out...somehow."

An uncomfortable silence followed her statement. After a few moments, Perry stood, crossed the floor, and disappeared into the refreshing room.

Jay shifted nervously in his seat, expecting someone to denigrate Perry while he was gone. No one did, but Paul rose and began pacing.

"Are you alright?" April asked him.

"The man's devastated," Paul said. "We shouldn't dump any more resentment on him...even if he deserves it."

"I'll leave it," Ellis agreed. "I only wanted to ensure he understood the enormity of what he's done."

"I think he realizes it," Jay said. "But remember that trouble's been brewing between the Ah-Ahey and the Dah-Ahey for a long time. Maybe a conflict was inevitable. Us showing up—and Carlson's stupid act—just took it to the next level."

Jay was going to add more, but became distracted when he noticed a pair of black hands poking through the room's entry portal to open it. Eah stepped through first, followed by Ahee, Uio, and Keah. It surprised Jay to see that both Eah and Uio had both changed their skin color to black. He had not seen them like that since their first meeting. Did the outward change have something to do with an inward one? Jay hoped the blackness of Eah's body did not represent a dark omen.

"Our first *step* away from Hourou is still far off," Keah explained as he joined the others in the sitting area, "so we may talk for a while."

Eah sat next to Jay, and he immediately felt tension surrounding her like heavy air that was hard to breathe. He wanted to take her hand as a symbol of comfort, but through touch she would sense his fear. She glanced at him from behind her cocoon of hair and offered a half-smile. It was something at least, so Jay grinned back and tried his best to make it look genuine.

"Have you found all that you need here?" Ahee asked, ever the gracious hostess.

"Yes," Yori replied. "It's just like the first wa-ah-ahea."

"Seem-eh-ler—similar—but not the same," Ahee said. "This one will pass through the atmosphere of Blue without being damaged."

"Then, after this trip, you'll be coming back to our world again?" Paul asked.

"I cannot make that decision now, Paul," Keah answered, sparing a glance at Jay. "Everything we do must reflect the Ways of Ahey, and that requires much consideration."

"What do you think will happen on Hourou?" April asked.

By then, Perry had returned and had taken a seat away from the others. Keah acknowledged him with a nod before answering.

"What has happened is new to us, April, and to the Dah-Ahey. How can we un-see what was seen? How will the people undo what has been done? I said the Dah-Ahey must not leave Hourou, but if they go on following the dark river... Opposing currents do not mix."

"Can't you do more to reconvert them?" April asked. "Teach them to be Ah-Ahey again?"

"We will try, yes. But the koyoyi has now worsened. The Dah-Ahey who continue doing the indescribable things we have just seen—those must not remain on Hourou."

"I see," April said.

"Always the people of Blue try to see what is ahead," Uio blurted. "The only knowing is about the thing that is. What is the word for this?"

"The word is *now*," Jay offered. "What you mean is that we keep guessing about the future instead of paying attention to what is happening in the present."

"Yes," Uio agreed. "This is something I do not understand. There is no knowing of what is ahead in a river that always bends and changes. Yet the people of Blue still try. Why?"

"That's an excellent question," Paul said. "It's impossible to predict the future, but we waste a lot of time and energy trying."

"But why must you do this?"

"I suppose we don't, but it's a problem we all wrestle with."

"It is not the Way of Ahey," Uio said in a whisper. Then, her puzzlement changed to curiosity. "Can the people of Blue *learn* the Ways of Ahey?"

Keah reached over and stroked Uio's hair. "Some Ways of Ahey already exist on their planet."

"But not everyone there accepts them," Paul added.

"Then...there are Dah-Ahey there, too?" Uio asked.

"I guess that's one way to put it," Paul answered. "In your eyes, there are both types of people on Earth. But those who are more like Ah-Ahey are still very different from you."

"This I already see, yes." She looked from person to person, studying each of their faces. "I also see the *waihohu*—the mark—of Ahey in all of you."

Keah explained something to her in their language and she nodded her understanding. "Until this moment, we have not discussed these things," he informed the group. "Uio has many questions about Earth."

"Is it alright to talk about this, then?" April asked.

"Yes," Keah replied, "I suppose we must...but with care." He gestured toward his daughters as a subtle request to consider their sensitivities.

"Of course," April agreed.

Keah turned to Perry, who looked as if he would rather not be talking about anything at the moment. "Perry Carlson, your people call you a lee-dah?"

"A leader," Perry corrected. "Yes, I am elected—chosen—by the people to represent them in our governing body, and I oversee certain functions of our government." He paused, noting perplexed glances between Keah, Ahee, Uio, and Eah. "That probably sounds confusing because your society is so different. If you need me to define—"

"Words are not the only messengers of ideas," Keah said. "We can see many of your meanings. Please continue. What do you believe has been happening on your planet since you have been away?"

Perry rubbed the back of his neck and grimaced at the tension he found there. "Well, there are two possible scenarios," he replied. "In the first one, your appearance—and our disappearances—would have been covered up, depending on how many people witnessed the events."

"How typical," Yori said. "Suppression of the truth. That's why most of us don't trust our governments anymore."

"To the unlearned and naive, it might seem that way," Perry jabbed, "but there is also a responsibility to maintain order and to protect communities."

Jay glanced around the seating area and saw tension return to the faces of his Earth friends. Keah, Ahee, Uio, and Eah, however, sat casually on their lounges and watched the altercation with curiosity and interest.

"Sometimes," Perry continued, "if the truth threatens to cause disorder and harm to people, choices must be made regarding how much of it is necessary to reveal. Those decisions are hard. It's a great responsibility, and most of us don't take the job lightly."

"So," Yori fired back, "even if there were credible witnesses to the events, there would be an attempt to conceal the truth to protect people from...from what? An alien invasion? Themselves?"

Perry ignored her question and spoke to the group. "In the second scenario, there may have been too many witnesses, making a cover-up impossible. In that case, I can't imagine the confusion and chaos. Consider your own reactions to learning about intelligent beings from another world—shock, fear, challenges to long-held beliefs. Now multiply that by billions. And, if fear and distrust take over, picture what we're going to be walking back into." He turned to Yori. "Miss Shimizu, could most people handle a quick shot of truth like that?"

"Probably not," Yori admitted.

"Right. So don't condemn the desire to suppress certain things in the name of peace. It's a bigger part of my job than you'll ever know."

"I suppose that includes *previous* evidence of alien visitations, too? Will all that finally come out, then?"

"I had hoped none of you were in the UFO conspiracy camp," Perry said with a derisive chuckle.

"There can't really be a conspiracy about it anymore," Ellis noted. "If there's been a cover-up about our disappearances, our return will certainly expose it. Likewise, if the entire world knows about what happened, denying past events is pointless."

"There *are no* past events!" Perry declared. "Despite what the well-meaning, but completely ignorant, conspiracy theorists might say, there have *never* been UFOs, recovered spacecraft, secret bases, contact with extraterrestrial life, or alien abductions."

"Until now," Paul suggested.

"Yes, until now," Perry agreed. "Everything else is either imaginative marketing or politically motivated, anti-government rhetoric."

"So," Yori said, "you expect us to believe, after our experiences, that there has never been some sort of contact with intelligent, alien life? We now know for certain they exist. Continuing with the same old party line is useless. You might as well just start admitting some of that stuff was actually true."

Perry abruptly stood to dramatize his growing frustration. "You still don't get it, do you? *Our* experience is the *first* time. Anything else you've heard is completely untrue."

"I'm no expert or enthusiast," Paul said, "but I've read some things that made *this* skeptic scratch his head and wonder. There must be *some* truth in all those stories. I mean, look around; we're sitting in a spaceship with a triangular shape. Besides flying saucers, haven't some people claimed to have seen black triangles?"

"Yes," Perry agreed, "along with floating lights, globes, pyramids, and even giant cigars." He turned to Keah. "Have you visited Earth before, Keah?"

"No," Keah answered.

"And there has been—for the lack of a better term—a travel ban against *anyone else* ever coming to our planet, right?"

"That is correct; no one may approach Earth."

"And that includes any *other* beings?" Ellis probed. "*Non-humans?*"

"There are no others, Ellis Minister...only humans."

"There you have it," Perry said in triumph. "Our planet has always been under an intergalactic travel ban. All the alien stuff you've heard is bunk."

"Isn't it possible that people from other planets *ignored* the ban?" Yori asked Keah.

"No," he replied flatly. "Those who can cross the expanse are few, and none of them would ever go against Ahey."

"But some from *Hourou* did," Yori protested.

"Yes," Ahee agreed, "but those were the first."

"How can you be so sure?"

"We would have seen it," Ahee replied.

"The only question then," Perry said to Yori, "is if you're going to trust the people who really know."

"What about those unexplainable stories, though?" Paul asked.

"Okay, look," Perry said. "Let me give you all a history lesson so you'll see it more clearly. You know about science fiction, right?"

"Yeah. We're living it now," Paul quipped.

Perry ignored the joke and continued. "The sci-fi genre grew in popularity soon after World War Two, fueled by post-war paranoia and excitement about major advances in science and technology. Ordinarily, it would have been just another fun, cultural phenomena, and it would have run its course like fads and fashions always do. But some smart defense people and crafty politicians got together and came up with a brilliant strategy to keep our nation's enemies in check."

"Please don't tell me you really faked the moon landing," Ellis joked.

"I am being very serious here, Minister," Perry rebuked. "Keah asked me about what is happening on our planet since we left. I believe we'll be walking into the beginnings of mass chaos and the restructuring of international power positions. I'm breaking an oath of office by telling you all these things. Fortunately, that doesn't matter anymore; everything is changing anyway."

"Please continue, Perry," April said. "I'd like to know what I'm going back to."

"Alright. So, this new defense strategy was to allow mystery, rumors, and accusations to flourish. They let everyone *think* things like UFO sightings, alien visits and abductions, crashed spaceships, and everything related to those were happening, while neither confirming nor denying them."

"What possible good would that do?" Yori asked.

"Besides our own people, our enemies would be watching all of this," Perry answered.

"Other nations would wonder if we really knew something," Paul surmised.

"Exactly!" Perry said. "And also if we *had* something."

"Had what?" April asked.

"Alien technology," Yori answered for Perry. "Some think the technological advances of the past seventy years came from studying it."

"People actually believe that?" April asked.

"Oh, yes," Perry answered, "and our government *allowed* them to."

"Why, though?" Yori asked, "What good would that do?"

"It created a deterrent," Perry said. "Other nations saw us advancing after huge technological discoveries. Then, they read about us finding crashed alien ships, and we let them see seemingly credible footage and photos of UFOs. In the end, they had to wonder if it was all true. We didn't need to do anything but stay quiet and maybe instigate the rumors a little here and there."

"And the so-called *UFO nuts* made it easier by keeping the conspiracy theories going," Paul guessed.

"Correct. It was, and has been, a useful defense strategy...until *now,* that is."

"Why?" Yori asked. "What changes? The government will probably just use our experience to bolster all that, anyway."

"It *all* changes!" Perry exclaimed. "They created a balance of power using that crazy strategy. Other nations eventually caught on and began their own UFO programs—allowing experimental aircraft to be seen, leaking stories about official UFO sightings, producing photos and video. A few of them even followed our lead by pretending they recovered crashed spaceships and alien bodies. Those countries were too late getting in the game, though, because we've been—and continue to be—the primary target of the conspiracy theories. Our use of the propaganda has kept us on top. When we get back, that all changes, though...unless our government figures out a way to use this *real* alien visitation, and our return, for national advantage, since it happened within our borders."

No one knew how to respond to Perry's shocking revelation. His last words were especially troubling. The idea of being used as leverage in a crazy game of international politics and intrigue did not sit well with any of them.

"So," Yori said, breaking a brief silence, "you're telling us that until this incident—until we were taken by people from another world—aliens have *never* visited our planet."

"Do you finally understand that now?" Perry asked. "It has *all* been false. And there has never been a big government conspiracy to hide the truth because there was never a *need* to do so. The truth has always been apparent. People just made up stories and their leaders let it all happen. And it still goes on today."

"That is irresponsible complicity or outright deception," Ellis said.

"Not *irresponsible*, Minister," Perry corrected. "It *has* kept the peace."

"So the doubters like me have been right," Paul stated.

Perry looked at him and chuckled. "You were taken by alien beings into an alien spaceship and traveled to an alien world. You were sur-rounded by thousands of other alien beings, witnessed alien technology, learned alien ideas, and are now sitting on another alien ship, headed back to Earth after visiting a different galaxy. That doesn't sound to me like the doubters were right about anything either."

Again, the room became quiet as everyone pondered what Perry had said. Keah began a hushed conversation with Eah, Ahee, and Uio, presumably to solicit some interpretations and explanations from Eah, who still understood more of the Earth language than the rest of her family. While they talked, Ellis rose and paced in front of the viewport. Hourou looked quite small now as the wa-ah-ahea sped away from its planetary system.

"Neither of your scenarios offers much hope, Carlson," Ellis said as he returned to the seating area. "So far, we've been talking about the world's reaction to our disappearances. Other than some people using it for their political benefit, what will our *reappearances* do to help or hinder the overall situation?"

"That depends on *how* we reappear," Perry answered. "Keah could return covertly, drop us off, recover his crashed ship and the Dah-Ahey castaway, and then leave. If that happens, the world will only have our individual explanations and stories. But if he does it all publicly and makes contact, there'll be support for everything we say, and it could usher in a completely new era for all of humanity."

"If they don't make contact, all this would've been for nothing," Yori said.

"Not really," April countered. "We each can tell about our fantastic experiences. And there were witnesses to our abductions."

"We'll be international stars," Paul added.

Yori did not find that reassuring. "What if no one believes us, though? Or what if the government demands that we keep it all quiet?"

"Either situation is possible," Perry answered. "But we can't know anything until we get back and see what is actually happening since our...departure. The rest is up to Keah and what *he* does."

All eyes then fell upon Keah. Sensing their staring, he ended his private conversation and turned to address them.

"Many of the words you spoke are unknown to us," he said, "but we understand your concerns about returning."

"Have you decided how *you* want to return?" Perry asked.

Keah shot a subtle glance toward Jay before answering. "No. There is still much to discuss."

An uncomfortable silence followed Keah's statement until April stood and addressed the Earth group. "Let's get back to what happens when *we* return," she suggested. "Despite what Perry said, I can't imagine everyday life changing all that much. Sure, our understanding of the universe has just taken a huge step forward, but unless we maintain contact with Keah's people, what does it matter? We can't travel through space like them. We can't visit other planets. So why should this knowledge make things worse for us?"

"Because it forces people to give up long-held beliefs," Ellis answered.

"Why should that cause widespread panic and chaos, though?" April asked, dropping back into her seat.

"I am curious about this, too," Keah admitted. "Why would the order of your planet change?"

"Fear often does that," Ellis noted. "People are afraid to think in unfamiliar ways. That causes an unwillingness to break with safe traditions, even when they're proved wrong. Carlson has painted a bleak political picture. But there are many other areas of life that must adapt to this new knowledge as well."

"Like what?" Yori asked.

"Like your own field of biological science, for one," Ellis suggested. "We've now got proof that life evolved in other places besides Earth. This could answer the big questions about the origins of life on our planet."

"How?"

"Since life has evolved on *other* planets, which many scientists have already postulated, then it is possible—even probable—that the seeds of life found their way to our Earth and brought us to what we are today."

"We aren't all evolutionists here, Ellis," Paul said.

"Then how does the revelation about life on other planets—especially *human* life—affect your own belief system, Paul?"

"I don't believe life was created on other planets and then spread to the Earth," he answered.

"I agree," Jay said.

During the long conversation, Jay had been content to just listen. Something about the current topic bothered him, though. His own beliefs were being challenged. On Hourou, he was too busy accepting his new environment and sorting emotions. He did not have time to consider his own worldview. Now, however, the ramifications of what he had been through were coming to light in his wearied mind.

"Paul," Ellis said as genially as he could, "if I, as an evolutionist, can accept humans evolved on other planets, synchronously with our evolution on Earth, why can't you, as a creationist, accept that your Higher Power could have created humans on other planets?"

"I *do* believe it's possible," Paul said. "But I don't think processes or beings from other planets seeded the Earth."

"Why not?" Ellis challenged.

Before Paul could answer, Keah stood and faced Ellis. "Life did not begin out here among the galaxies, Ellis Minister," he said. "It began on *your* planet...on Blue. All life began on Earth."

CHAPTER 34

Revealed

Jay was glad when Eah suggested taking a break from talking so the Earth guests could see more of the wa-ah-ahea. His friends' arguments over philosophical matters were getting tiresome. He could tell Keah and Ahee felt the same way when they eagerly agreed that completing the tour would be a pleasant distraction for everyone.

While the host couple led the group to the ship's power plant, Uio and Eah veered down a side passageway with Jay to show him other parts. Soon afterward, Uio took her leave on the pretext of needing to perform an important duty. Jay knew better, though; Uio was giving him and Eah some privacy.

"Well...I'm glad we're finally alone," Jay said, hoping Eah felt the same way.

"Yes..."

Eah's skin and hair matched the blackness of the ship's interior surfaces, making it hard for Jay to see her in the dark corridor. If not for the white eyes and teeth beneath her concealing mane, she would have been almost invisible.

Something's off, he thought. *She's usually a lot more talkative.* By now, her custom would have been to take his hand. "Eah, is everything okay?"

"Come," she said. "We will rest...and talk." At the end of the corridor, she stopped in front of an entry portal and gestured for him to enter the room beyond. "Wait in here. I'll be right back." With that, she turned away and her body faded from sight.

She used a contraction, Jay noted as he pushed through the membranous entryway. Eah and her family rarely used contractions when they spoke English; they did not understand combining words. Sometimes they would experiment, but only when they were trying to talk more like the Earth humans. *Maybe that's something good, then.*

Inside the room was a divan-like bed, a work table, some seats, storage nooks, and pieces of artwork in various stages of completion. Jay reclined on the soft divan and stared up at the black ceiling, wondering how the others were doing on their tour. He could still picture the shared expression of shock on everyone's faces after Keah revealed what he knew about the origins of life.

According to their host, a supreme being called Ahey created the universe and everything in it. On Earth, Ahey made the First Dyad—a human male and female—and then established doorways between habitable worlds so they could explore and eventually populate them.

The man and woman lived in unity with Ahey, but then something went wrong and they broke the bond between created being and Creator. Keah did not know exactly how the separation happened; the oral traditions of his people did not elaborate on it. All he knew was that the first humans rejected Ahey and chose to go their own way. Later, though, some of their children wanted to reunite with Ahey. This branch of offspring, known as the Ah-Ahey, used the space doorways to leave Earth and establish families loyal to the Ways of Ahey on other planets. Their rebellious siblings, the Dah-Ahey, remained on Earth, and conditions on that damaged world worsened. To slow their apostasy from spreading across the universe, Ahey closed every space portal and prohibited contact between the faithful people of the distant planets and the wayward humans of Earth.

Because the Ah-Ahey lived according to the Ways, their societies flourished. Ahey granted them superb health, long life spans, super-intelligence, and great wisdom. Within only a few generations, they discovered how to travel between galaxies. Soon afterward, they were visiting the other populated planets.

No one outside of Earth knew what life there was like. That apostates lived there was all anyone needed to know, and the Ways of Ahey were clear about how to treat that world; no human was to step foot on the planet called Blue. Ahey alone would manage its people, heal them, and restore them. The Ways spoke of this as a future salvation that would encompass the entire universe, bringing hope that Ahey would one day unify all humans and renew all worlds.

Keah's story was both astounding and familiar to Jay. He listened, along with Paul, April, and Yori, with great interest while Keah explained his religion's teachings. Perry and Ellis fidgeted during his long speech, but both men remained quiet. When Keah finished speaking, though, Ellis fired off a tirade of criticisms. The insensitivity of his comments shocked everyone. Paul, who was infuriated by Ellis's verbal attack, immediately rose to Keah's defense.

"Is it so hard to accept, Ellis, that the same people who possess such advanced scientific knowledge can also have a religion?" Paul had asked.

"Don't act like Keah's story doesn't affect you, Paul," Ellis shot back. "This has challenged *both* of our belief systems."

"Challenged?" Paul asked. "My religion hasn't taken a beating here —yours has! If what Keah said is true, those facts turn your beloved science on its head, while my beliefs remain supported."

"Supported by what? Similarities? Do you honestly think religious people back home will assimilate this knowledge into their systems of belief so easily? They'll reject such a questionable story! And it proves nothing—only that humans on other planets developed a religion strikingly similar to your own."

"What bothers you is that it might be *true,*" Paul countered. "Your adherence to the religion of science is being threatened. I can make peace with the idea of God creating other people and other worlds and—"

"I'm now agreeing with *you*, Perry," Yori said, interrupting Paul and Ellis. "This is but a small sample of the chaos you predict is happening back home."

Yori's comment ended the debate, which was threatening to turn into a heated argument. When tempers cooled, Eah stood up and announced her idea of resuming a tour of the wa-ah-ahea.

Even now, while Jay was lying on the divan and pondering everything Keah had said, his thoughts kept wandering to Eah. *At least our beliefs are compatible,* he thought. Her religion was, in fact, quite similar to his own. Besides the parts about life on other worlds and space doorways, the creation account was almost the same. *Could my God have allowed humans to leave the Earth and populate other planets?* he wondered. *It would account for the existence of Eah's people and the other ones I saw while we were in the city. How else could they have gotten to so many planets?* He rubbed tension from his forehead while he considered possibilities. *Did God create them out here? Ellis thinks they just evolved. If that's true, though, why do they all believe the same thing—the same story about Ahey?*

The earlier existence of space doorways made sense to Jay, and he was even more inclined to believe Keah when he considered the purity of the alien humans he had met. They never lied. *Also,* he thought, *evil hasn't touched them out here—at least, not until we showed up. There would be no reason to develop a religion just to stay in control of people, or to use as a crutch. They don't think in those ways. Their intentions are always good. Plus, they're extremely intelligent. With all their knowledge of science, why would billions of super-people choose to live by a myth—a lie?*

Jay knew there must be truth in what Keah said. At the moment, however, he was glad enough that the beliefs of Eah and her family did not contradict his own, and he counted that as a big win for his future relationship with her...if there was still to be one.

When Eah did not return right away, Jay rose and explored the room. The furnishings suggested he was in a studio where one could also rest. The divan was soft enough to sleep on, and the layout reminded him of his own multi-purpose bedroom at the youth ranch. *As much as I would miss Cody and a few other people,* he thought, *I can't go back there now—not after having experienced all this.* He poked his finger into the foam-like surface of a wall, and it brought back the memory of being aboard the other wa-ah-ahea, where he saw Eah for the first time. *I won't go back,* he decided. *Too much has changed. I've changed. If staying with her ends up being impossible, I'll have to find somewhere else.*

He waved his hand over some drawers to open them and found tools and miniature works of art. *So...an artist uses this room.* The pieces were beautiful—sculptures and small paintings created by a competent craftsman. Many of them were depictions of scenery and animal life on Hourou.

The last drawer was a long one that was built into the base of the divan. The first thing Jay discovered there was a painting that seemed to be made from dots of light instead of paint. It was a depiction of him in the forest—the time when he hiked through Hourou's wilderness with Eah and her siblings after their spaceship crashed. In this version of their journey, however, Jay was not wearing any clothing. He felt his face blush, so he put down the little picture and rummaged around to see what else was there.

Several objects were inside that he did not recognize, but two of them he did. Someone had found a fragment of his shirt and pressed it between translucent leaves along with strands of hair that matched his own. Further back in the drawer, there was a large piece of sheer material, saturated with an exotic flower scent. The cloth, in fact, smelled like Eah. It was only then he realized the purpose of the room. He was in Eah's quarters—her bedroom.

Hesitant to explore more, Jay closed the drawer and had just reclined on the divan again when Eah pressed her body through the entry portal. She was carrying a plate of food and two cups.

"You are hungry," she said softly, placing the cups on a table, "and so am I. Let us eat. Soon, we will make the first step away from Hourou, and it is better to eat *before* that."

Jay sat up. "How come?"

"Do you remember the steps that brought us to Hourou?"

"When I dematerialized and fell right through you," Jay recalled. "Yeah, I remember. So, it probably wouldn't be good to be eating or drinking when that happens again."

"I hear humor in your words," Eah said, smiling. "I am understanding more."

"Yes, you are." Jay decided to use an indirect approach to express his concerns. "I've, uh...been wondering if we'll be able to *continue*...learning from each other."

Eah wrapped herself in her hair and sat at the foot of the divan. "You speak about future things again. Yet..."

"No one can know the future," Jay stated. "That's true, but we're still both concerned about what's going to happen to us, aren't we?"

"Yes, but having concerns about what lies ahead is new to me, Jay."

"Then how do people on Hourou make plans?" he asked. "You have to consider what might be ahead so you can be prepared, don't you?"

"Yes. We study and contemplate, but we—"

"You don't obsess," Jay finished. "You don't worry about anything."

Eah nodded. "But now I am understanding more about worry," she admitted. "Have I learned this from you, Jay...or is it our *bonding* that causes worry?"

Jay scooted closer to her. "On my planet, bonding—love—causes many other emotions to surface. Some are enjoyable. But some, like fear of the unknown, are not. That makes us worry."

"Fear is something else I do not understand."

"I've seen that."

"Love—oha—does not cause fear or worry on Hourou. Such things cannot exist together with oha. Oha is...*pure* love."

Jay's gaze turned into a brief, blank stare as he recalled a powerful truth. "Perfect love casts out fear," he said in a whisper.

"What?"

"Perfect love casts out fear," he repeated. "It's something I was reading about back on Earth."

"In one of your...books? A collection of symbols that represent words?"

"Yes," Jay said with a chuckle. "But this is from our most *important* book...at least it is to me." He brushed some of her hair aside and, with a gentle motion, guided her chin so she would face him. "Eah, I want you to understand something. What you witnessed back on Hourou—what Carlson did—I would *never* do anything like that."

"I believe you, Jay."

"Good. I may not know a lot about the Ways of Ahey—at least not yet—but I can see how your beliefs and mine are almost the same. And, like you, I try my best to live by them."

Eah turned her body toward him, attentive to his every word.

"During our time together," he continued, "you've been showing me how similar we are as human beings. At first, I couldn't see it. We seemed so...different. But there's something that connects all humans wherever they live—no matter what color they are or how different they might seem on the outside. I think it's Ahey...and it's also love—*oha*. Does this make sense?"

Eah caressed his cheek with her fingertips as she spoke. "Yes. Ah-oha-nee, mee dyah."

"I love you, too," Jay said before leaning over and kissing her black lips. "I don't want to go back to my planet, Eah. I want to stay with you—to live with you and your people and learn more about the Ways of Ahey. I guess I've been...worried...that it might not happen now."

"Both of us must trust in the strength of our bonding," Eah insisted, "and in the purposes of Ahey. This is one of our tests."

"I understand, and I'm sorry for doubting. It's hard for me to have faith when my fate is being determined by other people."

"Only Ahey can determine your destiny, Jay. Your faith must be *there*." She offered him the plate of food she had brought as a way of changing the subject.

Jay took the hint. He scanned the selection and chose a fruit that resembled a purple strawberry. "I didn't know this was your room," he said between bites. "I've never been in a girl's bedroom before. Well, unless you count the time that the boys at our youth camp raided the girls' bunk house and tossed their stuff all over the place."

Eah raised a surprised eyebrow.

"You understood that, huh? Well, don't worry. The girls did a thorough job in the boys' cabin the next day."

"Such...raiding...is a game, then?" Eah asked.

"Yes. Something like that."

Jay grabbed a cup and gulped. By the time he placed it back on the table, a simultaneous flow of relaxation and invigoration was coursing through his body. To his astonishment and embarrassment, the sensation also caused a spontaneous physical arousal. He squirmed under Eah's gaze and tried to cross his legs. "What'd you put in that drink?" he asked with a chuckle. "It's, uh, pretty potent."

"It's the one April likes," Eah answered. "She said it makes her and Paul—"

"Never mind," Jay said, laughing. "I like it. It just has...strange side effects."

Eah giggled when she realized what he meant. After setting down the plate, she pushed her hair back and gazed at his body with admiration.

"I looked around the room a bit," he admitted. "I hope you don't mind."

"Mind?"

"I mean...I hope that was okay."

"Okay...yes."

Sometimes, she still sounded so foreign—so alien. Then there were times, like at present, when she mimicked his phrases and his language perfectly. Her utter humanness at that moment made Jay want to disclose more.

"Um...I saw your artwork," he said, watching for a reaction. "The one under your bed." Eah smiled, but because her skin color was such a deep black, he could not tell if she was blushing. "It's great," he continued. "On Earth, we'd say it looks like a photograph."

"Photograph?"

"An exact image. How did you make it?"

Eah reached down, opened the drawer under the divan, and pulled out the little painting of Jay. "I use tools to capture the light," she said as she ran her fingers over Jay's likeness. "Then I place the light onto the wood, and it holds the pattern."

"That's wood?"

Eah handed him the painting and closed the drawer. "Yes, the skin of a tree that holds light."

"For how long? I mean, how long will it last?"

"Long?"

"Sorry. I keep forgetting you measure time differently."

"Oh. Well...let me see. I think it'll last for *a good long time*."

Jay chuckled at her forced Earth-girl accent. "I'm glad." After she took the painting from him and placed it on the table, he gestured toward the base of the divan. "What about the other things in there?"

"Things? Oh...I..." She toyed with her hair and squirmed a bit.

So, he thought, *the Ah-Ahey* do *have some concept of privacy.* He decided not to pressure her about it. "It's okay, Eah. I don't mean to embarrass you." She flashed him a shy smile that expressed relief. "If that's a private drawer," he continued, "I'm sorry for opening it."

"Private means...exclusive? Personal?"

"Yes."

"Then it is personal to me, yes. We close our eyes with the things we cherish most."

"You mean...you sleep close to them?"

"Yes."

"Oh."

Jay recalled falling asleep in her lap when they were traveling through the forest. *That must have been when she took the piece of my shirt and the strands of my hair,* he guessed. It was also, he realized, when he felt the first signs of being in love. *I was so blind. She was already feeling that way and I couldn't see it.*

Eah motioned for him to recline on the divan. When he did, she cuddled next to him and draped her hair over them both like a blanket. They were quiet for a while, content to gaze into each other's watery eyes. When Jay could resist no longer, he kissed her, and Eah responded with a surge of emotion that almost overwhelmed his senses.

"Eah," he whispered, "I don't want this to change. I want—"

She pressed her lips against his, and the passion between them washed away any remaining concern.

"It will be okay," she said between kisses. "Remember...I love you, Jay."

* * *

Deep within the interior of the spaceship, Keah had taken Ellis, Paul, and Perry aside and was explaining how the vessel used the properties of dark matter to both propel and protect itself while traveling through space. In a different section, Ahee showed Yori and April the ship's spacious galley, a bathing area with a large pool, several rooms for recreation, and individual cabins for sleeping and storage. The women had just rounded the corner of a dim connecting corridor when they came upon Jay and Eah outside of Eah's quarters.

"Aha! So you sneaked off with Eah, huh, Jay?" Yori teased.

"Well, we just—"

"Why don't you join us?" April suggested.

"Sure."

Ahee shot a curious glance toward Eah before leading them all to a main hallway.

"Don't get them in trouble," April whispered to Yori.

"Oh, come on. We need a little levity around here. Everyone has become way too serious. Save all that for when we get back."

"I agree, Yori, but you shouldn't tease them. This might be their last day together."

Yori glanced at the couple behind them and frowned. "You're right. I hadn't thought of that."

"I'll be sad for them if they have to split up."

"Me, too."

Turning a corner, they met up with the other part of their group. Ellis and Perry were in the middle of a conversation about science, while Paul and Keah followed them and listened.

"What I don't understand," Perry was saying, "is how we're even walking. I didn't think about it during our first trip, but shouldn't we be floating around in here?"

"Oh. Hello, people," Ellis said to the approaching party. Then, back to Perry: "Carlson, you might not like my answer."

"Try me. What is it, artificial gravity?"

"There is some of that, right Keah?" Ellis asked.

"The wa-ah-ahea produces a force like gravity, yes."

"But it's not much," Ellis surmised. "You don't need a lot of gravity when you're using dark matter and semi-material objects."

"That is correct."

"Well, I *feel* material," Paul said as he patted himself down.

"If I have understood what you've shown us, Keah," Ellis said, "we have just enough physical substance to interact with our environment."

"What? We're like ghosts, then?" Yori asked.

"No, Yori," Ellis answered with guarded patience. "Remember on our first trip how I told you about dark matter?"

"Yes. You said something about turning matter inside out."

"Hiding normal matter within a shell of dark matter is more accurate," Ellis said. "However—and please correct me if I'm wrong, Keah—some of our normal matter remains exposed. That's why our senses still function and why we can interact with the minute amount of exposed matter in the spaceship and other objects around us."

"Yes, Ellis Minister," Keah said. "You understand much."

"When does the change occur?" Paul asked. "I've sensed nothing different."

"We were all changed as we boarded the wa-ah-ahea," Keah answered. "Within its walls, we remain this way."

"So it's automatic," Ellis surmised. "The whole idea baffles the mind a bit, but it makes complete sense."

"How so?" Paul asked.

"It makes traveling through space *safe,*" Ellis replied. "I'll explain more momentarily."

They had arrived at the entry portal of the main lounge, and several of them were already stepping through it. Once inside, they all settled into the seating area and stared at the massive viewing window. Since the lounge was in one of the wa-ah-ahea's triangular corners, they could look outward in multiple directions. Behind the ship, Hourou's nebula now resembled a distant purple cloud, and the planet itself was only a speck of light.

"You were saying something about traveling safely," Paul said to Ellis.

"Yes. Because the spaceship and its contents are somewhat immaterial, tiny solid objects floating around in space and harmful radiation pass right through. Neither the ship nor us can be damaged because a shield of dark matter is protecting our normal matter."

"What about damaging that small amount of normal matter?" Paul asked. "Wouldn't that cause a problem?"

"Obviously it doesn't," Ellis answered. "Otherwise, we would see each other get torn apart by dust particles, cooked by radiation, or pulverized by larger objects."

"It's hard to believe," April said. "I don't feel any different. How do our bodies keep functioning if we're, as you say, turned inside out?"

"To your mind and brain, you are still the same," Ellis replied. "Your body is quite real, and it works as normal within itself. You are fully here, April, but also hidden. It's a mystery to us, but Keah and his people have perfected the science. To tell the truth, it defies most of what I've learned and taught about physics."

"Sounds like we're now in the realm of *metaphysics*," Perry remarked.

Ellis smirked. "I think that's Paul's area."

"Hardly," Paul said. "But I study things that are beyond natural science."

"Paul is a professional student," April quipped. "When not teaching, he's studying something."

"And you...write...your knowledge in...books?" Eah asked.

"Very good, Eah!" April praised. "You've been learning about us! Yes, we write our words in books so others can learn by reading them."

"I understand," Eah said. "I would like to see some books from Earth."

"Well, when we get back, maybe..." A brief nonverbal exchange between Keah and Eah distracted April. It had something to do with Eah wanting to know more about Earth, but that was all she could interpret. "There, uh..." she continued, "is really so much more we could all learn from each other. Keah, will you want to meet others from our planet?"

Before he could answer, the surfaces of the room vibrated, and the ambient light dimmed.

"The first step begins now," Ahee said. "Soon, you will all be home."

* * *

Experiencing a brief period of immateriality while the wa-ah-ahea stepped into intergalactic space was not nearly as frightening for the Earth travelers as it had been during their first trip. Fear had been replaced by wonder, now that they knew a little about how the alien technology worked.

"How are we able to remain sitting?" Paul asked Keah. "Shouldn't we fall through our chairs?"

"Your seats are part of this vessel," Keah replied. "We build wa-ah-ahea from a material that has the properties of what you call dark matter. It maintains the structure of the wa-ah-ahea, keeps in air and light, and creates the force that holds everything in it together."

"I see." Paul tried to touch April, but his hand passed right through her arm.

"Now you try, April," Yori prompted, laughing.

"I'm afraid to! What if the step ends and my hand gets stuck in Paul's head?"

This time, Ahee laughed. "No, no, April. Such a thing could never happen. Your hand would be pushed away. Particles of matter, even dark matter, cannot occupy the same space."

As if to illustrate her point, Ellis's hand, which he had been holding inside his own head, was suddenly forced aside. When he touched his face again, he felt skin. "Extraordinary! Does this mean the stepping process is complete?" he asked Keah.

Keah rose from his seat. "Yes. We have stepped out of our galaxy and are now traveling to a point where we can step into yours."

"Keah," Ellis said. "Forgive my extreme scientific curiosity, but does this vessel *cause* the step?"

"The wa-ah-ahea makes small steps on its own, but to go further, we need the power of the ah-ey-ai."

"Ah-ey-ai are the giant cannons, right?" Yori asked. "Like the one that moved the mountain?"

"Yes," Ellis answered. "But the ones in space must be even more powerful. Am I correct, Keah?"

"Yes, because their energy crosses great distances. Each ah-ey-ai acts on a specific area of ahea—of space. We use some to create long rivers—channels—for the wa-ah-ahea to follow. Through those, we travel to points where the larger steps occur."

"So you make a series of jumps, from small to large?" Perry asked. "The ship can make small ones, the cannons make longer ones possible, and there are even bigger cannons to cover the greatest of distances?"

"That is indeed what Keah is saying, Carlson," Ellis said. "Thank you for translating it into layman's terms for the rest of us."

Perry ignored the jab. "Keah, why not build one big cannon rather than a bunch of smaller ones?"

Keah glanced at Ahee and motioned for her to answer. "The dark matter has limitations," she informed. "It is possible to use too much force on one point. When that happens, it will not bend. Instead, a hole forms that draws everything into itself."

"We call that a *black hole,*" Jay said.

"We do not wish to create more of those. Already, there are too many, and they can destroy worlds and galaxies. Our people are working on ways to close the holes, but we have not received the knowledge to do so yet."

"I am astounded by what you know already," Ellis praised.

"All knowledge is a reward from Ahey," Ahee stated, "and comes with much responsibility."

Keah took Ahee's hand and gave the group an apologetic bow. "We must leave you now to prepare for the step into your galaxy."

Eah, responding to a non-verbal signal from Ahee, rose and joined her parents.

"We will all return to you soon," Ahee said.

With that, the three of them left the room.

* * *

Ellis stood and paced the floor in front of the viewing window while the others either engaged in quiet discussions or sought refreshment in the adjoining galley. The Tadpole Galaxy now appeared very small. Ellis marveled at its splendor, but he still found the idea of traveling to a distant galaxy difficult to grasp. How could people with such intelligence also be bound by such archaic religious beliefs? In his mind, science and religion contradicted each other. Yet Keah acted as if the two were complimentary. How did he achieve so much while believing in myths and superstitions?

"Quite a view, isn't it?" Paul asked as he approached.

Ellis stopped pacing and stared at the swirling galaxy with its long tail. "That it is."

"If I'm not intruding on your thoughts, Ellis, I wanted to apologize for getting so angry earlier. You and I just approach things from different starting points. That's the reason we have a hard time understanding each other."

"There's no need to apologize," Ellis said. "I was getting heated, too. But please explain. What do you mean by 'starting points?'"

"Well...you look out there—at the universe—and start with an assumption, just as I do. You assume it all began with natural processes. I, on the other hand, accept that it all began with a supernatural process."

"You're talking about evolution versus creationism again."

"Yes. Two opposing starting points can't bring you to the same end point."

"Paul, you believe in the supernatural, while I only trust in the natural—what can be observed and measured."

"Exactly," Paul agreed. "You assume there's nothing more than that. But I'm willing to believe there *is* something more."

"If there are mysteries, it only means we haven't obtained knowledge about them yet. It doesn't have to mean they're beyond the natural or somehow unknowable. Given time, science debunks myth."

"Given time, science discovers and supports *truth*," Paul countered. "We're all searching for truth."

"And you think Keah has found that truth."

"You're a scientist, Ellis. Consider the results. Seeing the universe like Keah does has obviously propelled him far beyond us. While we still argue about evolving from apes, his people have been exploring galaxies."

Ellis chuckled. "True enough."

"Logically, should they be so far ahead? Why hasn't their religion held them back instead?"

"You want me to admit they may be right about some things, is that it?"

"I don't want you to do anything but consider what you've seen," Paul replied. "You're an observer. What do your observations lead you to conclude?"

"I can't answer that yet, Paul."

"I don't expect you to. There'll be plenty of time for that after we get home."

Ellis nodded slowly as he continued staring into space.

"And I'll be curious to hear your conclusions," Paul added.

"If that's an invitation to keep in touch," Ellis said, "I accept."

"It is. And thanks, Ellis."

"For what?"

"For your insights...and your friendship."

* * *

The Earth visitors remained alone in the lounge for quite a while before some of Keah's family joined them. Light conversation about space exploration seemed to relax everyone, and soon the young adults were offering to entertain their guests with tales of their family's adventures. Mahah and Maiha sang emotional duets about the beauty of a watery world called *Ieeay* where humans learned to live under the oceans. The loveliness of their singing brought tears to every eye. Then, Aai and Ua, as boys are apt to do, provided comedy by demonstrating their favorite wrestling moves. Tammah and Uio also had a turn at entertaining, showing off their works of art and telling fascinating stories about cultures on other planets.

Eah was the only sibling who had not returned to the lounge. Tammah said she must either have been busy working or with their parents. Jay assumed the latter, and his gut told him they were probably discussing her relationship with him. He wished he could be there to explain how he felt—that he loved Eah and wanted to stay with her. By herself, could Eah convince Keah and Ahee to accept her bonding? Would they dismiss it as an impossible fantasy, or would they at least let her try to make it work?

The step into the Milky Way Galaxy came and went without incident. From deep space, the spiraling mass of stars the Earth humans called home was a magnificent sight. Seeing it made everyone in the lounge feel a great sense of awe, and it was the only thing that could distract Jay from his worries.

"It's beautiful," April said while she and Paul stood in front of the viewing window.

"We're the first people to see our own galaxy like this," he noted. "Well...the first from Earth, at least."

"It looks so ordered," Yori commented, rising from her seat to get a better look.

"Indeed," Ellis agreed. "If I could venture a very *unscientific* observation—"

"Please do," Yori begged. "We've had enough science for one day."

Ellis chuckled. "I was only going to suggest that it looks...young."

"What makes you say that?" April asked.

"I don't know. It's just a feeling. Like I said...very unscientific."

"But still a wonderful thought," Yori praised.

Not wanting to be left out of the reverential moment, Perry rose and stood with them. "One step closer to home," he said in a whisper.

A soft noise at the entry portal behind them caused Jay to jump with anticipation. He spun around, hoping to see his elusive Eah, but it was only Tammah.

"Your eekaoa—your galaxy—is impressive," Tammah said. His black skin made it difficult to make him out until he joined them at the viewing window.

"We call it the Milky Way Galaxy," April said. "How many times have you been there, Tammah?"

"I have made many trips. It is home to several populated worlds, and we visit them as often as we can." He stepped closer to the transparent wall and pointed to an outer arm of the galaxy. "There is the planet called—well, we call it *Awheroea,* which in your language means pee-enk."

"Pink?" April asked. "Like the color pink?"

"Yes."

"You seem to name other planets according to their colors," Ellis noted.

"It's easier that way," Tammah said flatly. He gave a sly smile to show Ellis he was being jocular. "We will step into the Milky Way soon. I must leave now to prepare. You will be alone more often as we work, but if you need anything, send someone to us. You know the ways through the wa-ah-ahea."

"May I go with you?" Jay asked.

Tammah considered Jay's request for a moment and then nodded his consent.

"I hope you don't mind having me along," Jay said after they exited the lounge and headed down a long corridor. "I feel like I need something to do."

"No problem. I have to get the—what do you guys call it? The *hold?*—the hold ready for storing the rest of the other ship. You game for that?"

Jay grinned at Tammah's mimicry of his language and speaking style. Tammah had learned to use words and inflections to convey humor and camaraderie. It impressed Jay.

"I'm game," he replied with a chuckle. "How many pieces of the ship are still on Earth?"

"Only one large part," Tammah answered as they entered the cavernous cargo hold. "It contains the room for controlling."

"We call that the *bridge.*"

"Well, we could not retrieve the bridge section of that wa-ah-ahea. The crash must have buried it under *wheyuah*—the ground. Before we could get to it, Keah found where the Dah-Ahey had gone, so we left to search for them." Tammah walked to a control panel and waved his hands over its buttons and lights. "Sah was probably hiding in there. That's why he was not with Ria."

"Sah. Is that the one who was left behind?"

"Yes, *Sah.*" Tammah said his name with a hint of derision. "Ria told me about him when she was demanding to leave with us for Blue."

"It seems you don't like this Sah very much," Jay said.

"Like means to prefer?"

"Yeah. I guess so."

"Then, yes, I do not prefer Sah."

"Because he's Dah-Ahey?"

"No."

Jay expected Tammah to explain more, but he just kept working.

"From what Carlson said, it sounds like this Ria girl really wants to get Sah back. Is she related to him?"

"No."

Again, Jay waited for more information, but Tammah acted as if he was too preoccupied with his task to respond. Jay knew avoidance when he saw it, though; Tammah was only trying to look busy.

"You seem to know Ria pretty well," Jay said, continuing to probe. "I mean, to face off with her like you did when the Dah-Ahey showed up."

Tammah finished what he was doing and let out a long sigh. "Is everyone from Blue so per-sees-tent?"

"Persistent? No, but most of us are curious."

"Come then." He led Jay to a stack of crates and leaned against one while aiming a blank stare toward the empty hold. "It seems Ria intends to dyad with Sah when he comes of age."

"So, Sah is too young right now?"

"To you, Jay, Sah would look very young, yes."

"But Ria will wait for him to mature," Jay guessed. "When time doesn't matter, like on Hourou, and everyone eventually reaches the same level of maturity, waiting isn't a big deal, I suppose."

"Yes, Ria is good at waiting, but it seems she also promised to dyad with Wae."

"*Why-eh?* Is he the one who was with her in the field before we left? The one who she slapped?"

"Yes. That is Wae."

"Wow. That explains why Wae was so angry—Ria already planning to dyad with Sah. Is that even allowed?"

"No. The dyad is for two only...and for life."

"I understand. She was breaking the rules. Or was she hedging her bets?" Tammah looked perplexed by Jay's words. "Sorry. I mean, she set it up so that if one guy didn't work out, she would still have the other."

"So it seems, yes."

"On Earth, we call that playing the field."

"The dyad is precious, Jay," Tammah explained. "It is not to be promised with no thought and no caring. What Ria is doing—it is something the Ah-Ahey cannot even imagine. Do you understand this?"

"Yes. Many people on Earth, like me, take our relationships as seriously as you do."

"And the bonding...and the dyad...you understand these things as well?"

Now Jay was becoming a little nervous. He thought they were talking about Ria, but Tammah's questions sounded as probing as his own. Was this about Ria, himself, or about Jay and Eah?

"I think I do, yes," he answered. "We have similar customs on Earth. We promise ourselves to another, which we call getting engaged. Then we get married, which is sort of like your bonding."

"Do you also understand *breaking* the promise? When two promise it, but the dyad can never be?"

Jay took a moment to collect his thoughts. Did Tammah know about his bonding with Eah? If so, was he suggesting for Jay to break that bond? Was he saying their relationship was impossible?

Jay sat on a crate, stared at Tammah, and pushed strands of hair behind his ear, hoping the gesture would convey his desire to be candid. Tammah did the same, which told Jay he was ready to talk more openly.

"Look, Tammah," Jay said, "let's stop beating around the—I mean, let's speak clearly to each other."

Tammah cocked his head and leaned closer to listen. "Yes?"

"What are you *really* trying to tell me?"

"I am trying to explain a broken dyad, Jay. But how can I tell about something I do not understand?"

"*What* dyad?" Jay asked, bracing himself for the answer.

"My own."

Jay almost fell off of his crate. *So, it's about* him *and not me. But who would have been his dyad?* "Tammah, were you...did you bond with Ria?"

Tammah looked away, but his eyes had already exposed the ache in his heart. "You are perceptive, Jay," he said. "Yes, Ria and I had begun the bonding. We were to become dyad. But that was before she..."

"Before she became Dah-Ahey."

"Yes."

"I'm sorry, Tammah. I'm sorry for pushing, too."

"It's...okay."

"Now I understand a few things better. But why did Ria *become* Dah-Ahey? Why did she turn from the Ways of Ahey?"

"Those words I cannot speak right now."

"That's alright," Jay said. "But what about Uio? Eah said you and Uio were exploring dyad."

At the mention of Uio, Tammah brightened a bit. "Uio. Yes, Uio is a mystery. I burn for her, and she for me. But bonding with her has been…difficult."

"Eah says the two of you are much alike."

"Yes, I suppose we are. She is a beautiful *sohena*—a beautiful girl. I am very attached to her. She would make a good dyad, but I am not sure yet if we will complete the bonding. Some dyads are just not possible."

His last comment startled Jay. "I prefer to think that *anything* is possible, especially when it's right…and according to the Ways of Ahey."

"Yes," Tammah agreed, "and eventually we know. And if it is not meant to be, we must accept and keep searching."

"Sounds like relationships are the same no matter what planet you come from," Jay said with a chuckle.

An awkward silence remained after his statement. Jay wondered what to say next. Before he could think of something smart, Tammah stretched his arms and shook himself from any remaining pensiveness.

"Now, I must return to the bridge, and you should go back to your friends."

"You are also my friend," Jay said.

Tammah stepped close to him, placed his hand on Jay's chest, and looked deep into his eyes as he spoke. "We are *brothers*, Jay."

Jay smiled and repeated Tammah's gesture. "Brothers," he agreed. "No matter what."

* * *

Tammah's acceptance made Jay feel better about his chances with Eah, but as he followed the young man out of the hold, he wondered how much of their intimate conversation was also some sort of test. He could tell Tammah was reading him the entire time; there was a probing curiosity in his facial expressions and body language.

Halfway down the corridor, Tammah stopped abruptly and stared at the floor, deep in thought.

"What is it?" Jay asked.

Tammah did not answer, but after a few moments, a satisfied smile parted his lips.

"Is everything alright, Tammah?"

"Yes." He looked up at Jay and nodded. "Come, Jay. It is time."

"Time? Time for what?"

Taking Jay by the wrist, Tammah led him in haste to a nearby entry portal. When they reached it, he released Jay, smiled, and motioned for him to enter the room beyond. "You have given me something that I need, Jay, and now I am giving what *you* need."

"I don't understand, Tammah."

With a gentle push, Tammah guided Jay into the portal. On the other side, he found a small storage space stacked with colorful boxes. Toward the back, two white bodies glowed amidst the containers while they opened them and noted their contents. It was Keah and Ahee. When they looked up from their work, Jay could tell they had been expecting him.

"Jay," Keah said in greeting as he closed a small box. "Since Tammah sent you to us, we know he approves of your bonding with Eah."

Jay stood dumbfounded in front of the portal. "Uh...since Tammah...sent me?"

Ahee tossed her hair behind her back and stepped toward him, smiling brightly to ease his surprise and obvious discomfort. "He made you a brother, did he not?" she asked.

"Uh...I...well...yeah, he told me we're brothers."

"This is part of the bonding, Jay. Did Tammah explain more?"

"No, he just brought me here."

Ahee shared a glance with Keah and then continued. "When a woman initiates dyad, as Eah has done, the male sibling who is closest to her own age must recognize the bonding. That is Tammah...and he has recognized your bond."

"By *recognize,* do you mean *accept?*" Jay asked. "Does he have to approve of it?"

"There is no approval...beyond that of Ahey," Keah explained. "Tammah's recognition symbolizes his trust in the bond, and that is a sign to us. Am I using your words well?"

"Yes. Very well. But what about you? What about *your* approval? After all that happened on Hourou, I thought—"

"Jay," Ahee interrupted, "when things happen we cannot explain, we trust in the Ways of Ahey. We hope that as unusual as it might appear, it is still *within* the Will of Ahey. We cannot know reasons for everything...so we simply trust and wait. Do you understand this?"

"Yes. I believe that, too. But trusting in the Ways of Ahey isn't the same as blindly accepting what is happening, is it?"

"You seek our approval for a dyad with Eah," Keah surmised.

"Yes," Jay admitted. "That's usually how we do it on my planet."

Ahee wrapped herself in her hair and stepped back among the boxes. "On Hourou, there is no approval by parents. *Recognition* is a better word, or maybe *acceptance.* But this only comes after the testing. Did Eah explain this?"

"She mentioned a testing of the dyad, yes."

"There will be much for you to learn, Jay," Keah said.

Jay stiffened with anticipation. Did this mean they were going to let him stay with Eah...with them?

"Yes," Ahee confirmed, as if reading his thoughts. "If you still desire it, Jay, you may remain with us and continue the bonding, according to the Ways of Ahey. And we all must trust that our meeting, and your dyad, and all that comes afterward have been meant to happen."

Jay sensed a flood of emotion emanating from Ahee and mixing with his own feelings of relief and wonder. *I can stay! I can stay with Eah and this family.*

"This makes you happy?" Keah asked with a chuckle.

"Y-yes," Jay stammered. "I...I don't know what to say."

"Your eyes speak for you," Ahee said with a smile. "Using many words is unnecessary among our people."

"Right. I've been learning that."

"And learning is what you will continue to do," Keah said with firmness. "If you master the Ways and your dyad remains strong against the testing…you shall gain what you desire."

"Your acceptance of our dyad is all I want."

"Then learn," Ahee said with finality, "and build upon the Ways already inside you."

"I will."

With that, Keah and Ahee returned to their tasks, conveying the conversation was over. After a polite bow, Jay stepped backward and allowed the portal to swallow his body and move him out of the room. He then hurried down the corridor to search for Eah.

I'm going to make this work, he promised. *For all of us.*

CHAPTER 35

Home

With her coat pulled taut and arms wrapped tightly across her chest, Laura leaned on the rail of the high scaffold where she had perched herself earlier that night. *How long have I been up here?* she wondered. The first light of morning was just chasing the weaker stars from the sky. It was cold; she could see her breath. *Another all-nighter,* she thought. Cindy, her esthetician, would have her work cut out for her. Laura imagined the girl's lecture about sleep deprivation, saggy eyelids, and expensive treatment plans. She huffed, creating a puff of white vapor. *Why in the world am I thinking about beauty tips right now?*

Like an owl on the bough of a tall tree, her keen eyes darted along a wide radius, searching for signs of movement on the ground. Her perch was made of cold metal—fenced scaffolding that surrounded the Remnant. Now unearthed, the spaceship fragment resembled a giant triangle of light-absorbing obsidian. A squad of soldiers patrolled the inside of its encircling cage and guarded its only entryway. On the other side, military and civilian personnel continued to search the rest of the compound for the escaped alien child.

They won't find him, Laura's intuition told her. *He's long gone.* Because the boy could not return to the Remnant, which was the only thing familiar to him, his only choices were giving himself up or fleeing the site. It had been eleven hours since he disappeared, so it was clear he was not going to just turn himself in. That meant escaping was his plan. Laura believed he must have somehow breached all the layers of security and surveillance. *He could be miles away by now.*

As Laura saw it, there were only two downsides to being on the wall alone: she had too much time to brood over losing the boy, and there was no cover from the heavy dew that had fallen during the night. Her hair was damp and matted, and she hated to think how the rest of her must have looked. *I'm a mess,* she thought, *in more ways than one.* Scanning the busy compound yet again, she balled her hands into fists and frowned. "Where *are* you?" she asked in a whisper. "Don't you understand we're only trying to help?"

The sound of muted footsteps climbing a nearby metal spiral staircase seemed to answer her. She spun toward the noise and held her breath. *Could the kid have been in the scaffolding all this time?* She tensed and imagined herself pouncing on his invisible form like a cat. The footsteps stopped. A few seconds later, they continued. Laura stared wide-eyed at the top step, wondering if the universe was finally going to play fair by bringing the boy to her. When she saw a head of blond hair appear in the stairwell, she let out a long sigh and slumped her shoulders in defeat. *I guess today won't be my day.*

"Ah. There you are," Alex said from atop the last stair. "I have some good news."

"I can't handle getting my hopes up anymore," Laura snapped. "Just give me a plain old report."

"Yes, Ma'am," he retorted in an exaggerated official-like tone. "Oversight of the Remnant is now under Operation Fair Trade. Doctor Haines has yielded—with some reluctance—to orders that place the Agency in full authority at the site. Of course, the Colonel is still in charge of security, but this means the entire show belongs to you and the Agency."

Laura shrugged with indifference. "Good for us."

"Aren't you the least bit glad?"

"I'm not sure how to feel anymore, Alex." She turned away from him and glared at the Remnant. The light-swallowing blackness of its featureless surface seemed to mock her new authority. It dared her to try extracting its secrets. *We could spend years studying this chunk of alien scrap just to learn what it's made of,* she thought. *But the boy—if only I had him. He could tell us so much...*

Alex joined her at the railing. "What's wrong?"

"I'm afraid our little friend is gone."

"Why? What makes you say that?"

"A gut feeling. We should have been able to find him by now, even with his camouflaging ability. A mouse couldn't sneak around down there without setting off a sensor or being spotted."

Alex nodded toward the Remnant. "Could he have made it back into *that?*"

"No. They secured it long before he escaped."

"Still, he might have found a way."

"No. He's gone, Alex. I just know it."

Alex pulled out his phone and tapped on its screen. "Then I'll direct Jacobs to expand the search to the outside. She'll need more agency support teams. Also, priority designation to get defense cooperation."

"Better tell Colonel Richter right away," Laura suggested. "No one gets out of here without his approval." She pictured the lost boy in her mind. *No one except a strange bronze-colored alien child, at least.*

"I'll go to him first," Alex agreed, turning to leave.

"Alex." Laura took hold of his arm, but she kept staring at the Remnant. "Do whatever it takes. I want an airtight perimeter around this site covering a minimum of six miles."

"Alright. You'll get it."

"Think about how we can make our friend visible, too—spray something harmless on him so he can't disappear."

"Got it."

"From the air, too," Laura added. "Tell them to dust the open areas. That way, he might walk in it."

"Could cause quite a mess," Alex noted. "This is a nature preserve. There's bound to be pushback." The look on Laura's face showed him she did not care. "Alright. I'll find something safe that'll coat him as well as track footprints."

Laura faced him and her eyes bored into his as she spoke. "Whatever it takes. I want that boy back...before his friends come looking for him."

"We'll get him."

"That's what Richter said, too."

Alex frowned. "Laura, maybe we should also consider—" He stopped short when he noticed the surrounding air becoming charged with energy. "Um...what is this?" The hair on his arms and neck rose, then a tingling sensation crept through his entire body. From Laura's shocked expression, he could tell she felt it, too.

"Alex...we have to get down from here!"

Before they could reach the staircase, a powerful gust of wind blasted down on them from somewhere in the dark sky. Caught unprepared, Alex lost his grip on the railing and stumbled onto the catwalk. His knees hit the metal with a bang, but he twisted his body around in enough time to catch Laura as she tumbled over him. They struggled to get up, but the intensity of the windstorm had them pinned.

On the ground below, swirling gusts of wind tossed debris into the air while alarms blared all over the compound. Unsuspecting personnel toppled and fell as if knocked over by an invisible, immobilizing force. Those who found cover were gawking and pointing at the treetops where, through a cloud of dust and dirt, a massive black triangle hovered over them all.

When the buffeting subsided, Laura pushed herself off Alex and scanned the sky. Though its outline was hard to make out in the darkness, she saw the unmistakable shape of another alien spacecraft, and it was much larger than the one she had seen in photos. "They're...back," she whispered.

Alex jumped to his feet and joined Laura in gaping at the sight of the black triangle. "Something's happening," he murmured. Seconds later, a dark purple ray shot from the craft's belly and lit up the Remnant like a spotlight.

"No, no, no, no!" Laura cried when she realized what was about to happen.

The steady beam of energy lifted the Remnant from the ground and dragged it toward the underside of the spacecraft. Then, just before it made contact, the fragment of alien vessel dematerialized and vanished.

Laura yanked Alex's arm and ran to the staircase. "Come on!"

Alex followed her down, all the while keeping a wary eye on the spaceship through the scaffolding. When they reached the ground, Laura bolted to the middle of the compound, heedless of the buried sensors.

"Laura, wait!" Alex shouted, trailing behind.

Colonel Richter was already there, trying to bark orders to a squad of soldiers over the compound's blaring alarms. "...and shut off those blasted alarms!" When someone inside the main building did so, an eerie hum from the hovering spaceship replaced the cacophony. "You two should be behind cover!" Richter yelled to Laura and Alex as he surveyed the rest of the compound. "Major, take these two to shelter!"

The Major stepped toward Laura to usher her away, but she refused to move.

"Listen, Miss Turgis," Richter said, noting her obstinacy, "until we know what we're dealing with here, you and your people are going to do as I say. Now, clear the field!"

"I think we *all* had better do that, sir," Alex said, pointing upward.

Richter glanced up and saw a purple spot forming on the belly of the triangle. "Move!" he yelled.

Everyone in the center of the compound ran for cover just before another beam of energy hit the ground where they had been standing. Long seconds passed until something materialized within the light. It resembled a giant blob of mixed colors at first. Then it separated into six distinct, ghostlike figures.

Laura recognized each of them when their particles coalesced enough to show individual features. "Thank God they're safe," she whispered. Then she yelled to Richter: "Those are our abductees, Colonel!"

When the purple beam withdrew, Richter leaped from behind cover and motioned for his soldiers to advance with him toward the six fully formed people. Laura and Alex followed, as did Agent Jacobs, after Alex signaled her to join them.

"Are you people alright?" Richter asked the disoriented abductees. "Is anyone injured?"

A man stepped forward. "We're all fine," he replied.

Laura recognized him from her file photos. It was Paul Theele.

"You might find us some fresh sets of clothes, though."

Laura thought it was a strange suggestion until she noted the condition of their clothing. The fragments that were left hanging on them all looked threadbare, as if deteriorated by time.

"Right. I'm on that," Jacobs said, her mobile already raised to her ear.

"Are you sure no one needs immediate medical attention?" Richter asked the group.

"All of us are quite healthy, Colonel," replied another man. "I'm Perry Carlson, Congressional Armed Services Committee. Who's in charge here?"

"Military operations at this site are under my command," Richter answered. He gestured to Laura. "Director Laura Turgis—from The Agency—oversees all matters pertaining to the alien visitations."

"Very good," Perry said. "Director Turgis, we need to set up an immediate debriefing. I'm sure there will be some sort of quarantine, but we can't waste any time. There is much to discuss."

Not so fast, Congressman, Laura thought. She was not about to acquiesce to a pushy politician and recent abductee. Her agency had almost complete autonomy. She would have to make that clear to him, but not while standing underneath an alien spaceship. "I agree about a debriefing, Congressman," she replied, "but Colonel Richter and I first need information about the intentions of those who are in that object up there. Can you tell us about—"

"We'll take this one step at a time," Richter interrupted. "Right now, the safety of everyone here and the security of this site are *my* priorities."

He turned to address the abductees again. "I'll move you all to a safer location."

"We're in no danger, Colonel," said a woman who Laura recognized as April Theele. "*No one* is in danger."

Richter considered the hovering spaceship, but then motioned for his soldiers to take up strategic positions around the group. "Just the same, Ma'am, I have a responsibility."

"Excuse me, Colonel," Laura said. "I also have a responsibility." She flashed her identification badge at the former abductees. "My name is Laura Turgis. I oversee a special agency that has been investigating your disappearances. Can any of you tell us what the visitors intend to do? Are they friendly, or—"

"Miss Turgis..." Richter began.

"I'm sure their answers will have important security ramifications, Colonel," Laura interrupted.

"We can discuss this from an area of safety," Richter said, trying to hold back his temper.

"Excuse me," the other woman in the group said, "I'm Yori Shimizu. Can you tell us how long we've been away?"

"Four days," Laura informed. "This morning begins the fifth day since your disappearances."

The abductees glanced at each other as if taken aback by Laura's answer.

"Why do you ask?"

"We lost all track of time," Yori replied. "To us, it's been at least twice as long...at least."

"Absolutely extraordinary," said the man Laura knew to be Ellis Minister. "Like a time warp. The days were longer there, but time was slower here. It boggles the mind."

"I'm sure you all have many questions," Laura said, "and so do we, but the most important thing right now is what the visitors intend to do next."

A young man stepped forward who Laura recognized as Jay Harrison. "That depends on *you*," he said.

"What do you mean?" Richter asked.

"They want the one who was left behind."

Laura and the Colonel shared furtive glances.

"I see you know about him," April said. "You don't have to hide anything."

"There's nothing *to* hide," Laura shot back. April's probing stare was making her uncomfortable.

"I can tell that's true. Your words have a double meaning."

"Colonel?" Perry prompted.

"He's not here," Richter said.

Perry stepped toward him with a knowing look in his eyes. "You've seen him, then. Where is he?"

"This needs to be discussed in a debriefing," Richter stated, "and among people with the appropriate clearance."

"Colonel, there is no need to withhold information," Perry said in a commanding tone. "Director Turgis asked about the visitors' intentions. The crashed spaceship—and the person they left behind—are their only concerns. They have their chunk of ship back. Now, tell us about the boy."

"Carlson is correct," Ellis Minister agreed. "If the lad is in your care, they expect you to turn him over to them, right here...and right now."

"That's a problem then," Richter said.

"Why?" Jay demanded.

"Because we don't have him anymore," Laura answered, noting their individual reactions.

"Where he is?" Perry asked. "This is of the utmost importance."

"With all due respect," Laura replied, "your return, although hoped for and somewhat expected, has caught us off guard. We've been in the middle of—"

"I need to know," Perry interrupted. He pointed at the hovering spaceship. "*They* need to know."

Laura glanced upward. The alien visitors must have been watching them. *Why not come out and show yourselves?* she wondered. Perhaps, though, it was better for them to stay inside. How would they react to the news that Laura and her people found the little boy and then allowed him to run away?

"He was here as recently as eleven hours ago," she told the group. "During an examination, he disappeared and slipped through our fingers. We've been searching for him ever since. I fear he's left the site and is now somewhere within a six-mile radius. We were about to expand the search when you—"

"Paul," Jay interrupted as he turned toward Paul Theele. "You know..."

"Go ahead, Jay," Paul said, placing his hands on the younger man's shoulders. "We've got this."

April Theele approached Jay and gave him a hug. When she released him, he stood apart from the group and looked at each of them with great fondness.

"Wait!" Laura demanded. "What's happening? What's going on?"

"It's okay," Paul said. "Jay is an emissary. He needs to tell them about the boy."

When Jay stepped a little further away, Laura lurched in protest.

"Let them make the next move, Director Turgis," Richter suggested, taking hold of her arm.

Jay waved at the spaceship as a signal to bring him up. "Don't worry," he said to Laura, noting her anxious expression. A slim beam of purple light spotlighted him and lifted his body into the air. "I'll be fine." When he reached the ship's belly, he dematerialized and disappeared.

"Now...we should go inside, Colonel," Perry said. "Our priority going forward is to get that boy back for them, and I intend to see it done. I want a secure phone and a private place to talk." Richter and Laura both glared at him with blatant suspicion and defiance. "Okay. We seem to have a little authority problem here. My phone call will clear that up right away. Lead on, Colonel."

Richter wasted no time in steering the group toward the compound's command center. As they walked the short distance, he barked out orders to his soldiers. Some of them escorted non-military personnel to safety, while others took up protective positions underneath the floating alien ship.

Before they all entered the building, Laura noticed that Paul and April Theele had fallen behind and were looking up at the spaceship and waving at one of its corners. Laura froze as a sudden realization came upon her. Before she could react, a rush of wind blew down into the compound again and the giant vessel rose above the treetops. Seconds later, it shot away from the site in a black blur.

Laura ran to the Theeles and watched with them as the ship disappeared from sight. "You knew about this!" she accused. "What are you thinking? What about Jay Harrison?"

"He'll be fine," April said, wiping a tear from her eye.

The three of them gazed up at the empty morning sky.

"So that's it," Laura said. "They're gone?"

"They'll find the missing one before they leave," April replied with confidence.

"Carlson can look all he wants," Paul added, "but he won't find him. Of all people, he should recognize what he's up against."

"Will they ever come back? Will they return Jay Harrison?"

"We don't know if they'll be back," April answered, wiping away more tears. "As for Jay...he's finally found a family."

"A what?"

Neither of the Theeles offered further explanation. All around them, compound personnel recovered from their surprise and gawked at the empty place where the Triangle had been hovering.

"Paul! April!" Perry called from the doorway of the main building. "Let's go! There's work to be done here."

"Work? What is he talking about?" Laura asked.

"You tell *us*," Paul quipped. "What's been going on since we've been away?"

"You mean besides the whole world being thrown into chaos over the existence of alien beings?"

"That bad, huh?" Paul asked.

"Yeah...that bad."

"Nothing will ever be the same for any of us," April said. "Paul, how do we go back to our old lives after what we've been through? I feel changed...do you?"

"Changed how?" Laura asked. "Are you both okay? Were you harmed in any way?"

Paul chuckled. "We've just had a taste of Eden, Miss Turgis. Now...we'll have to live without it again. That's the only harm done to us."

"Director Turgis?" Two heavily armed soldiers had come up behind them while they were talking. "The Colonel wants to see you inside—all of you."

Laura nodded. "Yes, we'd better go in."

While following the escorts, one question kept nagging at Laura. She knew protocol demanded that she wait for an official debriefing. But the Theeles were here now, in a relatively private setting, and she would only have them to herself for about a minute more. "Mister Theele, Missus Theele," she said, "may I ask you something off the record?"

"You're wondering why they didn't show themselves," April guessed, "and why they didn't make contact."

"Yes." Laura was surprised by April's intuitiveness. How did the young woman read her so easily?

"Their people and ours are not very compatible," Paul answered.

"I see."

"We'll explain more later," Paul said. "For now, if you get nothing else out of this experience, at least you know for certain that there's other intelligent life out there. Who knows? Maybe someday, when the time is right..."

CHAPTER 36

All in Good Time

When Jay entered the bustling bridge, he found Eah's family already engaged in their search for the lost Dah-Ahey boy, Sah. *I may be a kind of emissary among them,* he thought, *but they sure didn't need a messenger.* As on Hourou, they had been listening to what was happening on the ground. As soon as Director Turgis announced Sah had fled, they prepared for the chase.

Eah was the only one to acknowledge Jay's return; everyone else was busy at their workstations. She smiled at him in her usual bright way and gestured toward Uio and Aai, who were standing in front of a viewport and studying the landscape. Jay joined them, hoping to be of some help.

"Welcome back, Jay," Uio whispered. She flipped her hair behind her body and Jay smelled the familiar fragrance of Hourou's tropical flowers. Yori had told him once that Ah-Ahey females did not use perfumes, and that the scent was actually human pheromones. He breathed in and smiled, pleased with himself for easily discerning the difference between Uio and Eah.

"Thanks, Uio," he replied. "I guess we have something in common now."

"In common?"

"We both found the perfect family to live with."

Uio grinned and poked Jay in the ribs with her elbow. "You do not fool me, Jay Harrison. You are here for more than just this family."

"What? What are you talking about?"

Uio nodded toward Eah, who was busy at work behind a flashing control panel.

"So, everyone knows about us now? Great." He returned her poke, which inadvertently contacted something a little higher than her ribs. Uio yelped in surprise. "Oops. Sorry!" He gave her an apologetic hug, but she kept examining and rubbing the spot to needle him into further embarrassment. "I can tell you're going to be a problem for me, Uio."

"Problem?"

"On Earth, we'd call you a show-off...a jokester."

"Problems are off-showing jokes?" she asked with a giggle. "Jay, the words you use are—"

Aai cleared his throat as an interruption. "Search now, Uio. Play with Jay later."

Uio huffed and went back to scanning the landscape. Jay chuckled and did the same, despite not understanding how they hoped to locate a small person from several hundred feet above the passing ground. As Jay stared through the viewport, though, he noticed that squinting sometimes brought hidden symbols and lines into view on its inside surface.

So, if you look at a viewport or window in the right way, he reasoned, *they become viewing screens. I wasn't able to pick up on that before.* Jay squinted and refocused until he could see the readouts on the glass with ease. Of course, what he saw meant very little to an Earth human who had no experience with their unusual technology. Still, Jay recognized that the symbols represented data and the lines formed a grid. *Uio and Aai aren't just searching with their eyes,* he surmised. *They're using instruments to scan the ground for Sah.*

Jay refocused on the passing landscape. He had always loved forests, but after experiencing the beauty of Hourou, the harsh woodlands of Earth would never again satisfy him. He marveled at the contrasts between the planet below him and the one he now affectionately thought of as the Planet of Eden.

Only minutes ago, he was standing with his friends on the hard ground in some sort of military compound. The surrounding air, once familiar and life-giving, smelled stale and lacking. Nature, which he once adored, was fierce and unwelcoming, not like that of Hourou, which radiated beauty and safety. The humans he encountered seemed more foreign to him, too. They were his people—those soldiers and government agents—yet after experiencing the virtue and peacefulness of the Ah-Ahey, they now resembled suspicious strangers.

I don't belong there. Never did.

Paul Theele said as much when the traveling companions were expressing their goodbyes in the hold of the wa-ah-ahea before Keah transported them all down to the surface.

"You belong where your heart is," Paul had said during their last moments together in the alien vessel. "Your heart is obviously here, Jay—with Eah and her family. So stay with them...and be confident that it's all part of a bigger purpose for your life."

"And," April added, "if there's a way, you'd better come back to visit us." She wrapped him in a tight hug and kissed him on his cheek as she pulled herself away.

"I will," Jay promised, though he wondered if he would ever see them again.

Yori rushed over and smothered him in her own embrace. "Jay, we may have only met a short time ago, but after all we've been through, I feel as if...well...you're like a brother to me."

"I know what you mean."

"You just take good care of that girlfriend of yours," Yori warned. "Eah deserves the best."

"Thanks. But I think we might already be past that stage."

"My, my!" Perry joked, offering a handshake. "Young Mister Harrison moves fast when he's inspired!"

Jay grasped his hand and smiled, unsure of what to say.

"Look, Jay," Perry said, "I hope you've forgiven me for offending you back on Hourou, and that you'll help Keah in cleaning up the trouble I started for him and his people."

"I'll try, Mister Carlson."

Ellis approached Jay last. The two men shook hands, and then Ellis pulled Jay into a big bear hug. "As the others have already expressed, this is like saying goodbye to a close relative, Jay."

"For me, too."

"You're absolutely sure about staying, then?"

"Absolutely sure."

"You could come back and be a star—a very rich one."

"No, thanks. I have everything I need right here."

Ellis followed his gaze to Eah, who was waiting nearby. "Yes, you do," he agreed.

Eah had changed her skin color from black to white. It was an apt change; she resembled the Eah they had all grown to adore during their visit to Hourou. Responding to Jay's glance, she joined the group in the center of the hold, where many hugs and kind words awaited her.

Soon, the rest of Eah's family arrived, and everyone expressed more goodbyes and well-wishes. When it was almost time to transport them to the surface, Keah and Ahee led them to a purple-colored portal on the floor and Keah told them of his plans.

"The remaining part of the stolen wa-ah-ahea is below us now," he said. "Your people have found it; there is even a large gathering of them nearby. Still, we will recover it before sending you down."

"I can tell you're concerned about them being there," April noted.

"Yes," Keah admitted. "I prefer for us and our activities to be unseen."

"I guess that means you've decided against opening relations between our two planets," Perry assumed.

"Yes. Jay will go down with you, but we shall remain here until he returns with information about Sah."

"I hope you change your mind someday, Keah," Ellis said. "Our people could learn a lot from you and the Ah-Ahey, and we'd be able to teach you about this planet you call Blue."

"I wonder about that," Paul mused. "If it was reciprocal, Keah would go down with us right now. As it is, I'm not sure we have much to teach *them* at all." Paul immediately regretted his words. "I'm sorry," he said to the group. "That sounded harsh."

Keah gestured toward Jay. "Jay can be a teacher among us, Paul. From him, we will learn more about your planet and its people. Then, if the Ways of Ahey permit it, we may return...*sometime down the road.*"

Keah's playful emphasis on the Earth phrase lightened the mood and offered hope.

"I like the sound of that," April said. "I can't believe meeting you all was just an accident."

"It wasn't," Yori agreed. "In my heart, I know this isn't an ending...but some sort of new beginning...for all of us."

Ahee hugged and kissed Yori a final time before ushering her family away from the transporting area. Then she stepped over to a control panel and waved her glowing white hands over its colored button.

"Ooo-oh-yee...sisters...brothers."

That was the last thing Jay heard before all sounds became muffled and violet light appeared all around him. A familiar tingling sensation numbed his entire body. Then the ship's hold disappeared. In the blink of an eye, he was standing with his friends in a lighted military compound with soldiers rushing toward him.

The memories of those last moments together would always remain special to Jay. Even now, back on the bridge of the spaceship, he still felt sad having to part with them. That was another unusual experience. In the past, it was easy for him to accept the inevitability of parting with people. When moving from family to family became routine, relationships were short-lived. Now, most dramatically, that had all changed. He had new friends, a new family, a new home, and a new love. This time, the change would be permanent. In his mind, there was no going back.

Jay stopped watching the passing scenery and gazed across the bridge at Eah. She could always sense that he was looking at her. Though busy working, she glanced his way and smiled to acknowledge his attention. So as not to distract her further, he gave a quick wink and turned again to the window. *If I were Sah, where would I go?* he wondered as he considered the forest below. Of course, Eah's family would find the boy. With their amazing technology, it was just a matter of time. What happened after that was the bigger problem. Sah was only a youth, but in the culture of Hourou, he still had a say in things. Would he agree to return with Keah, or put up a fight?

Fighting, Jay thought. *For all we know, the Ah-Ahey and Dah-Ahey are on the brink of a full-fledged war.* What was going to happen on that pristine planet now that the two people groups had witnessed and experimented with violence for the first time? How could Keah and the Ah-Ahey fix something that was caused by evil when they only knew good? *Maybe that's where I come in. I might be the catalyst for repairing Carlson's damage.* On a world untainted by hatred, deceit, and violence for thousands of years, one earthman taught them in a day how to lie and fight. To make things right, another man from Earth would have to unteach them. *How do I even start?*

Jay glanced back at Eah again and considered their relationship. Her customs were still so foreign to him. Her people had welcomed him as a visitor, but would they accept this alien as her mate? They were both human, but Eah was a superior one. Was he compatible with her in every way? Or would she always be comparing him to perfect Ah-Ahey men?

As if sensing his concern, Eah turned toward him and their eyes met. *I love you,* she said through their bond.

And I, you.

Though he had many questions, Jay allowed Eah to fill his mind with thoughts of the peaceful ways of her people, of their complete openness and acceptance, and of his new family. His heart warmed. Back on Earth, just before his unusual adventure, he was searching for a place to experience peace *away from* the rest of humanity. Now, he had finally found peace *with* humanity. There, in that spaceship, was everything he had ever wanted, and he no longer felt, nor desired to be, alone in the universe.

CAST OF CHARACTERS

(in order of appearance)

Jay Harrison

Twenty-two-year-old, male youth ranch counselor who lived most of his life as an orphan and has all but given up on his dreams of finding the perfect family.

Cody Milner

Sixteen-year-old youth ranch camper and friend of Jay Harrison.

April Theele

Thirty-something stay-at-home mother of two sons, Dex and Vince, and married to Paul Theele. April seeks to balance her life as a mother and a wife. She is devoted, caring, highly intuitive, and also competitive, having achieved much success in collegiate athletics.

Paul Theele

April Theele's husband. Paul teaches computer science at a local tech school while also pursuing a Master's degree. Paul dreams of slowing his life down a little so that he can enjoy more time with April and his sons.

Officer Brenan

Local police officer who witnesses the abduction of Jay Harrison and the Theeles.

Keah

Male alien human from the planet Hourou. Keah is a space explorer who travels with his wife, Ahee, and their children. His people consider him to be an authority on space travel.

Ahee

The wife of Keah. Ahee cares for her family while also performing important technical duties aboard her family's vessel. She is wise and nurturing, with an interest in interpersonal relations.

Eah

Oldest daughter of Keah and Ahee. Eah is a specialist in communications and an excellent artist. She has recently reached the age of mating and desires a husband, but she is saving her love for an unconventional man.

Tammah

Oldest son of Keah and Ahee. Tammah is a builder and craftsman. He is quiet and cautious, but also exhibits strong leadership. He is exploring a close relationship with Uio.

Uio

Female Ah-Ahey from another part of Hourou who is living with Keah's family during her formal education. Uio is a tomboy—bold and competitive, but she is also very feminine and fun to be around.

Aai

Son of Keah and Ahee. Aai is a born explorer and seeks to follow in his father's footsteps, traveling to distant galaxies.

Mahah

Female daughter of Keah and Ahee. Mahah is deeply caring and nurturing. She desires to be a mother like her own, having many children.

Ua

Male son of Keah and Ahee. He is a builder who especially likes to work at improving technologies.

Maiha

Female daughter of Keah and Ahee. Maiha is a quiet, wise thinker. She enjoys learning and has an impressive memory. She is also deeply connected to the natural environment of her home planet Hourou.

John Minister

Sixty-two-year-old professor of physics and British expatriate. He is curious and very scientific in his approach to everything. Grounded in the natural, he tends to reject religion and talk of the supernatural. He also does not like politics or politicians.

Yori Shimizu

Thirty-five-year-old female medical student of Japanese descent. Yori is fascinated by the workings of the human body and is a focused and driven student, yet she yearns to lighten up her serious life with fun and rest.

Perry Carlson

Fifty-nine-year-old career politician, congressman, and member of his government's defense committee. He is a cunning diplomat who over-uses his great leadership skills. His personality is often abrasive, but he is deeply patriotic and cares about people. Perry is a widower with an adult daughter back on Earth.

Director Laura Turgis

Director of a special and mysterious government department known as "the Agency" that investigates UFOs. Laura is proud of her career accomplishments and desires to leave her professional mark on the world before considering marriage and family.

Doctor Doug Haines

Director of the national space agency. Haines is in charge of investigating the alien visitation with his colleague Laura Turgis.

Captain Lawrence

Military captain who escorts Laura while at the alien crash site.

Colonel Richter

Colonel in charge of security at the alien crash site.

General Shepherd

General in charge of military activities after the alien visitation.

Alex Vaughn

Laura Turgis' Deputy Director, second in charge of their special agency, and her secret lover. Alex wants to settle down with Laura, even at the expense of giving up their careers. He is loyal to Laura and is respected within the agency.

Agent Jacobs

Female field agent who works in "the Agency" under Alex Vaughn.

Doctor Tannish

Military doctor overseeing an alien examination.

Ria

A female spokesperson of the Dah-Ahey. Ria has a mysterious past and Keah's family all seem to know her. She is conniving, but very wise. She is obsessed with life on Earth.

Yee

Male Ah-Ahey and friend of Eah, who is interested in Eah's sister Mahah. Yee likes to practice changing his skin to blend into various environments.

Wae

(pronounced Why-eh) Ria's Dah-Ahey boyfriend on Hourou.

Sah

Young Dah-Ahey boy who is left behind on Earth.

The language of the planet Hourou comprises three parts: verbal, visual, and perceptive. Only twenty-five percent is verbal, so words are few and limited mostly to vowel sounds. The rest relies on visual cues like gestures and facial expressions—what we call body language—and shared thought impressions, which are sensed through focused eye contact or direct physical touch.

The people of Hourou have advanced abilities in these areas, but, given time, Earth humans can learn to communicate this way, too. Some of us already do. For example, those who have honed the skill of intuitive touch understand that it is possible to convey emotions and intentions through physical contact. Likewise, two people who are familiar and open to each other can actually exchange feelings and even some thoughts through intense eye contact (i.e. "I know what you're thinking just by looking at you." "Your eyes give you away."). This sort of language requires alacrity, openness, and trust. Imagine if we Earth humans learned to communicate with each other in these ways...

In the following list, Eah, our communications expert, split up some words with dashes and added consonants to make pronunciation by Earth humans easier. She says this: "There are few consonants in my spoken language, but some words use them if you listen closely. To you, it would sound very soft, pronounced with soft lips and a lazy tongue. When you see a consonant, pronounce it lightly and hurry to the next vowel. For example, we say *mahree,* which means to calm the body. The *m* should sound like a soft hum. Emphasize the *ah* sound. Bend the tongue back, like you want to roll the *r,* but do not roll it—just say it lightly. Then drag out the *e.* Like this: Mmm-AH-rrr-eee. Very good!"

VOCABULARY (listed alphabetically)

Aaaaaah-ah-pah-sah - giant crab-like beast of Hourou

a-auh-hi-ooo-ah - trees, especially jungle trees

ae - yes

Ah-Ahey - Those with Ahey

ah-ey-ai [*ah-Ay-ah-Ee*] - canon-like device used to manipulate dark matter (literally means "giant mouth")

ah-ho-rho-to-Ahey - lighted plant on Hourou (literally "light inside from Ahey")

Ah-oha-nee - I love you

Ah-ya Ooo-oh-yee - a Hourou greeting that means "be calm, peace to you"

Aha - daddy; father; papa (informal)

ahea - space; deep space; created space beyond the planets

Ahey - God

aho - string-like fibrous plant that lives floating in the air and not on the ground; found in certain forest glades and mostly only visible at night

ahoonu - giant, nocturnal, tentacled, balloon-like creature that floats in the air and glows

ahua - general term for time

ai [*ay-ih*] - make love; intercourse

aihanyaah [*ay-han-yah*] - builder; crafter; creator; artisan

aophu [*ah-oh-foo*] - womb; sac; carry bag

Atsaahwua [*aht-sah-woo-ah*] - name of the most famous of Ah-Ahey cities (literally means "beautiful")

Awheroea [*uh-where-oh-E-uh*] - a pinkish planet

ayawaya - light beam on alien spacecraft used for transporting people and things aboard (literally means "ladder" or "bridge")

Dah-Ahey - bronze-skinned people group of Hourou (literally means "those without Ahey" or "those who run from Ahey")

Eeeeee-eh! - Stop it! Knock it off! (used lightly, not a harsh rebuke)

Eeeeemoo - multi-colored mosses that mark paths in the forests and jungles

Eeee-saah - of course

Eekaoa [*eek-ah-oh-ah*] - galaxies

ehe [*eh-heh*] - no

eu-uaua [*ee-you—you-ah-you-ah*] - muscles

fahee - large boat

Hasha-ah-ao - frozen

Hoono-heeoh - fuel; power supply

Hourou - name of the Eden-like planet (literally means "purple sky")

iao [*ee-ah-oh*] - crown

Ieeay [*eye-ee-ay*] - water-covered planet inhabited by humans who adapted to living in the oceans

kah-e-oh-ya - impressive

keer-eh-peee - fruit with a relaxing and slightly intoxicating effect

Kei-hee-ah-may! - an expression of wonderment, e.g. How wonderful!

koyoyi [*koh-yo-yee*] - to be turned against, perverted into direct opposition

mah-ree - to calm or relax the body

mahtee - small animal, cross between a monkey and a flying squirrel, brown with colorful striped patterns

meeroh - cotton-like plant that expands in water

oa-hah [*oh-ah-ha*] - ocean

oen - a calm wind; a light breeze

oha - love

o-hoo - belly

oho-ua - cavity; womb

ohri [*oh-ree*] - lizard-like creatures resembling small Earth dinosaurs

Oooooo-eee-ey-oi-i-heh - to join as friends

Ooo-oh-yee - a Hourou greeting that means "peace to you"

Seh! - Go for it!

soso-naaah-ha - coconut-like fruit with water inside

sohena [*so-hee-nah*] - girl

suisa [*swee-sah*] - general term for people

Tahah - Hourou's primary sun, closest to the planet (rises second)

Tameen - Hourou's secondary sun, furthest from the planet (rises first)

tay-oh-eee - town; civilization

tsahaihi [*ts-ha-hay-he*] - young boy

tsawee [*ts-ah-we*] - to hold back; to keep oneself from doing something

tsayooorua - valley

usu - hair

wa-ah-ahea - spaceship; vessel that travels through space

wa-hah-ho-yee-ho - a shallow vessel, like a ferry

waiehheh [*why-eh-heh*] - living waterfall

waihohu [*why-ho-who*] - mark; brand; symbol; sign

waiooua [*why-oh-uh-yah*] - soul; spirit; innermost being

wheyuah [*way-you-ah*] - ground; dirt

wiihee [*we-he*] - the watery outer atmosphere of Hourou (literally means "waters")

wooo-rooo-too - fruit that the ohri like to eat

yarae [*yah-ray*] - giant bird, like the prehistoric Quetzalcoatlus of Earth

yeh-heh-yeh – forest

DAN WHICKER believes that the best stories leave you feeling hope, no matter what galaxy they take place in. Drawing from his degrees in marketing and theology, as well as over 27 years working as a professional communicator, Dan has developed a writing style that leads the reader to experience a story primarily through the dialogue of its characters.

Though he loves fiction, Dan also enjoys subjects as diverse as modern culture, metaphysics, philosophy, religion, biology, business, leadership, and relationships. He has written many articles for various periodicals and online channels.

When Dan is not behind a computer, he is honing his singing voice and teaching himself to play the guitar. Often, you can find him beach-combing in Florida where he lives with his two sons.

Make contact at danwhicker.com.

www.ingramcontent.com/pod-product-compliance
Lightning Source LLC
Chambersburg PA
CBHW021328310726
48971CB00001B/26